THE
ALPHA
SPECIES

ALSO BY WW MORTENSEN

W W MORTENSEN

THE ALPHA SPECIES

TERROR HAS ADAPTED

HOUSE OF THE
SUN

AUTHOR'S NOTE

This book is the successor to EIGHT and follows on from the events of that story. For maximum enjoyment of THE ALPHA SPECIES, it is recommended you first check out EIGHT.

ACKNOWLEDGEMENTS

Special thanks go to Julie Sampson, Jeroen ten Berge, Rob Siders, and Ben Mortensen. To Craig, Kelli, Bill and Betty, thanks for the feedback, support and encouragement.

For Sophie and Sam

PROLOGUE
α

It had passed without trace—no telltale tracks, no scuffed earth or broken twigs. Nothing.

Impossible.

Mbambuk shook his head, certain he'd missed something. All animals leave a trail, even the most cunning predators.

Not this one, it seemed.

At the edge of the clearing, surrounded by the flared roots of giant lombi trees and an ever-deepening gloom, Mbambuk knelt and scanned again. The afternoon storm, although brief, had brought drenching rain, and the earth was soft, ideal for tracking. There should be signs everywhere.

There were none. Not here, anyway.

The sound of light footfalls caused Mbambuk to turn.

Hunched and treading lightly, Nlaka, his brother, crept forward, a bow clenched in his left hand and in his right, several arrows. He crouched beside Mbambuk. "Aya reached the edge of those trees, right over there," the younger man whispered, gesturing over his shoulder. "But then… *nothing.* It makes no sense."

Mbambuk squinted at the opposing treeline, where the last of the child's prints were pressed deep in the mud, clear and unmistakable. By the length of stride, the shape of the tread, she'd been moving fast.

Running for her life.

Then she'd vanished.

Where are you, child? And what were you running from?

As though reading his brother's thoughts, Nlaka said, "Not a leopard."

Mbambuk agreed. At first, a leopard had seemed likely: the animals were sometimes drawn to the village, tempted in part by hunger or desperation, but mostly opportunity, and they had stalked the children before. But a leopard kills fast, and their four-toed prints are distinct. No animal tracks, leopard or otherwise, had been found—only Aya's, well beyond the village, where she had last been seen.

The children had been returning from the river, having spent the morning there swimming. The oldest, Iteri, had said that somewhere along the path, Aya must have fallen behind. They hadn't noticed this at first, but then from somewhere deeper in the forest her screams had risen and in fear, the group had turned and run home to summon the adults. This was the story Iteri and the other children had relayed, and yet Mbambuk was unsure. The path was familiar to Aya, and she knew not to stray. She was a good child, and wise for her age.

Almost certainly, she had been lured away.

More movement from behind. Akelo was the same age as Nlaka, and his brother's closest friend. Stout and yet fleet of foot, Akelo had matured into a fine warrior, a master of the bow, and—like Mbambuk—a future leader of the hunt.

"It grows dark," Akelo said, crouching next to the brothers. "We should turn back."

"We cannot," Mbambuk said.

Akelo hesitated. "With night, the trail is lost. Soon, it will be too dark to track."

Mbambuk brushed a final time at the muddy, leaf-covered floor and stood. "It matters not, Akelo. There is nothing *left* to track."

With that, Mbambuk turned and jutted his chin. As smoothly as untethered shadows, the five remaining hunters rose from the undergrowth and moved into the green veil at the clearing's edge. For the moment, Mbambuk and his young charges let them pass, and did not follow.

"If that is true," Akelo whispered, drawing upright to stand on Mbambuk's left, "then the shaman is correct."

Mbambuk did not answer, and Nlaka, who was the last to stand, simply turned to the trees, equally mute but suddenly restless, too.

Akelo looked from brother to brother and his gaze hardened. "So, we hunt a demon."

Grimly, Mbambuk nodded. What further proof did they need? The child had been taken—of that they were certain—and with a furtiveness no earthly creature possessed. Before leaving, the shaman had warned the hunters of the nature of their quarry. And yet he had not called it a demon. He had called it something else.

Mbambuk was familiar with the tricksters. As a child, he'd heard the stories. Nlaka, too. Their parents had said the tricksters were forest spirits. Mostly, these spirits were good and kind, but not the tricksters—they were cruel and cunning. It was said they could take many forms, both physical and otherwise, and took pleasure in luring unsuspecting children to their deaths.

A trickster had lured Aya from the path and had snatched her away.

Was she still alive?

He prayed so. Either way, they could not abandon her.

Turning to Nlaka, Mbambuk said, "We need to go there... to the place father told us about."

"It is forbidden," Nlaka replied.

"Aya will be there."

Akelo listened to this exchange and his face paled. "The men will not follow."

"They will," Mbambuk said. "They are good men. Come."

With a wave of his hand, Mbambuk motioned them forward, and neither Nlaka, nor Akelo—who were themselves good men—needed further urging. Together, they caught up to the others, and once more Mbambuk took the lead.

In spirit form, the tricksters could not be tracked, but Mbambuk wasn't deterred.

He knew where they lived.

Night closed, and under its spreading blanket, the hunters, like spirits themselves, covered much ground. The men must have realised where they were headed, for Mbambuk sensed in them a growing unease. Still, they said nothing. They were brave.

They had to be.

The last of the strangled light drained away. Though his eyesight was strong, Mbambuk was forced to navigate by instinct. His fortunes improved when overhead, the canopy thinned, allowing shafts of silver to spill through. The rising moon was large and full—a hunter's moon.

A good sign, Mbambuk thought, and pushed harder.

As they neared the forbidden place, Nlaka whispered, "Do you remember father's story?"

Mbambuk did. How could he forget? As a young man, their father had led a hunting party like this one, not in pursuit of a child or a spirit, but in search of red-tailed monkeys. This was before the tricksters had arrived, and before Komba had forbidden them. That night, under the same full moon, their father had come this way, perhaps down this very path, to a spot not far from here, when, without warning, a line of fire had streaked across the night sky. Their father had called it a Fire Snake, because it had a long tail that had shimmered, and a head of flame. The Fire Snake had grown, its flames so bright the hunters had to shield their eyes as the jungle flared and night became day. Then with a hiss and a whoosh of air the apparition dived below the line of the canopy and disappeared. As darkness returned, a boom and a rumble of thunder rode with it, causing the ground to shake, and as his companions murmured in alarm, their father knew that Komba had been roused and was angry. It was not wise to anger Komba, and fearing his wrath, the men fled, never to return.

Mbambuk drew to a halt and looked up. Behind him, the hunters paused.

The trees. Mbambuk wasn't sure why, or in what way, exactly, but ahead, the forest looked different. The trees were familiar—strong and towering, with huge, flared roots at the base—and yet somehow unusual.

It was said the trees in the forbidden place can be found nowhere else.

This is it, Mbambuk thought, *the place where the Fire Snake had come to the world.*

The home of the tricksters.

Arrows gripped tightly in his clenched fist, his palm slick with sweat, Mbambuk turned to his companions. The men, who stood unmoving, waiting for instruction, met his gaze with wide, doubting eyes. Perhaps Aya's disappearance was Komba's will, and in coming here the men were opposing the will of the Creator.

The tricksters do not serve Komba, Mbambuk thought. And while the men, too, knew this, they began to murmur nervous prayers.

A voice—a whisper—rose from somewhere deep in the forest. The hunters spun, seeking its source.

"Komba?" one of the men asked hopefully. Mbambuk wished the man had stayed silent.

Komba would not whisper.

The voice came again, low and murmuring. Chanting? Mbambuk could discern no words, the sound wisping through the trees like an exhalation of breath carried on a light breeze.

The sound stopped.

Anxiously, the men also fell silent, and when the forest creatures—the birds and insects and monkeys—ceased their own chorus, Mbambuk wondered if the clenching fist of night had throttled not merely the light, but now all sound, too.

The snap of a single branch broke the hush. On its heels, the strange vocalization that may have been a whispered chant rose again, too, and then more branches cracked, and boughs shivered.

Something large approached, pushing through the trees.

The men fell into a tight circle.

"Nlaka, do you see anything?" Mbambuk said, his gaze darting.

"No! Nothing!"

The chanting, closer now, and louder, was not human, and in fact, more a rasping vibration—animal-like, and yet unlike anything Mbambuk had heard before. Bows creaked, and the men, back to back, pressed even closer. One of them—Djingi, who was standing behind Mbambuk—said something inaudible, his voice stressed and full of fear, but before Mbambuk could urge him to hold his nerve, he sensed a rush of movement overhead and then a large, physical presence near to him, and by the time he had turned the presence had vanished… along with Djingi.

Chaos erupted, and panicked cries. A volley of arrows hissed blindly into the shadows.

"No!" Nlaka cried. "Hold!"

Hearing his brother's voice above the tumult, Mbambuk swivelled—and saw his sibling's bare legs, and then his feet, whoosh upwards, hauled skyward by some unseen force.

"*Nlaka!*"

Reflexively, Mbambuk reached for him but missed. Nlaka's body disappeared into the wildly shuddering canopy.

No!

Dazed, his eyes blurring with tears, Mbambuk sensed another large presence swoop in—this time from a different angle—and haul Akelo away, and then after him, yet another man, each of them drawn vertically into the canopy. Spinning with each attack, Mbambuk tried to sight the enemy, but was too slow. Where his men had stood, only shadows remained.

Shadows! The spirits—the tricksters—were shadows, not one but many, coming for them at will.

High in the trees, men screamed as the demons fed.

Mbambuk realised he was running. The foliage ripped at him, and he slapped it away.

Something thundered through the brush behind him.

As a child, Mbambuk's days were spent in the treetops. He was an accomplished climber, and he was fast. Drawing on those skills, he scurried up the bole of a giant lombi, using the hanging, vine-like lianas for leverage. It was a practiced move and in a single breath he was safely in the branches of the massive tree, hugging the bole close, blending in. Desperately, he wiped tears from his eyes and scanned the ground below. There were no paths through this part of the forest, but he saw clearly where he had burst from the underbrush.

No demon emerged in pursuit.

Had he eluded it?

Mbambuk's heart rapped hard in his chest, loud in his ears. His mind reeled. He thought about the hunting party, and Nlaka and Aya, and came to a terrifying realisation.

The tricksters had drawn them here.

Aya had been lured so the hunters, in search of her, could in turn be enticed. It had been a trap all along.

How could I have been so stupid?

As a child, Mbambuk had been warned of the tricksters' cunning and yet now, as an adult, he'd fallen for their ploy.

I must warn the village.

He moved to leave, but above him, from higher in the tree, the terrible clicking sound—that rasping vibration—came again, but this time, more like a hiss. With dread, Mbambuk turned his gaze upward, and his lower lip trembled.

The demon that had come for Aya had left no tracks on the ground, because it had hunted her from the trees.

Poised above him, Mbambuk saw now the creature's true form—a form of flesh and blood and multiple, wide-spread legs.

"J'ba Fofi…" he breathed.

And with that the blackness shifted and came for him, and he screamed.

$$\alpha$$

"This is the place."

Ray Drexler paused and balled a fist in the air. Behind him, the team froze, and when he released his fingers, noiselessly dispersed. As the men hustled for cover, Drexler slipped ahead, to the man whose voice had crackled through his earpiece. Nico, on point, slung his weapon as Drexler hunkered beside him.

"Down there," Nico whispered, signalling with his binoculars through the waist-high fernery.

Ahead, the forest floor fell away, the jungle sinking into a bowl-like depression hundreds of feet wide. Poised high on its rim, Drexler ran his gaze down the slope and thought, somewhat wistfully, that the earth had drawn a breath it had yet to exhale.

"Looks like a meteor crater," Nico said.

Apt, but not accurate. An impact crater, yes—but not the result of a meteor strike.

Nico knew this, too, and passed Drexler the binoculars. "Check it out."

Zooming in, Drexler swept the binoculars back and forth, adjusting the focus.

Christ.

"A lot to take in," Nico said.

That's understating it, Drexler thought, still scanning. Poking through the sea of green like the bleached and scattered bones of a gargantuan beast were chips of jagged stone.

"That's the city… the remains of it, anyway," Nico said.

"Intihuasi," Drexler replied, nodding. "The House of the Sun."

"That's what they called it. Check the middle—dead-centre."

Drexler panned back. On the crater floor, nestled in the bowl's deepest point, sat an ancient pyramid. The structure towered more than a hundred feet high and stretched at least twice that distance across the base, although its exact dimensions were unclear. This was partly due to the concealing vegetation, but mainly because of the shroud of silver-grey netting. The gigantic web radiated from the pyramid, its tendrils forming broad sheets that spread to the crater walls.

Incredible.

"They weren't kidding, were they?" Nico said.

No, they weren't. Drexler cast his mind back to the briefing, less than three hours ago. Straight up search and rescue, they'd said. Of course, that was bullshit, and it seemed his gut was on the money. This wasn't a search for survivors—it was a recovery mission.

"We need to get closer," Drexler said, and turned. Signalling for the team to move up, he swivelled back to Nico, whose green-and-brown-streaked features were coated in a light sheen of sweat. "They said there was a vantage point not far from here. Find us a path."

Nico checked his M16 and moved to stand, but Drexler caught him by the arm.

"They use the trees, remember? Stay frosty."

"In this heat?" Nico joked, and disappeared.

The others assembled to a chorus of disbelief. Drexler gave them a moment to settle; hell, they'd seen some weird shit before, but this was next level. After several seconds, he called for focus. "Remember, they camouflage themselves, but they also fluoresce. Switch to UV."

The soldiers reached for their specially tooled goggles and moved out. As they did, it began to drizzle, and in the distance, thunder growled. Drexler fitted the hood of his poncho and hustled after them.

Catching up to Nico, the team skirted the crater's rim, weapons trained on the suffocating green maze. They moved swiftly, faster than before, and soon came upon a crude shelter of camouflage netting strung amongst the trees. This was the makeshift hide the science team had used to study the nest, the place they'd dubbed the north-western vantage point.

A short distance away, down the slope, lay a crumpled Black Hawk UH-60 helicopter.

"Nico left, Box right," Drexler said. "Wolfe, Quinn—get down there, single sweep, thermographics and video." As the four men dispersed, Drexler turned. "Merc, you got LIDAR?"

Kneeling in the light rain, Merc typed commands into a ruggedized laptop and nodded. "Transmitted just now via satellite uplink." He spun the device. "Check it out."

A 3-D topographic map dominated by orange hues and contrasting striations of yellow and blue filled the screen. The image—a digital representation of the crater below, minus the jungle and the web, which had been stripped clear—provided a detailed picture of the underlying terrain.

"You can see the buildings scattered throughout," Merc said, wiping droplets from the screen. "And there, in the centre, is the pyramid."

Studying the desolate image, Drexler mused that if not for the spread of ancient ruins, he may well have been staring at a crater on the moon. LIDAR operated like radar, but with light; while he and his team were en route, a low altitude, fixed-wing UAV had overflown the site, saturating the huge bowl with laser light and measuring the reflected pulses with onboard sensors. From that data, an image of the crater and its contents had been generated.

Committing the city's layout to memory—entries, exits, obstacles—Drexler patted Merc on the shoulder and straightened.

Merc looked up at him. "You think anyone's alive down there?"

Turning, Drexler urged him forward. "Let's find out."

As expected, the Black Hawk was empty: no survivors, no bodies. Drexler's focus, for now, was the city below.

Already, Wolfe had unpacked the WASP. The mid-sized, rotary wing UAV was aptly named: squatting on the jungle floor, the drone's resemblance to a large, robotic insect was uncanny, with its eyelike camera lenses and its six jointed legs spread in a starburst beneath its belly. While LIDAR had provided Drexler with a plan of the city, the WASP-6—or Wide-area Autonomous Surveillance Probe—would confirm the presence, or absence, of survivors.

Or just as importantly, *hostiles*.

After running some diagnostics, Quinn gave the thumbs up, and Wolfe worked the handset. With a quiet whine, the WASP's six rotors engaged, and the vehicle lifted into the air. Guided by the first-person view through his goggles, Wolfe steered the drone through a gap in the canopy, across the treetops, and down the crater's sloping wall.

Beside him, Merc punched commands into his laptop. "Okay—we've got video."

Moving behind Merc to peer over his shoulder, Drexler scanned the monitor. The site loomed large on the video feed, the ruined, stone buildings poking up through the sea of silk and vegetation in high definition.

"Get closer," Drexler said. "Aim for the pyramid."

Piloting the UAV to the bottom of the slope, Wolfe levelled out and skimmed the canopy, heading for the pyramid's truncated peak, on top of which sat a dark, stone temple. There, he slowed the WASP to a hover.

"Down a little," Drexler said. "Show us the base, 3 o'clock."

Wolfe tilted the camera. On the pyramid's northern face, top to bottom, a yawning hole had been torn into the silk and vegetation, as though each had been clawed away by some immense beast. With both gone—destroyed, in fact, by the devastating events of the previous day—the team had an unobstructed view. At the base of the huge structure lay a flagstone plaza, and in the middle of that, two large objects.

"Jesus…"

Battered and crumpled, a single-engine floatplane rested lengthways on top of an equally mangled helicopter, the second of the two downed Black Hawks.

Mashed together like this, the two machines looked like a single, twisted hybrid.

"Man," Nico said. "They told us about this in the briefing, but still…"

"This is close enough, Wolfe," Drexler said. "Hatch them."

Wolfe flicked a button and instantly, the hovering WASP released its cargo, dropping from each its legs a sphere the size of a baseball. Like a small cloud of insects, the six micro air vehicles—or MAVs—swarmed momentarily before abruptly scattering.

"The data's coming through," Merc said as the small vehicles, flying independently of the mother drone, spread low over the city.

"Anything on the FLIR?" Drexler asked, scanning the monitor for thermographic information transmitted via the MAVs' forward-looking infrared radar.

Merc shook his head. "I'm getting subtle differences in ambient temperature, but no heat signatures. If there are survivors down there, I'm not picking them up."

"What about the bugs?" Box asked from behind.

Quinn smirked. "They're not bugs, man."

"The hell they aren't," Box said. "Six legs, eight legs—they're bugs, and this is a goddamned bug hunt. You get that, right?"

Merc typed commands without looking up. "Bugs or not, they won't show on thermal."

"What?" Box said.

Still grinning, Quinn said, "You passed grade school, yeah? They're cold-blooded—they don't generate body heat. They're ectotherms."

Box scoffed at him. "You're kidding, right? *Ectotherms*? So, you're a frigging lab rat, now?"

Ignoring the two of them, Drexler said quietly to Merc, "What about UV?"

Merc rapped at the keyboard. On the screen, multiple images flashed up, washed in ultraviolet. "Nothing. On the surface at least, the joint's a ghost-town. They could be underground, inside the nest."

No, Drexler thought. They're on the move—*just like she said.*

At that, he straightened. "Call it through," he said to Merc. "Tell them she was right."

8 HOURS EARLIER

α

Rebecca Riley pushed through the jostling bodies, searching desperately for the woman. A gloved hand fell on her shoulder and tried to pull her aside, to make room, but she shrugged it off and swivelled. The woman was a doctor, right? She'd told them that—they'd been the first words out of her mouth, the first thing she'd uttered when she and the others had swarmed from the chopper. Rebecca had rushed to meet her, but then the crowd had converged, and the woman was lost in a shifting sea of yellow.

"Blood pressure is low," a male voice said.

Rebecca turned to it, but her view was obscured by two men in hazmat suits.

"What are his symptoms?" This time, a female voice, sounding distant, artificial.

Sidestepping the men, Rebecca found the voice's owner, the woman—the doctor—crouching beside the Zodiac. She, too, was dressed in a yellow, synthetic polymer hazmat suit, fully integrated with a mask and a clear, hard-plastic face shield, but the woman's features were obscured by the reflected glare. Then the woman barked out something else, a command directed at the others in her company—at least a dozen of them, probably more—and bodies swung into motion. The woman must have been talking over two-way radio, her voice amplified by a speaker in the mask.

Not amplified enough, Rebecca thought. She barely heard it over the thumping rotors, and as she glanced at the US Army helicopter, perched on the gravelled riverbank not fifty feet away, debris from the spinning blades mushroomed outwards. Rebecca copped an eyeful of dust and recoiled from the stinging pinpricks.

"*What are his symptoms?*" the woman repeated, looking to the man beside her, the man who wore jungle fatigues instead of a hazmat suit, and a grave expression instead of a mask. Alex Kriedemann's mouth moved, but the Green Beret's words were lost in the noise and confusion.

"Breathing is shallow," another amplified voice said. "He's going into shock."

Overhead, a deeper thumping arose, and a second Black Hawk appeared, skimming the treetops. Like the blades of that aircraft, Rebecca's thoughts spun, and suddenly dizzy, she wavered, light-headed. She sensed a slowing, as though time was grinding to a halt, and through a sting of tears not solely a result of the swirling dust, she glanced again at Ed—on his back, eyes closed and pale-faced, his body cocooned in an emergency foil blanket and trembling on the floor of the Zodiac. They'd beached the vessel on the same curving stretch of riverbank that had served as the landing zone for the first—and soon-to-be second—rescue chopper. The bank was narrow—barely enough room to land a single aircraft, let alone two—but there was a wide, and rare, break in the canopy. Caught in the downdraft of the second Black Hawk, water blew in rings across the river, away from the bank, causing the stern of the Zodiac to bob and the surrounding vegetation to ripple, but none of this seemed to be in real time. Rebecca viewed the scene from afar, as though from outside her body.

Then someone called out. It was Alex.

"He was in pain, severe and increasing," Kriedemann yelled to the woman, and the volume and abruptness of his voice jolted Rebecca from her daze.

Ed needs me.

Time sped up. Rebecca rushed forward, closer to Zodiac and Ed's prone form. "He'd been complaining of abdominal cramps," she said urgently to the woman. "Increasing in intensity. Then he became feverish."

Movement behind her—medical personnel closing in. Another gloved hand landed on her shoulder, and beside her, a gurney appeared. The paramedic wanted her to lie down. She shrugged him away; she didn't need a stretcher.

She spoke again to the woman. "He began drifting in and out of consciousness. He was envenomated—unknown type, but probably a neurotoxin. I have a sample. He seemed okay at first, but then his condition deteriorated. Fast."

Multiple gloved hands forced her onto the gurney, and unable to resist, Rebecca sat, but remained upright. She wasn't sure if the woman—who hadn't looked up—had even heard her; if she did, she said nothing. More bodies, more hazmat suits, swarmed the clearing, this time from the second Black Hawk. Like the others, they were clearly medical personnel but likely military, too. A familiar and yet desperate voice called out, and Rebecca turned as members of the first team lifted Jessy—lying flat on a gurney, with her broken leg secured—and hauled her away. As she went, heading towards the first chopper, Jessy called to Ed again, but over the whump of the blades, Rebecca couldn't make sense of what she was saying. Then Owen's gurney was on the move, too, and as she directed her attention to him, Rebecca heard someone say something about infection. Owen had been without proper medical treatment for several hours, and there was every chance the spear wound to his abdomen had become infected, but as she scanned the sea of hazmat suits, Rebecca realised the statement may have referenced a different kind of infection. Was it possible? Had they been exposed to something? All of them? Then her view was blocked and suddenly Owen was gone, too.

And Sanchez.

Down in the cave system, Robert had been attacked and bitten, just like Ed. He hadn't exhibited the same symptoms as Ed, though, hadn't suffered cramps or become feverish or faded in and out of consciousness. He'd seemed okay. Then again, until a few moments ago, so had Ed.

Chad, too, had disappeared.

Everyone had been spirited away—even Kriedemann's men, Tag and Bull. The people in the hazmat suits weren't taking any chances.

"We need to get him back," the woman said.

Rebecca turned. "Back *where*?"

She got no answer, and two suited men promptly lifted Ed's gurney from the Zodiac. A third person held a drip high. The group, including the woman, hustled for the chopper.

"*Who the hell are you people?*" Rebecca called out to them, trying to swing her legs from the gurney, but hands held her back, more forcefully now.

"Ma'am, you need to lie down."

Rebecca ignored the man and called again to the woman. "Where are you taking him?"

Halfway to the chopper, the woman—the one who may or may not have been a doctor, but was clearly the leader—hesitated, turned, and through her face mask fixed Rebecca with a pair of hypnotic brown eyes. The woman, Asian, smiled, and her voice floated robotically over the speaker. "Don't worry, he's in good hands."

With that she turned to bark out more orders, remaining behind while the first chopper—the chopper into which Ed had been loaded—lifted away. Rebecca glanced desperately at Kriedemann, who was still standing and arguing with two men who were trying unsuccessfully to get him, like her, onto a gurney. "Alex! *What's going on?*"

He glanced over, his mouth working, but she didn't hear his reply.

The sting was small, sharp, quick.

Rebecca flinched, turning and thrusting a hand to her neck. "What the hell?"

Gloved fingers—a syringe held between them—loomed large in her field of view, and then the world tilted as Rebecca fell backwards onto the gurney, her vision swimming as the sedative took effect. Prone now, she saw swaying foliage above her, and a clouding sky, and sensed movement, a kind of up and down jolting as the hazmat-people carried her towards the second chopper. Voices rose, but then the thump of the blades swallowed them, and she was suddenly inside the aircraft, surrounded by medical equipment—dials and monitors covered in plastic sheeting, probably some sort of biohazard control.

We're sick, aren't we? All of us. Not just Ed.

She realised she and her companions had been separated, split between the two choppers. She wondered if there was a reason for that other than simple logistics, but she was slipping rapidly into an oily blackness and her head had become too heavy to lift, so she couldn't crane her neck to see who of her friends might be in here with her. At the very least, Ed was in the other aircraft, and as she processed this, she realised that Priscilla wasn't with her.

Oh God.

Rebecca felt a muted flush of panic—she remembered passing the tiny monkey off to Tag, just before rushing out to meet the hazmat-suited woman. But she hadn't seen Priscilla since.

Was she still with Tag?

The chopper lifted off the ground. As the Black Hawk wheeled about, Rebecca's stomach rolled with it.

Though she fought it, sleep finally took her, and her eyes fell shut. As she drifted off, she heard a voice, close to her ear. It was the woman—the doctor—and when she spoke, her words seemed to come from far away, echoing her earlier sentiments.

"Just relax, Ms Riley. Trust me, all of you are in good hands."

THE
AFTERMATH

1
α

The rhythmic whump of an approaching chopper stirred Rebecca from a light sleep.

She opened her eyes, suddenly alert, and listened.

A supply chopper? Perhaps. They still made daily runs. This one, while distant, was closing fast, the growing thud of its blades cutting through the afternoon's heat-induced hush.

The aircraft converged from the north.

Rebecca sat up. The bunk's metal frame shifted, creaked, and the paperback she'd been reading before drifting off slid from her chest, evading her grasping fingers to land with a thud on the laminate floor. Rebecca wondered, momentarily, how long she'd been dozing, before returning her attention to the growing rumble outside.

How many today? Five? Six?

At least that. Maybe seven. Either way, more than usual, and all from the north.

She waited.

With a roar, the chopper buzzed overhead, low, like the others. Though robust, the walls of the CHU shuddered as it passed, and then it was gone, its thunder fading into the distance.

Not a supply run, she decided. There were less of those now, a lot less. Not since the first two weeks—when maybe a dozen birds a day had been commonplace—had there been this much activity. Not necessarily a big deal, but none had landed… or returned.

Something was up.

Movement caught Rebecca's eye, and she spun as a brown shape darted from beneath the single chair in the room's corner, low to the ground and moving fast. The slender-limbed Capuchin leapt high and hit Rebecca in the chest, forcing her backwards. Giggling, Rebecca struck the mattress with the tiny monkey on top of her. "Hello there, princess!"

In her familiar, sing-song way, Priscilla chirped excitedly, grasping Rebecca in a playful headlock.

"Hey! Take it easy!"

More grappling, and vigorous jumping, too, and although the monkey wasn't much taller than a foot, she was strong. Her curling tail whacked Rebecca across the face. Clearly, she was up for a wrestle.

Laughing—but having none of it—Rebecca gave Priscilla a playful push, and taking the cue, the monkey sprang away to the far end of the mattress. There, she calmed.

"Much better," Rebecca said, a little short of breath. "We'll play later, hey?"

Understanding, Priscilla chittered briefly, and fell silent. Tranquillity restored, Rebecca lay for a moment, listening. She could hear no more activity, no choppers in the distance, only the insects and their ever-present heat-chorus.

Rebecca sighed, and the final remnants of her smile dissolved. She didn't have to check her watch to know she'd slept long enough, that she should get up, but already, the inexorable heaviness had returned, that dreaded weight, unwelcome and yet familiar. Always, it seemed to find her, as tangible now as a block of stone on her chest.

Just a few more minutes.

Rebecca rolled onto her side. The bunk's metal frame creaked out its usual complaint. It always goddamned creaked. The mattress felt lumpier than usual, and she rolled the opposite way. Finding no comfort, she rolled onto her stomach, and finally, once more, onto her back.

Goddamn it.

Unblinking, Rebecca stared up at the plain white ceiling. The air-conditioner hummed softly. Of her few conveniences, she was most thankful for that. The days, even the nights, were relentlessly humid, and still, she hadn't adjusted. Usually, she kept the climate-control pumped up to max. She had to; she'd roast in here otherwise. At a mere eight feet wide and a dozen yards long, her claustrophobic living quarters were susceptible to the heat. They'd moved her into a Containerized Housing Unit—CHU for short and pronounced 'shoe'—a month ago. The soldiers called the pre-fabricated houses 'cans', which was an apt description. The units were simply glorified shipping containers.

Still, it was a step up from the inflatable fabric shelter she'd originally been allocated. The infirmary was in a secluded area of the base, in the south-eastern quadrant, a high-risk zone with access limited, for the most part, to certain healthcare personnel. In there, she never saw anyone without protective gear. Like the others, she'd had her own tent, with a bunk, toilet and shower, and a window through which medical staff in hazmat suits would peer. Separation from the rest of the group was mandatory, they'd said. They'd also said they'd be there for 72 hours, which was apparently the minimum quarantine period, and standard protocol for both civilian and military personnel. After her initial resistance, she'd seen the sense in that. She figured a period of isolation—or, as the medical staff had called it, 'close monitoring'—was to be expected. The need for caution was understandable.

But then everything had changed. Close monitoring had escalated to 'controlled monitoring'. This new level would last for 21 days, to ensure they were beyond the incubation period.

That, she'd baulked at. Incubation period? Again, the questions arose. Had they been exposed to something inside the nest, beneath the pyramid? Maybe a toxin or a pollutant, or an infectious agent of some kind, or even one of those viruses that jump between species, animal to human? It was possible. They'd spent time, however briefly, without protection in a biologically contaminated environment; they could have been exposed to any number of things. For that reason, standard disease containment strategies and infection control procedures had kicked in, and again, as a scientist herself, she got that—they had to be sure. Still, it had played on her mind.

They'd spent the three weeks of controlled monitoring in a larger area, together, as a group. Everyone except Robert.

And Ed.

Through pursed lips, Rebecca slowly exhaled. That familiar pang of loss, of overriding emptiness, hit her again, hard, and she took a moment to steady her breathing.

She'd moved out of the infirmary more than a month ago, and had spent the weeks since in here, her new digs.

By then the constant supervision, the consultations, the enquiries, had started to ease. Not just the attention from the doctors, but from the suits, too. Right from the start, there'd been dozens of interviews, most of them in those early days when she and the others had been separated, unable to see or talk to each other. Always, it was just her, firstly from inside her isolation tent, then later at a small table in a small room in some secluded part of the base. She'd found out afterwards that the others had been interviewed, too, but like her, always individually. Most of her interviewers had been army personnel, or so she'd been told—or presumed. She'd seen so many IDs, had so many ranks and positions and department names thrown at her she'd lost count. Mainly doctors at first—there'd been a plethora of medical types, including shrinks—but after the first few interrogations, she'd lost interest; she didn't care who was sitting across from her. Some had been civilians, government types—State Department, DEA, Department of Defense, US-AMRIID, maybe even CIA. The government people usually came as a pair, initially in PPE, then later more casually, suit-jackets discarded in the heat, ties loosened, sweating and uncomfortable but appropriately straight-faced, nodding their understanding even though what she told them was outrageously unbelievable. There'd been others, of course. Academics. Scientists. She recognised those types—she was one of them, after all. All of them had variously recorded her statements on audio devices and on video and had taken copious handwritten notes. She didn't embellish anything, just told them all the same thing. She sensed, at times, they wanted the story to change. But why would it? Hell, it happened. It was scarcely believable, yes, and even she had trouble processing everything. But it happened.

Some groups were more interested in Aronsohn and his men, others wanted to know about Oliveira and *his* men. Many were focused on the pyramid. One pair asked about the diamonds. She couldn't remember her answer to that. Maybe she'd feigned ignorance.

Plenty of her interviewers had asked her about the sphere.

And plenty more had questions about the arachnids. They had lots of questions about them. Some of the shrinks had asked her about her childhood. At first, she'd been evasive. What did her childhood have to do with anything? Then they'd circled around to the disorder, her phobia, and she'd understood. She still hadn't given them much, not at first—it was none of their goddamned business. But then she'd realised the best way to get rid of them was to comply. Give them what they want. So, she'd changed her approach, and told them what they wanted to hear, and since then, the interviews and the constant questions had eased. Now they'd stopped altogether.

Good. She was tired of talking about it. She didn't want to talk about anything, anymore.

Priscilla hopped onto her chest.

Rebecca moaned. "I'm sorry, honey, I'm beat. Go to sleep."

Not giving up, Priscilla responded with a series of high-pitched squeaks, tickling Rebecca's face while peering down at her with a concerned tilt of her black-cowled head. When that failed to elicit a reaction, she hopped away, bolting under the chair. She returned a moment later rustling a brown paper bag.

Curious, Rebecca sat up. Priscilla offered her the bag, and obligingly, Rebecca eased it from her grasp and peeked inside. "Pistachios? You've been sneaking into the chow hall again, haven't you!"

Priscilla lowered her gaze.

"Don't worry, your secret is safe," Rebecca assured her, scooping out a handful for each of them. Together, they tucked in. Priscilla masterfully shelled her own.

Through a mouthful, Rebecca said, "You know, for future reference, a bag of choc-chip cookies would also work."

Mid-chew, Priscilla hesitated, tilted her head.

"Just saying," Rebecca said, pausing for effect before breaking into a wide smile. "I'm kidding! You did good, girl. Real good."

Priscilla raised her hands in apparent exasperation and resumed chewing.

"I mean it," Rebecca said, scratching the monkey's chest. "Thanks for lifting my spirits."

Together, they finished off the bag. Rebecca crumpled it and placed it on the mattress. She considered lying down again but didn't. She was indeed feeling better, and today, she'd slept long enough.

Long enough these past two months.

Rebecca glanced down at the floor, to the fallen paperback, the front and back of which had pitched a tiny A-frame tent. She retrieved the book and smoothed the tattered, iconic front cover with its lone female swimmer and the toothy maw looming up from below. Rebecca placed the book next to her pillow.

"What do you say? Time to visit Egbert?"

Gulping her final pistachio, Priscilla thrust her hands over her eyes.

"I know you don't like him," Rebecca said, "but I should get to work. You can stay outside, like you always do."

Priscilla slumped, chattering disapprovingly as Rebecca swung her bare feet from the bunk and stood. Despite the heat, the laminate was cool from the air-conditioning. Beyond this room, with its single bunk, bedside table and chair, was a small bathroom. She was lucky to have scored a wet CHU—regular units don't have a bathroom and the luxury was normally reserved for the officers. She was thankful for the privacy.

Crossing to the basin, she turned on the faucet, filled a glass and took a long swig while appraising her reflection in the mirror.

What a mess. Tired, pale. Her skin was flushed. Her dark hair, tied in a ponytail, needed washing.

At least the cuts and bruising had healed. There were scars, though, physical and otherwise. In the early days, when the wounds were red and raw and verging on infection, she'd avoided the mirror. The sight of De Sousa's brutal handiwork wasn't a deterrent, not directly, but the nightly visions her injuries inspired were enough to keep her away.

For several weeks now, she'd slept okay. Free of nightmares, anyway.

She glanced at the amber pill bottle beside the faucet and considered reaching for it when a rhythmic chopping sound rose suddenly—another bird, again approaching from the north. Judging by the heavy whump, it was close and low, aiming for the compound.

Intrigued, she went to the door to peek out. As she opened it, she found a thirty-something woman standing there with her hand raised, ready to knock.

"Oh, Helen—Dr Worboys—hello," Rebecca said. "I didn't realise you were out here. Don't tell me I've missed another appointment."

Dr Worboys, wearing fatigues and a buzzcut, opened her mouth to answer, but the sound of the chopper landing unseen on the near side of the compound was too loud.

As it powered down, Dr Worboys smiled. "If I didn't know better, I'd assume you were avoiding me."

"I'm sorry, Helen. Please, come in." Rebecca held the door wide and stepped aside. As she did, she glanced across the compound, past the CHUs lined up beside hers, to the ever-present wall of green pressing at the perimeter fence. Towering above the razor-wire, the tall, dense trees blocked the sky and cast deep shadows across the compound's bare earth.

Initially, Camp Delta had been a much smaller affair, full of quick-erect shelters and rapid-deployment, inflatable tents. It had grown substantially since then, the tents replaced by more permanent structures. Before their rescue, on the *Tempestade*, Bull Harper had referenced a map location, referring to it as 'rally point Delta'. At the time she'd understood it to be a meeting point, a predetermined location the Special Forces team could fall back to when things went south. She'd never worked out if the two locations were in fact the same place but figured there was a connection. They were still in Brazil, she knew that much, although where, exactly, she wasn't sure. She supposed a base of this size could not have been built without local consent, but whether it was a joint venture, a result of closer US-Brazil defence ties, or some deal or agreement between the two governments was anyone's guess. Certain information, she'd discovered, was hard to come by.

A Humvee rolled past, kicking up a spray of thick, red mud. In the jungle, the ground never dried out fully.

Rebecca closed the door behind Dr Worboys, who strode over to give Priscilla a quick pat.

"Again, I apologise," Rebecca said. "I mustn't have heard my alarm."

"Another nap?"

Rebecca didn't answer.

Dr Worboys dragged the chair to the bunk.

"I wasn't avoiding you," Rebecca said, perching on the edge of the mattress.

"Don't sweat it," Dr Worboys said. She changed the subject. "How have you been?"

"Good."

Fixing Rebecca with a long, probing stare, as though searching for something, Dr Worboys hesitated, and then nodded. From her bag, she retrieved a stethoscope. Placing the tips in her ears, she pressed the head against Rebecca's chest, beneath her shirt. The metal was cool. Seemingly satisfied, Dr Worboys removed the eartips and let them fall, before retrieving an ophthalmoscope and holding it up to Rebecca's eyes.

"Priscilla and I were just about to head over to the lab," Rebecca said.

"Uh-huh," Dr Worboys said. "You've been sleeping a lot, Bec."

"Yeah?"

"Too much." She checked Rebecca's blood pressure.

"I'm pushing hard at work, I guess. But I can handle it."

"You've been away from home for a long time."

The statement, out of nowhere, struck Rebecca as odd, perhaps premeditated. She tilted her head. "You're not here for a physical, are you?"

Again, Dr Worboys hesitated, and then packed her gear away. In the process, she glanced sideways at the paper bag lying crumpled on the bed. She frowned at Priscilla. "Pistachios, young lady? Honestly, I don't know how you get away with it."

As though understanding, Priscilla raised her eyebrows, feigning innocence.

"I wish you'd pinched *me* a bag," Dr Worboys said. She tickled the self-satisfied monkey under the chin and stood. Glancing at Rebecca, Dr Worboys opened her mouth to speak, but then closed it again.

"Helen, is everything okay?" Rebecca asked.

Hesitance dimmed Dr Worboys' face, as though she had something on her mind, something she wanted to say—maybe even something personal—but wasn't sure how to broach it. Then the look faded and she reverted to her more natural, professional approach. "It's not uncommon during long periods of isolation to experience anxiety, depression…"

"Helen…"

"And what you went through down there… it's perfectly normal. Understandable. In fact, it's to be expected."

"I get it," Rebecca said, a little sharply. "PTSD and all that. We've been through this before. Many times. I'm fine."

"What happened down there, what you found—"

"We found nothing. You know that."

"If you want to talk about it…"

"We're under orders," Rebecca said. "You know that, too."

Dr Worboys blew air through her teeth. "Doctor patient privilege, remember?"

Rebecca pursed her lips. "I realise you're doing your job, Helen, and I appreciate you looking out for me, I really do. But I'm fine. The disorder, the phobia… it's gone. The nightmares, too."

"I know," Dr Worboys said, and smiled. "On the outside, if you need someone to talk to, it can be arranged."

"Outside?"

A knock at the door interrupted them.

Before Rebecca could answer it, Dr Worboys promptly—and unexpectedly—leaned in for a hug. "Take care of yourself, Bec."

Rebecca frowned. "Helen, I don't understand…"

But Dr Worboys said nothing further and without looking back, let herself out. Confused, Rebecca hesitated, then glanced through the door, which Helen had left ajar.

At the threshold, wide grins plastered across their faces, stood Jessy Baxter and Owen Faulkner.

2
α

Rebecca didn't ask them inside. Instead, she squealed and hurtled through the open doorway, drawing both friends into a tight hug. "Oh my God, what are you doing here?"

"You need to ask?" Owen said, stepping back and pushing his glasses up his nose. Like always, he was dressed in board shorts and a Hawaiian shirt. His Miami Marlins baseball cap, now looking a little worse for wear, sat backwards on his head, and wild curls of hair stuck out on either side. "We figured you were due some visitors."

"When did you get in?"

"Just now," Jessy said, smiling.

Rebecca nodded, recalling the chopper she'd heard just moments ago. "Well, it's a wonderful surprise, I gotta say." She leaned back to appraise the younger woman. Jessy had ditched her trademark—and once-blonde—pigtails for a shorter, sensible ponytail. "You've dyed your hair. It's darker. I love it!"

"A change is as good as a holiday, right?"

"And your leg?"

Gingerly, Jessy raised her left foot to show off the moonboot encasing the calf. "Still doing my best Robocop impression. But I'm walking."

Jessy's injury had been serious—a spiral fracture of the tibia and fibula. Fortunately, there'd been no skin penetration, but back in the jungle she'd put too much weight on it—unavoidable, given the circumstances—and that had slowed her recovery. On arrival at Camp Delta, she'd had the leg cast and for the first couple of weeks had been confined to a wheelchair. The doctors had told her she'd be back to half-strength in a month or two; at least, that was how long it would take for the bones to heal. The ligament damage would take longer. But she was young and strong and by the looks of it, ahead of schedule.

Another Humvee rolled past. A handful of soldiers walked the opposite way, along the perimeter fence. Absently, Rebecca noted two more in the tower. At this time of day, most of the soldiers would be in their cans, or lazing under the communal tarpaulin of the rec area, trying to stay cool.

"It's hot out here," Rebecca said. Sweat rolled from her forehead, and she wiped it away. "Let's go inside. I've got aircon. And beer."

Owen and Jessy followed her inside and sat side by side on the bunk.

"I'm not even going to ask where—or how—you got your hands on these," Jessy said as they opened a round of Rebecca's secret stash of *cervejas*. She'd barely said the words before Priscilla flew into her arms, almost knocking her over in her desperation for a cuddle. Excitedly, the tiny monkey then bounded across to Owen, hugged him, and back again to Jessy, repeating the process.

Rebecca laughed, smiling fondly as the three reunited. Absently, she scratched her arm.

Jessy peeked past Priscilla and cringed. "Not another boro, I hope."

"God no," Rebecca said, and stopped scratching. She clicked her fingers and Priscilla leapt over to her and calmed, giving Jessy and Owen some peace. "But I had a few more, soon after you guys left."

"Me too," Jessy said, catching her breath.

"How many?"

"Another three," Jessy said. "Eighteen in total."

"*Shit.*"

None of them had escaped unscathed, it seemed. In the early weeks, Rebecca's doctors had been just as concerned by the numerous red lesions dotting her body as they had for her facial injuries. Some of those lumps had discharged fluid. The medical term was *furuncular myiasis*, but Rebecca had no need for an official diagnosis. To her, the signs of the boro were familiar, and already, she'd concluded that multiple botfly larvae were growing beneath her skin, feeding on her flesh. Back at Advance Base Camp, one of Oliveira's men, Luis, had extracted a single larva from her arm by blowing smoke into the creature's breathing hole and, through that hole, forcefully ejecting the inch-long maggot by applying sharp, sudden pressure with his thumb and forefinger. Of course, there were other options for removal of the parasites, most of them more appropriately advanced. The infirmary doctors, worried about infection, had ruled out allowing the maggots to mature and drop away naturally. Surgical extraction had been an option but wasn't without risk. In the end, they'd settled on an ingenious method. Using a venom extractor—basically, a plastic syringe—they'd simply sucked out the larvae; again, through the punctum, or the breathing hole.

From her, they'd extracted twelve of the things. Two from her scalp, one from behind her left ear, another two on her neck. They'd found one under her left armpit and had then pulled six from her legs. Disgusting. Even now, the thought of it made her stomach roll.

Jessy glanced at Owen and nudged him with her elbow. "Tell her."

Rebecca sensed what was coming. "How many, Owen?"

Owen swallowed hard. "Thirty-seven."

"Oh God."

"I forgot my repellent," he said grimly, before breaking into a half-smile.

Although trying to stay serious and empathetic, Rebecca returned the grin, which grew into a snigger. Before long, the two girls were in full-on hysterics.

"Yeah, yeah," Owen said, shaking his head, "laugh it up, why don't you?"

"It's not funny, I know, but…"

"It's a little funny," Jessy said, erupting into more laughter. This time, Owen joined in.

Eventually, the moment petered out, but Rebecca's smile remained. "God, I've missed you guys."

"We missed you, too," Owen said. "It's been a while."

"Still no phone?" Rebecca asked.

Owen shook his head. "Not that OPSEC would have transferred my call."

"You're probably right," Rebecca replied, nodding. For operational security, all personal communication devices—phones, tablets, laptops—had been forfeited as a matter of procedure; overkill, given the absence of cell towers on base. Personal calls had been allowed, via sat phones in the comms tent, but all information, both incoming and outgoing, had been monitored. She'd spoken to her siblings a couple of times, and her parents. Not wanting to worry them, she'd told them she was still on assignment—exciting discovery and all that, but she couldn't reveal anything just yet. She wasn't lying as such, just stretching the truth. That's what she told herself, anyway.

"You heard anything on the outside?" Rebecca asked. "Anything in the media?"

"A few snippets, nothing much," Jessy said. "Not exactly front-page material, right?"

Owen nodded. "I read one, just a paragraph or two, about a multinational team of scientists that had discovered a lost world deep in the Amazon jungle, in the process uncovering several new species of animal, including a number of insects previously unknown to science."

"Insects?" Rebecca said. "Where do they get their information?"

"You know where," Jessy said. "Anyway, there's been nothing on TV. Some international outlets ran a similar piece online, likely from the same press release."

"It's being carefully orchestrated and controlled," Owen said. "I found something else about a team of US-led scientists who'd uncovered a previously uncontacted lost tribe. Not connected with the other article."

"But that's all there's been," Jessy said.

The three friends sipped their beers, falling into a moment of silence.

"Have you heard from Robert?" Rebecca asked eventually.

"No."

"Chad?"

"I heard he'd come back down here, looking to get his hands on another boat, to start over," Owen said. "But otherwise, nothing."

Rebecca nodded. Confiscated phones, monitored communications, misinformation—it was no surprise they'd lost track of each other. Feeling a twinge of sadness, Rebecca wondered if she'd ever see Chad or Robert again.

She took another swig of beer. Aware she was no longer able to avoid the obvious question, she looked at Jessy. "You've heard from Ed?"

"Yes."

"Is he okay?"

Jessy glanced at Owen, and her mouth twitched momentarily.

"Jess?"

Jessy lowered her eyes. "Bec, he's okay. But I should tell you… Ed and I broke up."

A wave of conflicting feelings hit Rebecca hard, devastation at the demise of her friends' relationship, but also relief at the news of Ed's return to health. "I'm so sorry, Jess. Are you okay?"

"Yes, I'm fine. I'm okay. It's okay. It was amicable, and mutual."

"When did this happen?"

"A few weeks ago."

Rebecca fell into a moment of silence before speaking again. "And Ed? He's good? He's holding up?"

"I don't suppose you would have heard," Jessy said. "The doctors cleared him. Physically, he's recovered."

Thank God. "But…"

Jessy shifted her weight, and the bunk creaked. "He needs time, and space, is all. What happened down here—the incident… it was intense."

An understatement, if ever there was one.

Jessy went on. "At the time, in the heat of the moment, I guess it forced me and him closer, but then out of that environment, back home, we struggled. *He* struggled."

Rebecca wasn't sure how to respond. Soon after the river evacuation, Ed and Robert had been extracted to another location, but she hadn't been told where this was. None of them had. They found out later that Ed, at least, had been evacuated to the States for specialist treatment at a larger facility. Robert, a Brazilian national, had apparently been taken to a local hospital. Although she'd received ongoing assurances—both from the infirmary doctors and a variety of agency suits—that the two men were fine and doing well, Rebecca hadn't spoken with either of them since that day on the river. No direct contact, anyway, just some relayed well-wishes from the staff while the men were recovering; again, more smoke and mirrors. She'd struggled with the separation and the lack of information, especially in the early days, just like she'd struggled with a lot of things since then, and she couldn't remember at what point everything had become too much and she'd simply stopped resisting. "So, back in the States, they released Ed… they told me that, but…"

"He got out of the facility about the same time as Owen and I got out of here—when we left for home," Jessy said. "We met up, but it was… *he* was… different."

"Different?"

"In hindsight, we should have taken more time," Jessy said. "Taken things slowly. But we picked up where we left off, and it wasn't the same. Maybe we didn't try hard enough, or maybe we tried *too* hard; I don't know. But thinking back, he wasn't ready. Neither was I. It was too soon, too rushed, things were still raw. It was difficult."

Owen reached over and gently squeezed Jessy's knee, and then looked at Rebecca. "For the last two or three weeks, we haven't heard from him."

"What? Nothing?"

Jess shook her head. "He hasn't returned my texts, my calls."

"He just dropped out?" Rebecca said.

"He needs time."

Rebecca felt her face flush warm, surprised by—and unable to control—the sudden flare of anger. "This is so like him, isn't it?"

"Sorry?"

"Ed, he's so goddamned *selfish* at times."

"Bec, that isn't fair," Jessy said.

"Are you kidding?" Rebecca fired back. "He abandons you and disappears? Doesn't return calls? He only thinks of himself. This is so typical."

"Bec…"

It's what he did to me when we broke up. Took off and disappeared. It's what he does.

"It's been hard on all of us, Bec," Owen said. "Take it easy."

Rebecca drew a sharp breath, but she wasn't done. "I shouldn't be surprised. The way he behaved—"

"None of us can be proud of our behaviour," Jessy said, lowering her eyes. "You know, since we got back… what happened… it's played on my mind. A lot. We all let professional ambition get in the way, to cloud our judgment. We're all to blame. We all made mistakes."

Rebecca glanced away. Jessy was right—Rebecca had struggled with this herself. In one way or another, they'd all acted selfishly. Ed had dropped them in the shitter, sure enough, but each of them had willingly followed him down; God knows they could have made better decisions. People had died, and they were all responsible. They all had to live with that.

"Ed needs time. We all do," Owen said, as though picking up on her thoughts. "It's why you stayed behind, right?"

Rebecca looked at him, and her eyes narrowed. "I didn't leave with you guys because there was work to be done here. You get that, right? I wanted to continue my research. Egbert's here."

Owen nodded. "Yes, of course." He glanced at his watch, then at Jessy, and the atmosphere inside the CHU seemed to shift.

Rebecca looked at her friends in turn. "I never thought I'd see you guys down here again. Not after what happened."

Again, Jessy and Owen traded glances.

"Bec, listen," Jessy began.

"Why *have* you returned?" Rebecca interjected. Something was off. "Are you checking up on me?"

Owen shook his head. "We can't stay."

"What's wrong?" Rebecca asked.

"Bec," Owen said, leaning forward and lowering his voice to a whisper. "They made us sign non-disclosures. When we left, we couldn't get out of here without them. Nor could we get *back*."

"What's going on?"

Jessy reached out and took Rebecca's hand in hers. "They gave us a few minutes to come say hello, Bec. But we gotta go; we're heading out within the hour. They said they'd fill you in."

"They? Who? What do you mean? What's going on?"

"We can't say," Jessy said. "But you need to get over to the lab."

Rebecca's heart skipped a beat. "The lab? Why?"

"Just get over there, Bec. It's about Egbert."

3

α

Clutching Priscilla to her chest, Rebecca hurried across the compound, dodging puddles of mud and water, clusters of soldiers, and the occasional zigzagging Jeep. Owen and Jessy weren't with her—they'd stayed with the two soldiers Rebecca discovered had been stationed, for their entire visit, around the corner of her CHU.

Another chopper approached the facility. It must have been flying low, because she couldn't yet see it above the trees. Under the circumstances, she wouldn't have paid it heed, but this one sounded different. After two months of listening to them coming and going, she'd grown accustomed to the variations. Most were Black Hawks. This wasn't. This sounded bigger and heavier.

She was right.

A deafening roar of rotors washed over her, and the trees at the camp's southern edge flattened outward, succumbing to the powerful downdraft. A moment later, a dark shape rose ominously above their crowns, blotting the sky. Clearing the treetops, the aircraft settled into a hover above the bare patch of earth that was the helipad, causing leaves and loose debris to mushroom outwards.

The helicopter was conspicuous for a couple of reasons. First, and oddly, it was painted entirely black, with no identifying markings. The second was not so much the aircraft's size—although that was notable, because it was one of those heavy-lifting Chinooks with the tandem rotors—but because of what it transported.

Heavy lifting, indeed.

Beneath the chopper's substantial belly, swinging at the end of multiple sturdy tethers, was a shipping container.

Rebecca's heart leapt. The chopper was here to collect something.

Egbert.

The compound was comprised of a series of semi-permanent shelters. Rows of closely stacked shipping containers—living facilities and accommodation for the service personnel, including soldiers and support staff—dominated the north-eastern quadrant. This was where CHUville was located. The north-west was mainly administrative—a combination of demountable buildings and rigid inflatables, most of which were interconnected. She'd heard that a sprinkling of civilians, scientists and government employees were housed in their own facility in the south-western quadrant. She didn't know this for sure—it was fenced, and she had no access to the southern zones.

She had access to the lab, however. Using her prox-card, Rebecca burst inside. An observation window separated the viewing gallery—where she stood—and the cleanroom, all white and stainless steel. Inside that area, beyond the glass, men in biohazard suits moved about.

"What the hell?" Rebecca asked. She didn't have a clear view of what was happening in there, but she could guess.

Two armed soldiers with wired earpieces and dressed in black body armour and fatigues with no insignia blocked the airlock door. Another two guarded the gowning area and changerooms.

"This is my lab," Rebecca said, crossing to the airlock. "Let me pass!"

Neither soldier moved.

"Dr Riley." The voice came from behind.

Rebecca turned. Like the other soldiers, the owner of the voice was dressed in unmarked, black fatigues, with a sidearm holstered low on his thigh. Fit and broad-shouldered, he looked to be half a dozen years older than her, maybe more—his close-cropped hair, high and tight, was grey-flecked at the edges. Judging by his confident stride, he was the ranking officer.

"What's going on here?" Rebecca demanded, turning back to the window. Inside the cleanroom, two men slid open the specimen drawers, and frigid air looped and spiralled in a ghostly mist.

The holding cell door was open.

"You're taking him," she said, spinning back to the man. She noted, in his left hand, a manila folder. "You're taking Egbert."

"The live asset, yes. And the dead ones, too," the man replied.

"*Everything*? You can't do that!"

Behind the glass, the men in biohazard suits opened more drawers, pulling out specimen trays and canisters and loading all of them onto multiple stainless-steel gurneys.

"*Who the hell are you people*?" Rebecca thundered.

"Come with me, Dr Riley," the man replied. "I'll explain everything."

4
α

Near to the lab was a mobile command centre, and adjoining that, yet another prefabricated, drop-in shipping container. It was into this building that the man strode at pace. Rebecca hurried to keep up.

Inside, the demountable was basic and sparsely furnished, sporting a single desk, a metal filing cabinet, and three chairs, two on one side of the desk, the other behind it. Behind that chair, on a pole, hung a US flag.

She'd been here before.

"Where's Petersen?" she asked.

The man crossed to the other side of the desk but remained standing. "Please, have a seat, Dr Riley."

Rebecca ignored him. "This is the base commander's office."

"General Petersen won't be joining us today. Please, sit down."

The air-conditioning wasn't on. The air was heavy and hot, stirred only by a small desk fan. Rebecca stayed on her feet.

Regarding her with sharp blue eyes, the man smiled and held out his right hand. "I'm afraid I have you at a disadvantage. My name is Beckett."

No rank? She scanned his uniform for identifying marks, but again, found none. She doubted Beckett was this man's real name and concluded she was still at a disadvantage. "What branch are you with? Clearly, you're military."

Beckett smiled, but didn't answer. His face, handsome in a hard way, bore the scars of tough life experiences, and most likely battle. Clearly realising his current battle was unwinnable, he conceded and lowered his hand. Again, he gestured to the chair.

This time, Rebecca sat. Priscilla leapt into the other chair. Sitting himself, Beckett placed the manila folder on the desk and opened it. Silently, he flicked through the papers within.

Figuring the best way to wrest the advantage was to seize control of the conversation, Rebecca blurted, "Egbert is mine. The research is mine."

Beckett cleared his throat. "Yes, research," he said, picking up one of the pages and scanning it. "I must say, you're an accomplished researcher. Highly experienced, Dr Riley."

"Let's get this straight," Rebecca said. "I'm not a doctor."

"My apologies."

"No need to apologise," Rebecca said. "But I'm guessing you were across that detail already."

Beckett didn't look up. He flicked through more pages. "Ah, here it is. No, you're not a doctor, but you've been working towards it. You're part of a PhD programme."

"Yes."

"You have two degrees, Masters, no less—one in Science, another in Biology. Your specialty is predator-prey dynamics. That's your field of research."

"Yes, Mr Beckett, but I'm not sure—"

"I see you've completed all your coursework and were putting the final touches on your dissertation representing a report of independent research. What the hell is *Troglodytic*?"

"It means cave-dwelling," Rebecca answered. "My dissertation focused on predator behaviour in cave-dwelling spiders. I had arranged to complete my doctoral fieldwork in Venezuela, with the *Ciudad Universitaria de Caracas*."

"And?"

Rebecca glared at him. *This is bullshit.* "I missed it, because I was stuck down here."

Beckett nodded thoughtfully.

For some reason, Rebecca felt an urge to explain. "The thesis is written and completed. There's still the oral exam and dissertation defence before the study committee. Then I present my results to the department."

Beckett tried to feign interest, but judging by the way his eyes glazed over, he was anything *but* interested. "You've made perhaps the biggest discovery your field has ever seen. It's a shame they can't give you credit for your fieldwork."

"I don't think it works that way. And anyway, they'll never know, will they? Non-disclosure, right?"

He nodded again, but more to himself, as though he wasn't really listening.

"Going back to what I said, Egbert is mine. The research is mine."

"Egbert is an unusual name," Beckett stated.

"I named him after a character in a comic strip I used to read."

"Uh-huh," Beckett said, turning pages. "*Megarachne Amazonas*. That's Egbert's scientific name, right? You also came up with that, didn't you?"

Rebecca nodded.

"I haven't seen the specimen yet, but I hear it's impressive. And big. Damn big. Soldier caste, am I right?"

"Yes."

"A soldier. That's interesting."

"Mr Beckett—"

Beckett raised his eyes. They shone coldly. "Colonel," he said. "Let's get that straight."

His expression and his tone threw her, and in that instant, she sensed that any advantage she may have been fighting for was gone. "Colonel—"

"The asset is the property of the US government, Ms Riley," Beckett said sternly. "It isn't yours, nor is the research. It never has been."

She opened her mouth, but he thrust up a hand.

"Do I need to remind you, Ms Riley, of your agreement? Of the reason you were permitted to stay, while the others returned home to their families?"

She said nothing and instead, looked away.

Beckett leaned back, and his chair creaked. For a long moment, he was silent. "I knew this guy once, back in Nebraska. You ever been to Nebraska?"

"No."

"Nice place. Anyway, this guy, he was a no-hoper. Career criminal, but petty stuff. You know the type."

"No, I don't."

"Well, let me set the scene. All his life, this guy was in and out of the big house. He gets out again, but this time, less than a week after his release, he gets into this argument in a bar, right? Somewhere on the border, maybe even down in Kansas. Anyway, he beats up this guy; beats him to death, in fact, with an eight-ball! Brutal stuff. And when I say that he got into an argument, I mean, he picked it—over nothing, apparently—but there was intent, they say he planned it, so it was felony murder. So, here's this low-life, with nothing more serious on his rap sheet than a few break-and-enters, in and out of the pen, and now, suddenly, he's a lifer, in for good, down in Leavenworth." Beckett leaned forward and fixed her with a hard stare. "Do you know, Ms Riley, why he picked that fight? Why he killed that man?"

"He was afraid," Rebecca said without missing a beat. "Afraid of life on the outside. And this was his ticket back in."

Beckett smiled, and again, leaned back. The chair creaked. "Good," he said. "But you're only half-right. He was a coward, sure. Couldn't adjust to life on the outside, so he chose life on the inside. But fear didn't drive him to murder—trust me, he was motivated to do it."

"Yeah?"

Beckett again leaned forward. "What he wanted, Ms Riley, was to *hide*. From himself."

Rebecca looked at him, and for a moment, silence fell between them, only the noise of the desk fan turning slowly. Eventually, she broke the hush. "What a load of BS."

"Sorry?"

"Nice story," Rebecca said, "but I think you made it up to illustrate your point. You're suggesting that I'm afraid, right? Unsure of my next step? Maybe a little rudderless? And instead of owning that and facing up to it, I'm hiding down here, because that's the easy option. Is that what you think, Colonel?"

Again, Beckett smiled, and his eyes shone. "What I think, Ms Riley, is that you should be asking those questions not of me, but of yourself."

Rebecca clasped her hands in her lap. It was clammy in here.

Beckett returned to his papers. "There are protocols for this, Ms Riley."

"For what?"

"For the discovery of certain scientific… *anomalies*."

"I'm sure there are."

"For your safety, and for the safety of medical personnel and the soldiers at this base, not to mention the general populace, you and your team were kept under observation for an indeterminate period. The base commander was under direct orders from the Army Chief of Staff. That period ended five weeks ago."

"I asked to stay on and continue my research."

"And your government thanks you for your work. Truly impressive."

Rebecca frowned. "Colonel, I'm an Australian citizen, and my work was part of a privately funded expedition."

Again, Beckett glanced down at the manila folder. "Yes, I'm aware you're an Australian national." He shuffled to another page, ran his eyes over it, and went on without looking up. "For the past four years, you've lived in New York, and have been employed at the American Museum of Natural History. I haven't been there myself—the museum, I mean—but I hear it's well worth the visit."

"Colonel, I fail to see the relevance—"

"As an Australian professional in a specialty occupation, you're in the States on an—" he scanned the page— "E-3 visa." He looked up at her. "Is that right, Ms Riley?"

"Yes."

He nodded, glanced back down at the paper. "This is not my field of expertise, of course, but I understand there's a validity period of 24 months for this particular visa classification. You've had an extension already, by the looks of things, but in the next month or so it's up for another renewal. Do you anticipate applying for renewal, Ms Riley?"

Rebecca felt her cheeks flush warm. What did he mean by that? Was he threatening her?

"Ms Riley?"

Careful to maintain her composure, Rebecca drew a calming breath. "Colonel, what are you trying to say?"

Beckett set the piece of paper aside and tented his fingers. "I'm sure you can appreciate the sensitive nature of your work down in GR-43."

GR-43. That was a mapping term, a grid reference.

"Ms Riley?"

Rebecca puckered her brow. "Sorry. Grid Reference 43. Intihuasi, you mean?"

"The investigation into the events at Restricted Area GR-43 is ongoing," Beckett said.

Restricted Area. So, it's under military control. Of *course* it is.

"Ma'am?"

"The investigation," Rebecca said. "You mean into the civilian deaths, and the deaths of those soldiers."

"There was substantial loss of life, yes," Beckett replied. "The fifteen men who perished in service to their country have families, and those families deserve answers."

Rebecca agreed. "Yes, of course."

Beckett nodded. "But none of what went on here, or down in GR-43, is for public consumption. None of it, either real or imagined."

"Imagined?" Rebecca stammered.

Beckett didn't flinch. "Let me summarise," he said, clearing his throat and reading from another page. "Deep in the Brazilian Amazon, a multinational team of scientists uncover a mysterious object with strange and unusual powers, guarded by a deadly species of animal—a *superspider*, no less—both of unknown, possibly extraterrestrial origin." He lay the page on the desk. "How does that read to you?"

"You forgot the bit about the ancient city, and the lost tribe. Oh, and the diamonds... and the drug runners. Otherwise, it's on the mark."

"It's absurd."

"It *sounds* absurd, yes," Rebecca corrected. "But every word is true, and you know it."

"It's fantasy."

"Not to me or my team," Rebecca said. "Or those fifteen soldiers."

Beckett's jaw clenched, and slowly, he leaned forward. "Let me reframe things, then. The incident, the discovery—it's classified. Top-secret. Quite simply, as far as you're concerned, it didn't happen."

A low throb beat at Rebecca's temple and she reached for it. He was kidding, right? Full denial? She'd figured they'd lock things down for the duration of the investigation—hell, she'd agreed to non-disclosure herself as part of her arrangement to stay on base and continue her research—but not this. Not long-term public concealment. Those who lost their lives deserved better than that.

"Ms Riley?"

Rebecca blinked. "Let me guess. You're suggesting it was… what? An unfortunate training accident?"

Beckett shrugged. "That's more realistic, wouldn't you say? But of course, it's all conjecture. The investigation is ongoing; I can't pre-empt its findings."

"You're sweeping it under the carpet," Rebecca said slowly. "And you're asking me to lie."

Beckett's gaze hardened. "I'm not asking you anything. I'm *requiring* you to understand."

"Understand?"

"Make no mistake, you need to understand. My job is to *make* you understand."

Rebecca shook her head. Again, this was bullshit. "I get it, Colonel."

"Do you? To ensure we're singing from the same hymn sheet, let me state it nice and plain: you are bound to secrecy, under penalty of prosecution. Should you break that secrecy, you will be prosecuted to the full extent of the law. This is serious. It carries jail time. Am I clear?"

"Crystal," Rebecca said, and with that, the throb in her temple intensified. She should have seen this coming. Maybe deep down, she had. But still, this was wrong.

"Are you sure?"

"You're not asking me to lie. You're requiring me to keep my mouth shut."

"No, not me. US law requires that."

She thought to ask if that applied to her as an Australian but didn't.

"Ma'am?"

"I get it."

"Good." Beckett held her in his stare, his cold blue eyes boring into her, as though assessing her commitment to the cause. Eventually, the intensity behind them faded, and breaking the gaze, he returned to the papers. "Now, back to your friend Egbert, and your research, and why we're here today."

Rebecca didn't want to be here at all. She wanted to get up and run.

"We're absorbing the project, Ms Riley," Beckett announced. "More accurately, we're relocating it. You're through down here. Shut down, effective immediately."

The air in the room seemed to thin. Rebecca baulked, feeling a shortness of breath as a deeper, more alarming truth hit her. "This isn't just about Egbert," she said, her voice cracking.

"I have your release papers here—"

"You're cancelling my visa. You're sending me back home. To Australia."

Likely sensing Rebecca's change in demeanour, Priscilla leapt from her chair, scampering up Rebecca's arm to hug her around the neck.

His lip curling at the edge, Beckett half-smiled at the scene. "You've become quite attached to that monkey of yours."

"She's not mine," Rebecca said slowly, absently, still trying to process this latest turn of events. "Not strictly, anyway."

Again, Beckett consulted his notes. "I understand we haven't been able to track down Enrique Paulo's family. The Capuchin is currently in your care."

"Yes… that's correct."

"What are your plans for her?"

Plans? For Priscilla? Right now, any plans she may have had for her, for *anything*, seemed dead and buried. Not that she'd thought too far ahead—to be honest, she'd avoided the subject for fear of the inevitable.

Now, Beckett confirmed those fears. "I'm not sure of the regulations in Australia, but there are CDC regulations prohibiting importation of NHPs into the US, specifically as pets."

Rebecca's body shot through with weakness. "NHPs. Non-human primates." Tears blurred her vision, but she fought them. "I don't understand why you're telling me this. The US? None of this relevant."

As though not hearing her, Beckett turned to his notes, scanning the pages. "It says here that there are importation allowances for permitted purposes—scientific, educational, exhibition. However—" he flicked back to a previous page, "you've been residing in New York. Capuchin are prohibited in New York, Ms Riley."

"Colonel, please, I'm not following."

Still focused on his notes, Beckett read from another page. "While the CDC's Division of Global Migration and Quarantine administers the regulations about importation, the laws concerning the possession of exotic animals in the US are not uniform." Anticipating an objection, he held up a hand. "So, while NHPs are banned in New York, the regulations are less stringent in other states. States like Nevada, for instance." Oblivious to her frown, Beckett sighed and leaned forward in his chair, to more creaking. "Let's back this up, shall we? You jumped to conclusions a moment ago, which, quite frankly, seems unusual for a scientist, especially one of your calibre."

A fog, thick and swirling, had settled in Rebecca's head, clouding her ability to think straight. *What the hell is he talking about?* "Colonel…"

"You're not being deported, Ms Riley. Quite the opposite, in fact. You've been seconded. Dr Worboys has cleared you for duty. She signed the medical certificate."

Rebecca hesitated, caught off-guard. *What? Cleared me for duty*? Was that the reason for Helen's spontaneous and slightly awkward house call earlier? Had it been a final check-up? A final goodbye?

Beckett cleared his throat. "You need to sign some papers, of course."

"Hang on," Rebecca said, needing a moment. None of this was making sense—it was as though time had jumped forward a few seconds and left her flailing in its wake. "You said I've been seconded?"

"Reassigned. Professor Hayward has organised everything."

At the mention of that name, Rebecca's head spun ever faster, and she suspected that if she hadn't already been sitting, she may well have collapsed on the spot. *Frank*? What the hell? Francis Hayward was the museum's curator and head of the Entomology Department—not just her boss, but her mentor. She considered him a close friend. A couple of months ago, on the back of Ed's incredible discovery down here in the jungle, she'd begged Frank for some time off work, giving him almost zero notice and even fewer details. But he'd obliged, no questions asked. Afterwards, she'd struggled with the fact she hadn't revealed to him the true nature of Ed's discovery—to be fair, at the time, she'd been in the dark herself and had decided, for the moment at least, to keep her cards close. But her subterfuge had ashamed her. Frank had been curious, of course, but to his credit had helped rush through the paperwork. His efforts had been instrumental in getting her down here.

Now, was he trying to get her back *out*?

"We've kept Professor Hayward availed of your situation. He's excited about your return to work."

"I don't understand," Rebecca said. "How is Frank involved?"

"That's obvious, isn't it?" Beckett replied. "We approached Professor Hayward partly because of his connection with *you*, and as one of the eminent minds in your field, he came highly recommended. He's heading up the research team."

"*What* research team?" Rebecca asked. She felt numb, stunned by the never-ending stream of revelations. In a daze, struggling for clarity, she cast her mind back over the past two months, trying to recall the two or three conversations she'd had with her mentor during that period—monitored, of course. She'd told Frank only what the script had permitted—a partly true story about a new species of Salticid she'd discovered down here, very exciting and all that, and she'd need another few weeks and it'd be good for the museum, but the account was deliberately vague and barely scratched the surface of what she was really up to. At the time, she'd agonised over how far she was willing to take this, where the line between white lies and outright deceit lay, and she'd concluded that maybe there was no line at all and that she was simply repeating the shameful errors of her past. But she'd been bound to non-disclosure, right? Classified information. Need-to-know. She'd had no choice—that much was true, wasn't it? Frank, she was certain, had known more than he was letting on, and she'd been desperate to speak to him freely, but General Petersen had assured her that she needn't worry about Frank or the museum, that she needn't get bogged down with the details because everything had been handled on her behalf—in fact, he'd told her not to worry about *anything* back home at all. To be honest, that had suited her, because if she believed Petersen, if she trusted that everything had been handled and everyone had been kept in the loop and she was only doing what she was required by law to do, she could sleep at night—fitfully, if nothing else. So, she'd blindly put her faith in Petersen and towed the line and been assured Frank and the museum had sanctioned her work down here and the funding was approved and all that, but she wasn't permitted to discuss those details, not over the phone, which in hindsight made no sense at all but again, everything had been *handled*—they kept telling her that. What, or how much Frank had really known she couldn't be certain, not then. But if Beckett was telling her the truth *now*, Frank had been privy to a great deal. In fact, it seemed he'd been keeping as much from her as she from him. "You mentioned Nevada…"

Beckett nodded. "We have a research facility there. State-of-the-art. Like I said, your project has been absorbed, and you have clearance to join Professor Hayward's team. You can continue your work with Egbert." He pointed at Priscilla. "Now, as I was trying to say, we've cleared your pet, too, all in line with Nevada's regulations. She's passed quarantine, had all the tests done. We've arranged for her entry into the US for miscellaneous purposes."

Miscellaneous?

"Everything's been arranged, Ms Riley. We're extending your visa, and you're free to take Priscilla."

"To Nevada…"

"Yes. To your new posting."

"My new posting," Rebecca repeated slowly, probingly, as though the phrasing was alien and unfamiliar. "And Frank organised this? Can I speak with him?"

"Not at this time," Beckett said. "Professor Hayward is out of town for a few days. That's part of the reason we want you up and running by the morning." With that, Beckett slid the papers into the manila folder, closed it, and stood.

"The morning?" Rebecca stammered, scrabbling to catch up. "*Tomorrow* morning?'

Sweeping his right hand in the direction of the door, Beckett nodded. "We have a chopper prepped and waiting. We'll brief you in transit."

5
α

Exiting the room, Beckett strode quickly down the adjoining corridor. Rebecca struggled to keep up—and not just physically.

Why was she only learning about all of this *now*? And why hadn't she been told there was research being conducted parallel to hers? She needed time to think.

Stall him.

"You wanted me to sign some papers?"

"We'll do that en route," Beckett said, outside now.

Rebecca exited behind him. On her shoulder, Priscilla hopped about anxiously.

Out the front was a parked Jeep. Beckett made for it.

"Wait," Rebecca said. "Please, hold up. I want to know what I'm agreeing to, what my work will entail, what kind of facility we're talking about. Frank will take my call."

At the Jeep's door, Beckett paused and turned. "Ah, yes, that reminds me… your phone. Once we're in the air, I'll ensure it's returned to you. If you're inclined, you can call Professor Hayward on the way."

Rebecca considered asking Beckett for another phone. Any phone. Even *his*.

"You're overthinking this, Ms Riley," Beckett said, as though reading her mind. "Let's be clear: You don't have the resources down here to keep the project moving forward—Professor Hayward, on the other hand, *has*, and he's moved mountains to get you clearance and bring you on board. Not just you, to be fair, but Egbert, too. You should be pleased."

Should I?

"We're merely progressing with the plan, Ms Riley."

"The *plan*… right," Rebecca said. "But Intihuasi… the nest… everything is down here."

"There's nothing for you down here. Not anymore."

The tone of that last sentence seemed eminently insurmountable. Still, Rebecca opened her mouth, about to argue, when overhead a chopper roared past, silencing her and giving her a moment's pause. When it had gone and she had her chance to reply, she didn't. Who was she kidding? She was powerless to stop this. Beckett was seizing her research, seizing Egbert—which *sucked*, because she was losing control—but he was also extending her a lifeline, one that seemed fair and attractive: a renewed visa, entry back into the country, with Priscilla, no less, and a golden opportunity to continue her work, all with the backing of Frank, and by extension, the museum.

Like he said, she should be pleased. So why wasn't she?

Because Beckett's railroading you. He might even be threatening you.

Was he? It certainly felt that way. If nothing else, he was herding her in a direction over which she had zero control. And maybe that was the crux of it.

Control.

Maybe, right from the start, *everything* had been stage-managed—the whole thing, ever since her arrival. Sure, she'd asked to stay on to continue her research, and had been given unlimited access to Egbert—to date, the only live specimen they'd managed to acquire. But perhaps things had fallen into place too easily. Had Beckett's people been behind that? Had they orchestrated the approval? Clearly it was possible, if not probable—Beckett, or whoever the hell he worked for, seemed to wield significant power; enough, no less, to kick a General out of his own office. If those same people had wanted to control her—just like they'd controlled the media and the public, even their families—it made sense to keep her here, to keep tabs on her until they needed her.

They needed her now, seemingly.

Maybe she should tell them where to stick their proposal.

Tempting, but counterproductive.

You'll lose everything. And you've lost enough already.

Slowly, Rebecca crossed the muddy ground to the Jeep, her boots making sucking sounds. If Frank was involved, he'd have her best interests at heart. This man Beckett couldn't be trusted, but Frank, she trusted implicitly.

She opened the door, and another realisation dawned. She wouldn't admit it, not to Beckett, anyway, but through all the posturing and manipulation he'd forced her to confront an awkward truth. He was right.

She'd been hiding down here.

It was time to come out.

"I should pack," Rebecca said, taking a seat.

Beckett smiled, sliding behind the wheel. "No need. Your things have already been collected."

Right. Of course. She should have objected to Beckett's audacity, his presumption, or at least been riled at the thought of someone handling her personal effects without her permission. Instead, all she felt was a numbing, inescapable force, an inexorable pull to a future she couldn't resist.

Again, Priscilla, on her shoulder, chittered nervously.

Rebecca reached up to reassure her. She wondered if taking the tiny monkey to the States was the right thing to do. Maybe Priscilla was better off down here, or even back in the wild. The latter seemed unrealistic—she was too domesticated for release. And the former? Who could she leave her with? They'd had no luck tracking down Enrique's next of kin; Sanchez might know how to find them, but he, too, had dropped off the radar—Rebecca hadn't heard from him in two months. And anyway, who's to say they'd even want her?

Priscilla has bonded with me. She seems happy. You're her family now. Take her, and track Robert down when you can. Decide what's best after that.

Head spinning, Rebecca buckled up. As she did, Beckett's words came back to her; how he'd said he'd return her phone once she was on the plane. When she had it, she'd start making calls. Her first would be to Frank, to get some answers. Once she'd spoken with Frank, things would be clearer. She'd have options.

If you want, you can call Ed, too.

Dodging Humvees and trucks, Beckett drove to the helipad onto which the Chinook had earlier lowered a shipping container. Both the Chinook and the container had disappeared, no doubt with Egbert on board. On the helipad now, in place of the container, was a powerful looking, grey-coloured

HH-60 Pave Hawk. She'd seen several of these during her time here. On the side of this aircraft, in white, were the letters USAF.

An air force chopper.

"Climb aboard," Beckett said, helping her from the Jeep. "I'll be with you shortly." He turned and hurried to a group of black-clad soldiers loading crates and duffel bags into the aircraft.

Feeling dazed and somehow removed from her body, Rebecca looked past them, to the edge of the helipad where, several yards from the group of soldiers, a second Jeep was parked. Beside it stood Owen and Jessy. Beckett, she noted, had his back to her.

Snapping out of her stupor, Rebecca hurried to her friends. "Why didn't you tell me about Nevada?" she asked as the Pave Hawk's rotors powered up. She stood close so that Owen and Jessy could hear her, but she kept her voice out of earshot of anyone else.

Owen frowned. "Nevada?"

Jessy swallowed. "They told us they were absorbing the project, but nothing more. We knew they weren't giving us the full story, but our hands were tied… Beckett's an asshole."

"Did Beckett say *where* in Nevada?" Owen asked.

Rebecca looked at him. "No, just some research facility. Why are you surprised by this?"

Jessy lowered her gaze. "Bec, we're not coming with you."

"What?"

"Ms Riley?" It was Beckett. Seemingly annoyed she wasn't on the chopper, he started walking over.

Quickly, Owen pulled Rebecca into a close hug, pressing his lips close to her ear and angling his head to hide his words from Beckett. "I'm sorry, Bec, but we weren't permitted to discuss it. We're heading back to Intihuasi."

What the hell?

Owen didn't miss a beat. "Something big is happening. Need-to-know, so we're not up with the full story. But they need experts down there, specialists in a variety of fields. I guess we're it, and we know the site. Once we're there, we'll work out how to get in touch with you. Remember, the phones are monitored."

With that, he broke the embrace. His face was ablaze, perhaps with shame, but also something else. Anxiety?

Beckett drew alongside them. "Your luggage is loaded, Ms Riley. We need to get moving—the rest of your team is awaiting pickup."

Rebecca wondered, fleetingly, who that might be, but with Owen's revelation still ringing in her ears, didn't pursue it. Beckett didn't elaborate, either, and simply turned and left. As he went, he barked instructions to one of his men, who moved to ease Priscilla from Rebecca's embrace.

"She needs to go in a carrier for the flight," the soldier said.

"I'll do it," Rebecca snapped, keeping hold of Priscilla and turning back to her friends.

"Bec," Jessy said, reaching out to gently squeeze Rebecca's hand. "I'm so sorry…"

Rebecca opened her mouth, but no words emerged. She could feel that her own face had flushed hot, just like Owen's, but for a different reason; she was angry, but she was mostly hurt and confused. Owen and Jessy were heading back to Intihuasi *without* her? It made no sense: she'd asked to remain here with the specific aim of returning there as soon as practicable, and yet here she was, about to head in the opposite direction while *they* returned? It wasn't surprising that Beckett had kept this under wraps; if he hadn't, he'd never have attained her consent to Nevada.

Nevada. That's where he wanted her. Frank, too. It all came back to that.

"Owen," Rebecca said. "What's in Nevada? A moment ago, you reacted to that."

Owen pursed his lips, unsure. "Beckett said it was a research facility?"

"That's what he told me. What do you know?"

"Nothing," Owen replied, his voice low. "But your ride, it's an air force helicopter."

"The others have been army," Rebecca said. "So?"

"I'm not sure how many facilities the air force has in Nevada, but I know of at least one, just outside Vegas: Nellis Air Force Range. Groom Lake."

Rebecca raised her eyebrows. "You think *that's* where I'm going?"

Jessy frowned. "Groom Lake? What are you talking about?"

Owen turned to her. "Detachment 3, Air Force Flight Test Center, also referred to as Groom Lake. It goes by other names, too: Paradise Ranch, Dreamland, Watertown, Homey Airport, Area 51—"

Jessy's eyes widened. "You're kidding, right?"

Glancing nervously at Beckett, who was still barking orders nearby, Owen said, "Bec, you should go. I'm sorry it went down like this."

"Me too, Bec," Jessy said. "Please forgive us."

That deep sense of shame flared again in her friends' eyes, and Rebecca wondered why Beckett hadn't simply flown the two of them straight to Intihuasi, bypassing her altogether. Bringing them here was risky.

Control, remember? Beckett's using them. He must have his reasons.

Rebecca pulled the two of them into a tight hug. "There's nothing to forgive. It's okay."

"Take care, Bec," Owen said.

Rebecca smiled faintly, still a little hurt, and turned for the chopper, her mind abuzz as she hurried beneath the spinning blades. Climbing aboard, she considered the timing of this latest twist. It was no coincidence that on the very day she was reassigned—two long months after her arrival—Owen and Jessy show up on their way back to Intihuasi. Owen had said that something was going on down there, and no doubt something was unfolding in Nevada, too. Beckett was rushing; everything was connected.

She took a seat, joined in the rear of the chopper by four black-clad, stony-faced soldiers. Beckett moved up front.

She'd barely finished locking Priscilla into her carrier—calming her with a few soothing assurances—before the Pave Hawk rose amidst a swirl of debris. Rebecca looked down at the patch of cleared jungle, at the make-shift roads and low buildings she'd called home for the past two months, and at the edge of the helipad, the figures of her companions, each with an arm raised protectively against the eddying detritus.

She waved, and they waved back, and then another chopper swept in from the side, their ride to Intihuasi, no doubt, and suddenly her own chopper banked sharply and peeled north and then the compound was gone and so were her friends, replaced by a wash of green. Seized by an instant sense of loss, Rebecca turned, desperate to look back, but the chopper had righted itself and her view was forced to the horizon.

No looking back. Just forward.

How poetic.

Rebecca swallowed, still gazing ahead but for the moment not really seeing anything. She sensed she was speeding towards an uncertain future, and when at last she focused, she noticed dark clouds stacking high in the distance. A storm was building.

She hoped it wasn't an omen.

In the carrier beside her, Priscilla babbled softly. Rebecca poked a finger through the wire and stroked the monkey's chin, comforted by the touch. She avoided eye contact with Beckett's men, who sat without speaking.

Still caressing Priscilla, Rebecca sank against the headrest. Her thoughts roved, eventually returning to Owen and Jessy, and into her mind's eye came the image of their tiny forms waving to her as she departed.

Could Owen be right about her destination?

It was possible.

What the hell have we been dragged into?

Rebecca wondered about that as the chopper carried her away.

6
α

FIELD CAMP 2, JUST OUTSIDE KUNLUN STATION
EAST ANTARCTIC ICE SHEET, ANTARCTICA
AUSTRALIAN ANTARCTIC TERRITORY

The Kamov Ka-32 thundered across the ice sheet, low to the ground.

Leaning forward, Wei Zhou scanned the sea of white. "There," he said, pointing past the pilots and through the windshield at a cluster of dark shapes in the distance. Out here, with little to provide contrast, it was easy to lose perspective, but as the chopper closed on its target his confidence grew. "That's the site."

Sitting opposite him, the South African squinted ahead and spoke into his throat mic. Zhou wasn't privy to the order, but the accompanying soldiers—like their commanding officer, dressed in winter camo and heavily armed—checked their equipment. Zhou swallowed nervously. The Antarctic Treaty prohibited all military activity down here, but this, it seemed, was of no consequence to his superiors.

The chopper slowed, descending. As it did, the South African removed his gloves, flexing his fingers for warmth. Zhou glanced down and noticed, tattooed across the man's right hand, four letters, one per knuckle: CASH. Across the knuckles of his left hand, another four: ONLY.

Appropriate, Zhou thought, before sensing a gaze upon him. He raised his eyes to find Dwayne Cash staring back at him, unblinking.

"You are… I see you're…married," Zhou stuttered in English, referencing the band of gold on the South African's ring finger, just below the tattooed 'L.'

Cash said nothing in reply, and simply slipped the ring from his left hand to the third finger of his right.

Feeling foolish, but even worse, fearing he'd spoken out of line, Zhou's breath caught in his throat.

Cash held the stare, his cold, green eyes shining, and although a broad grin slowly opened across his bearded face, he maintained his silence. Since departing Kunlun, the man had barely said a word.

Zhou wished he'd kept quiet himself.

The chopper landed. One of Cash's men slid open the door, and a swirling gust blew loose snow inside. Then the soldiers piled out and were gone. Fitting his goggles, Zhou jumped out after them. Ahead, across the ice, a couple of RDS inflatables struggled in the gale. Parked beside the shelters was a yellow track vehicle with an integrated drilling rig. In front of that, waving, was a man in thick-layered, cold-weather gear.

"Bai Chen, I presume?" Zhou called to him above the wind, reverting to Mandarin.

The man nodded and held out his hand. "Dr Zhou, it is an honour." He jutted his chin. "Unfortunately, your companions did not wait… they are already inside."

"And the drill team?"

"Down below."

Noting tracks in the snow, Zhou moved to follow Cash and his men, but a hand gently held him back.

"I was expecting you, Doctor," the younger man whispered. "But mercenaries?"

"We have orders," Zhou said in a low voice. "You should know better than to question them."

Chen bowed apologetically, and Zhou hurried ahead, tracking the footprints to a large inflatable tent pitched over the ice. No flags fluttered at its entrance, which wasn't surprising. This was a temporary field camp, situated in Australian territory. By rights, they shouldn't be here at all.

Chen seemed to sense his concerns. "We are a long way south; the satellites rarely pass this region. We have time."

"The heat blooms were detected by satellite," Zhou countered.

"Yes—one of ours. But it will be many hours before foreign eyes are above us."

Drawing back the tent flap, Zhou ducked his head. "Then I guess there is no time like the present."

They stepped inside. It was good to escape the wind, but it remained bitterly cold in here, the kind of cold that ached deep inside the muscles. Underfoot, most of the loose snow had been cleared away, exposing the ice, and Zhou was careful not to slip as he moved to the centre of the shelter, where an array of halogen lights encircled a large round hole maybe six feet in diameter. Descending not merely into that hole, but into deep, blue-hued shadow, was a steel ladder. Cash and his men weren't here; they must have gone down.

"We covered the site, not just to protect it from above, but from the elements," Chen said, his breath puffing out in a misty cloud. "We noted accelerated ice melt."

Zhou nodded. The Antarctic ice sheet was melting faster than ever, but Chen's observation had nothing to do with global warming. "And the air?"

"Breathable, but you should wear this." Chen passed Zhou a face mask. "Are you ready?"

Zhou fitted the mask. "Lead on."

Their boots clanked on the ladder's steel rungs. In cold-weather gear, the descent wasn't easy, and again, Zhou was cautious. He felt like an astronaut making the slow climb from a lunar module onto the surface of the moon and thought, wistfully, that this place was as harsh and alien as the environment encountered by the men of Apollo 11.

"It is fortunate Kunlun had an eminent geophysicist on hand, Doctor," Chen called up from several rungs below. "You won't be disappointed."

"How long has it been down here?" Zhou called back.

"Longer than you'd think… the depth suggests a few thousand years. But we won't know for certain until we get the core samples back."

"And the recent activity?"

"This, I admit, is strange," Chen said. "It seemed to just… *wake up.* Then…"

His voice trailed off.

About twenty feet down, the drill team had cut a shelf into the ice, leading to another opening, and another ladder. Following Chen, Zhou climbed into this new hole, his breath coming now in misty, ragged heaves.

"We're here, Doctor."

At the bottom, Zhou turned… and stifled a gasp.

A void in the deep-blue ice opened wide before him—effectively, a cavern with sheer, angular walls. Partially buried in the floor, its upper half exposed, was a large—and clearly foreign—object.

"*Incredible…*"

The sphere was at least twenty feet across, and made, it seemed, of a dark alloy—though what this was, Zhou couldn't be certain. Curiously, protruding from its exposed outer surface were several crystalline growths, almost like rods of glass. The object's shape, in combination with the studded protuberances, made it vaguely reminiscent of those old floating sea mines.

"*Incredible*," Zhou repeated, but in truth, his attention was split. He was drawn now to the surrounding ice.

Radiating from the sphere for several feet in all directions was a succession of strange ripples—like those in the disturbed surface of a pond, but unmoving—and Zhou suspected the ice surrounding the sphere had recently melted and refrozen. Crusting these rings was a huge, green-black stain, a substance that resembled tar, but was at the same time also like mold, or even lichen or fungus—it seemed to be all of these—and as he inspected it more closely, Zhou realised it wasn't just on *top* of the ice, but *within* it, because he could see long, snaking tendrils deep beneath his feet, spreading through the ice and across it and up inside the walls, and he couldn't help but feel the distinctly plantlike substance was an organism of some kind.

An organism—trapped within the icy bowels of an Antarctic cavern, hidden from light, hidden from the sun. It wasn't possible.

"We need to work quickly—"

Zhou cut himself off, realising Chen hadn't spoken since entering the cavern. Sensing a presence to his left, he spun.

Several yards from the sphere, in a void off the main chamber, stood Cash and his men, all four of them, guns out. Kneeling in front of them was Chen and the five members of his drill team.

"What… what is this?" Zhou stammered. His gut squirmed.

Pressing his sidearm to Chen's temple, Cash said, "You hit the nail on the head, Doctor—we *do* need to work quickly. Governments will kill for what's inside this chamber, you know that."

"Please, no," Chen begged, his chin quivering. "We did what we were told. We maintained radio silence. Please… I have a family."

In the confined space the gunshot was deafening. Instantaneously, Chen's head erupted, a fountain of blood spraying across the ice, red on blue. His body slumped, but before it had even hit the floor more shots rang out; Cash's men executing the rest of Chen's team, and there were more gouts of red and Zhou put his hands to his ears as the soldiers put a further round into each man's heart. Then there was silence and Zhou, certain he was next, held up his hands in submission, recoiling in fear… only to watch the South African holster his weapon.

"What… what have you done?" Zhou asked, trembling.

"I've given you plausible deniability," Cash answered, turning to speak into his throat mic, maybe to the pilots in the chopper above. He then addressed his men. "Prepare the object for extraction. Leave the bodies."

"Leave them?" Zhou stammered.

Cash turned to him. "You don't want your nation involved or implicated."

"But these men. They're citizens…"

"Precisely," Cash said. "You wouldn't do this to your own citizens, right? And you certainly wouldn't leave them down here. Quite obviously, this is the work of a foreign entity—perhaps the Australians, but probably the Americans. Like I said, governments will kill for this."

"But they were digging…"

"They were surveyors, and they had permission."

Moments later, he and Cash were topside. Obviously, Cash needed reception above the ice, because from a pocket in his vest, he retrieved a sat-phone; no doubt the device was secure and encrypted. In the howling wind he entered a number and after a brief pause, spoke into the mouthpiece. "We have it."

Zhou wasn't aware the South African was fluent in Mandarin.

Another pause, then Cash said, "Affirmative. The sleepers are awake. Odysseus has been activated."

7
α

An hour after departing Camp Delta, the Pave Hawk landed at an airfield on the outskirts of a small jungle town with simple roads and buildings with corrugated iron roofs. Slinging her knapsack and sports bag—the two pieces of luggage she'd brought with her from New York a lifetime ago—Rebecca hoisted Priscilla's crate and leapt onto the sealed tarmac.

On the runway ahead sat a large, drab-grey cargo plane, evidently a Hercules. Its loading ramp yawned. Various personnel—some pushing equipment-laden hand-trucks, some performing pre-flight checks—milled about. Flanked by soldiers, Rebecca headed for the throng.

On the nose of the aircraft, stencilled in white, was a series of letters and numbers: USAF C-130J.

Just like the Pave Hawk, the Hercules was the property of the US Air Force. Rebecca wondered if that was the branch of the military Beckett worked for.

Movement caught her eye. On the other side of the plane, a heavy-duty forklift peeled away, heading towards a series of hangars. In front of those buildings sat the black Chinook, and next to that, on a truck trailer, was the shipping container the chopper had conveyed to and from Camp Delta. The hinged door to the container was slightly ajar.

Inside that container, Rebecca knew, had been Egbert's crate. Egbert must already be on the plane.

Juggling her luggage and Priscilla's carrier, Rebecca scampered up the incline and into the shadowed belly of the Hercules.

Overtly utilitarian, the cargo bay was a combination of padded canvas walls, exposed steel struts, and cargo netting. It wasn't as large as she'd expected, maybe forty feet long and ten feet across, but big enough to accommodate several vehicles end to end if needed. Presently, it housed a couple of pallets loaded with unmarked, polycarbonate equipment cases. Some of those, no doubt, stored the specimen drawers from her lab.

Running beneath the pallets, along the floor, was a roller system. Beyond the pallets, towards the front of the plane, sat Egbert's crate.

Dodging more personnel, Rebecca hurried for it. Strapped down tight, the white, cube-shaped pen was unmarked and non-descript. No holes or windows were cut into its eight-foot-long steel walls; air was recycled through a ventilation system and cameras had been mounted internally to assist observation. Fully integrated and secure, this was the very same, purpose-built crate that had been used for Egbert's initial transfer from Intihuasi to Camp Delta. While she hadn't been personally involved in that operation, she'd been granted full access to the specimen following its capture. She'd named him, and as the onsite head of research, she'd considered him hers. Until today.

On the side of the crate, built into one of the corrugated walls, was a monitor and interface. A man in fatigues, tablet in hand, stood before it.

"He's sleeping," the technician said without looking up. With a stylus, he ticked various checks on the tablet. "Chemically restrained, of course."

"Isoflurane?"

"Eight percent. Low anaesthetic depth. Just a light sleep."

Chemical immobilization was the only way to safely transport Egbert, who, it had to be said, had a grumpy reputation. It was safe enough—commonly, carbon dioxide was used to anaesthetise regular-sized spiders so their venom could be milked. Carbon dioxide worked for Egbert, too, but isoflurane had proven superior, causing him less agitation as he was going under and a calm recovery as he was coming out. Back at the lab, they'd purpose-built an inhalation chamber capable of administering the gas. The transport crate had the same feature.

"Vitals?" Rebecca said.

"Normal. Here… have a look." The technician stepped aside so she could check the monitor.

Placing her luggage and Priscilla's carrier on the ground, Rebecca accessed the touchscreen, navigating through biometric data and pausing occasionally to assess the information. Everything checked out.

Finally, she opened the high-definition video feed.

In the middle of the crate, on its back and unmoving, lay the animal she'd nicknamed Egbert—a male subadult of the species *Megarachne Amazonas*.

Washed in ultraviolet and with his legs in the air, half-bent, he looked almost comical.

He was anything but.

Four feet from head to tail. Seven-foot leg-span. Even in this position, Rebecca could make out part of his shell-like dorsal area, or carapace. Under regular light, the carapace was bright red, a striking feature peculiar to the soldier caste, just like the two spiked and scythe-like raptorial legs, which, in his current position, lay partly splayed. Resembling the forelegs of a praying mantis, the prominent limbs, sitting just behind the pedipalps, were devastating weapons. Prior to Egbert's arrival, she hadn't seen an example of the soldier caste, not up close, anyway. Back in the jungle, during the event later termed the Incident, she'd seen several of the creatures from a distance, climbing up from the river, onto Chad's boat, the *Tempestade*. But she'd been too far away to capture detail. Alex had told her the creatures had used their forelegs like swords.

"He looks dead, hey, lying like that with his legs in the air," the technician said.

"This will be the longest we've had him under," Rebecca said.

The technician nodded. "We're actively monitoring anaesthetic depth, and every ten minutes, we're checking the righting reflex. Hell, he's probably dreaming of those egg-layers as we speak."

Rebecca tapped the monitor. "We don't want him waking up mid-flight. Keep the temperature low." Keeping it cold would slow the metabolic rate.

The man nodded and moved away when Beckett came over.

"Ms Riley, I trust everything is in order? I need you to take a seat."

Satisfied Egbert was sleeping safe and sound, she turned to Beckett. "You said I could have my phone back."

"That's precisely why I'm here," Beckett replied, passing her a large envelope. "Your restricted items, including your phone. Please sign here, to confirm I've given everything back to you."

He offered her a pen, and she signed where indicated.

"Once we're in the air, we can go over those release papers," Beckett suggested, "including the Customs paperwork."

"Happy to, once I've spoken with Frank."

Beckett grinned. "We've been cleared for take-off, Ms Riley. Please, any seat will do." He left her to stow her luggage.

Rebecca turned. Flush against the wall was a long row of red jump seats. Currently upright, they could be lowered when needed. Passenger comfort, it appeared, wasn't a priority.

"I'm guessing they don't serve free liquor on this flight," came a voice.

Beyond one of the crates, further down the row and already strapped into one of the seats was a bespectacled, goateed man, likely in his mid-thirties. Dressed in cargo trousers, a polo shirt, and a baseball cap, he looked more civilian than military. Prior to this moment, she hadn't noticed him.

Rebecca smiled. "No liquor? Damn. And I thought I'd booked first class."

She grabbed her gear and Priscilla's carrier and shuffled over, figuring here was as good a place as any to sit. She held out her hand. "Rebecca Riley."

The man fumbled with his harness, attempting to stand, but got clumsily entangled. Blushing, half out of his seat, he gave up and clasped her hand in his. He nearly crushed it. Rebecca tried not to wince, stunned by the enormous strength surging through his grip; it was like a transfer of electrical current.

"Holtorf," the man said. "Charles, L. My friends call me 'Chuckles'. Get it? Charles—*Chuck*—L...?" He released her hand and folded down the seat to his right.

"Clever," Rebecca said, plonking down beside him and discreetly wringing her fingers. She doubted Holtorf had meant to squeeze her that hard, surmising it was an unintended consequence of supreme fitness—the man was seriously ripped. Hell, he may well have been carved from a block of granite. Maybe he was military, after all.

Holtorf nodded at Priscilla. "Your pet?"

"Chuckles, meet Priscilla," Rebecca said. She was glad Priscilla was safely inside a carrier and shielded from a possible hand-crushing.

"Cute," Holtorf said, trying to stick a thick finger through the carrier to tickle Priscilla.

As he was doing this, Rebecca sensed a gaze upon her and looked up. Across the way and several seats down, lined up along the wall and facing inwards, sat Beckett's men, half a dozen in total, all in black combat fatigues and body armour. Beckett wasn't with them—he'd probably moved up front.

At least one of the soldiers seemed overtly amused by Holtorf's awkwardness. Chuckling, shaking his head, the man murmured something to the soldier next to him, who was busy clipping his fingernails. At this range, the comment was out of earshot, but judging by the fingernail-clipper's rough guffaw, the observation was less than complimentary.

Unimpressed, Rebecca looked away.

Holtorf seemed not to notice. He gestured at the crate. "So, in there… is your other pet?"

"Egbert? Not a pet, no."

"Funny name," Holtorf said. He swallowed hard, maybe nervously. "It's real, then?"

"Yes, he is," Rebecca said. "Clearly, you know what's in there."

"I've been briefed… sort of. You're an entomologist. Specifically, an arachnologist. Can I meet Egbert?"

"He's asleep," Rebecca said, deflecting him. For all she knew, such decisions were now Beckett's to make. More pressingly, she was curious as to how this man knew her profession. "Were you at Delta? I can't say I've seen you around."

Suddenly, an alarm blared through the cargo bay and a red light washed over them. With a hiss of hydraulics, the loading ramp started to close.

Holtorf didn't answer her question, and instead began a frantic search of his trouser pockets. He seized an object just as the ramp sealed shut and then rested his hands, clenched into tight fists, on the tops of his jiggling knees.

"You don't like flying?" Rebecca asked, buckling in as the engines fired up and the plane taxied forward.

Holtorf smiled uneasily, his face turning a light shade of green. "Actually, I love flying," he said, raising the object of his search as the plane thundered down the runway. "But taking off? Not so much."

On cue, the Hercules lifted off the ground with a powerful, stomach-rolling lurch, and with that, Chuckles chucked his lunch.

8

α

The item Holtorf had pulled from his trouser pocket was a sick bag. As he hurled into it, Rebecca turned away to give the poor man some privacy.

Finished, Holtorf wiped his mouth and swigged from his water bottle. "I must say… it's nice to be in the air."

Obviously, he was trying to make light, so Rebecca followed suit. "So… I'm guessing landings are okay?"

"Landings are peachy."

"Can I get you anything?"

Holtorf shook his head and took another swig. While he drank, Rebecca glanced across at the soldiers. Predictably, Holtorf's misfortune had given them great amusement.

"Assholes," Rebecca murmured under her breath.

Holtorf didn't seem fazed. "It's all good. Looks like I made their day."

The men, still chuckling, noticed Rebecca's scowl and broke eye contact. Rebecca scanned the group and wondered what unit they were from. Smart asses aside, they were, to a man, typically serious, a demeanour that seemed almost standard for guys like these. What wasn't standard, however, was their appearance. Some of them had longer hair, and a couple sported full beards. At Delta she'd learnt more about the military than just helicopters. When it came to appearance, the rules for some units were relaxed. These guys were likely a special operations team.

Holtorf must have picked up on her thoughts. "Security detail," he said. "For that asset of yours."

"You know these guys?"

"No. But I've heard the leader is an asshole."

"News travels. So, you're part of the research team?" Beckett had said they'd be picking up more members.

Holtorf hesitated, as though unsure how to answer. "I'm in the transport industry. Logistics, I guess."

"Right," Rebecca said. *Here we go.*

Holtorf shifted uncomfortably. "I'm not so good at this, am I? To be honest, I'm not usually in the field. Pencil pushing is more my thing."

"So… you're CIA," Rebecca half-joked.

Holtorf laughed. "Nothing that exciting, trust me." He leaned in close. "Technically, I suppose you could say I'm OGA."

"Right," Rebecca said again. "Other Government Agency. Some of your colleagues paid me a visit."

Again, Holtorf squirmed. Lowering his voice, he leaned forward. "As you're aware, several agencies have a stake in this. I was here at Echo on unrelated business, and my superiors arranged for me to hitch a ride. My role is to ensure a smooth transfer."

"Mine, or Egbert's?"

Holtorf smiled but didn't answer. Removing his cap, he ran a hand through his hair. It was longer on top, high and tight, as the soldiers back at Delta had called the favoured style.

At that moment, Rebecca remembered the envelope in her lap. Her phone! Parting the seal, she slid the contents into her hand. Nothing much there, other than her passport and her phone. The cell felt peculiar; foreign. Turning it over, she tried switching it on.

Dead, of course. It hadn't been charged in weeks. She got the feeling Beckett would have counted on that, the son of a bitch.

"I can charge it for you," Holtorf said. "Wirelessly, from my phone."

Wondering if, after all this time, it would still work okay, Rebecca passed him her cell, figuring she had little alternative. Retrieving his own phone and placing the two devices back to back, Holtorf set them on the ground beneath his seat.

"It'll take a while," Holtorf said. "But if you'd rather use my phone in the interim…"

Rebecca considered this. Maybe she should take advantage of Holtorf's offer; after all, Owen had said they were still being monitored—maybe Beckett had planted a bug in her phone. On Holtorf's phone, she could speak freely.

Unless Holtorf was being monitored, too.

You're being paranoid.

She declined his offer. Hell, she didn't know anyone's number off the top of her head, anyway. "I wonder how long the flight will be," she said, changing the subject.

"About twelve hours, give or take."

"No inflight entertainment, I'm guessing."

"Doubtful," Holtorf said, "But plenty of time to sleep, if you can."

Tempting. And probably a good idea, but not yet. "What do you know about Nevada?"

"Gambling springs to mind."

"And our destination? The research facility?"

"Not much—I'm guessing less than you. I was told to expect a full briefing on arrival."

"What about Egbert? What do you know about *him*?"

For a moment, Holtorf said nothing and simply held her in his gaze. It was a surprisingly hard stare that highlighted the more austere aspects of his face. Now, his features seemed more angular and weathered. A kink in his nose suggested it had been broken more than once, and a couple of scars she hadn't noticed earlier collectively hinted at a tough upbringing. "Well, now that you ask," he said eventually, "it seems to me you've captured your very own J'ba Fofi."

Rebecca raised her eyebrows. Outside of those with at least a passing interest in cryptids, few would have heard of the legendary great spider said to stalk the forests of the Congo. Of course, J'ba Fofi, with its alleged five-foot leg-span, was a myth—and from a different continent, no less.

Still, the similarities with Egbert were obvious.

Holtorf held the stare, waiting for a response.

Rebecca gave none. In that moment, she wondered about the bespectacled man beside her; this man with a funny nickname who was somewhat awkward and prone to airsickness and who spouted pseudoscience with a straight face; this man who, on the flipside, was also supremely fit and strong, hard-looking with probing ice-blue eyes and maybe government or military connections running deeper than he cared to reveal.

The contrasts intrigued her.

What unnerved her, at least a little, was the realisation that this man was here specifically because of her—and Egbert.

9

α

For several minutes, they made small talk. Rebecca probed for information, but Holtorf either had none, or chose not to share. After a while, she suspected the former.

Eventually, Holtorf asked if she'd mind if he worked—she didn't—and he pulled out a laptop and started to type.

Rebecca turned her attention to Priscilla. The small monkey lay curled in a ball inside her carrier, her tiny chest rising and falling rhythmically. The gently shuddering plane had lulled her to sleep.

Maybe I should sleep, too.

Not yet. You need to check on Egbert. And it won't be long before your phone is charged. You need to call Frank.

But Rebecca's eyes were growing heavy, and she closed them, just for a moment.

She did, in fact, fall asleep. Several hours later she woke as the plane descended for a brief refuelling stop. It was dark outside. She checked on Egbert, as she should have done earlier. He was stable and sleeping soundly. No visit yet from Beckett. They took off again.

Her phone was charged. Back in the air, she called Frank, but the call diverted to voicemail. Beckett had said Frank was out of town—maybe he was out of range, too. She left a short message.

By her calculations, it was mid-afternoon in Australia, and after checking in with her parents and her sister, Charlotte—disappointingly, her brothers missed her call—she spent several minutes replying to old text messages. She then scrolled through her contacts. When she hit Ed's name, her finger hesitated, and she realised the fingers of her other hand were at that moment resting on the pill bottle she'd earlier retrieved from her luggage and shoved into her shorts pocket.

No messages or missed calls from Ed.

Rebecca frowned, perplexed as to why he hadn't tried to contact her.

You haven't contacted him, either. Call him now.

She couldn't. Why, she was only partly sure. It didn't matter anyway—the cloud that had hovered over her hours earlier rolled in again; that familiar, crippling emptiness that made her want to roll into a ball and push the world away. When it came for her, there was only one sure-fire way to exorcise it.

She slept some more.

Hours later, the whine of the engines swelled and woke her. The plane was descending again. She checked her watch. Minus the stopover, they'd been on the move for almost fourteen hours, airborne for nearly twelve.

Behind her jump seat was a small window, round like a porthole. For much of the flight, only blackness had pressed against it. Now, subdued light filtered through. Releasing her harness, she twisted around and peered through the glass.

In truth, she hadn't expected to see a spreading metropolis below—clearly, a military plane with top-secret cargo was never going to land at a civilian airport. But she hadn't expected this, either.

Beneath the Hercules, a lonely, alien landscape stretched endlessly into the distance.

Cut into that landscape, bathed in muted yellow light, was a tarmac, at the end of which lay a cluster of drab-coloured, low-lying buildings, several hangars, and a control tower. It looked remarkably like the airfield from which they'd originally departed, except that facility had been surrounded by vibrant green jungle.

The airfield below lay in the middle of a barren desert.

You're kidding me…

Owen was right.

10
α

The lonely facility stretched beneath the descending Hercules. Rebecca peered down at the spread of buildings, then checked her phone, seeking a GPS location. Strangely, nothing. No service—in fact, the device appeared to have frozen.

She glanced at Holtorf. His face was its normal, healthy shade; true to his word, it appeared he was indeed fine with landings.

"Out there—it's not what you're thinking," Holtorf said above the engine-whine.

"How do you know what I'm thinking?"

With a harsh jolt, the Hercules touched down, shuddering under brakes. Rebecca craned to look back out the window and caught a blurred view of bunched, single-storey buildings. She saw no signs of activity.

"Your phone," Holtorf said, his voice still raised.

"Sorry?" Rebecca replied, turning back. She followed his gaze to her cell. Still no service.

"Cell phone jammer," Holtorf explained. "They're jamming the service. And GPS, too."

"Who? The military?" *Who else could it be?*

Slowing, the Hercules eased to a gentle taxi, and the noise in the cargo hold dramatically diminished.

"It's illegal to interfere with cell phone transmissions in the US," Holtorf said, his voice lower now, almost a whisper. "But with permission, federal facilities can use this type of technology."

"So, it's a federal facility," Rebecca said. "Groom Lake, right?"

Holtorf shook his head. "There's a push to use this technology in prisons, to stop inmates communicating with the outside using contraband phones. So, sure, the tech exists. But despite the secrecy, this isn't Groom Lake or Paradise Ranch or whatever you want to call it." He released his harness and joined her at the window. "The configuration of buildings… it doesn't match."

Rebecca again glanced outside, wondering if the desert beyond the glass was in fact the Mojave or one of several other possibilities. "Okay… so, where *are* we, then?"

At last, the Hercules halted. As its engines powered down, the plane became a hive of activity both inside and out.

Beckett appeared, directing his men. Rebecca hadn't seen him all flight. He ordered everyone off.

"What about Egbert?" Rebecca asked.

"There's a transfer crew waiting outside—he's in good hands," Beckett replied. "We'll get you over to the terminal and take it from there."

"And Priscilla?"

"You can bring her."

Beckett left them. Holtorf slipped into his backpack, grabbing Rebecca's luggage so that she could carry Priscilla. Exiting the Hercules via the loading ramp, they hit a wall of suffocating, dry air. The afternoon sun, full of heat and glare, beat down remorselessly, and white light reflected off the desert floor so harshly that Rebecca was thankful she'd packed her shades.

Holtorf refitted his cap. "Man, it must be 100 degrees."

At least that, Rebecca thought. Although not as humid, she sensed it was even hotter here than in Brazil.

At the bottom of the ramp, a scorching wind rose without warning, cutting across them. Pinpricks of dust stung Rebecca's face and she turned, ducking her head until it passed. When it had, she glanced about.

Talk about the middle of nowhere.

For the most part, the land was low and flat and covered in scrubby bursage and creosote bush. In the near distance, the terrain undulated, with low hills shrouded in the same vegetation, but interspersed with a few taller trees, maybe cholla. Further afield, haze painted larger hills in smoky blue hues. Beyond those peaks rose taller mountains, and directly above these, dark clouds, pregnant with rain, had begun to smudge an otherwise pretty dome of azure.

Voices called out instructions. Sensing movement beside her, Rebecca turned. Rumbling into position at the edge of the tarmac, heading for the ramp and surrounded by Beckett's men, was a truck crane. On its tray was one of those magnetic arms used for lifting shipping containers.

Egbert's transfer crew, no doubt.

Her transfer vehicle, sitting on an unsealed, dirt road running parallel to the tarmac, came in the form of a long white bus with blacked-out windows.

"This way," Beckett called.

Juggling Priscilla's carrier, and with Holtorf in tow, Rebecca followed Beckett. In front of the bus was an unmarked pickup—a large Ford F-150—also white. Behind the bus were two more of these vehicles.

Odd. Rebecca had expected to be greeted by Humvees or jeeps. It looked like a convoy of civilian vehicles.

Off the tarmac, the ground was parched. Sandy gravel crunched underfoot. Once more, the dry wind stirred, blowing swirls of dust across the group, hot and stinging.

As they covered the final few feet to the bus, Holtorf nudged Rebecca with his elbow. "Over there." He motioned in the direction of the distant hangars, maybe a hundred yards away. Interestingly, a plane, perhaps a 737, sat outside one of the buildings. Save for a band of red running nose to tail, the aircraft was white and otherwise unmarked. Again, Rebecca got the impression it was a civilian aircraft. Several workers moved about, as though preparing the plane for take-off. Contrastingly, they were dressed in military fatigues.

This is an airfield, Rebecca thought. *Where the hell is the research facility?*

With a hiss, the bus door opened. "Please, if you will," Beckett said, gesturing with an open palm. Rebecca climbed aboard. The driver wore sunglasses. He also wore fatigues, further indication this was, indeed, a military installation. He said nothing as she and Holtorf moved down the aisle.

Towards the back of the bus, sitting together, were two dark-skinned men, civilians, judging by their clothes, chatting animatedly and seemingly unaware of the new arrivals. Rebecca took a seat in the middle rows. The smell of vinyl filled her nostrils, taking her back to her childhood and the bus she used to catch to school. Holtorf sat across the aisle, so that Rebecca could place Priscilla's carrier on the seat beside her.

Two of Beckett's men moved to seats up front, just behind the driver. Beckett and the remainder of his men jumped into the lead F-150.

Rebecca saw this through the windshield. Through the blacked-out windows running the bus's length, she could see nothing. She glanced at Holtorf and shrugged, and as she did, caught movement in the corner of her eye. One of the two civilian men jumped up and slid into the row behind her, leaning over the back of her seat and thrusting out his hand. "Spencer Raymond," the man said, chewing gum furiously. "I know, confusing right? Like I've got two first names, and they should be swapped around. But please, call me Spencer."

Rebecca twisted in her seat, causing the vinyl to creak. The man, in his thirties, was short, with thick, frizzy hair. Emblazoned on his dark shirt were the words 'Zombies Hate Fast Food' and an image of several lumbering undead on the tail of a running figure.

Spencer caught her looking. "Yeah, my 'Squatch and Soda' shirt is in the wash."

Smiling at the Bigfoot reference, Rebecca shook his hand, introducing herself as the other man joined them.

"You'll have to excuse my colleague," the second man said. "He's socially unaware. Wyatt Raymond. Pleased to meet you."

"Colleague? Or brother?" Rebecca asked.

"Both."

Holtorf leaned over to shake the hands of both men, again introducing himself with a reference to his nickname.

"Whoa, that's some grip, Chuckles," Spencer said, wringing his fingers and chewing more furiously than ever.

Comfortably dressed in a suit jacket and jeans, Wyatt, who was notably taller and thinner than his brother, shot his sibling an exasperated glance. "Can you give it a rest?"

Spencer rolled his eyes, then winked at Rebecca. "I should take it easy on him. He has misophonia."

"I do not!"

Spencer leaned closer to Rebecca and tapped his forehead knowingly. "Undiagnosed. But trust me, he has it."

"And you have an oversharing disorder," Wyatt shot back.

"Misophonia?" Rebecca asked.

"Sound-rage," Spencer said.

"He reckons I have sensitive hearing," Wyatt said, sighing.

"He can't stand certain noises," Spencer clarified. "Some sounds bug him, like the sound of me chewing gum. Chewing anything, for that matter."

"That, I agree with," Wyatt said. "You sound like a goddamned cow."

Spencer lowered his voice, leaned even closer to Rebecca. "He also reckons I breathe too loudly. And he hates it when I do this." He pushed a closed fist against the palm of his other hand, making the knuckles crack.

"There'll be more knuckles cracking if you keep this up," Wyatt said, clearly uncomfortable.

The bus took off. As it gunned down the road, the F-150 ahead of it spewed a thick trail of dust.

Spencer changed the subject. "Your accent… Australian, right?" He didn't wait for a response. "Cute monkey. Capuchin?"

Rebecca nodded. "Meet Priscilla. So, I'm guessing you guys are part of the project team?"

"Of sorts," Spencer said.

"We're in the private sector," Wyatt explained, undoubtedly pleased for the shift of topic. "Our company dabbles in a few areas. Our latest is food security."

Rebecca frowned.

"We consult to URS," Wyatt said.

"I don't know it," Rebecca said.

"They're a large defense contractor," Spencer said. "You heard of DARPA?"

"Now *that*, I've heard of," Rebecca said. "It's the government's scientific research agency, tasked with developing cutting-edge military technology."

"Essentially, yes," Wyatt said. "The Defense Advanced Research Projects Agency is an arm of the Pentagon."

Spencer smiled. "They have a lot of money."

"Let me guess… that's where your company comes in," Rebecca said.

"Partly," Wyatt said. "I like to think it's more than that. Are you familiar with biomimicry?"

Rebecca raised her eyebrows—she'd certainly heard of it. Also known as biomimetics, biomimicry was, essentially, the science of imitating nature to produce better technologies, like looking to birds to design more aero-dynamic aircraft, or termite mounds for self-regulating ventilation systems, or even gecko feet for more efficient adhesives. It was a fascinating field of research with plenty of crossovers with her own work.

"We deal with robots, with a focus on the imitation of specific organisms, mainly insects," Spencer said.

"Dr Riley is an entomologist," Holtorf said.

"I'm not a doctor," Rebecca corrected.

"But you're an entomologist, right?" Wyatt said. "So, it's true, then… what you found? We've been briefed."

"Sort of," Spencer said.

"But what you found… it's real?" Wyatt asked.

"It's real."

Wyatt blew air through his teeth. "Wow. That's interesting. I bet you'd be fascinated by our range of wasp and ant drones. Really impressive."

"You mentioned food security?" Rebecca said.

Wyatt nodded. "We're studying plant-eating insects, with the view of one day using nanobots to transmit scientifically engineered plant viruses—"

"Helpful viruses, of course," Spencer interjected.

"—to strengthen food crops and defend against threats to the food supply."

"By threats, you mean bioterrorism," Holtorf said.

Again, Wyatt nodded. "Exactly."

"So feasibly, bioterrorists could use their own nanobots to spread *harmful* viruses," Holtorf said.

"Feasibly," Wyatt said, shrugging.

Rebecca looked ahead at the billowing dust thrown up by the lead F-150. "So, what do you know about this place. Where are we, exactly?"

"You don't know?" Wyatt asked.

"Excellent," Spencer said, rubbing his hands gleefully. "I mean, it's not surprising, really. That's what they do."

Rebecca looked quizzically from one brother to the next. "I don't follow."

"They like to keep things compartmentalised," Wyatt explained, "so you don't get the full picture—the less you know, the better. That way they control the flow of information."

Spencer chewed furiously. "So, they get you to work on your piece of the puzzle, and *only* your piece, and they don't tell you jack shit about anything else. But we're not stupid." He gestured towards the front of the bus, where Beckett's men were seated. "You know who those guys are?"

"They're a security detail," Rebecca said.

"Of sorts," Spencer said. "At first glance, they hold themselves like D-boys."

Unfamiliar with the term, Rebecca tilted her head.

"Delta Force operators," Spencer explained. "Still, I'm figuring OGA—part of the military but operating outside the normal chain of command. Those guys do their own thing."

Rebecca shot a glance at Holtorf, who shrugged.

Spencer caught the look. "What? *You're* OGA?"

"I'm in logistics," Holtorf answered.

"So, you're CIA, then," Spencer said matter-of-factly, chewing fast. He didn't wait for a reply and turned back to Rebecca. "I'm sure you noticed those guys have no insignia. And I bet when they arrived, there was a black chopper somewhere."

"There was an unmarked Chinook."

Spencer rocked backwards and clapped his hands together. "Yes! I mean, they mightn't be wearing black suits, but as I said to my brother… I think these guys are a take on the iconic 'men in black.'"

Rebecca started to laugh, thinking he was joking, but stopped herself abruptly. He was serious. "Men in black? Those Government guys that turn up after a UFO sighting and threaten witnesses to keep quiet?"

"That's them."

"They're real?"

Spencer shrugged. "Do you believe in UFOs?"

"You mean aliens?" Rebecca clarified. Up until recently, no. She considered telling him that, but let it slide.

Spencer let it slide, too. "Did you see the white plane before?"

"The 737?"

"JANET Airlines," Spencer said. "'Joint Air Network for Employee Transportation'—or as I prefer, 'Just Another Non-Existent Terminal.'"

"The airline is owned by the USAF," Wyatt explained. "Highly classified. It's used to ferry contractors and government workers from Las Vegas—"

"To Groom Lake," Rebecca mused.

"Area 51! It's *always* that, right?" Spencer said.

The bus hit a bump in the road and turned down a small incline. Rebecca glanced at Beckett's men, wondering if she and the others should be talking so freely.

Wyatt didn't seem fazed, and said to her, "You're partly right. JANET *does* fly to Paradise Ranch, but this isn't that facility."

"Everyone thinks of that place first," Spencer said. "But there are others. A few years back, they built a mysterious landing strip at Area 6, about twelve miles from Area 51."

"So, we're *there*?"

Wyatt shook his head. "There's been more work, too. That's the point. This whole area is huge. Massive ground-space—more than a million hectares. And you're talking nearly 5,000 square miles of restricted airspace above it. We're in the vicinity of Groom Lake, no doubt, but not Area 51 itself. That place is nothing more than a convenient smokescreen."

"So true!" Spencer said, clapping his brother on the back. He was buzzing now.

Wyatt smiled. "As you can tell, this is a pet interest for my brother—he's a sucker for this stuff."

Spencer nodded. "You could say I'm a believer."

"You said Area 51 is a smokescreen?"

"I did," Spencer said energetically. "The place has a near-mythical status. And why not? A top-secret test site for experimental weapons and aircraft, reputedly home to captured alien technology—exciting, right? But it's not the most secretive area, or even the most interesting. And it serves a purpose."

"It draws all the attention," Wyatt said. "Takes the heat, so to speak."

"Hell yeah," Spencer said. "Meanwhile, the other sites, the *real* sites, fly under the radar. Trust us, there are multiple, even more secretive installations not only right here in Nevada, but across the country. Utah. California. Man, there's one outside Fresno."

This sparked something in Rebecca's memory. "There's that urban myth about a secret base in Colorado where they reverse-engineered alien technology."

"I think you mean Dulce Base. It's in New Mexico."

True to his nickname, Holtorf chuckled quietly. "I love a conspiracy as much as the next guy, but if any of that were true, then a hell of a lot of people are staying silent."

The comment, although fair, rang hollowly, and Rebecca wondered if Holtorf had more to share on the subject. He didn't get a chance, because suddenly the bus slowed. Ahead, through the windshield, a cluster of demountable buildings appeared, not unlike those at Camp Delta. Behind them sat a larger structure that looked like a huge concrete bunker, seemingly decades old and to be honest, a little rundown. Drab-coloured and cube-like, its standout feature was its lack of windows.

Surely this wasn't the state-of-the-art research centre Beckett had promised…

With a hiss of airbrakes, the bus drew up in front of the bunker. Dust clouds billowed and swirled before dispersing in the hot wind.

"Honey, we're home," Spencer said.

"I still don't know where home is," Rebecca murmured, standing and hefting Priscilla's carrier as Beckett's men herded them from the bus.

Outside, the mysterious building loomed large; a box in the middle of the desert. No guards or personnel were posted externally. Nothing stirred in the heat.

Beckett, alighting from the lead pickup, led the group to two solid steel doors running flush with the structure's façade. Like the rest of the building these were windowless and painted in sand-textured hues. Rebecca wondered if it was an attempt at camouflaging.

Above the doors, covering the entrance, was a CCTV camera.

As they approached, a light on a metal plate over the doorhandles flashed green. A loud click suggested the doors had been electronically unlocked.

Beckett pushed them open. "After you," he said to Rebecca with a sweep of his open palm.

Glancing from him to Holtorf and finally at the brothers, Rebecca shrugged, hoisted Priscilla's carrier, and entered.

11

α

The chopper circled the clearing and descended, its rotor-wash playing havoc with the inflatable shelters below. From one of these, a figure emerged, long grey hair billowing in the downdraft. Waving to Owen and Jessy, the man hustled over as the chopper landed, crouching beneath the blades and opening the door. "Dr Ethan Perez. We spoke on the phone." He shook Jessy's hand first, and then Owen's. "Your timing is impeccable."

Raising his voice above the still-turning rotors, Owen asked, "Timing?"

"We're heading out to the site. Please, follow me."

Alighting, Owen and Jessy slung their backpacks and followed Perez, a tall, thin man in his sixties, to the edge of the clearing, where a troop carrier awaited.

"I trust you had a good flight," Perez said without turning. "This way."

The truck had a canvas back, although the side-flaps had been rolled up. Perez climbed deftly into the tray and assisted Owen and Jessy in turn. Safely seated, he clapped an open hand twice on the back of the cab. Up front, the driver gunned the engine and the truck heaved forward, rumbling down a makeshift track cut into the steaming jungle. Rudimentary at best, the road was just wide enough for passage.

"I didn't think we'd be heading out so soon," Owen said. He had to raise his voice above the grinding of gears.

"We wanted to get you up and running as soon as possible," Perez replied. A world-renowned spelunker and geobiologist known for his work in microbial ecology, the celebrated doctor was the team leader here at Encampment 6. More importantly, he was their guide out to the site.

"So… it's true then?" Jessy asked as the truck bounced and jolted noisily. She braced one hand against the wooden bench seat, the other against the exposed metal ribbing over which the canvas normally lay.

"True?"

"About Intihuasi."

"That… yes. It's true."

The truck hit a muddy pothole, slid alarmingly sideways, then regained traction, engine revving. On either side of the track, walls of green loomed, vegetation clawing at the vehicle as though attempting to halt its egress.

"What about the others?" Owen asked. "The rest of the research team?"

"You're the last," Perez said. "For now, anyway. It seems like they're bringing in new people every day. Experts, specialists—the operation is growing exponentially. You ask me, they had no idea what was down here."

"You have people on the ground at both sites?" Jessy asked.

"Of course. There's an operation at Site 1, as you call it—the place where your team discovered the single moai. And at Site 2, where you found the spheres—"

"You mean the large sphere buried beneath the pyramid of Intihuasi, and the smaller one up top, in the temple, cradled by the moai," Jessy clarified.

"Yes," Perez said. "At Site 2… well, let's just say our interest there has been piqued."

Jessy studied his face closely. "And what you told us earlier…"

"Following your rescue, we searched the city. It wasn't long before our investigations pushed us further afield."

"Beyond the crater," Owen said.

Perez nodded. From his backpack, he pulled a tablet. Peering over his glasses, his tanned, wrinkled face a picture of concentration, he tapped the screen. "Have you heard of LIDAR?"

Jessy nodded. "Light Detection and Ranging. A mapping tool, commonly used in my field."

"Mine, too," Perez said. "The new laser technology is wonderful. Here, look at this." He spun the tablet for their benefit, nearly losing his grip as the truck hit another pothole.

On the screen, dominated by hues of brown and orange, was a full-colour, three-dimensional scan of the crater. The jungle had been stripped away.

"The topography is fascinating," Perez said. "As you can see, beneath the canopy, there's a lot going on. Both natural… and otherwise."

Indeed. In addition to the expected ridges and undulations, Owen noted an abundance of shapes not readily found in nature: square and rectangular forms, straight lines. Ruins, blanketing the bowl.

And of course, in the centre, the pyramid.

"I agree it's fascinating, but we're familiar with the city," Owen said.

"Yes, but not this," Perez replied. He reached over and zoomed the image out. "This is what I told you about."

More straight lines—*buildings*—well beyond the crater.

"The site is bigger than we thought," Jessy said in a low voice.

"You mentioned something else," Owen said. As he recalled his earlier conversation with Perez, his heartrate accelerated in anticipation. "There's more."

"Much more," Perez said, his grey eyes flashing with wonder. "Trust me, GR-43 is the epicentre of something incredible."

"What did you find there?"

Suddenly, the truck slowed, and as it did, Perez looked forward, and then back at each of them. His expression turned grim. "I should warn you to prepare yourselves. It's not as you remember."

"What do you mean?" Jessy asked.

"Look for yourself," Perez said, pointing out the side as the truck lurched to a full stop. "We're here."

12
α

Owen leapt from the truck, instantly overcome with déjà vu. "Holy shit… will you look at that…"

He'd made a similar comment the last time he was here. Back then, standing with Ed and the others in this exact position—the place they'd ultimately dubbed the north-western vantage point—he'd been struck with awe at the sight of the ancient city buried inside the web-enshrouded crater. Now, that stunned sense of wonder was just as great, though it was tinged with other emotions, too.

Perez had warned them that things had changed, and he was right.

"My God," Jessy whispered.

Intihuasi was vastly different to how they'd left it. Much of the surrounding forest had been cleared, especially around the rim of the smaller bowl within which the Mayan-like pyramid lay nestled. Here, a makeshift road had been gouged, encircling the pyramid in spiralling dirt tracks like those dug into an open pit mine. It was an apt comparison, because numerous vehicles—many of them resembling mining vehicles—moved along the crater's rim and down its sides. Some had tip-trays, but there were other types, also—loaders, cranes, excavators—some yellow, most khaki-coloured, all of them obviously airlifted in.

Incredibly, floodlights had been erected in a ring around the smaller crater, facing inward, towards the pyramid.

Outside of that, spread along the sloping sides of the larger crater, tents and inflatable shelters dominated. The area was home now to two cities: the ruined, ancient city of Intihuasi, and a modern-day tent-city.

The scale was mind-blowing.

Tears welling in her eyes, Jessy shook her head. She looked up and she and Owen traded a glance. Words weren't necessary.

We're too late…

Owen closed his eyes. Before accepting Beckett's offer to come here, the two of them had made a pact. No-one else, just him and Jessy. They'd kept it from Beckett and Perez, of course, but all along, their primary motivation for returning, for agreeing to trade their insight and assist with what was going on here, was to secretly get back and protect the truth; to safeguard Ed's dream, and the site.

They'd failed.

"What have they done?" Jessy murmured, her voice cracking.

Owen opened his eyes. Like the surrounding vegetation, the web had also been cleared to make way for the spiral-road. This zone was fenced, and armed soldiers patrolled the perimeter. Everyone *within* the demarcated area—Owen saw people moving up and down the pyramid and around the plaza out in front—was dressed in a hazmat suit. Some carried small boxes, maybe radiation scanners or monitors. Others carried equipment into the tunnel running from the plaza, down beneath the pyramid; still more carried equipment out of it. Trolleys loaded with polycarbonate crates wheeled in and out in endless lines.

They were gutting the place.

Owen shook his head. Even now, weeks later, they were bringing stuff out. It'd take time to pack and document everything, no doubt.

This wasn't the archaeological dig he'd been praying for.

He scanned the courtyard. The floatplane and the Black Hawk helicopter, Raven One—the two aircraft that had crashed into the plaza that fateful day several weeks back—had been removed. For that matter, so too had the second Black Hawk, Raven Two, which had come to rest not far from here. Presumably, the wreckage of all three had been airlifted out—in those early days at Camp Delta, he'd noticed several choppers buzzing past with shipping containers swinging beneath them.

He'd known something was going on down here, just not to this scale.

Where were they taking it all?

"I thought they'd clear some of the jungle for ease of access," Jessy said, dabbing at her eyes. "But not this. It's even worse than we feared."

"I know," Owen said. "This isn't right."

"Ed predicted this. It's why he wanted to keep it a secret. Intihuasi is a natural treasure, a sacred site."

Needing no reminding, Owen nodded, and for a moment thought about the Yuguruppu, the indigenous people with whom, weeks earlier, he'd had a life-threatening encounter. In those early days, as he recuperated from his various wounds, he'd fought hard to suppress his bitterness—he'd nearly died at their hands, after all—but with the passing weeks, that anger had waned. As of this morning he'd harboured little if any resentment, and he'd been more than ready to return here. Now, after seeing this, he realised the last kernel of negativity had in fact dissolved, and in its place had taken root not only a deep sadness, but a growing sense of hopelessness. Like Jessy had said, this land was sacred; it was to be treasured and respected, not destroyed. At a time when indigenous Amazonians faced a grim future, at a time when the irrepressible tide of miners and loggers and oil companies continued to push the forest people closer to extinction, this was a real kick in the guts. This was devastating.

Devastating, yes, but hardly surprising.

He turned to Perez, who stood several feet behind them, giving them time and space. "They're not interested in preservation," Owen said, "and they're not here to study."

Perez lowered his gaze and his voice. "From afar, it looks bad, yes. But they're more interested in those things than you realise."

Jessy spun on the old man. "We've been brought here under false pretences. You asked for our help, but this is wrong, we can't be a part of this." She fixed him with a hard stare, her eyes narrowing. "Hell, is this even *legal*?"

It was a good question. This was foreign soil. Owen couldn't see any flags, US or otherwise, but the site was clearly under US military control. Were the local authorities a part of it? They had to be.

Perez shifted his glasses up his nose. "As you were told, there's more to this place than meets the eye." He cleared his throat. "Let's get you into suits and beneath the pyramid. I want to show you what's really going on here."

THE
SITE

13
α

Behind the group, the steel doors closed with a soft hiss.

The interior wasn't what Rebecca had been expecting. Outside, the building was an unremarkable concrete block; dated, almost rundown. Inside, it was all white walls and glass and exposed anodized girders—for the most part utilitarian in design, but also modern, and in good condition. Equally surprising was the temperature. In stark contrast to the heat outside, it was cool in here, almost icy. The sudden change caused Rebecca's skin to ripple in gooseflesh. She shivered.

The foyer was small. Ahead, metal detectors flanked a long security desk, above which sat a screen of glass. Standing in the foyer on this side of the security desk was an elegant Asian woman, perhaps in her mid-thirties, with jet-black hair tied in a sensible, no-nonsense bun. Over her dark pant-suit was a white lab-coat, to the lapel of which was affixed a plastic sleeve containing a photo ID.

"Welcome," the woman said, ignoring the security entourage and bee-lining for Rebecca. She held out her hand. "My name is Cassandra Li, but you can call me Sandy. I'm one of the senior researchers here. You must be Dr Riley?"

Rebecca shook her hand. "Rebecca. It's a pleasure to meet you."

Li bowed slightly. "The honour is mine. Professor Hayward told me all about you."

"Is Frank here?" Rebecca asked.

"The professor is out of town," Li said. "I've read your report—your work down in Brazil…quite frankly, it's stunning. Again, this is a great honour."

Before Rebecca could respond, Li turned and introduced herself to Wyatt and Spencer, and finally Holtorf. To Beckett and his men, she smiled and nodded politely, but said nothing; clearly, she and Beckett were known to each other. Without waiting, Beckett led his team to the security desk, which was manned by two soldiers, both of whom drew upright and saluted.

To Rebecca and the brothers, Li said, "Unfortunately, I must ask that you surrender your cells. I'm sure you understand." She turned to Holtorf. "Will you be joining us, sir?"

Holtorf nodded. "I'll surrender my phone, too."

Chewing loudly, Spencer frowned at Li. "There's no coverage here. Does it matter?"

"It's standard procedure," Li said. "No civilian cells are permitted on base."

On base. As suspected, a military establishment.

Rebecca reached for her phone, glancing at it before passing it over.

Li must have sensed her hesitation. "Don't be concerned. It'll be locked up securely and returned to you when you leave."

Rebecca nodded. The phone's screen remained in that odd state of flux—still no service. And still no reply from Frank, either. Maybe he'd returned her call and gotten a busy signal while her cell was offline—with the jammers in place, she wouldn't know this anytime soon. Deciding to save the battery—already, her cell felt warm, probably working hard to connect—she turned off her phone and reluctantly passed it to Li.

Li tossed her a wink. "I know how you feel. We're so dependent on these things that giving them up is like losing an arm."

"Talk about separation anxiety," Spencer said, passing off his cell, too.

Li smiled. "You'll be issued with secure, approved and encrypted duty cells in due course."

Rebecca wondered how that worked, guessing the duty cell network must have antennas beyond the range of the jammer signal, bypassing it. Was that feasible? She wasn't sure; technical stuff wasn't her forte.

"Of course, recording devices are also prohibited," Li said. "Video, audio. I don't presume you have any?"

"Just my phone," Rebecca replied.

Li nodded. Glancing at Rebecca's luggage, then the carrier, she said, "You can leave everything here at the security desk. Unfortunately, that means Priscilla, too."

"She's been holed up for a long time," Rebecca said. "She needs a break. I can't take her?"

"This is a secure environment," Li said. "Professor Hayward has asked I provide a short orientation; the tour won't take long. You can return here after that and we'll sort something out."

Rebecca understood and bent down to Priscilla. "I'm sorry, girl," she whispered, feeling terrible about leaving her behind and wondering again if she'd erred in bringing her here. Reaching through the wire, she scratched the monkey under the neck and then passed the carrier and her luggage to one of the burly guards. She gave a tentative, faint wave. "I'll be back soon, I promise."

Chittering softly in response, Priscilla slumped onto her haunches and sighed.

Broken-hearted, Rebecca straightened and turned back to Li. "What about Egbert? Where is he?"

"Once the transfer team has him secured, I'll take you to him," Li said. "Mr Holtorf, too, so he can sight the asset. Please, this way."

The brothers had already shed their backpacks and passed through the security gate, so too Beckett and his men, who, Rebecca noted, had retained their sidearms.

At the gate, a guard waved her down with a metal-detector wand. Once she'd passed through, Li handed her a visitor lanyard. Rebecca slipped it over her head and waited for Holtorf to come through.

"This way, if you'll please," Li said.

As a group, they vacated the security area and entered an adjoining elevator hall. Rebecca was momentarily confused; the building was no more than a single storey high.

The elevators go down, not up.

Rebecca swallowed. Of course. The base is underground.

This is some real secret shit.

In total, there were four elevators, two on each side of the hall. Li hit the call button. With a ping, a door opened. Khaki padding lined the cab's interior.

"Freight elevator," Li said. "Protects the inside, and the cargo. Please, if you will."

Including Beckett and his men, the group was twelve strong. Freight elevator or not, the cab was small. Beckett ordered two of his men to stay behind.

"We can make room," Li said.

"They don't need to come down," Beckett replied bluntly. He punched the close-door button, cutting off his charges.

Shrugging sheepishly at Rebecca, Li held her access card to the reader and pressed the single floor button, labelled SL1. Sublevel, obviously.

"Well, this is cosy," Spencer said, reaching into his pocket for another stick of gum.

Before he could pop it into his mouth, Wyatt snatched it from his sibling's grasp and pocketed it.

The cab descended.

It seemed to move at a crawl, but Rebecca guessed that was a matter of perception. For all she knew, they were in fact moving quickly. She wondered how far below ground they had to travel.

Looking about, she realised she'd been herded centrally into the elevator. Li stood slightly in front of her, so too the brothers. Behind her left shoulder was one of Beckett's men, and behind her right, another. Beckett and Holtorf had taken position between them. At the front of the cab, on either side of Li and the brothers, stood the remaining two soldiers. Interestingly, all four men, one in each corner, faced slightly inwards.

Gone was the bravado from the plane. Still, she sensed their coolness was a pretence—they were like coiled springs at the ready. Were they concerned about her? Or Holtorf or the brothers? Why? *We're on the same team, right?*

She figured it was none of that. This was their default behaviour: hyperalert, hypervigilant. Still, something seemed amiss. Why they were even here? Beckett and his men were a security detail, tasked with protecting and delivering an important government asset: Egbert. Shouldn't they be with *him*?

At last, the elevator pinged, and the doors opened. For a moment, jostling bodies obscured Rebecca's view. She could see part of a wide corridor ahead. Hurrying out, she made eye contact with Spencer, who was in the process of retrieving an alternate pack of gum from his pocket.

Popping a stick into his mouth, he smiled at her. "You always need a Plan B, right?"

The corridor was deserted and otherwise silent, save for the hum of ducted air conditioning. The walls were white and plain and devoid of decoration. The overhead fluorescents were reflected in the polished, laminate floor. Rebecca was reminded of a hospital.

Following Li, the group worked its way past various doors, all closed, and most numbered. Labs, Rebecca thought, but she couldn't see inside because they were windowless. There were no windows anywhere, in fact, and she reminded herself they were deep underground. At that, she suddenly felt claustrophobic.

Not a hospital. More like a submarine. Or a tomb.

She shivered. It was cold down here. "It seems a little quiet. Everyone out to lunch?"

"This may be a military facility," Li replied without turning, "but most of our on-site personnel are civilians. Over the weekend, we keep a skeleton crew only."

Of course. It's Friday. Rebecca recalled the unmarked 747 they'd passed earlier, which looked like it was being prepped for take-off. It was early afternoon, but the day shift must already be knocking off.

Li confirmed her suspicions. "We have a night shift, starting soon. Security personnel mainly. Anyone not rostered tonight is already finishing up."

"Hitting the bars, no doubt," Spencer said.

"We have a couple of those on base," Li replied. "If you're so inclined." She turned left. "This way please."

More corridors. Gradually, Rebecca tuned into her environment. Soon enough, she heard something she hadn't noticed before; a strange humming sound, vibrating through the walls. Air filters? The sound seemed to pulse, ebbing and flowing. She imagined some huge piece of machinery thrumming from deeper within the complex, maybe beneath them. Several weeks earlier, back in the jungle, she'd heard a similar sound; a strange pulse emanating, as it turned out, from the mysterious sphere they'd found beneath the pyramid.

At last, they stopped at a door with a proximity reader. Li pressed her card against it and it beeped and flashed green. With a hiss, the door opened, and they followed her into a dimly lit, almost dark room—the main source of illumination radiating from the glowing faces of multiple flat-screen computer terminals positioned side by side on top of a long, curving counter.

Looks like mission control at NASA.

The console screens, facing the back of the room where Rebecca and her group currently stood, swam with all manner of images: some held graphs and formulas and what may have been lines of code, others crawled with squiggly lines like those on an EEG monitor. More than one screen, she noticed, looped through CCTV images, seemingly from various angles, although at distance, Rebecca struggled to see detail. The chairs to all terminals—maybe half a dozen or so—were empty, except for two. At these were hunched a pair of silhouettes, perhaps technicians, also in white lab coats. They had their backs to the group and didn't turn or look up from their keyboards.

"What is this place?" Rebecca said to Li, stepping forward. To her right, banks of servers ran along the walls. It was cool in here, even cooler than the corridors. Probably for the servers.

"Let me show you," Li said. She walked up to one of the technicians and issued instructions. The man's fingers danced over his keyboard.

Slowly, the wall in front of them slid back to reveal a large observation window—extending floor to ceiling, it was several yards long. Just below it, on the other side of the glass, ran a steel structure. Rebecca guessed this was a viewing platform, mainly because of its shape and position. The platform sat high above a colossal open space lit by stadium-like towers of LED lights.

The space looked to be a massive subterranean hangar.

And while the hangar's left and right edges extended into impenetrable shadow, in the centre, where it was brightly lit, was an incredible sight. Rebecca gasped.

Li smiled and spoke in a breathless whisper. "Welcome to the Farm."

14
α

Stunned, Rebecca gazed out through the observation window.

In the centre of the massive lighted space—positioned two-deep and four across on the floor of the colossal hangar—sat eight huge, white hemispheres. Each of the opaque domes was as big as a football field, maybe bigger, and crisscrossed with hexagonal, beehive-like ribbing. They looked like giant golf balls cut in half. Rebecca was reminded of the distinctive white radomes at military spy stations, specifically those at the Pine Gap joint defence facility back home in central Australia.

Similar, but also vastly different. Something else entirely.

"No frickin' way," Spencer said, chewing in slow motion, "this is incredible."

More than incredible, Rebecca thought. On the outside of the domes weaved a network of galvanised steel walkways, staircases, and gantries—again, all brightly lit—which gave a sense of scale and proportion. Rebecca could see no-one on the catwalks, but anyone down there would have appeared ant-like. In its entirety, the structure looked like a futuristic lunar-base, the effect heightened by the gloom pressing at its edges like the coldness of deep space. These same shadows concealed the underground hangar's exact dimensions, so she couldn't be sure of its size. But clearly, to house something of this magnitude, it must have been gargantuan.

"What the hell are those things?" Wyatt asked Li. "The domes…they look like huge glasshouses."

"Not glasshouses," Li said. "But close. And not glass, either. The domes are largely thermoplastic."

"You mean acrylic, like Plexiglas?"

"Correct," Li said. "Hard plastic, essentially. Thick, too. About 60 milli-metres, in fact, or nearly two and half inches. The material is super-strong. They use the same stuff in oceanariums around the world."

"What?" Holtorf queried. "This is *aquarium* tech?"

"Tweaked for our requirements, of course," Li replied. "The engineer-ing really is outstanding. Lots of cool technical stuff I could tell you about but won't bore you with."

"*Please*, bore us," Spencer said. "This is fascinating."

Li smiled. "Some other time, maybe. Suffice to say, we've laid more than a mile of acrylic cylinders, and tons of acrylic sheeting. Most of the materials were prefabricated and assembled on site. Because of that, we got the structure up and running quickly. But it's not finished yet—some of it is still under construction."

"This is all very interesting," Wyatt said. "But again, what the hell is it?"

"Like I said, we call it the Farm," Li answered, turning back to the win-dow. "Essentially, it's a vivarium."

"*What*?" Wyatt said.

Rebecca baulked, stunned. "You're kidding, right?"

"No, I'm not," Li replied. "Down there, inside those domes, is a place of life…an ecosystem like nothing you've ever seen before."

15
α

The sound of his own breathing was loud in Owen's ears. The facemask amplified the effect, so he reached up to shift it into a more comfortable position. He'd never worn a biohazard suit before, and the garment, complete with an air-purifying respirator, felt bulky and awkward. He'd happily ditch it, but no-one was permitted here without one.

Still fidgeting, he peered into the semidarkness ahead. Although sodium lights were strung along the passageway's length, they glowed only faintly. Through the beam of his headlamp, motes of dust drifted on invisible currents of air.

"Relax, Owen," Jessy said, her voice preceded by an amplified click in his ear.

Owen nodded. Not only was his breathing loud, but it was fast, too. Obviously, Jessy could hear it through her speaker.

"This way," Perez said, moving to the front and leading them deeper underground. Over the two-way, his voice sounded distant and clinical.

Earlier, the old man had led them from the north-western vantage point to a perimeter checkpoint, and from there, to a gowning area in a large temporary shelter. After suiting up, the three of them had headed down to the plaza in front of the pyramid, where the mouth of the tunnel that burrowed deep beneath the structure yawned.

Ahead, the tunnel curved. Owen wondered how far below ground they were. Underfoot, his boots scuffed softly on the stone. He reached out a gloved hand and brushed the wall. It, too, was stone, comprised of large bricks cobbled together.

Along the floor, running beneath the string of lights, was a large ventilation hose, and overhead, a thick bundle of conduit and power cables. All of it ran down from the surface.

"This is the same tunnel Bec followed to gain access to the nest," Jessy said.

"And the same one she and Kriedemann used to extract Ed," Owen said, trying to steady his breathing. "The burrow must be down here somewhere." With his mask on, he couldn't know how it smelt in here, but he sensed it must have been earthy and animal-like.

"When Bec was in here, it would have been pitch black," Jessy said. "And it hadn't been cleared of the residents."

Owen nodded. How Bec had summoned the courage to traverse this place, not only in impenetrable gloom, but under the crippling personal circumstances of her re-emerging fear, was beyond him.

"She faced her demons," Jessy said, reading his mind. "She's strong."

Owen said to Perez, "Our friend, Rebecca—she wasn't wearing a suit while she was down here."

"The air is perfectly breathable," Perez replied from up ahead, his voice floating over the speaker. "But there are protocols for working in such environments. Okay, we're here."

Rounding a slight veer in the passage, they entered a large natural cavern, maybe a hundred feet across and brightly lit. Above their heads, torn into the ceiling, was a gaping hole, roughly circular, with steep, sloping sides.

"Wow," Owen said, swivelling about.

"This must be the funnel Bec told us about," Jessy said, tilting her head to run her gaze up the slope. "And up there must be the pyramid's interior."

Owen shivered, recalling Rebecca's story. Somewhere up there, high above their heads, loomed a huge domed chamber at the top of which a mass of spiders had roosted in a grotesque, pulsating ball. With Oliveira and his team, Rebecca had climbed the funnel and unknowingly walked beneath them. Now, Owen raised an arm to his eyes, shielding them from the bright light flooding from above. Because of its intensity and angle, he couldn't see into the pyramid itself, but he sensed the domed chamber high above. What he *could* see was a steep metal staircase that hadn't been present when

Rebecca was here, running up one side of the funnel. The stairs provided access into the pyramid.

Owen said to Perez, "The sphere was in here. The funnel up there is where it punched through the forest floor, but down here is where it came to rest."

"And where it stayed for some time," Perez said, nodding. "Long after the pyramid was built overhead."

"So where is it now?"

Jessy interrupted. "Owen, check this out."

Owen turned. Across the floor, fenced now for safety, was a large hole. A ladder descended from its steel-reinforced rim.

Crouching at its edge, faintly lit by the light shining up from below, Jessy said, "This must be where Rebecca fell through the floor. And down there is the cavern she told us about."

Perez nodded. "From what I hear, she didn't see what was down there. Not everything."

"No," Owen said. "Are we heading down?"

"Please do," Perez said.

Jessy said to Owen, "After you. Watch your step."

Straddling the ladder, careful of his footholds, Owen descended. About ten feet down was a narrow earthen ledge. Another seven or eight feet below that was the floor of the cavern proper. Reaching the bottom, he turned outward as Jessy, following, descended the last few rungs behind him.

"Holy mother of God," Owen gasped.

The supercavern stretched in all directions, so large that despite the presence of multiple mobile light towers, its extremities remained in shadow. For the most part, the space was wide-open, but in places rocky outcroppings, not quite stalagmites, soared upwards into darkness. Around these, on the floor of the cave, a patchwork of steel walkways zigzagged. Moving across them, headlamps jolting, were dozens of hazmat-suited workers, those in the distance looking tiny but giving scale to the place. The more Owen scanned, the larger the cavern seemed to grow.

"Incredible," Jessy said. Over the two-way, her breathing sounded fast and ragged. "How far does it extend?"

"This chamber alone is nearly a thousand feet long, and three hundred feet wide," Perez said. "You could fit half a dozen 747s in here with ample room to spare."

"Man…"

"As for the size of the overall system, we're not certain," Perez went on. "We're talking multiple huge chambers and connecting passageways. We're finding new rooms every day."

"You're still mapping?"

"Yes. We've conducted multiple sweeps with the laser scanner, but it takes time to penetrate every nook and cranny—we're working through the data gaps as fast as we can. Please, follow me."

Starting out from the base of the ladder, Perez crossed to the nearest walkway, his boots clanking on the galvanised steel mesh. Jessy went next, and Owen followed, panning his head about. Deep shadows interplayed with blinding lights, somewhat confusingly. On the side of the cavern nearest them, partially lit, a sloping mound of jagged rocks, likely from a previous roof collapse, rose to a distant point. The gigantic formation was at least one hundred feet high and twice that across the base.

Almost as large as the pyramid above them.

"I can't believe this was beneath us the whole time," Jessy murmured.

Owen could scarcely believe it himself. The cavern was Rebecca's discovery; she'd found it by chance after falling from the chamber above. Later, she'd explained that it must have run deeper and wider, but with only her night-vision goggles to aid her and not having ventured farther, its true scale had eluded her.

Over the two-way, Perez said, "For years, we've suspected there were dozens of undiscovered caves here in the Amazon, hidden beneath the jungle. Maybe hundreds. But this is something else, eh?"

Owen nodded. Almost certainly, this was part of the same network of caves from which he and Sanchez had escaped following their capture by the Yuguruppu.

Incredible.

Suddenly, Jessy drew up and lifted a gloved hand. "What's that over there?"

Owen followed her pointing finger to the huge rockfall he'd noticed a moment ago. What he *hadn't* noticed, but saw now, was the vast, oily blackness at its base, extending into the penumbral shadow behind it. "Is that water?"

"Water, yes," Perez said, leading them to a better vantage point. "But not just any water. Here…take a closer look."

Owen squinted through the gloom, and as he watched, the water seemed to shift and slide deeper into the cave like a serpent disturbed from its slumber.

"It's moving," Jessy said breathlessly. "It's a *river*."

Perez nodded. "Have you heard of the Rio Hamza?"

Owen shot Perez a glance. "The Hamza? It doesn't exist."

Perez shook his head. "It's real."

Jessy transferred her gaze from one man to the other. "The Hamza?"

Owen turned to her. "Rumour has it that directly beneath the Amazon River flows another, even bigger river—"

"Wait…*what*? Beneath it? You mean like the Amazon's *twin*?"

"Allegedly," Owen said. He turned to Perez. "But the Hamza isn't a conventional river—at best, it's slow-moving groundwater. And it's a theory, anyway."

"Not a theory," Perez said. "It's real. But I agree, the Hamza isn't a river in the traditional sense. That said, we've found…something else."

"Something *else*?"

Perez cleared his throat. "What if the stories were true? Picture this: a pair of mighty rivers, one above the ground—the Amazon—and the other below it, the two of them running parallel to each other for almost 4,000 miles, west to east, from the Peruvian Andes all the way to the Atlantic. Incredible, wouldn't you say?"

"You've found this? Another river?" Owen said. "The Amazon's *twin*?"

"There are signs," Perez answered cryptically.

"But we're far from the Amazon," Jessy said. "We're not beneath it. Not here."

"Think of it as a massive subterranean basin," Perez said. "The Amazon's secret sibling, if you will, and the Hamza, and even this waterway here, all part of the same system, all feeding into each other from hundreds of miles in every direction." He pointed to the expanse of water in front of them. "This is a tributary; we call it the Rio Sombra."

"The Shadow River," Jessy said. She turned to stare across the inky waterway. "Apt…and a little creepy."

Owen said to Perez, "You need a research team in here for this alone."

"We have one," Perez replied. "The river, and the cave system itself—everything down here is bigger than we could have imagined, and it'll take years to fully map and explore. But already, we've collected some fascinating data. Did you know that under the right conditions, a river can flow uphill? Amazing, right? Capillary action, pressure, siphoning—all those things can contribute. But I haven't brought you down here for a potamology lesson."

With that, he hurried forward again, towards the far side of the chamber, boots clanking. Owen and Jessy rushed to keep up, ignored by the many hazmat-suited workers. Some of these, Owen noted, collected rock samples, which were then loaded and wheeled out on trolleys and hand-trucks. The cave echoed with the sounds of metal on stone.

Before long, the cavern narrowed. Perez led them into the bottleneck, squeezing between several closely spaced stalagmites that sparkled wetly in the beam of his headlamp. Here, between the converging walls, cracks and openings into other chambers yawned. The place was a huge, labyrinthine maze.

Soon, the walls widened again. Off to the side, the Sombra slithered silently beside them, as though following their progress.

Perhaps spooked by its false gaze, Jessy thrust her head about nervously. "And the nest…you've cleared it, right?"

"The megarachnids?" Perez said. "Why, of course. That'd be a serious workplace health and safety issue, eh?"

He snuffed a laugh and pushed ahead. Owen glanced about. The spiders had nested not only in the pyramid above, but in the caves beneath; Rebecca had told them the supercavern had been covered in silk. Owen could find no remnants of that now, and in fact, noted a series of dark smears on the walls, possibly scorch marks. The place hadn't merely been cleared; it'd been torched.

The path opened into a small chamber. Away from the workers, it was quieter, and Owen heard water dripping eerily. On the far side of the space lay another dark passage, at the mouth of which were parked several electric carts. Perez selected one, waited for Owen and Jessy to slip into the back seat, and accelerated. Lit intermittently, this new tunnel bored downhill in a straight line, burrowing deeper into the earth. Along the way, Owen noted several adjoining, natural alcoves, some of which housed generators and pumps and maintenance equipment. Within minutes, the tunnel ended, opening into another wide space. This new supercavern was almost as large as the one directly beneath the pyramid.

"*Whoa…*" Jessy said, sliding from her seat as the cart rolled to a stop.

At the far end of the space rose an immense wall of rock. In front of it, on stilts several feet above the ground, was a large metal platform, circular, with connecting stairs and catwalks. Gathered here—some standing, some seated at workstations but all facing the wall—were several personnel in yellow hazmat suits. On either side of them, flanking the platform and supported by scaffolding at least two storeys high, towered racks of powerful LEDs, arranged like stadium lights. These, too, faced the wall.

Owen circled the cart, his gaze fixed ahead. In an alcove to his right, just a few feet away, he sensed, more than saw, several rapid-deployment shelters and heard, somewhere close to them, the sound of a waterfall, perhaps the Sombra tumbling from above into an unseen pool. His attention, however, was locked on the huge rock wall. Though his view was partly obscured by the large metal structure in front of it, he discerned a gigantic, vertical crack in the rockface, maybe one hundred feet high. Despite the concentration of lights, this fissure remained impenetrably dark.

"What the hell is *that*?" Jessy asked.

Perez spoke, but he didn't answer the question. "This is as far as we go. The site is emitting low levels of radiation. Not harmful, of course, and likely latent. But for now, this will do."

"Emitting?" Jessy said. "You mean from inside that crack?"

As she asked this, Owen thought he heard a low moan, almost a buzz, and cocked his head—the sound seemed to be emanating from the cleft, as though a breath of wind was passing through it into the cavern. He said to Perez, "You sure that's all it is emitting?"

Before Perez could reply, a female voice interjected over the two-way. "Let me tell you an interesting fact about the Amazon."

Sensing movement behind him, Owen turned. A dark-skinned woman in a hazmat suit emerged from one of the inflatable shelters, speaking as she walked. "Did you know the Amazon wasn't always a lush rainforest? In fact, as recently as 2,000 years ago, it was dominated by savannah. Picture the Serengeti, in Africa." Stepping beside them, the woman smiled. "I'm Dr Yolanda Mbye, project leader. Welcome aboard."

In turn, Owen and Jessy shook her hand and introduced themselves.

"You mentioned the Serengeti," Jessy said.

Dr Mbye nodded. "It's fascinating, really. The Amazonian ecosystem used to be vastly different—now, it's all dense, impenetrable rainforest, right? But pollen found in river sediments suggest that as recently as two millennia ago, most of this region was *grassland*. The question is: What happened 2,000 years ago?"

The relevance of this escaped Owen, but he played along. "We know what happened. Shifts in the Earth's orbit around the sun caused the climate to become wetter, promoting tree growth—"

"That's been suggested, yes," Mbye said.

Jessy hesitated, her brow furrowing. "I get the impression I'm missing something."

Turning to the fissure, Mbye lifted a gloved hand. "You asked what that was. We call it the Vent, and we're fairly certain it appeared 2,000 years ago."

"*Appeared*?" Owen queried.

Mbye smiled. "The creatures you found, the megarachnids—they're a fascinating discovery. I'm aware of your theory on how they got here."

"It's Rebecca's theory," Jessy said. "They were brought here by the sphere, the one she found in the chamber beneath the pyramid."

Mbye shook her head. "No. They came through the Vent. And they didn't come alone."

16
α

Rebecca blinked and stared blankly into the huge chamber beyond the observation window, trying to wrap her head around Li's revelation. "You said *ecosystem*?"

Before Li could respond, Wyatt interrupted. "Wait…those domes, that structure down there…you're telling us it's a giant *terrarium*?"

"Essentially, yes," Li said. "Technically, it's a vivarium, which, as you're probably aware, is the overarching term for an artificial habitat for studying animals. But a terrarium sums it up. Cool, huh?"

"*Animals*?" Spencer said. "What kind of animals?"

A disquieting weight settled in Rebecca's gut. She turned to Li. "Tell me you haven't done what I think you have."

Li frowned. "You don't approve?"

"You're kidding, right?" Rebecca shot back. She spun on Beckett, who was sitting on the edge of one of the terminal desks. "Egbert's not the only live specimen you've collected. Correct?"

Beckett returned her gaze, but in the room's low light his expression was unreadable, and he made no attempt to reply. His silence spoke volumes.

Rebecca hesitated, alarmed, but also feeling foolish and betrayed. For a moment, she couldn't speak.

Looking perplexed, perhaps sensing the tension, Li answered on Beckett's behalf. "I apologise…I thought you were aware. But yes, you're correct,

Egbert isn't the only live specimen we've recovered…we have many, and that structure is their home."

"Jesus," Spencer said.

Wyatt shook his head. "Right…so you're telling us you've created a giant underground terrarium and filled it with *giant* spiders."

Perhaps thrown by the simplistic description, Li drew a breath. "It's more than that—a lot more. Like I said, we've built an ecosystem."

Chewing, Spencer turned to Rebecca and shrugged. "Well, that's a relief. An *ecosystem*. Much better."

"It's fully secure, if that's your concern," Li assured them. "Like I said, we sourced the acrylic from oceanarium contractors, so it's able to withstand massive pressure—you can imagine the stress requirements. We don't have anywhere near the same forces to deal with."

"I'm only concerned that it's strong enough to contain the residents," Wyatt said. "It *is*, right?"

"It's *more* than strong enough," Li replied. "The structure is titanium-reinforced. To be honest, it's impregnable."

Rebecca only half-heard this. In a daze, she was still trying to process the implications, still trying to process *everything*. She gazed through the window. Sitting there clustered together, the white domes looked like a knot of plump mushrooms.

"Aquariums are transparent," Holtorf said. "The domes are opaque."

"We call them habitats," Li said. "They're tinted and shuttered. We can alternate between opaque or transparent as needed. Right now, the external shutters are closed to simulate night. But we have full control of light and shade."

"If it's an ecosystem, I assume you have plants, too?" Spencer asked.

Li nodded. "And they have everything they need, all controlled and optimised: water, nutrients, sunlight."

"Sunlight? We're below ground."

"We use sun pipes and photovoltaic cells to collect sunlight from the surface and feed it inside. And we have supplemental grow lamps, to help with photosynthesis."

"What about the resultant by-products?" Wyatt said. "What about air filtration? Is the humidity an issue? And what about mold? I used to keep frogs as a kid, so I know a little about this. Closed terrariums need to be aired to discourage mold."

Li nodded. "We have a filtration system, fans and filters to cycle fresh air. Very advanced. We also pump air directly into the soil to inhibit mold spore production."

Again, Rebecca only heard some of this; to be honest, she didn't care about plants or mold or air filtration. "You didn't think this through."

"Sorry?"

"What happened in Brazil…you're aware, right?"

Li hesitated. "I've read your report, of course. We've planned—"

"I've seen what these things are capable of," Rebecca interrupted. "This isn't a good idea. It's a *terrible* idea."

Once more, Li rallied, smiling gently and reassuringly, the way a parent might to a frightened child. "We have emergency measures and contingencies."

"Including termination? You can destroy them?"

"In the event of an emergency, yes," Li deadpanned. "As I said, the habitats are fitted with an advanced filtration system—they're essentially large inhalation chambers. If needed, we can flood the domes with carbon dioxide."

Rebecca nodded. "You need to put that contingency into immediate effect. You can't keep them here. You need to terminate them."

At that, Beckett rose from the shadows and stepped forward, the computer terminals lighting one side of his face. "That's not going to happen," he said simply. He locked gazes with Li and a wordless conversation seemed to pass between them.

Nodding, lowering her eyes, Li transferred her gaze to Rebecca. "I understand you have questions, but if you'll follow me, I'm sure I can ease your concerns."

17

α

A door to the right of the control room's observation window provided access to the external viewing platform, which itself lay at the base of a short steel staircase. Descending, Rebecca followed Li with the brothers, Holtorf, Beckett, and two of his men—the fingernail-clipper, and his asshole buddy from the plane—in tow. It was semi-dark out here, the only source of illumination some emergency lighting and the diffused glow from the distant habitats. Rebecca gazed out at them. Although troubled by what Li had described, she was nonetheless keen to view the domes up close.

Running from the platform and down to the hangar floor were two yellow-painted pylons, within which was housed a glass-walled elevator. The group squeezed inside. Tapping her prox-card, Li punched the down button.

"I still don't understand," Rebecca said to her as the elevator descended. "I mean, why bring them here? Why go to all this effort? I get that you want to study them. But—"

Li's brow wrinkled. "That's just it—how could we *not* do this? You've gone to great lengths yourself with Egbert."

Rebecca wanted to argue that this was different…but *was* it? "This species has unique attributes. It can't be taken lightly."

"And we haven't," Li replied. "Far from it, in fact. This is a massive undertaking."

"It's an unpredictable, and inherently dangerous species."

"Hence the precautions."

Rebecca drew a slow breath. Beyond the glass, the habitats shimmered like a distant underwater base. Thinking of Egbert, she said, "These are large, complex animals. If nothing else, you have their welfare to consider."

Li turned. "We have taken all necessary precautions and measures. Our research team—headed up by your mentor, your *friend*, Professor Hayward—is top notch. And now you're a part of it."

The elevator reached the bottom. The doors opened into a clear space: utilitarian and industrial-looking with a dimly lit workstation and computer terminal off to the left. No personnel were in this area—in fact, the place was eerily quiet. One hundred yards away, on the other side of the hangar, the habitats shone brightly. Between here and there, low-level, recessed lighting marked a path on the polished concrete floor; in the near dark, it looked like a runway. At the head of this path sat a yellow burden carrier, like an airport baggage-carrier but without a trailer and big enough for all of them. Taking a seat up front, next to Li—who took the wheel—Rebecca cast her gaze about. The hangar was for the most part scantily lit, preventing her from getting a true sense of scale, but it was clearly huge. The ceiling, well out of range, loomed like a starless night sky. Rebecca sensed the enormous weight of the earth pressing down on top of her.

"For such a large space, it can feel oddly claustrophobic," Li said as she drove, as though reading Rebecca's thoughts.

Rebecca nodded, and turned to her. "So…was it difficult getting the animals past border control? I imagine there are CDC regulations about importing exotic species into the US."

"There are Federal Quarantine Regulations regarding the importation of biological specimens, including invertebrates," Li said. "But equally, there are allowances for scientific research. I'm sure the appropriate clearances were acquired."

"Sure?"

Li shrugged. "To be honest, those details are above my paygrade."

Rebecca wondered if a top-secret government project would be hampered by simple regulations or quarantine protocols.

They observed quarantine protocols when they detained us in Brazil, didn't they?

"I've heard about your work with Egbert," Li said, changing the subject.

"Yeah, that," Rebecca said unhappily, jutting her chin at the domes. "Turns out the last two months of my life are officially redundant."

"Oh, not at all," Li said. "Quite the opposite, in fact; our projects complement each other perfectly. Your experiments…they aren't merely ground-breaking, they're incredibly relevant."

Rebecca turned to her. "My report documents everything up until the Incident, and nothing more. I haven't reported on my work with Egbert. You're aware of it? The specifics, I mean?"

"Your theories are fascinating," Li said indirectly. "I'm looking forward to discussing them in depth."

Rebecca was about to question her further when Li drew the carrier to a halt and in the same smooth motion, slid from the vehicle. Behind her, the others exited, too. Leaving the conversation for another time, Rebecca followed suit.

"Man…get a load of *this*," Wyatt said, panning his head about.

Surrounded by metal catwalks and observation decks, the cluster of opaque white domes loomed high above them—up close, they were even bigger than Rebecca had imagined. Stepping forward, she craned her neck upwards.

"More than 200 feet high," Li said. "Enough to clear the treetops. We've got some tall vegetation in there. We had to replicate the environment as closely as possible."

"Had to?" Rebecca queried. She hadn't noticed before, but the air seemed stale, hard to breathe. She swallowed to rid her mouth of a coppery, metallic taste.

"Initially, we had some issues with integration," Li explained. "Replicating their environment fixed that."

Chewing loudly, Spencer stepped up behind them. "Great White sharks have never been successfully kept in captivity. They keep banging into the walls, losing their appetite. Some say they suffer depression. Bottom line is, for some species, imprisonment doesn't work."

"Fortunately, we're not working with sharks," Li said, walking now. "This way."

Running between the first two domes—effectively joining them together—was a solid-looking, bunkerlike structure. In the middle of the bunker's façade was a closed steel door.

"That's the habitat entry?" Holtorf asked.

"Indirectly, yes," Li replied. "Beyond that door is Research Center 1, which services H-1 through to H-4. There's another entry like this further along for Research Center 2, which primarily services H-5 and H-6. A third center is currently under construction, along with H-7 and H-8."

Rebecca noticed cranes and trucks sitting idly in the distance. The domes down there looked to be externally complete but were surrounded by scaffolding. For now, the building site was quiet.

"Direct access to the habitats is via airlock and cleanroom," Li said, still walking. "Class 1."

Increasing her pace to catch up, Rebecca nodded. Clearly, the habitats were controlled environments—the cleanrooms serving as a barrier to ensure pollutants weren't tracked in or out.

"So, we're going *inside*?" Wyatt asked.

Li smiled. "No, definitely not. But I thought I'd show you our H-1 observation tunnel."

The entrance to this tunnel—which evidently ran through the middle of the habitat—lay to the left of the research center, behind a separate steel door. It was in front of this that Li finally halted and turned, waiting for the group to assemble.

Rebecca observed, affixed to the tunnel door, a yellow, diamond-shaped sign with a black border. In black writing were the words, 'Spiders at Work'.

"Funny…sort of," Spencer said, noticing it, too.

"We're scientists, what do you expect?" Li replied, holding her proxcard to the reader. It flashed green. "Okay, let's see if they're up for visitors."

18
α

On the other side of the door, extending into the distance, was a long, cylindrical passageway: polished concrete underfoot, and reinforced, curved acrylic overhead. It was dark in here, save for muted floor-lighting and a purple-green glow that seeped through the plexiglass like a ghostly mist. Rooted to the spot, Rebecca gazed about, stunned.

For all intents and purposes, she was standing in the middle of a rainforest. On the other side of the rounded, transparent wall—inside the habitat—she saw vegetation: *thick* vegetation, but only hints of it, mainly broad green leaves, but then her eyes adjusted, and the huge, flared roots of a larger tree came into focus, snaking through the leaf litter. Because of the low light and condensation on the plexiglass—suggesting it was steamy on the other side—she was unable to get a clear view, so she rushed to the other side of the tunnel hoping for better visibility. It was the same there, just a collection of shadows and dark shapes looming out of the phantom mist. She discerned a fringe of vine-like lianas, no doubt hanging from an unseen canopy, and the pressing, slate-grey shadow of an understorey. Not much, but enough to suggest there were larger things in there, mysterious things lurking in the darkness.

She saw no movement and couldn't be sure if this caused her disappointment or relief.

"Man…this is awesome," Spencer said, his face childlike and glowing as he pressed closer to the plexiglass. "Just like the shark tunnel at SeaWorld."

"Enough with the sharks already," Wyatt said slowly, his voice laced with wonder. "But yeah, you're right…it's awesome."

Rebecca ran her fingers along the warm, curved acrylic. It *did* look like an aquarium tunnel, except down here—or rather, out there, stalking the shadows—were predators unmatched by any theme park on Earth.

"Can you turn on the lights?" Spencer asked. "Help us see better?"

"We can, but not now, unfortunately," Li replied. "The cycles are timed."

"Cycles?"

"I should explain," Li said. "Everything is carefully controlled to simulate their normal environment. So, to promote a healthy circadian rhythm, like I mentioned earlier, we cycle night and day. Now, we're replicating night, so everything in the visible spectrum is at a low level, not much brighter than starlight. But we've just activated the blacklights; they're warming up as we speak."

"Blacklights," Wyatt said. "You mean UV-lamps."

Li nodded. "UVA has no impact on the cycle, but we use it sporadically. To be honest, we often go a step further, actively filtering UV from white light to promote tree growth. But for now, the lamps are on because it helps us see them."

"This species is nocturnal," Rebecca said. "They'll be active now."

"Unusual for a species with such good eyesight," Li said, agreeing. "But it's true. So, fingers crossed, we'll see some action soon. As for the cycles, I should let you know that we also control the climate—temperature, humidity, air quality and filtration. Even precipitation."

"Rain? A sprinkler system, you mean?" Wyatt asked.

Li nodded. "We have an irrigation system; the main storage tanks are beneath the domes and feed up to smaller tanks on top. Two in every three days, we simulate rainfall; it's a rainforest, after all."

"What about storms?" Spencer asked, his voice mirroring the childlike wonder plastered across his face. "Lightning? Thunder? It's a jungle, right?"

Li smiled faintly. "No storms, but we can vary the intensity—light showers, heavy rainfall—all computer controlled, of course. The water drains away and is collected by the tanks beneath the dome and recycled. There's no wastage. It's quite ingenious."

"You mentioned temperature," Wyatt asked.

"We keep the operating temperature steady, usually around 80 degrees Fahrenheit, but can fluctuate this as required. Generally, nothing outside a band of 75 to 85 degrees."

"That's the average year-round temperature for a tropical rainforest," Spencer said.

Around 24 to 29 degrees Celsius, Rebecca calculated. "Average humidity?"

"80 to 90 per cent," Li said.

"How do you control that? Either the temperature, or the humidity?" Wyatt asked.

"It's surprisingly simple, really," Li said. "We steam water, and pump that steam inside. It's a controlled process. Again, it's quite ingenious."

As you keep saying, Rebecca thought. At that moment she realised Holtorf was conspicuously quiet and turned to find him hunched slightly and with a finger to his ear. When he noticed her, he shrugged and whispered, "Sinusitis. My ears, they tend to block occasionally. I'm good."

She turned back, curious now about Beckett and his men, and saw them a long way ahead; they'd progressed down the tunnel, leaving the sightseers behind. She refocused on the brothers, who continued to talk in excited tones.

"I gotta admit, it is pretty cool," Spencer said to Li. "Scary, but cool."

Next to him, Wyatt nodded. "It's an extraordinary setup, for sure. So, going back to what you were saying earlier about seeing some action. The spiders…they're in H-1? They're in this habitat?"

"They're in here, yes," Li said, starting down the tunnel. "Let's keep walking."

Rebecca held back, once more scanning the foliage inside the habitat. Nothing caught her eye, and shrugging, she hurried ahead. Once she'd caught up to the others, she said to Li, "I'm guessing they know we're here."

"Like all salticids, they have superb eyesight, as I mentioned before," Li said. "And their vibration sensitivity is acute. Sometimes when we're in here, they test the plexiglass."

"Whoa," Spencer said. "You mean, they *attack* the tunnel?"

"They're territorial," Li replied. "I'd suggest it's more of a reminder."

"Sounds like a warning to me," Wyatt said. "So, you think they're watching us *now*?"

"There's a good chance, yes."

"*Whoa,*" Spencer said again, chewing loudly. "I wonder what they're thinking when they look at us."

Wyatt threw him a frown.

"What?" Spencer shot back. "Maybe they see us as big and threatening…shark tunnels distort size; the curved acrylic creates a diverging lens which makes everything *on that side* appear smaller to us. Maybe we seem bigger to them."

Again, Wyatt frowned.

"You get where I'm going, right? Anything beyond the plexiglass, anything in there, is bigger than it appears," Spencer said, clearly feeling the need to explain. "Just saying."

At that, Wyatt shied uneasily from the tunnel wall. "Useful information, Spencer. Really useful."

Chewing loudly, Spencer shrugged. "Like I said, just saying." He followed this with a sharp guffaw. "Hey, remember when we were kids, that day in the car when that big huntsman crawled across your window and you were showing off and stuck your face against the glass, thinking the spider was on the other side…only it wasn't on the other side? You remember that? You remember when it jumped at you? Right at your face?"

"Yes, I remember, Spencer," Wyatt murmured, shaking his head.

"That was so funny," Spencer said, and laughed again. "Real funny. Good times."

Sudden movement caught Rebecca's eye—a dark, streaking blur on the other side of the plexiglass. Spinning, she sought it out, but saw nothing unusual, only a tangle of roots and some fern fronds, one of which swayed gently back and forth.

It's not swaying. You're imagining it.

Leaning closer to the acrylic, she squinted into the jungle.

"So, what do you think?"

Startled, Rebecca jumped. Li had stepped up beside her. Concluding there was nothing out there—at least, not anymore—Rebecca turned from the plexiglass. "It's certainly impressive, I'll give you that." She hesitated. "So impressive, in fact, I don't know where to start. I mean, how on Earth could you get this up and running in just two months? It doesn't seem possible. And the cost must have been astronomical. Which begs an even bigger question, something we haven't yet established."

Li's eyes shone curiously. "And that is?"

"Why you're doing this. Why you've collected them, why you've spent all this money and gone to such an effort," Rebecca said. "We haven't established the end-game."

Li nodded, understanding. "Well, the answer to that is simple. We're going to harvest the silk."

19
α

The Farm, Rebecca thought, feeling foolish for having missed the connection. "On the door back there, the sign about the spiders. You're farming silk."

Li held up a hand. "Not yet; we're still building the infrastructure. But that's the intention."

At last, the pieces were starting to come together. Rebecca was reminded of a conversation she'd had with Ed, weeks back, in which she'd espoused the value of silk-harvesting. To her, it was inevitable; as one of the world's toughest natural fibres, spidersilk is not only ultra-strong, but light and flexible, a future building material for everything from ballistically tolerant body armour to super-lightweight aerospace components. But to date, commercialisation hadn't been successful; on the one hand, the fibre is difficult to synthesise artificially, and on the other, most spiders are solitary, so throwing together a heap of territorial, cannibalistic arachnids simply isn't feasible. Here, however, was a game-changer: a eusocial species capable of producing silk naturally and in vast quantities. "It's all about scaling; finally, the business model is viable."

Li's eyes gleamed. "Biotechnology is the future. We're entering a new era of consumer biotech; we're talking consumer-driven advancements in all sorts of fields—pharmacological, medical, industrial—and shortly, we'll be at the forefront of all of that."

"That may be true," Rebecca said, "but this is a *military* facility."

"As you've highlighted, we're dealing with an intrinsically dangerous species," Li explained, walking once more. "There are security issues to consider, safety obligations to comply with. It's also an extremely expensive undertaking, as you mentioned. Positioning the project within a military framework was a necessity, but I assure you this is a civilian operation. The government is committed to scientific advancement."

Rebecca wondered about DARPA and *its* commitment, specifically the development of technologies for military use. But she let it slide, for the moment more concerned about Egbert's role in all of this.

Clearly Wyatt, walking closely behind, had been listening to the conversation. "So, essentially, this is a giant biofabrication lab? Or will be?"

"As I mentioned, there's much to do before we're fully up and running," Li said. Turning to walk backwards, she addressed both brothers now. "So, your input is welcome, gentlemen."

Spencer chewed thoughtfully. "Well, I guess now that you ask…and I kinda feel like a buzzkill for even mentioning it, but…isn't this a little redundant? I mean, they've already engineered *silkworms* to produce spidersilk. You ask me, it'd be much safer to web-farm a few of those—less chance of getting eaten."

Li stifled a laugh and turned forward again. "It's a quaint idea, but this kind of silk is *well* beyond the capacity of an engineered silkworm."

They reached the end of the observation tunnel. There was no door here, just an opening into a large room, essentially a lab with several workstations, monitors and servers lining the walls. Three technicians in lab coats, two men and a woman, were seated at terminals. Beckett and his men stood behind them.

As Rebecca's group caught up and filed in, Li's comment lingered.

"What you said just now about the silk," Rebecca probed. "I'm sensing more."

Li walked over to one of the lab-techs, issued instructions, and then turned back to Rebecca. "We discovered something. The silk, it's more than a simple building material. It has other properties."

"You mean antiseptic qualities," Rebecca said. When she'd rescued Ed from inside the pyramid, he'd been cocooned in swathing-silk, which she'd noted at the time had kept his wounds clean and protected. "The silk has medical applications."

"It's one of the areas we're investigating," Li said as the technician—a fresh-faced young man looking barely out of grad school—passed her a pen and a clipboard with several attached pages. As Li browsed the document, she continued her conversation with Rebecca. "Spidersilk has been used to mend nerve damage in patients, so the medical potential *is* exciting. But that's not what I was referring to. We've discovered something unexpected, and quite frankly, even more incredible."

Beckett cocked his head. Pressing a forefinger to his earpiece, he muttered something into his throat mic and strode over. "We need to wrap this up. The transfer has been completed, and the asset is waking. Your assistance has been requested, Ms Riley."

Rebecca nodded. While she wasn't finished with Li—she still had a million questions—Egbert was her priority. Readying to leave, she looked to Li to lead on, but had to wait for her counterpart to scrawl her name at the bottom of the clipboard's final page. Li never finished, however, because halfway through that action, without warning, the world suddenly tipped on its head.

20
α

As Li scribbled, a hand flew over her shoulder from behind, snatching the pen from her grasp and sweeping it through the air in a short, fast arc, dagger-like.

Holtorf lodged the ballpoint deep into Beckett's neck.

Someone screamed—maybe more than one person—and there was a blur of panicked movement and then Beckett, his neck jetting blood and his eyes bulging in surprise, staggered backwards, reaching with one hand for the pen, and with his other, his sidearm. But Holtorf was too quick, and as Beckett unholstered his weapon, Holtorf sidestepped and disarmed him, locking his victim's wrist, and then twisting him to the ground in a single fluid movement. Rebecca watched in horror, stunned and confused as all this unfolded in what was no more than the blink of an eye, and in the same instant in which Holtorf felled his target she registered a scuffling sound beside her and heard a loud, bone-shattering crack, and one of Beckett's men—the fingernail-clipper—crashed to the floor at her feet, writhing in pain and spraying blood all over the laminate from some unseen wound. She spun, but the remaining soldier, the one who had just ambushed his companion, had already closed the gap, his pistol raised high above his head. She had no time to defend herself.

"This is going to hurt," the man said, and with that he drove the pistol into her face and Rebecca knew no more.

21
α

Muffled voices. At first, mere fragments of sound, but eventually the syllables coalesced and became full words, then short phrases, and yet still they were unclear and seemed to be coming from far away, floating, but then maybe that was just how it seemed because Rebecca's ears were blocked and ringing and a hammer pounded deep inside her skull, distracting her.

"…*ake*…*up*…"

Something cold against her cheek. Rebecca realised she was on her side, prone on the laminate, and then she remembered Holtorf and the other soldier and what had happened and tried to sit up, but she couldn't lift her head—it hurt, and for some reason her cheek seemed to be stuck to the floor. More words. She sensed people, the owners of the voices, nearer now, and through the auditory haze swirling around her, she heard one of them, a female, calling softly.

"…*becca*…*wake up*…*you*…*kay?*"

Grimacing, ignoring the pain, Rebecca pulled her cheek from the floor—the skin glued there by dried blood—and forced her eyes open. Through a watery blur, the room swam slowly into focus, but it wasn't the room at the end of the observation tunnel; this was an unfamiliar room filled with lockers and hanging hazmat suits and at its far end, a hatch of polished steel with an acrylic porthole, strong and sturdy and designed to seal tight.

What the hell?

"Rebecca?" It was Li.

Still rising, Rebecca tried to leverage herself into a sitting position, but her hands wouldn't work—they were stuck behind her back. "What's going on?" she croaked, and that simple act of speaking made her head pound harder, made her want to lie down again. "How long have I been out?"

"Fifteen, twenty minutes," Li said in a low voice from somewhere beside her. "I was worried about you. Rebecca, you need—"

"They threw them inside…they fucking threw them inside. Oh God, this can't be happening." It was Wyatt, somewhere behind her, his voice full of fear. There were other voices, too, shocked voices, and someone sobbing.

"What?" Rebecca's head swam and her eyes lost focus. She was heavily concussed, not fully awake, and sensed she was about to go under again.

"Rebecca, stay with us…" Li said, speaking fast now. "There are others here, other men…they're with Holtorf. They threw them inside—Beckett, and the other soldier. Rebecca, they had—"

The rest of Li's sentence trailed into oblivion and Rebecca's eyes closed and her head lolled, and she felt like she was sinking, as though the floor had turned to quicksand.

Inside? Inside what?

New sounds roused her back—shouting, from beyond this room—and Rebecca thought she recognised one of the voices but she had to be mistaken, it wasn't possible, and she opened her eyes at the same time that a door to the room opened and men—soldiers, at least three of them dressed in tactical gear, together with Holtorf—entered, but she was confused, not only because she'd never seen these men before, but because between them they held a struggling figure against his will, an older man in his late sixties, dressed in business clothes, and there was blood in his grey-flecked beard and down the front of his tousled shirt, and while a part of her wanted to know what the hell was going on and why Holtorf was doing this, most of her was focused on the older man—

—her mentor, her friend—

—and when she recognised Francis Hayward, she tried to call to him, but her mouth wouldn't work.

This can't be real…Frank's here? He shouldn't be here…he wasn't meant to be here!

"I did everything you asked of me!" Frank cried, struggling fiercely, but he was no match for his captors. "For God's sake…*no*—"

"Frank?"

At the sound of her voice, the man ceased thrashing and turned his head, locking gazes with her as the polished steel hatch swung open behind him, and in that fleeting moment it was just him and her, as though time had stopped.

"Bec, I'm so sorry," Frank said, his grey eyes moist with both shame and fear. "I'm so deeply sorry. I didn't want to drag you into this…I tried not to. I hope you can forgive me."

"Frank…please, what's going on? What do you mean? I don't understand—"

And then time sped up and Rebecca realised with horror that they must have been in the research center, because the hatch was in fact an air-lock door, an entry into the habitat, and Holtorf had used Frank's prox-card to open it…

No, please no…

Violently, abruptly, Holtorf shoved Frank hard in the chest, pushing him through the opening and into the room beyond.

"No! You don't have to do this!" Rebecca shouted at Holtorf as Frank, off-balance, tripped and crashed to the ground. As he went down, Rebecca tried to stand, and through sheer force of will got to her knees, but the door was already swinging closed and she knew she couldn't get to him, she couldn't help him…she could only lock eyes with her friend, and no more. And with that, Frank seemed to accept his fate, and as he got slowly back to his feet, he said a final goodbye…and then the hatch closed shut with a resounding clang.

"No!"

A light above the door went red and Rebecca, crying freely, realised there was an air shower in there, and she heard a hiss as the room vacuum-sealed and there was a click of vents and she sensed the air pressure being equalized, and then the light above the hatch went green, and Frank was not only on the other side, but he was inside the habitat.

Oh God…no…

She tried to rush Holtorf, but before she could, an arm snaked around her neck, from behind, choking her and bringing her to the ground. As confusion and despair washed over her, blackness again threatened, and she relented, yet even as she did, the man behind her refused to. She could find no air, but somehow, she held on, and still conscious, she looked across to the plexiglass wall at the same moment that someone shrieked, startled by

Frank's sudden appearance as he threw himself against the acrylic in abject terror. On the other side of the curved material, surrounded by dense vegetation, his ghostly image was distorted, but judging by his wide eyes and even wider mouth, he was begging, crying for help. Rebecca heard none of that—no cries or pleading, only the faint, muffled drumming of his fists as he beat them upon the plexiglass. The barrier was too thick to convey sound, other than by direct contact, and even then, it was muted. She did, however, hear the sustained cries of anguish behind her, maybe Li's, maybe more than one person. Then Frank's soundless screams appeared to stop, perhaps because he realised they were in vain, or because on his side the noise was attracting attention. He turned away, pressing his back against the plexiglass, and when he did this, Rebecca got the impression he'd heard something behind him and had turned to face it, raising his arms to shield his face—

Francis Hayward vanished.

No!

It was swift, as though he'd never been there at all, except he had been, and there was proof because up against the acrylic, right where he'd been standing, was now a long smear of blood across the inside of the plexiglass.

His blood.

Rebecca hadn't seen what had swooped in, hauling her dear friend into the darkness, but she knew what had claimed him.

A low moan bubbled up inside her and somehow, despite the arm around her throat, a piercing wail escaped her lips, a terrible sound even to her ears, and again, she wanted desperately to get to Holtorf, wanted to kill him, because that was what she was going to do—she was going to kill him—and even though she was still pinned from behind she managed to twist her head ever so slightly as Holtorf's man tightened his grip. As she did, through her free-flowing tears, Rebecca saw the brothers, and Li, and the three lab-techs, all of them, like her, sobbing, with guns to their heads and their hands zip-tied behind their backs, being lifted roughly from their knees, forced by Holtorf and the other men—the soldiers, or whoever they were—to their feet.

It was a terrible sight to behold—despairing, frightening, confusing—but in that fleeting moment she saw something else, something that was somehow worse.

Something impossible.

When her brain cut through the bewildering haze and recognised the man, when it made the connection and unlocked his name, the jolt to her system was simply too much to bear. She'd just witnessed the murder of her friend and now, standing here beside his killer, was the last person on Earth she expected to see. It made no sense at all.

Concussed and deprived of air, Rebecca could no longer resist the coming blackness, but the ultimate cause of her loss of consciousness was *shock*. As she went—as darkness rolled over her, enfolding her in sleep—she focused her last ounce of strength, her last breath, on a single question. A single word.

"Ed...?"

22

α

With Jessy in tow, Owen hurried after Mbye and Perez, heading for the cluster of inflatable shelters tucked into the cavern's corner. As he went, he glanced again at the huge, shadowed crack in the cave wall—the Vent, as Mbye had called it—his mind galloping.

The spiders had come through there, she had claimed. But so too had something else.

What did she mean by that?

At the shelter, Mbye held back the flap, ushering them inside. Dominating the brightly lit room beyond was a large table replete with multiple laptops and surrounded by several chairs. The space resembled a war room; Owen figured it was a command post. On the far wall, a giant flatscreen TV hung beneath a large, digital countdown clock, which was currently ticking backwards from just over three hours.

"Three hours until *what*?" Jessy whispered.

Zipping shut the door, Mbye said, "I know you have questions, but first, let's rid ourselves of these." With that, she leaned over and removed her facemask, placing it on the table. "Please, it's perfectly safe. Just don't tell anyone—they hate it when I fly in the face of procedure."

Perez was already in the process of removing his own mask. Shrugging, Owen and Jessy followed suit. Relieved to be free, Owen took a satisfying—if not slightly metallic-tasting—gulp of air.

Mbye, revealed now as an attractive woman in her late forties, smoothed her neat cornrows and gestured to the chairs. As the group moved to sit, a soldier entered from a connecting room, still wearing his facemask but seemingly unfazed by their own non-compliance. He saluted Mbye. "Major, we're running the final diagnostics now, but it looks like we'll be green for launch."

Launch? What did he mean by that? Owen's gaze was again drawn to the bright red digits of the countdown clock. Did this have something to do with the Vent?

Requesting water for her guests and issuing further instructions to the soldier, who promptly departed, Mbye moved to the head of the table and booted up a laptop.

Owen said to her, "What you said a moment ago, Doctor…or do you prefer Major?" Obviously, Mbye held both a military rank and a PhD.

"To be honest, I prefer Yolanda," Mbye replied.

"Doctor…I'm sorry, Yolanda," Owen stuttered, "what you said about the Vent…I'm stunned, and a little confused."

Not waiting for a reply, Jessy chose a more direct line. "Major, what's on the other side of that fissure? And what else came through?"

Mbye opened her mouth just as the soldier returned and issued bottled water. Still standing, she waited for him to leave and said, "Let me start with what we know. Approximately 2,000 years ago, this area was witness to an extraordinary event. Ground zero, if you will."

Owen turned to Perez and whispered, "When we first got here, back in the truck, you mentioned that Intihuasi was the epicentre of something incredible—"

"What kind of event?" Jessy asked Mbye.

"A hypervelocity impact," Mbye replied.

Jessy nodded. "Yes, we know. You're talking about the sphere, the one Rebecca discovered beneath the pyramid. That was her theory—that the crater housing Intihuasi was caused by an interstellar impact. The sphere, crashing into the jungle."

"I've read your reports, including Ms. Riley's," Mbye said. "They're good, and you're partly right. But the crater wasn't caused by that sphere; not solely, anyway. The debris field covers hundreds of square miles."

"Wait…debris *field*?"

Mbye turned to Perez. "Ethan, if you please."

Using a remote control, Perez dimmed the lights and turned on the TV. On the screen, a satellite image flashed up, showing the massive depression and dozens of square miles of surrounding terrain in high-resolution true-colour. Overlaying this were graphics, including range lines and co-ordinates.

"As you can see, the jungle has swallowed everything," Mbye said. "But if I strip away the vegetation—" she clicked the presentation remote and another image flashed up— "the story becomes clearer." This second image, devoid of vegetation, showed a barren, pockmarked topography not unlike the surface of the moon. On the outskirts of the huge central crater were long scars and numerous, smaller depressions.

"Impacts," Owen said. "Multiple, by the looks."

Mbye nodded, highlighting each with the laser pointer. "In total, eight measurable ancillaries."

Jessy's jaw fell. "Eight spheres? What, like a meteor shower?"

Mbye shook her head. "Not all spheres; mainly random debris. Picture a single, catastrophic event. Just outside this shelter is the epicentre, the main impact site. And around that are the ancillary impacts, caused by fragmentation."

"Something large breaking up in the atmosphere," Owen said. "You mean—"

"A craft," Mbye explained. "A very large craft."

Owen baulked, stunned. This was new. All along, he and Jessy and Rebecca had thought there'd been just the two objects—the larger sphere buried beneath the pyramid, and the smaller object cradled by the moai up in the temple, which had been destroyed when Ed had set off the satchel charge. That sphere, they'd assumed, had been removed from the larger object below. Now, Mbye was suggesting a different scenario, one that involved another, even more mysterious object.

This is getting better all the time.

"Wait a second," Jessy said. "Let's get this straight. You're saying a large craft, I'm guessing damaged and out of control, enters Earth's atmosphere, and on the way down it breaks apart and the spheres fly off and everything crashes here with one almighty bang, yeah? And this craft, it's still down here, buried somewhere beyond the Vent? And all this happened 2,000 years ago?"

"The timing is correct," Mbye said, nodding. "Like I said before, sediment analysis shows that at the time of the impact, this part of the Amazon was savannah. Shortly after, everything changed."

Jessy's brow furrowed. "You're suggesting the crash *caused* the shift? Changed the ecosystem? That's a stretch even for us, and trust me, we've grown used to stretches."

Sliding out a chair, Mbye sat, tenting her fingers on propped elbows. "You know, about 540 million years ago, there was an explosion of life, a sudden burst of evolution. Abruptly and inexplicably, almost all major animal phyla appeared in the fossil record. Prior to that moment, life on Earth consisted of remarkably simple organisms, but after it, and over a short geological period, the entire ecosystem disappeared…and was replaced."

"The Cambrian Explosion," Jessy said. "You're linking that event with what happened here in the Amazon? The timing is *way* off."

"I'm not suggesting a direct link," Mbye said. "But some believe the Cambrian event and the sudden burst of biodiversity that followed was the result of an *encounter*, that it occurred when something—ancient microbes, or a retrovirus that had been borne across space and time— impacted with Earth, rewiring everything. Creating, if you will, Earth's new DNA."

Half-joking, Owen said, "Yeah, supposedly we're all Martians, right?" He glanced at Mbye and grew serious. "You're referring to the Panspermia Hypothesis."

"Interstellar seeding," Perez agreed, jumping in. "The notion that life is distributed through the galaxy by meteors and asteroids."

"Or spacecraft," Jessy added. "Cross-contamination by microorganisms. Like I said, this was Rebecca's theory, that something hitched a ride with the sphere."

Owen nodded. Soon after their rescue, when they'd been isolated for three weeks of controlled monitoring with ample opportunity to try and make sense of what had happened down here, he'd discussed this very idea with both Rebecca and Jessy. At the time, none of them had thought the Panspermia Hypothesis was a perfect fit, not in the traditional sense, anyway. It was unlikely that contaminant in the form of bacteria, or a microorganism attached to the exterior of the sphere, could have survived the freezing cold of space or the heat of atmospheric entry. Even an extremophile, able to thrive in severe conditions, seemed farfetched. So, the chances of something more complex surviving the journey—like a cluster of eggs, for instance—was even more improbable. *Impossible*, in fact. So, logically, the organism—whether a passenger, stowaway, or otherwise—had to have been *inside* the sphere, protected like a seed in a pod. And then, after surviving the crash, it was released, or simply escaped. Tilting his head, Owen said, "So, for the record, you agree there *were* organisms on the larger craft?"

Mbye pursed her lips. "The Panspermia Hypothesis is one explanation of how life might spread through the universe. In this case, the hypothesis fits." Clearing her throat, she fixed him with a long stare. "But what if there's another scenario? What if that craft didn't bring anything at all?"

Baffled, Owen frowned. "But…we *know* it did."

Mbye traded a knowing, sideways glance with Perez.

"The spheres are drones," Perez said. "That's our theory. We believe they're part of a larger—and intrinsically connected—swarm. They crashed here, along with the swarm's unmanned mothership."

What?

"The larger craft…" Jessy said.

Perez nodded. "Multiple drones, like the two you found, followed the mothership down. The impact created the huge crater and the wider debris field…and something else, too."

"Something else," Owen murmured. "You mean the Vent."

"An anomaly," Mbye clarified. "A rip in space and time, an opening—"

"Through which the arachnids passed," Jessy finished, slowly, disbelievingly. "This is incredible."

Mbye nodded, agreeing. "A variation of the Panspermia Hypothesis. Transpermia, if you will."

Staring blankly, Owen took a moment to absorb this new information.

This changed everything—not just his understanding of what had happened here, but his wider understanding of the universe itself. Mbye's theory was mind-blowing.

The megs weren't *transported* here at all—they didn't crawl from that crevice after escaping a damaged probe or errant sphere or even the bowels of a fallen and now long-buried mothership.

They'd crossed through, yes…

But from somewhere else entirely.

23

α

The room swam before his eyes, shrinking, then expanding. Speechless, Owen blinked, struggling to refocus.

A rip in space and time, an opening…

A shiver coursed down his spine, his skin prickling at the thought of what lay outside, looming beyond the shelter.

Jessy seemed just as alarmed. "An opening…you mean a gateway of some kind. But…it's closed now, right? I mean, it must be…I'm guessing it closed shortly after the crash, but it was open for a while, long enough to let things through, to let the megs through." She leaned forward. "*What else came through?*"

The answer was strangely obvious, and Owen realised it had been staring him in the face all along. "Flora," he said simply, glancing from Jessy to Perez and finally to Mbye. "That's it, right? 2,000 years ago, the ecosystem changed. When you said that something else came through, you meant plant life."

"Of all the biota known to have emerged, *Megarachne Amazonas* is the alpha species," Mbye replied.

"Plants," Jessy said slowly. "The megs…and *plants*."

"Non-indigenous and invasive, somehow dispersed from the Vent," Owen explained, nodding as he mulled it over. It was plausible, wasn't it? If the megs had crossed through from some other place—if that stunning revelation was in fact true—then why not plants, too? Why not a cloud of spores floating through the air, or seeds or pollen carried by water above and below ground and distributed God knows where, ultimately conquering the landscape? Redefining it?

Jessy, leaning back, murmured drily, "Well, I guess it's better than another monster."

Agreeing, Owen shrugged.

Turning from him, back to Mbye and Perez, Jessy shook her head, bit her lip thoughtfully. "It's still a stretch, but I get it. And in a way, it makes sense. Trouble is, *where* are these plants? We never saw anything like that down here. Nothing out of the ordinary."

Still reflecting on the idea, trying to see it from all angles, Owen scratched his chin. "You know, I'm not so sure."

"Sorry?"

He leaned towards her. "Remember what Rebecca said about arthropods being one of Earth's most successful lifeforms? That of all animal phyla, Arthropoda is the most dominant? It's because the design works. And if it works here on Earth, it's conceivable that *extraterrestrial* lifeforms may follow a similar blueprint. That's what she said." He looked to Mbye, and then Perez. "The megarachnids are an example of convergent evolution."

Perez nodded. "Unrelated organisms, faced with the same environment, the same set of circumstances or stimuli, adapt the same way. They develop similar traits and features; wings, fins, bone or eye structures…or the parts of a plant or tree. There are only so many ways for life to evolve, so many patterns, and the best, most efficient designs are adopted. The most successful prevail."

"Unfortunately, it's not that simple," Jessy said, shaking her head. "I see where you're heading, sure. Yes, the megs and regular, known species here on Earth are similar, and there's no reason the principles of convergent evolution couldn't apply to the local plant life as well. The thing is, despite the similarities, there are fundamental *differences* between the megs and regular spiders, size notwithstanding. These differences are obvious. If there was anything else out there, any other non-indigenous life, the differences would be clear. We would have noticed."

"No," Perez said. "Not necessarily. I'm assuming you're familiar with the concept of inattentional blindness?"

"We miss what we don't expect to see," Owen said. "You mean—"

Perez nodded. "What if all along everything in front of you, everything you thought was native, was in fact a visitor? If you didn't know otherwise, if you were of the opinion—the *belief*—the plants were regular, native species, then that's exactly what you would see."

"The 'theory-ladenness of observation,'" Owen said. "What we observe, is influenced by a preconceived understanding."

Jessy frowned. "So, what are you saying? That we didn't see the forest for the trees?"

Mbye leaned forward. "The Amazon, as you know, is home to countless unique species, both flora and fauna. Many of those species remain undiscovered, and just as many—some of which aren't local—have been hiding in plain sight, up there, inside that crater. This part of the Amazon, and maybe more, is fundamentally an ancient, alien landscape. And it's been under our noses the entire time."

Owen and Jessy traded a glance. It was a lot to take in, almost too much, but it was at the same time thrilling, too. Cross-contamination through the Vent, from some other world…the homeworld of the arachnids, a world of primordial rainforest, a primitive ecosystem of dense jungles looking just like the Amazon itself—

No, not *like*—the *same* as the Amazon…

Incredible.

He realised that Jessy was speaking, "—so this flora had lain dormant, and when the atmospheric conditions became more favourable—when the Earth's orbit changed, and the climate became wetter and more suited to tree growth—"

"There was a perfect storm of conditions," Perez said. "And the non-indigenous species thrived, and suddenly you go from savannah, to lush—"

"Non-native jungle…" Jessy finished.

Mbye nodded. "The examples were all around you. We've collected many. The botanists at our research facility are having a field day."

"This is insane."

"It gets better," Perez said. "When the swarm entered the atmosphere, it lost integrity. Some of the spheres followed the mothership down. Others got stuck in a decaying orbit, travelling further afield as the Earth rotated. Many of those errant drones crashed a long, long way from the mothership."

Again, Jessy frowned. "How could you possibly know this?"

"Because we've found them," a graveled voice said.

Together, Owen and Jessy turned as the voice's owner entered through the same door the young soldier had used before. Judging by his apparel—fatigues, instead of a hazmat suit—this man was also a soldier, and a high-ranking one at that.

"Colonel Belding," Mbye said, trading a nod, but no salute.

"Major."

Stern-featured and solid-framed, Belding strode to the head of the table, greeted Perez, and then used his formal rank of lieutenant colonel to introduce himself to Owen and Jessy. The operations commander already knew them by name.

"Colonel," Jessy said. "You said you've *found* other spheres?"

Seating himself on the edge of the table, Belding swept his hand at Perez, indicating that the older man still had the floor.

"It's true," Perez said, nodding and picking up from where he'd left off. "Like I mentioned before, the swarm is intrinsically connected. Think of a neural network, a hive mind. Recently, that mind—the swarm—woke up."

Jessy turned to Owen and clicked her fingers. "Oliveira. The swarm woke when Oliveira activated the sphere in the temple. That's gotta be it."

Owen, still considering the implications of multiple, scattered spheres, only half-heard this. Just how far from the mothership had they drifted? He turned to Belding. "The other spheres…how did you find them? Some sort of signal or transmission? Heat signatures? More to the point, *where* did you find them?"

"We have data on numerous locations," Belding replied. "Investigations are current, and the retrievals are SCI-classified. But I'm authorised to tell you that one, at least, crashed in the continental United States."

"The *States*?" Jessy blurted. "*Where* in the States, exactly?"

"The same place that's now home to our new lifeforms," Mbye said, her voice low. "Nevada."

24
α

He peered down at her with glistening, deep brown eyes, concern etched into the rugged contours of his face. His hair was longer than she remembered, and he was bearded, which surprised her. He doesn't have a beard.

He does now.

Kneeling, he leaned closer, his lips moving, but Rebecca heard nothing; strange, because earlier, her hearing had been the first of her senses to return.

What are you saying? I can't hear you.

Wake up, Rebecca.

She opened her eyes—*a little confused because she was certain they had already been open*—and her vision swam. Beside her was a figure, on its haunches, but it was blurred, hazy.

"You need to get up," the figure said. A male voice—but not Ed's.

Where's Ed? He was here, wasn't he? Just now?

The man helped her into a sitting position. "Careful…you got a nasty knock." Although he whispered, he sounded urgent. Incrementally, his features sharpened and resolved.

"Wyatt…?"

"We have to move," Wyatt said. In his hands was a cloth, maybe a torn piece of shirt, stained red.

Blood…

"Yours," Wyatt explained. "I've stemmed the flow."

Rebecca's cheek tingled, a kind of burning sensation, and she tried to reach for it, but her wrists were stuck behind her back and as she struggled to part them, she became aware of voices, fearful and confused and arguing.

"…we're dead!"

"You need to calm down…"

"Don't tell me what to do!"

She glanced towards the source of the conflict, to where Spencer and three strangers—no, not quite strangers, the three lab-techs—were huddled, maybe half a dozen yards away. Spencer was behind them, his back to her and his arms working in a sawing action, but Rebecca's attention quickly shifted to the platform of steel grating on which the four of them stood and the curved metallic ceiling above their heads—dim and shadowy despite an array of emergency downlights. She and Wyatt were on the very same platform, beneath the very same overhang, but her surroundings puzzled her and when she shot her gaze beyond the alcove and saw waist-high fernery her stomach flipped—

No…

"We're in trouble," Wyatt blurted, confirming her fears. "They threw us in here…just like the others…*we're inside the goddamned habitat.*"

His voice was laced with barely disguised terror and cracked as he said this, but Rebecca scarcely registered his distress, turning—

Frank…

—to glance over her shoulder at the plexiglass wall behind her, where Frank's blood, still fresh, had traced long, sticky rivulets. Her eyes fell shut, burning with tears, a cocktail of despair and anger and vengeance again washing over her, but she steeled herself, fought hard to hold it in check because she sensed that if she didn't—if she lost it now in front of the others, who themselves clearly bordered on panic—things could get a whole lot worse, and fast.

"Rebecca?"

She opened her eyes and again looked beyond the crescent-shaped alcove, which was unwalled along the edge that sloped down to the forest—

…the habitat…we're inside the habitat…this is bad, this is unbelievably bad…

—affording her a wide view of her surroundings. Overall, the forest was dark, simulating night, but the ultraviolet lamps, likely fixed to the structure above, must now have warmed up to full strength because against this inky backdrop the dense foliage glowed more brightly than before. Still present was the ghostly, purple-green aura that had earlier flooded the observation tunnel, only now it was stronger, and she saw more hues, vibrant indigo and pale white and even shades of pink and blue. If her situation hadn't been so dire, she would have basked in the sheer beauty of it all. Instead, she scanned the sea of colour in desperation, searching for danger. "Where are they?"

"The spiders?" Wyatt clarified, moving behind her. "I don't know…I thought you would know…they were here before, they must have been, because they took him…took *them*…but they've disappeared—"

"Where's *Li*?"

"Gone…they took her."

"The spiders?"

"No, Holtorf and his men," Wyatt explained, wrenching at her cable ties. "They grabbed her…took her hostage and left…there's just us now, the six of us in here…God…you know, Beckett and the other soldier, they were still alive when they were dragged inside…just like Professor Hayward—"

"There was another man," Rebecca said, turning again to the plexiglass but this time squinting past Wyatt and into the cleanroom beyond.

"I didn't see anyone else."

Searching the room, Rebecca saw monitors and lockers and the entrance to the air shower, but no people. "He had a beard, he was with Holtorf. You sure you didn't see him?"

"No, just Holtorf and the soldiers, but I wasn't looking for anyone else…I was scared, and everything happened so fast—"

Too fast, Rebecca thought, wondering if she'd made a mistake. Perhaps it hadn't been Ed after all—hell, she'd been concussed and confused, not thinking straight. Could it have been one of Holtorf's men instead?

It was possible. She had certainly been wrong about Holtorf.

"What do you think he wants?" Wyatt asked. "Holtorf, I mean? He seemed to be in charge." He continued to work on her ties.

"I don't know," Rebecca replied, only half-listening as she fought the familiar pall of loss that in recent times always accompanied her thoughts of Ed. "The attack…it came out of nowhere."

"It was an ambush," Wyatt said. "What happened…it was horrible…beyond words. You think Holtorf's a terrorist? He's CIA, right? Maybe he's gone rogue."

Before she could respond, Spencer separated from the others and hurried over, an odd blend of relief and terror upon his bloodless face. "Bec…thank God you're okay. Those things…they've disappeared, but I'm guessing they'll be back, right? We need to get out of here. Let me help you with those ties."

As he moved behind her, she noticed in his right hand a sharp-edged, slate-like stone, obviously collected from the forest floor. Judging by his grazed and bleeding wrists, he'd used it to slice his own ties—probably with someone's help—before attending to those of his brother and the three lab-techs.

As he started on hers, Rebecca looked up at Wyatt, who'd moved back in front. "What you said just now—the ambush. It caught Beckett by surprise, too. And one of his men—"

"Is a traitor," Wyatt finished. "It was a well-orchestrated incursion. Question is: *why*?"

Why indeed. What the hell was Holtorf up to?

Movement caught her eye and Rebecca glanced over at the three young lab-techs, all of them looking fresh out of college and even more out of their depth. They'd gathered in front of the airlock door, where the woman—red-headed and athletic and facing the hatch—was jumping up and down, waving her arms at the overhead CCTV camera. Her companions, maybe worried about attracting attention, faced outward, their gazes nervously roving the world beyond the alcove.

"You're making too much noise!" one of them—a tall, slender man, maybe of Indian descent—said.

"I'm not!" the woman shot back, still waving. Unlike her two companions, she'd ditched her lab-coat. "I'm telling you, they'll come for us! Once security sees where we are, they'll raise the alarm. They'll send help."

Rebecca thought about that. Holtorf's agenda was unknown, but she got the feeling he would have planned for this; most likely, he'd have seized control of the cameras or even disabled them entirely. He could do it, too; he had people with him, soldiers, and one of Beckett's men. Maybe even more than one; a couple of them, she recalled, had remained at the security counter after Beckett had ordered them off the elevator, and two more had stayed at the control room. Any number of them could be involved.

What if Beckett had been a part of it, too, and Holtorf had betrayed him?

Again, it was possible. Either way, they had to assume that Holtorf had annexed the facility; if not the whole thing, then at least key parts of it. It wasn't as farfetched as it sounded; Li had said that over the weekend the facility was run by skeleton staff, and on top of that, a change of shift had been imminent. No doubt Holtorf's team had taken advantage of this, the timing deliberate. Neutralizing the lobby security guards to enable the ingress of a larger force would have been the first step—

Priscilla is up there, at the security desk…

The thought hit Rebecca hard, almost like a physical blow, and she winced.

"Hey, you okay?" Wyatt asked her.

Rebecca gritted her teeth, and when she spoke, her words were even and controlled. "No-one is coming for us."

The woman, hearing this, stopped jumping and turned. "What?"

There was a snap as Spencer severed Rebecca's cable ties. Immediately, Rebecca stood, massaging her wrists. Her legs were rubbery, unsteady, and her head throbbed at the sudden change of position, but she was focused now and infused with purpose. "How long since the ambush? Thirty minutes?"

"At least," Wyatt said. "Long enough for Holtorf's crew to get down here."

"And long enough for security, too, don't you think?" Rebecca glanced at the woman. "We're on our own."

The woman hesitated, clearly mulling this over, unwilling, it seemed, to accept the truth. Then her head dropped.

"Christ," the youngest-looking of the three lab-techs—an overweight, nerdy type—murmured, fidgeting and pushing his glasses up his nose.

Rebecca wasted no time and hobbled across the platform to introduce herself. The woman—heavily tattooed and gravel-voiced—was Carlisle. She didn't give a first name. To the two men, Dave Fitzgerald and Naziem Singh, Rebecca said, "Keep your eyes peeled, and call out if you see anything."

Both men nodded as Rebecca made for the cleanroom entry. Underfoot, the metallic grating was caked with dried mud and leaves; clearly, researchers or maintenance personnel came through this area, the alcove probably serving as a wet room where they could wipe their boots before entering the air shower from this side. "The exit," she said to Carlisle, gesturing to the polished steel hatch with its acrylic porthole. "You've checked it?"

"Yes, but they've taken our access cards," Naziem interjected, turning from the trees to look over his shoulder. His voice trembled, suggesting he was barely holding it together.

"Sorry?"

"The proximity reader; you need your card to get out. The soldiers took our cards, our duty cells, everything."

Rebecca realised, absently, that her lanyard was missing, too. Stepping up to the thick steel portal, she pushed hard. As expected, it was sealed tight. "There must be an emergency override."

"There is. Here." Carlisle gestured to the right of the door, specifically a touchscreen panel, with the numbers zero through nine. Beside that was a large red button. "We've already tried it. It's jammed."

Just to be sure, Rebecca punched it.

"You have to enter a four-digit code first," Carlisle explained. "Prevents an accidental door-release if a crawler bumps the button."

"Crawler?"

"That's what we call them … the assets."

"That, or fuzzies," Fitzgerald said.

"The code works," Naziem said, "but they've jammed the lock. We can't get out."

"Emergency exits?" Rebecca asked.

"This *is* the emergency exit."

"We're in trouble," Wyatt said, echoing his earlier sentiments.

Rebecca pressed her ear to the hatch. The clunk of both inner and outer vents and vacuum pumps, likely used to control pressure, resonated faintly. Standing on her toes to glance through the porthole, she saw another door just a few tantalising feet away, and between the two steel portals, the air shower. Stepping back, she scanned the exterior. Usually, there was a manual crank handle in case the motor or electrics failed —

There was, in the centre of the hatch.

Yes!

Rebecca pulled on the handle, but it was stuck solid.

"They've jammed that, too," Naziem said.

Great, Rebecca thought, spinning and searching for alternatives. The plexiglass—which extended from both sides of the hatch—she ignored; according to Li, the acrylic was more than two inches thick.

Impatient and on edge, Spencer ran a hand through his hair, chewing faster than ever. "We don't have time for this. Once those things are finished with the others—*whatever the hell they're doing right now*—they'll be back. We need to move."

Wyatt spun on his brother. "For Christ's sake, that *chewing*…seriously? Can't you shut your mouth?"

"Hey, take it easy," Rebecca said, turning to them both. "Cool heads, okay?"

"It's plain rude!"

"It's not deliberate!" Spencer shot back, transferring the sharp-edged stone nervously from hand to hand.

More arguing, louder now and drawing in the rest of the group, but Rebecca pushed it into the background as the throb in her temple suddenly intensified. For an instant, she feared she might faint and steadied herself with a hand on the hatch until the feeling subsided. She wished she had some water; her mouth was awash with the stale, coppery taste of blood, and her throat burned where the soldier had choked her.

"*…have no idea!*"

"Quiet!" Rebecca barked, startling the group into silence. "Enough! Spencer's right. We need to move."

Yeah, but move where?

"Somewhere…anywhere but here," Spencer said, reading her mind.

Biting her lip, certain she was missing something, Rebecca straightened, her thoughts racing. Needing a moment to get them in order, she again turned to Naziem and Fitzgerald, urging them to keep their eyes on the trees before pulling Carlisle aside. "We gotta work this through," she said in a low voice. "You need special clearance to access the habitats—to get in and out. Right?"

"Right," Carlisle said. "But the three of us, we don't ever come in here…we're microclimatologists, Fitzy's a meteorologist; our job is to maintain the life support system, keep tabs on air quality and temperature and humidity and—"

"Sure, but you have access…you have clearance."

"Yes."

"And Holtorf had clearance like the rest of us—otherwise, he wouldn't have been allowed on base."

"SAP clearance, yes," Carlisle said. "Special Access Program, to be clear. It's specific to this project, so we all have it, and it includes top-secret security clearance. But you need SCI clearance to enter—"

Naziem turned from the jungle and threw Carlisle a questioning glare. "Um…should we be speaking about this?"

"They have SAP clearance, Naziem," Carlisle fired back, "the same as the rest of us." She turned back to Rebecca. "Don't mind him. It's our training. Outside these walls, we're janitors. That's what we're instructed to tell people."

"This facility has a lot of janitors," Fitzgerald said.

"As I was saying," Carlisle resumed, speaking fast, "you need SCI clearance for the restricted areas, or to open certain doors. Visitor access is limited."

"SCI," Spencer said. "Sensitive Compartmented Information. Sub-clearance, within the general band of top-secret. That's what I was talking about in the bus earlier. Need-to-know."

"That's why Holtorf needed Professor Hayward," Wyatt reasoned.

Makes sense, Rebecca thought. Days ago, Holtorf's men must have kidnapped Frank, probably forced him to concoct a story that he'd be out of town on business, then once the incursion was underway and the guards were neutralized, used him to access not only this level, but the habitat as well.

"And now they've taken Li," Wyatt said. "Why?"

"Good question," Spencer said. "They have Hayward's prox-card. They can access everything. Why not dispose of Li, too?"

"Holtorf needs her," Rebecca said. "But he doesn't need the rest of us."

"What, so he throws us in here to destroy the evidence?" Wyatt asked.

"Let the spiders do the dirty work," Spencer replied, shaking his head. "Fucking CIA."

"There could be another reason for taking Li," Fitzgerald said, his tone nervous but thoughtful. "Biometric authentication."

"Sorry?"

"SCI level two and above," Fitzgerald explained, momentarily turning from the jungle. "Some of the restricted areas run on biometrics: facial recognition, voiceprint analysis. Management and senior staff with at least

SCI-2 clearance have access. There's a reader in H-4, which is one of the primary research pens. Point is, for most of the base you need your card, but Li has both. Maybe Holtorf needs her to access one of the restricted areas."

On edge, Naziem shook his head. "That makes no sense. Biometric authentication is simply a backup system, another means of access; we're talking the same security level as the prox-cards, no more. This guy Holtorf has our cards, but more importantly, he has Hayward's. That's all he needs to access everything on this level."

Wyatt shrugged. "Maybe Holtorf took Li to prevent her from helping *us*. You know, stop her from using biometrics to escape."

Again, Naziem shook his head. "Still makes no sense—if he was worried about that, he could have just knocked us off and dumped our bodies. It doesn't add up."

"It doesn't have to," Rebecca said, struck by an idea. She turned to Fitzgerald. "You said there's a biometric reader at H-4. Why there, and not here?"

"We work in Research Center 1," Fitzgerald replied. "Basic SAP clearance, which gives us access to the first four habitats only. The reader in H-4 gives you cleanroom access to RC-2, which is restricted—"

"Can we get there from here?" Rebecca asked.

"Not normally…we segregate the fuzzies, control their movement. Each dome is separated from the next and connected by gates—"

"But…"

"But Li opened the gates to the first four habitats," Carlisle said, jumping in. "Not standard procedure, but she wanted the crawlers to move freely, wanted you guys to see them in all their glory—not that it worked. So long as Holtorf hasn't closed the gates, we can get there. But without authentication…"

She trailed off. Rebecca's mind spun rapidly.

The megs were quick to get to Frank and the others, but they haven't yet come for us. Why is that?

When the answer presented itself, she turned to Carlisle. "This isn't their normal feeding site, is it?"

"What?"

"The assets…where do you feed them?"

Carlisle shrugged. "There's a live feeder at H-4. Goats, mainly. They like to hunt."

"Christ," Spencer said.

"Where do they take their kills?" Rebecca asked.

"There's a nest—"

"They have a *nest*?" Wyatt asked.

"Of sorts," Carlisle answered. "They take their prey to a central feeding area, near to where they roost…we call it the chow-hall. But they rarely kill the goats outright…mostly, they envenomate them, you know, paralyse them, keep them alive for later."

Rebecca straightened. "The individuals that took Frank and the others were scouts; I'm guessing three or four at most. They don't normally hunt here, which is why they weren't present in greater numbers. It's also why they haven't returned."

Wyatt processed this. "They don't know we're here…"

"Not yet," Rebecca said. "Which means we have a window, but it's small…and closing." She looked at each of them in turn and got the sense they knew she was building to something. She was. "I think I can get us out of here."

"*Hayward*," Spencer said, clicking his fingers. "The professor's still alive, and he has biometric access; that's what you're getting at, yeah? But…all that *blood*."

"Maybe he's just injured," Fitzgerald said, his voice climbing with expectation. "I mean, the fuzzies don't kill the goats. There's a chance…"

Not wanting to falsely inflate their hopes, Rebecca tried to downplay her response, yet she couldn't help but be reminded of Ed's rescue from the nest back in Intihuasi. Could it be like that again? "If he *is* alive, we have to get to him. We have to try."

Energised, Wyatt said, "If he's alive, we can get out of here."

"He doesn't need to be alive," Carlisle murmured. "I mean, there's facial recognition…we just need—"

Fitzgerald's eyes flew wide. "You're kidding, right? That's messed up. *Seriously* messed up."

"I'm just saying!"

"No…*no!*" Naziem blurted, raising his arms, palms out. "Don't you think we're getting ahead of ourselves? Like *way* ahead? You reckon we're just going to march in there and snatch the professor—dead *or* alive—from right under their noses? Just like that? That's insane. And that's only part of it…if the gates are closed or the locks are jammed, the plan's shot from the get-go."

"If you have a better idea, Naziem," Carlisle fired back, "then share it."

"I *do* have a better idea. We dig in here and wait it out. Someone will come for us."

"We've gone through this already," Spencer said. His tone was low and even, perhaps to rein in the rising emotions. "Maybe Holtorf doesn't know about the gates, or figured we'd be killed outright and overlooked them. The plan's a good one. The exit at H-4 is our ticket out of here."

Naziem shook his head. "That's assuming, of course, we can make it to the nest, find Hayward, and then get to the reader *undetected*, which is quite obviously impossible! Can't anyone see that?" He swallowed hard, his eyes wide and imploring. "Please, you have to listen to me; you're not thinking this through. Behavioural studies have shown that when assessing risk, 80% of people are prone to optimism bias."

"Leaving one in five overly pessimistic," Carlisle taunted.

"That's not what it means," Naziem said, clearly stung. "It means most people overestimate their chance of success. Trust me, we gotta ride it out. Someone will come eventually."

"Those *creatures* will come eventually," Spencer retorted. "We can't stay."

"No, we can't," Wyatt agreed. "If they think there's food here and that this place is a new, alternative source, they'll be back, and we'll be sitting ducks. We've gotta go before the window closes. It's worth a try."

"It's worth more than that," Rebecca said. She turned to Naziem. "This isn't just about us now, or about getting out. Frank's out there…it's about him, as well."

"And Beckett and the other man," Wyatt added. "If they're still alive."

Rebecca nodded. "Them too." Momentarily, she thought about all three of them, but her mind settled on a single image, one of Frank alone out there in the dark, still alive and suffering and trembling with fear—

Naziem started to pace. Rapidly. He looked agitated, increasingly desperate.

Catching him gently by the wrist, Rebecca drew him to a halt. "Hey, just relax, okay?"

Locking gazes with her, Naziem nodded, took a deep breath. "I get it, I really do," he whispered, verging on tears, "but this is nuts, Bec. The feeding grounds…the heart…trust me, you don't want to go in there. You know how many are in there, right?"

No, she didn't. Lightly placing her hands on his shoulders, she lowered her voice to mirror his tone. "It's okay. Talk to me—I'm listening." She needed him to calm, but he'd raised a good point. This could be helpful information. "The megs…how many are we talking about?"

Fidgeting, Naziem drew another deep breath, but before he could reply, Carlisle interrupted. "Two dozen weavers," she blurted.

"Weavers?" Rebecca asked, turning to her, but with her hands still softly holding Naziem. "You mean the workers?"

"Yes," Carlisle said. "The workers are the primary web-builders, so that's what we call them—weavers. They're essentially drones, if you think of them in the same way as the caste system of ants—"

Rebecca nodded. "Yes, I know. What about jumpers?"

"You mean hunters?"

"If that's what you call them," Rebecca said, urging her on.

"It's just that they range out from the nest, and hunt—"

"How many?"

"Twelve."

"Trapdoors?"

"Three."

Rebecca stepped back from Naziem. Now that they were listening to his concerns, he'd started to relax. "What about alphas?"

This time, Carlisle hesitated, and Naziem answered. "Two alphas, one of each. A male and a female."

"But they're not in here," Fitzgerald explained. "They're segregated, kept in H-5 and H-6 with the others."

"Others?"

Carlisle nodded. "The dominant female resides over a small egg-laying caste—"

"How many egg-layers?"

"Eight."

"And the male?"

"He has six soldiers."

Great, Rebecca thought. Soldiers, like Egbert. Potentially even more aggressive than the jumpers.

"But like Dave said, the royals are segregated from the rest," Carlisle clarified, clearly sensing Rebecca's unease. "Those habitats are sealed. Only the subordinates are in here."

"Um…*only*?" Wyatt said. "By my count that's still—"

"Thirty-nine, in here with *us*," Spencer said. "Fifty-five in total."

"This isn't good," Wyatt said.

Rebecca kneaded her brow, then touched a clammy hand to her cheek. The spot where the soldier had hit her had started to tingle again. It felt tender and swollen, and tentatively, she worked her jaw up and down, hoping the tissue was simply bruised and that no bones had fractured. Suspecting the worst, but with no way of knowing for sure, she hid her discomfort and turned to the three lab-techs. "The weavers, I understand. And I also get that you need egg-layers and a dominant male to fertilise them. But why the rest? The soldiers and the hunters and the trapdoors?"

"We started out with weavers only, but they wouldn't nest," Fitzgerald explained. "Their instinct to build, to weave silk, simply wasn't there. It was only when the rest were introduced, when it became a fully functioning society, that things changed. Nature's balance had to be restored, and it was only then that it worked."

"But you said the alphas and the betas are segregated," Rebecca said.

"There were concerns about controlling the alphas, particularly the male, who for some reason had killed a number of the subordinates," Carlisle said. "So, they had to be removed, put in their own pen with the betas. But they were still needed, so we harvested the female's mandibular glands—"

"The Queen Substance," Rebecca said, nodding. "You extracted the pheromone."

"Yes…and we infused it throughout the habitats via a purpose-built system running parallel to the air filters," Fitzgerald said, hefting his pants over his substantial belly. "We monitor the levels, of course; it's one of our tasks."

Rebecca understood. "The alpha secretes the pheromone, just like a queen bee. It confirms her presence in the nest and helps maintain colony integrity."

"Right. Without it, the colony would break down," Carlisle said.

"And by infusing the pheromone in here, you trick the weavers into believing the alpha is present, even though she's in another pen entirely," Rebecca said.

Again, Fitzgerald piped up. "More recently we started injecting a synthetic version of the pheromone. The weavers don't know the difference."

Wyatt shifted nervously, glancing about. "Listen, this is highly fascinating, sure, but can we move it along? They're still out there, remember?"

"Yeah, all thirty-freaking-nine of them," Spencer added.

At that, Carlisle clapped a palm to her forehead and spun to Fitzgerald. "Shit! I totally forgot! You've got to be kidding me."

"What?"

"The shed!"

Fitzgerald's face contorted and his jaw fell. "Yes! Of course!"

"Hang on…what?" Rebecca asked. "*What* shed?"

Carlisle bit her lip. "It never occurred to me until now, because we were so focused on exits and getting out of here—"

"*What shed?*"

Carlisle cleared her throat. "Like I mentioned before, we don't come in here, not us, but others do, like when there's maintenance to be done or samples to collect—"

"And then for safety reasons, they herd the assets into another dome," Fitzgerald said. "It's not something we're involved in ourselves—"

"Herd? How?"

"They're moved out with fixed ultrasonic repellers," Carlisle said. "They're essentially fences; the soundwave interferes with the chordotonal organ—"

"Yes, I know," Rebecca said. Back in the jungle, they'd used ultrasonic devices—X40s—to repel the creatures. The units were particularly effective at close range, emitting high-intensity ultrasonic soundwaves which agitated the creatures' nervous systems, causing them extreme irritation. By the sounds of it, a similar system had been implemented here.

Spencer clicked his fingers. "If we could turn on the fences—"

"We can't, not without system access," Fitzgerald said. "That's not part of our role."

"No, but there's something else," Carlisle said. "Something that might help. We know when the assets have been successfully herded—and contained—because at any given moment, we know where they are."

"You track them," Rebecca reasoned. "How? Microchips?"

Fitzgerald nodded. "Implanted directly into the carapace. Provides data on all sorts of things—not just position, but circadian rhythm, behavioural patterns. They're not just social, but also hierarchical—"

"Guys! The point?" Wyatt blurted.

"Over in H-2, there's a maintenance shed," Carlisle said. "There's equipment inside—mobile trackers, tablets. If we can access the shed, we should be able to get a fix on the assets, find out where they are. It might be useful."

"More than useful," Naziem said, suddenly snapping from his stupor. His face had brightened, suggesting he was finally buying in to the plan. "They store handheld herders in the shed, don't they? Ultrasonic prods? We mightn't be able to access the fences, but if we can get our hands on a couple of those…"

"We can use them as a shield," Fitzgerald finished. "Push our way through."

A sense of hope rippled through the group, leaping from person to person.

Rebecca turned to Carlisle. "This shed. Do you know where it is?"

Carlisle nodded. "Yeah, I do. It's not far."

Needing no further convincing, Rebecca gathered the group close. "Right, so we're agreed, then? That's the plan. Get to the maintenance shed, load up, and make our way to the feeding grounds. Then we find Frank and get the hell out of here."

THE HABITAT

A CROSS-SECTION

H = HABITAT. **H-2** = HABITAT-2

BIOME >> TROPICAL RAINFOREST << | ATMOSPHERE >> HOT, HUMID << | PRECIPITATION >> HIGH <<
VEGETAL BIODIVERSITY (SPECIES OF TREES AND HIGHER PLANTS) >> UNKNOWN <<

PRIMARY ASSETS >> WEAVERS << | SECONDARY ASSETS >> HUNTERS <<

SHELL CONSTRUCTION >> THERMOPLASTIC / TITANIUM-REINFORCED <<
MAINTENANCE BUNKER >> 1 <<

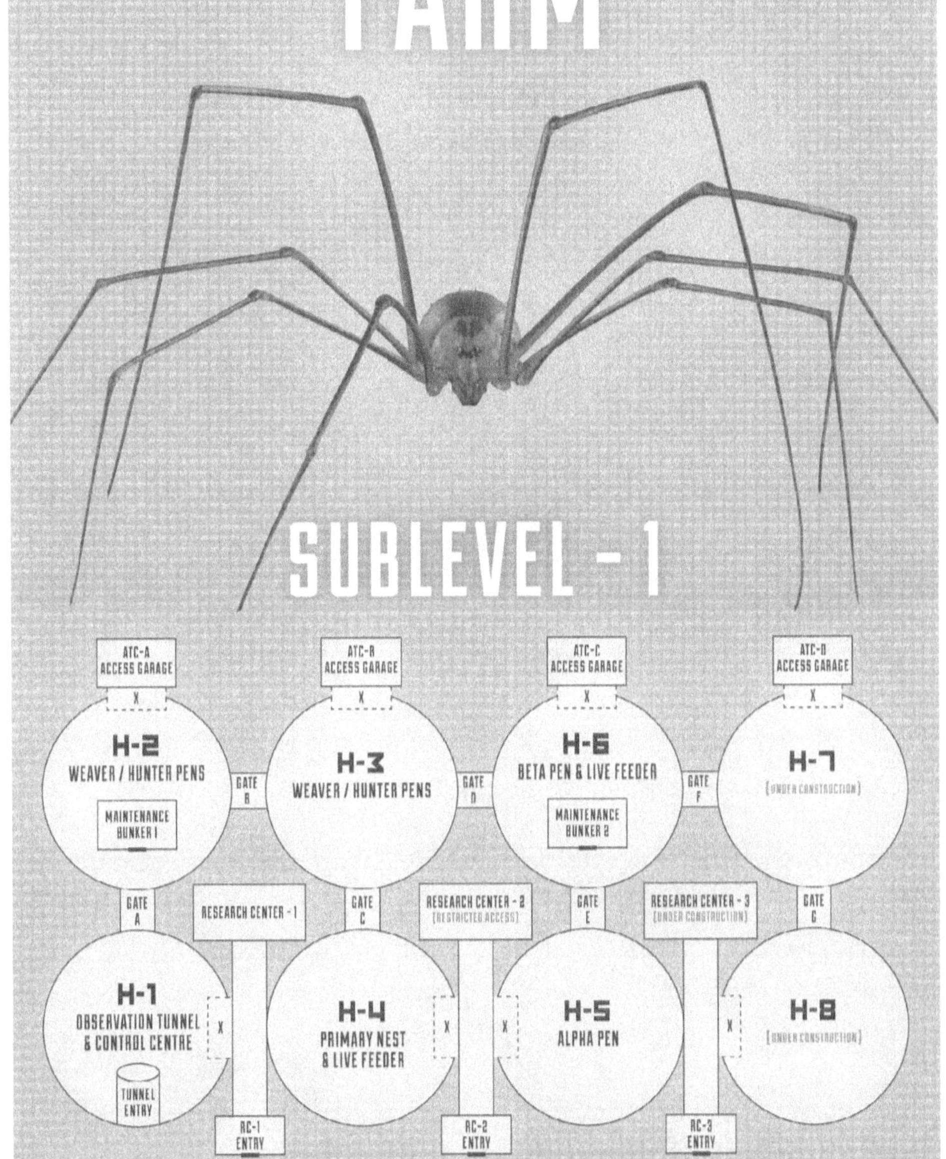

THE
FARM
SUBLEVEL - 1
ATC-A ACCESS GARAGE
ATC-B ACCESS GARAGE
ATC-C ACCESS GARAGE
ATC-D ACCESS GARAGE
X
X
X
X
H-2
WEAVER / HUNTER PENS
MAINTENANCE BUNKER 1
H-3
WEAVER / HUNTER PENS
H-6
BETA PEN & LIVE FEEDER
MAINTENANCE BUNKER 2
H-7
[UNDER CONSTRUCTION]
GATE B
GATE D
GATE F
GATE A
RESEARCH CENTER - 1
GATE C
RESEARCH CENTER - 2 [RESTRICTED ACCESS]
GATE E
RESEARCH CENTER - 3 [UNDER CONSTRUCTION]
GATE G
H-1
OBSERVATION TUNNEL & CONTROL CENTRE
TUNNEL ENTRY
X
H-4
PRIMARY NEST & LIVE FEEDER
X
X
H-5
ALPHA PEN
X
H-8
[UNDER CONSTRUCTION]
RC-1 ENTRY
RC-2 ENTRY
RC-3 ENTRY
X = CLEANROOM & AIRLOCK ENTRY

25
α

The gate rose with a jolt, slowly at first, because it had never been opened before, then picking up speed. This was despite its size and weight and sturdy construction. On both sides of its bunkerlike housing, humming within the solid concrete frame, large motors drove the thick door higher, lifting it on wide, vertical tracks. From the gate's lower edge, clumps of muddy earth rained. Woody vines, clinging stubbornly to its base, snapped free, or simply lost their grip and fell.

Within moments, the door separating the two habitats was at its maximum height, where it halted with a clunk that echoed loudly before dying. Into the ensuing silence, a series of softer mechanical sounds intruded, vents opening and closing and vacuum pumps kicking into gear, equalizing the pressure.

Then they, too, fell quiet.

At the aperture, seeping like a softening wall of oil, shadows spilled. No light challenged them. This was a place where light rarely shone.

For an instant, the deep blackness and even deeper silence reigned. Then, roused by noises outside, something stirred.

Curious, sensing opportunity, it scurried for the opening.

26
α

Darkness, and then a gasp—a sharp intake of air, followed by an even sharper exhalation that caused something warm and wet to explode from his lips.

…air…more air…

Desperately, he drew another whistling breath, but the liquid bubbled back around his nose and mouth and down his throat, and instinctively, fearing he might drown in his own blood, he gurgled and spluttered until he could breathe freely again. There was a sensation of movement, and indeed, above him and to the sides, strange, glowing streaks flashed by, lights in the darkness, and at the same time something slapped at him, and he realised he was on his back and being dragged by the feet. Although he couldn't move his head, he got the feeling the slapping-things were leaves, undergrowth of some kind, and he must have been in a forest, but that made no sense, not until an image flashed into his mind's eye and he recalled the attack on the Colonel and being hit himself, hit by that fucker Davies who'd come from nowhere and nailed him with his Glock and then—

You're inside the goddamn dome, the greenhouse, or whatever the hell it is. Get up. Now. Do something!

Again, he tried to lift his head, if for no other reason than to see what was dragging him along the jungle floor, but his neck wouldn't bend or lift. In fact, he couldn't move *any* part of his body, neither his arms nor his legs, nothing at all, and when he realised he was paralysed he wondered if his back was broken. Deep down, of course, he knew it wasn't—shit, deep down, he knew *exactly* why he couldn't move, and what was dragging him. If only he could get up and fight! But he couldn't. He was done for. Now, all he could hope was that death would come quickly and—

Everything stopped.

He sensed, more than felt, a release, and above him, the glowing streaks paused and resolved and became bright, white fronds, and although the strange shining foliage was now static, a blur of movement caught his eye; colourful, but at the edge of his vision and too fast for him to gather detail. A skittering sound arose, followed briefly by silence, and he wondered if they had gone—the creatures, all of them, because he was certain there were more than one—leaving him here to bleed out to a slow death. Then he heard a light scurrying, more like a soft padding sound, off to the side, his left, and another to his rear, behind his head, and then something took hold of him again and this time he was bumped and tugged, pulled and prodded where he lay, and there were sounds that could have been things puncturing flesh, sharp things, *biting* things, but thankfully he felt nothing. He didn't think they were feeding—

—*please not feeding*—

—but he did think they were ripping and flaying skin and smothering—

—*wrapping*—

—him.

Fuck!

Not like this. Just end it!

It didn't end. Not yet.

In the distance, he heard a loud, heavy shiver of leaves, and branches cracking, and as this noise grew, there was another noise closer to his ear, a low vibration, almost a barking sound. The two sounds overlapped, building on top of each other until the sound of the large thing thundering through the trees grew to a crescendo and won through, and as it did the fern fronds above his face shook as the things that had dragged him here dispersed, leaving him there on his back, alone. Into his mind's eye came an image—it was just a flash, and in that instant, absently, he had a concurrent thought about how strange it was that the mind could reach for a comparison even at a time like this—and the image was that of a pack of hyenas forsaking their prize at the approach of a larger, fiercer predator, a lion, because that was precisely how these things had fled, like animals that cared no longer for their hard-fought kill, animals that now cared only for self-preservation.

They had abandoned him because a fiercer predator had scared them away.

He heard a massive thud as something dropped from the trees to land unseen behind him. It came for him, a heavy scurrying, and although he had no hope of craning to see it, his imagination gave it form and his terror climbed. He sensed it close in, clicking as it moved, and heard a huffing sound, maybe an exhalation of breath, and he could tell by the depth of that sound that whatever it was, the creature was large. Again, the barking sound arose, now in the mid-distance, as though the hyenas had regrouped, readying to approach once more, but he also heard something closer, much closer, a frighteningly loud cry, not quite a shriek or a hiss and in truth, incomparable to anything in his experience. It chilled him to his core, and for what seemed like an eternity these sounds—the barking and the hissing—continued back and forth, the opposing parties threatening each other, fighting over who had the rightful claim to him, and then suddenly he was grasped and there was a lightning-blur of movement and he was hauled bodily into the trees. There, somewhere in the canopy, the larger thing, the lion, wedged him across a forked branch, stretched him prone along a thick limb so that he faced the ground. He sensed the creature above and behind him, not quite pressing down on his back, but astride him nonetheless, and his body shuddered, shook back and forth as the thing ripped at him but again there was no pain because he was still numb and paralysed. The ferocious tugging persisted as the thing continued its frenzied assault, and as he coughed and spluttered blood he heard a horrible, wet, wrenching sound and realised the creature had torn a piece from his body and was now feeding.

Whatever the hell it was, this was a different animal to those that had dragged him here—the things that had crept back to circle restlessly on the ground below, in the place where his blood now dripped and pooled. He knew this, because those things fed by pumping their victims with digestive fluid before sucking out their liquefied organs. This wasn't like that. This was different. This was primal, full of rage. He heard the godawful rend and snap of ligaments and the crunch of bones as the animal continued to feed, eating him alive, and although it had seemed like forever, he sensed that all of this must have passed in no more than a few seconds.

The creature let out another high-pitched shriek. This time, the call was as much a cry of victory as it was a warning to the things now crowding in the darkness, the things not just crawling on the ground but also in the trees nearby, the unspeakable things attracted by the scent of blood and hungry for the feast but still not daring to approach, even in numbers.

That shriek, shrill and alien, was unlike any sound he'd heard before, and as he fell mercifully into a looming black void, he thanked God he'd never hear it—or *anything*—again.

27
α

At the edge of the platform, Rebecca froze.

What the hell was that? A scream?

Maybe. High-pitched. Way off in the distance.

Inclining her head, she listened.

It was nothing, and even if there had been something, there's nothing there now. Don't spook the others, Bec. Just get moving.

Heeding the voice of reason, guessing her imagination had gotten the better of her, she took another step, but at the edge of the glowing rainforest faltered, still unsure.

Hardly an inspiring start, Rebecca thought. Turning, she goaded the group forward. She hadn't coveted the leadership role, but her companions, on board with the plan yet loath to depart the alcove, were even more opposed to going first. Someone had to do it.

"No-one comes in here without a suit, or with the assets roaming freely," Naziem reminded her. "This is nuts." His voice trembled, and although he'd agreed to the plan, he seemed to be doubting his decision.

"We need to be quiet," Rebecca whispered.

He said something else, but Rebecca thrust a finger to her lips. This time, he complied.

Pausing for a moment, she shifted her gaze to the rest of the group. Fear rippled from person to person like an electric current. Looking further afield, past the ashen faces, she eyed the hatch. The clunk of vents and pumps still echoed.

So close to freedom, and yet so far.

Stop stalling.

Turning, she stepped from the overhang and into an alien world.

Waves of colour engulfed her. Up close, the effect was intense, the tones more vivid than ever. It was hard not to be stilled by awe, yet she managed to spin slowly on the spot. Under regular light, greens and browns would likely have dominated, but beneath the wash of ultraviolet, those hues receded into the background. Shadows still lurked, dark blues and deep blacks cloaking the taller trees and filling the spaces between the foliage, but at ground level, where shrubs and ferns ruled, and in the understorey, where orchids and bromeliads and lianas jostled and climbed, it was all indigo and teal and glowing reds and whites. The light seemed to be concentrated here; bright, lively, and luminous. The rainforest had a magical, otherworldly feel.

"I must be tripping," Spencer said. He still carried the sharp-edged stone and shifted it from hand to hand, full of nervous energy.

Panning her head, Rebecca agreed. Psychedelic and beautiful…but inherently dangerous, too.

A faint buzz cut through the hush. Chirping, high-pitched. Beneath that, another sound, lower in pitch, more like a chorus of croaks. There were insects in here, and frogs.

And other things, too.

Keep moving.

She pressed deeper, fronds of dazzling azure brushing featherlike against her legs. She glanced over her shoulder, hoping she hadn't lost anyone. Naziem brought up the tail, with the alcove now a dozen feet or more to his rear. The metal platform had ended at the jungle's edge, extending from the main structure in a fading gradient before plunging beneath the soil. Rebecca assumed it didn't end there but instead ran throughout the habitat a yard or two beneath the surface. Where she strode now was over another section of grating that ran flush with the forest floor. No more than a yard wide, the steel-mesh walkway formed a path that disappeared into the glowing foliage ahead.

The scientists use this to navigate the habitat, Rebecca thought. While the path was strewn with leaves and scatterings of soil—and in places, overgrown with roots that looked like petrified snakes—it was sufficiently clear. This was good; a defined path eliminated the risk of straying. Carlisle had said that about ninety feet along the walkway was a junction, and another path that cut across the habitat on a direct line to the gate. From there, they could pass into H-2, which housed the maintenance shed.

Easy. Stick to the walkways, keep it simple, break it into small, attainable steps.

The first step is getting to the junction.

Hyperalert, Rebecca led the group forward, listening and scanning as she went. A line of sweat dribbled into her eyes, hot and stinging, blurring her vision. It was warm in here. Blinking rapidly, she wiped her eyes with her shirt. As she did, her attention was drawn overhead. Despite the ethereal glow at ground level, an abundance of shadows clung to the canopy above them.

Wyatt must have sensed her trepidation. "We'll see them, yeah?"

Turning to him, still blinking, Rebecca nodded, reminding herself that the arachnids were covered in tiny scales that reflect ultraviolet light. This was the sole reason for the UV lamps and the most efficient method of combating the creatures' unique camouflaging ability.

See them or not, if they come for us, we won't be able to defend ourselves.

Feeling exposed but desperate to project confidence, Rebecca set her jaw, fighting against a return to the alcove and its illusion of refuge. "The sooner we get to the junction, the better," she whispered, as much to herself as to Wyatt. "It can't be far."

As though trying to reassure them both, Spencer chimed in. "Another forty feet. Fifty, tops."

Rebecca acknowledged this and pushed forward, confident that at any moment, the cross-walkway would appear through the foliage. Presently, however, visibility was low; so low, in fact, that she could see no more than a few yards in any direction. Squinting, she scanned her surroundings more closely. The jungle was denser here, more suffocating. Something else caught her attention, too. Some of the plants looked a little strange. At first, she wasn't sure why, then concluded that several species appeared less terrestrial and more like those found at the bottom of the ocean, like kelp or seagrass or even algae. She wasn't a botanist, but she possessed a degree in biology, and many of these plants were unknown to her. In any other situation, at any other time, she'd stop and investigate. Right now, however, that wasn't an option.

Still, it was strange. *Very* strange.

Suddenly realising how quiet it was—almost always a bad sign—she turned, just as a wheezing sound arose from behind.

Fitzgerald, at the rear with Naziem, had drawn to a halt, his substantial frame hunched. He had a hand pressed to his thick chest.

"Hey, you okay?" Spencer asked, the first of the others to hurry back.

"Asthma," Fitzgerald stammered, trying to steady his breathing.

"He doesn't have his inhaler," Naziem told the group. "It's back in the office."

"I'm okay…it's mild, it's not a problem," Fitzgerald wheezed. "Keep moving."

Spencer turned to the rest of the group. "Mold spores, for sure. They can trigger an attack."

Reminded of Naziem's earlier comment about hazmat suits, Rebecca realised she was holding her breath. She released it and inhaled; slow and tentative, as though testing the air for the first time, and in a way that was true because before, when the adrenalin had been coursing through her veins and she'd been focused on making sense of their predicament, some of the finer details had escaped her. She'd already noted the temperature, but now, she sensed something else; the atmosphere seemed heavy, like that of a greenhouse. Briefly, she wondered about spores and toxins and other air-borne contaminants but expelled the thought, moving as she did to comfort Fitzgerald. "Can we help? Are you sure you're okay?"

Still hunched, Fitzgerald hitched his pants over his wide hips and gave her the thumbs up.

Watching this, Wyatt stepped beside Rebecca and whispered in her ear. "Maybe he should wait for us back at the alcove. We can move faster. Once we're out, we can circle back and open the airlock."

Overhearing the comment, Fitzgerald heaved his large frame upright. "What are you saying? I'm slowing you down?"

"I'm sorry—"

"I'm not staying here by myself," Fitzgerald said, breathing deeply. "I'm good. I can keep up." As though intent on proving this he trudged off with another loud, panting gasp, almost a whistle, which caused a fleeting, pained expression to contort Wyatt's face. Rebecca sensed that Fitzgerald's ever-increasing nasal-wheezing was stirring Wyatt's misophonia.

"I'll keep an eye on him," Carlisle said, hurrying after her companion.

Rebecca turned to Wyatt, pondering this new dynamic and feeling the sharp bloom of a migraine. "You okay?"

Perhaps embarrassed, Wyatt nodded without making eye contact and moved past her, down the walkway. Shrugging, Spencer hastened after his brother.

Rebecca watched them go. To Naziem she turned and said, "We're in an enclosed dome. We've got enough clean air, right?"

"It's safe, and in ample supply," Naziem said, his voice low and even. "Right now, inhaling a few mold spores or running out of oxygen are the least of our concerns."

With that, he left her and hurried after the others. Hesitating, trying to wrap her head around everything, Rebecca stood a moment, watching and listening. Under the multiple boots of her companions, the steel mesh clanged; softly, barely noticeably, but she imagined rings of vibrations fanning outwards into the habitat, the way a pond ripples when hit with a pebble. She wondered if they should leave the path and travel adjacent to it, and to that end pressed a boot to the side of the walkway to test the ground. Underfoot, the rich, dark soil felt soft and damp, but suitable for walking.

A thrum pulsed up from the ground and into her heel.

Rebecca jerked her foot away, startled, as though she'd been hit with an electric shock. She hadn't, but it wasn't dissimilar. Intrigued, she eased her boot back to the soil. There it was again, a vibration from somewhere below, like the faint, almost mechanical tremor she'd felt upon entry to SL1. Here, though, the thin, almost buzzlike energy seemed to rise and crackle around her—as though it was not just in the ground, but in the air, too. In that moment, she sensed there may also have been an audible component, a low hum reflecting off the unseen walls of the dome, but of that she wasn't certain.

Either way, the source of the vibration was clearly underground. It wasn't biological. It could be pumps, air filtration, climate control.

It could be something else, too.

Again, her thoughts circled back to when she'd exited the elevator on SL1. Then, the thrum had reminded her of the pulsing sphere she'd discovered deep beneath the pyramid.

It couldn't be that, could it?

No, this isn't a pulse, as such. This is steadier, more consistent. She decided it was low frequency, like the hum of electricity. The sound made by a power transformer. Yes, that was it. There must be all sorts of machinery beneath the habitat.

Rebecca glanced about, scanning the trees. If she needed any further convincing that this wasn't a real jungle, wasn't a true rainforest, the realisation that powerful machinery thrummed underfoot was enough to seal the deal. But it was a perplexing notion, too, because otherwise, this place *did* look real, *did* look like what she'd encountered in South America. And that was it, wasn't it? An artificial, fabricated ecosystem, a synthetic environment that was at the same time entirely real. The trees were real trees, the plants and vegetation, the kapoks and lianas and bromeliads, all real. The temperature, the humidity, the feel, the smell. Again, all real. With the alcove long gone and the plexiglass dome fully hidden by the screening vegetation, the illusion of reality was heightened.

But there was a difference, and it was stark.

Suddenly, Rebecca felt oppressed, closed in. She couldn't see the ceiling above the canopy, in the dark more than two hundred feet above her, but she could sense it looming there, like she'd sensed the ceiling of the cavern earlier, pressing down with real weight. All that heaviness above her, the dome, and the earth, all that pressure. Like the weight of the ocean at depth.

This is how it would feel to be trapped at the bottom of the sea, or in a mine, or in an icy tomb with no way out. No hope. Nowhere to go—

You have somewhere to go.

Do I?

You will get out.

An image came to her, a flashback to the burrow beneath the pyramid, weeks ago, when she'd slithered on hands and knees through the earth, fully enclosed in that tight space. Now, she was there again, with that same stab of claustrophobia that had caused her world to shrink and her breaths to come in heaving, ragged gasps, and suddenly she couldn't breathe and put a hand to her throat and—

For Christ's sake, keep it together!

She gasped, still overbreathing.

You know what to do. You've overcome this before. Deep breaths. Slow, steady.

Rebecca stood there, stock still, going through her exercises, and in moments got her breathing under control. She calmed. The world expanded.

"Oh, God."

She was glad the others weren't here to witness her moment of distress. Of weakness.

Losing control isn't an option. It's never an option.

Absently, she reached up to her neck and the chain with the gold cross at the end of it, rubbing the item between her thumb and forefinger. At the same time, with her other hand, she swept away the moisture that had pooled at the corners of her eyes. Clearing her throat, she took a moment to smooth her clothes.

In her shorts pocket, the pill bottle bulged. Retrieving it, she shook out two tablets, reflected on that, and opted for a third. She swallowed all in a single gulp.

She waited for them to kick in, lingering until the physical symptoms of her anxiety had passed. It didn't take long.

Composed again, back where she needed to be, Rebecca gritted her teeth and hurried after her companions.

28
α

"There it is."

Leading once more, Rebecca paused. Ahead, no more than fifteen feet away and just beyond the huge, flared roots of a soaring kapok, their path ended, merging with another that cut across it perpendicularly.

"Yes!" Fitzgerald said, wheezing softly. His face was dotted in sweat, and his glasses had steamed up. "That's the junction." Still keen to prove his health, he started for the tee-shaped intersection, but Rebecca pulled him into a crouch.

"Hang on," she whispered.

Several feet beyond this new path, running parallel with it, rose the top half of a curved acrylic tube.

"That's the observation tunnel," Carlisle murmured, hunkering next to them.

Rebecca had figured as much. There was little to see through the plexiglass—the tunnel's interior was mostly dark—but to that she paid scant heed, anyway. Of primary interest was the area *outside* the tunnel. Here, the foliage was thinner, the forest floor more open; most likely, the space was regularly cleared to improve visibility for the observers inside. This had a knock-on effect. Li had said the arachnids would test the tunnel wall, meaning they weren't merely aware of the structure but associated it with intruders. Looming *over* the tunnel, crowding the cleared area, were taller trees. These offered ample cover.

The megs are ambush predators. If they're here now, watching, waiting, then this is the perfect kill zone.

She heard a slapping sound behind her and turned.

It was Wyatt, swatting wildly at his face and neck. Upon realising the eyes of the group were upon him, he paused.

"Mosquitoes," Spencer whispered, nudging Naziem with his elbow. "They love him. You should see him when we go out squatchin.'"

"Squatchin'?"

"You know, bigfoot hunting," Spencer explained. "More red lumps than a bowl of cherries."

Wyatt shook his head. "Anything about me you *haven't* divulged yet?"

"I haven't told them about your fear of snakes."

Glaring at them, Rebecca thrust a finger to her lips before turning forward again, searching. Threading through the canopy overhead was a network of crisscrossing girders. To this, an array of UV lamps was attached, which meant that while it was dark above and between the foliage, the vegetation itself still glowed. By this light, she scrutinized everything, but saw nothing in the trees, either at the mid-forest level, or in the over-storey. Turning her attention to the forest floor, she again noted nothing of concern. Listening, she caught the chirp of insects and frogs, but no quaking leaves or branches snapping under duress; nothing to indicate movement. Transferring her gaze to the cross-path, she looked for signs of recent activity, and found none. Earlier, Carlisle had said that this walkway would lead them to the gate separating H-1 from H-2. She turned to Carlisle now. "The gate," she whispered, "how far?"

"From here, maybe 180 feet, give or take."

Okay. That's not far. Keep breaking it down, just like before. We can do this.

"Fingers crossed Holtorf hasn't closed it," Wyatt murmured, still slapping at his arms and face, but quietly now.

"It'll be open," Spencer said.

Looking to Rebecca for direction, Carlisle asked, "So, we're good?"

Rebecca nodded. "From now on, we stay off the path and go through the trees." She figured they could keep the path in view and walk adjacent to it, on this side, which was denser than the open side next to the observation tunnel. No-one questioned her, evidently aware of the need to trade speed for cover. "Stay close."

Without further delay, Rebecca stepped from the path and scampered forward. As she went, she couldn't help but tense, anticipating an attack, feeling exposed and defenceless; the way an antelope might feel heading down to a waterhole.

Not the image you want in your mind, Bec.

She cast it out, and for the moment at least, the attack never came. At the junction, she turned right and made for the gate.

29
α

The next few minutes were a blur. That's all it took to get from the habitat's mid-point to the northern wall, but Rebecca, lost in a heightened state of hypervigilance, recalled little of the journey. Thankfully, it was uneventful. A part of her wondered how this could be, how they could have gotten this far without incident, and she couldn't help but draw parallels to her mission inside the pyramid when she and Oliveira and his men had been allowed to venture unopposed before everything had gone south.

But this was different, right? That had been a trap; back then, they'd been lured and herded into the clutches of the alpha female.

There are no alphas in here.

Putting her faith in that, praying she was right because God knew she couldn't afford to repeat her mistakes, Rebecca focused on what was immediately in front of her. As they neared the wall and the large, hemispherical structure set into it, she relaxed a little, even though her body ached with a fatiguing throb of adrenalin.

Into the dome-like edifice was a concrete, square-shaped gate-housing. It was unobstructed. The gate was raised.

"Thank God," Wyatt said, exhaling.

The opening was larger than Rebecca had anticipated, at least thirty feet high and wide. Big enough to drive a truck through.

Big enough for other things to slip through, too.

Beyond the gate, through the opening, was H-2. She saw more jungle in there, gloomy, just like here, but also bathed in ultraviolet light.

There was no reason to delay, and they didn't. Bunched together and moving quickly, they entered the gatehouse. On either side of the structure rose large vertical tracks. A shadowy space lay above. Rebecca couldn't see the gate or what it was made of, but no doubt it was strong and sturdy and sitting somewhere up there in the darkness.

Leaving H-1 behind, they crossed into H-2.

Ahead, on a direct line from the gate and just eighty feet across a swathe of flat, open ground, was the shed. It looked like a concrete bunker. Surrounding it was a ten-foot-high chain-link fence that held the thick, broad-leafed foliage at bay. Set into the side of the shed and in line with the track—which, come to think of it, resembled a dirt road—was a large roller-shuttered door. Again, big enough for a truck.

"The door is down," Fitzgerald said. "You think it's locked?"

"Only one way to find out," Carlisle replied. Throwing caution to the wind, she broke into a run.

Refusing to be left behind, Fitzgerald hurried after her, and Naziem followed. Rebecca turned to the brothers, about to urge them forward, and saw that one of them was missing. Her heart leapt. "Where's Wyatt?"

Awkwardly, Spencer hooked a thumb over his shoulder. "He had to pee."

At that moment, Wyatt burst from the undergrowth, still zipping himself up. "Sorry," he said sheepishly, turning and adjusting his belt before frantically waving the two of them over. "You have to come see this."

Rebecca took a couple of steps towards him and then wavered, glancing back over her shoulder at Carlisle and the others, who had already passed through the gate in the chain-link fence and were almost at the shed door.

"Quickly," Wyatt said, gesturing impatiently before slipping back into the bushes.

Hesitant to split the group but intrigued by Wyatt's urgency, Rebecca followed him beyond the treeline, a few paces behind Spencer. She found the brothers at the top of a slight incline.

"I came in here, and saw this," Wyatt whispered. "Look…down there."

Ahead, down the slope not ten feet away, was a disturbance in the leaf litter. It was difficult to discern in the semidarkness, but scuff marks had clearly been gouged into the soil's surface, not deep, but several feet long and looking as though something had been digging—or at least clawing—at the ground.

"What the hell?" Spencer whispered.

"It gets better," Wyatt said. "Check this out." He bounded a pace or two ahead and parted the feathery underbrush. On the ground beyond was a pile of assorted detritus, most of it in a small, heaped mound, but some of it lying further afield, randomly scattered, glowing faintly.

"Are those shells?" Spencer asked.

"That's what I thought," Wyatt replied. "But they can't be shells, right? Why would there be shells in here?"

Slowly, Rebecca approached the pile. "Not shells," she said, kneeling and gently lifting one of the larger pieces from the dirt with her thumb and forefinger.

No way, this doesn't make sense.

The piece was at least two inches wide, lightweight, and a reflective brown colour. It was hard, too. Shell-like, but not as rigid as a shell. "This is chitin."

The brothers crowded behind her. "What?" Wyatt asked.

Rebecca looked back over her shoulder. "The gouges over there, the scuff marks…and then this. This is feeding activity. These are remains."

"Whoa, no," Spencer said, glancing about and clutching his sharp-edged stone as tightly as a security blanket. "*Remains*? Remains of what?"

"An insect," Rebecca said.

"*One* insect? You mean dozens of insects, right? Those pieces—"

"Are huge," Rebecca said, nodding. "But there's no doubt. These are the remnants of an invertebrate carcass. A *single* carcass."

"No freaking way," Spencer said.

"Look," Rebecca said, picking through the mound, selecting various bits and placing them in order. "This here is part of the carapace, here's part of a wing casing…we have sclerites, leg armour…"

"No," Wyatt said, shaking his head. "It can't be that. It's way too big to be an insect."

"She's an entomologist, Wyatt," Spencer said, sighing. "If she says it's an insect, then it's a goddamned insect." He hesitated, then tapped Rebecca on the shoulder. "But…are you *sure* it's an insect? My brother's right. It's way too big to be an insect."

"You're both right," Rebecca said, standing and scanning the trees. "It's an insect, but it's way too big. We need to get back to the others."

"You're spooking me," Wyatt said. "What aren't you telling us?"

Rebecca didn't want them to panic, but she needed to give them something. Throwing her gaze about, she spoke calmly yet quickly. "I don't need to tell you this isn't a regular invertebrate. Judging by the wing casings, the flattened body and carapace, this is an animal that keeps low to the ground. My knowledge of ancient species is a little rusty, but it reminds me of a Blattoptera, maybe a large Archimylacris. It looks like a roachid of some kind."

"A cockroach?"

"A primitive cockroach, yes," Rebecca replied. "But most blattopterans, including Archimylacris, weren't anywhere near this big. They were comparable with modern cockroaches."

"This one is a foot long, head to tail," Wyatt said.

"A giant freaking cockroach," Spencer murmured. "They never said anything about giant freaking roaches."

No, they didn't, Rebecca thought. She glanced at the gouges in the soil.

Wyatt was sweating profusely. Wiping at a line dripping from his brow, he said, "So…the giant cockroach is super-mysterious and all, but is anyone troubled by whatever *ate* the giant cockroach? The spiders, right? Seems like they weren't keen on those bits and spat them out. But they were here…and they might still be around. We've gotta go. We've gotta go *now*."

A twig snapped, followed by a loud scratching sound, somewhere close.

"Oh shit…*oh freaking shit…*" Wyatt whispered, scrambling backwards. As he did, something pushed through the undergrowth, heading towards them. "*The spiders…*"

"No, not spiders," Rebecca murmured.

The bushes in front of them burst violently apart.

At first, Rebecca caught only a shiny, curved side as the animal arced through the foliage, but that fleeting glimpse was enough to conclude the thing was huge. Maybe six or seven feet slid past, low to the ground, flat and snakelike, but it wasn't a snake. The body, at least two feet wide, was not scaled; instead, it was heavily armoured, covered in an array of interlocking, chitinous plates, like shields. Most notably, clicking and writhing beneath those plates, were dozens of segmented legs.

"Holy shit!" Wyatt cried. "*What the hell?*"

At the sound of his voice the great body turned and the creature's head—rounded, insectoid, with two large waving antennae and obsidian black eyes—burst from the foliage, swerving towards him on a direct line, no more than a dozen feet away and closing swiftly.

Again, Wyatt stumbled backwards. "It's a *centipede!*"

The creature halted and reared. This time the resemblance to a snake was heightened, the front half of the animal's body rising from the ground like a cobra poised to strike. Hissing, it flared its multiple legs wide in a menacing threat-pose.

"Jesus!" Spencer said, raising his stone—his comfort object—as though readying to hurl it at the creature. Just as quickly, though, he lowered it, clutching it to his chest and scooting backwards like his brother.

Agitated by this, the creature redirected its attention to Spencer. Although it remained rooted to the spot, it leaned forward, expelling more air, another hiss. Its legs waved and clicked.

"Keep still!" Rebecca ordered. *This is incredible.* She'd seen this arthropod before, or at least something like it. But only in the history books.

It can't be…

It looked like an Arthropleura—the gigantic ancestor to both centipedes and millipedes.

Wyatt made to run, and the creature spun towards him.

"No!" Rebecca cried, catching him by the arm and halting him. She was fearful of triggering a chase response. While Arthropleura wasn't dangerous—that species was in fact herbivorous—this wasn't Arthropleura; hell, she had no idea *what* this was. At a minimum, given it had snacked on a roach, it was insectivorous. Maybe that's all it ate. Maybe it was nothing more than a harmless scavenger. Then again, it could just as easily be a predator. Either way, she had to assume the worst, that no matter what it was, it was dangerous, maybe venomous, maybe armed in ways she couldn't imagine and if nothing else was willing to violently defend itself if need be.

Most of all, she couldn't know what might prompt these defences, or how fast the thing might move.

"Listen to me," she whispered. "Back away slowly. Now."

Still rearing, the creature waved hypnotically back and forth, warily watching the group as Rebecca, arms spread, herded the brothers away.

Eventually, they'd retreated far enough that the creature, apparently no longer threatened, eased to the ground. As it touched down it scampered towards the road, disappearing swiftly. Twigs snapped and leaves shivered in its wake, and then all was still.

"Holy shit," Spencer said. Like his brother, he was sweating copiously.

"We need to get back to the others," Rebecca said.

"Hell yeah," Spencer agreed.

But for the moment, none of them moved. Rooted to the spot, they stood wide-eyed, panting in disbelief.

After several seconds, Wyatt shook his head. "That thing was seriously armoured. You saw that, yeah? Why does something that big and scary need such full-on defences?"

It was a fair observation, but Wyatt, like everyone, knew what else lurked in here.

"It headed up to the road," Spencer said.

Rebecca nodded. "It did, but I don't think we'll see it again." She paused, reflecting a moment. "Still, I think we'll take the long way around."

"Fuck yeah to that," Wyatt said.

THE
BREACH

30

α

"What I'm about to tell you is on the public record," Major Yolanda Mbye announced.

Fidgeting, leaning forward in his chair, Owen only half-heard this. His thoughts hadn't stopped spinning.

A sphere had crashed in Nevada.

Rebecca is in Nevada…

"The public record?" Jessy queried. "What do you mean? You mentioned another sphere."

Lieutenant Colonel Belding, still sitting on the edge of the table inside the command post, nodded at Mbye, who clicked the presentation remote. On the wall monitor, an image flashed up, a new topographical map showing what appeared to be the western United States.

"In the latter half of 1940, a small parcel of land in southern Nevada was withdrawn from the public domain," Mbye began. "It was immediately designated a wildlife preserve. While sudden, this occurred without fanfare or publicity. Over the next two decades, more parcels were acquired, vast tracts of adjoining land, some of which was privately owned. These reclamations drew far more attention, sparking both interest and suspicion. With time, the wider area gained an ever-increasing foothold on the public imagination."

"The rumour-mill fired up," Owen said. "People heard what was going on there. You're talking about Nellis Air Force Range, and the Nevada Test and Training Range. You're talking about Groom Lake."

"The rumour-mill, as you say, is exactly that," Belding interjected. "A ragbag of stories, fabrications, and urban myths."

Mbye nodded, and said to Owen, "In recent decades, the wider area you refer to has earned a growing profile, unlike the initial withdrawal of land, which from the very beginning went largely unnoticed. Today, that original parcel remains a federal preserve, restricted from public access, but effectively ignored. This is where the public record ends."

"Let me guess," Jessy said. "It's not really a preserve."

Standing, Belding walked to the head of the table, leaning over it, and transferring a hard stare from Owen to Jessy and back again. "The following is SAP-classified. Top-secret. At this point, I remind you of your obligations." Straightening, he turned to Mbye and gave her the go-ahead.

Again, Mbye clicked the presentation remote, causing the image to magnify. "In early 1940 a survey team working for the Nevada State Parks Commission, operating in a remote region of the southern Mojave between the Pintwater and Sheep Ranges, stumbled upon an object of unknown origin or purpose in a previously unmapped cave system. That system is located on what is currently restricted land."

"The preserve," Owen said.

"Reports state that radiating from the object—later tagged as object N-439478—was a mass of unidentifiable and long-decayed organic material," Mbye said. "The nature of this material, which was too degraded for sampling, remains unclear. Best estimates, however, suggest that both it and the object had been inside the cavern for upwards of 2,000 years. In the weeks following its discovery, N-439478 was moved, under the auspice of the now-closed Project Greenfield, to a top-secret, purpose-built facility in this area here." She clicked again, and the image on the screen zoomed in further. "Note the subdivisions, particularly grid reference 71."

Owen squinted. "All I see is desert."

"There's little to see above ground," Mbye said. "But I can tell you that N-439478 was housed in this location, gathering dust, for more than eight decades. Two months ago, it woke up."

"The object. It's a sphere, right?" Owen said. He turned to Jessy, whispering excitedly. "Just like you said: when Oliveira activated the sphere up in the temple, the Nevada sphere probably started pulsing and flaring with the same energy. But the question is: *how*? They said the drones are connected, but across continents?"

"'Spooky action at a distance,'" Jessy whispered back to him.

"It's a little spooky, yeah."

"No, I mean, that's what Einstein said."

"Sorry?"

Raising her voice, Jessy said to Mbye, "When Einstein talked about 'spooky action', what he was referring to—what *you're* referring to—is quantum entanglement."

Owen slumped. "And with that, you've officially lost me." He folded his arms. "Just so you know, I don't understand anything with the word quantum in front of it… or anywhere near it, for that matter."

"Neither do I," Jessy agreed, patting him on the knee before transferring her gaze back to Mbye. "But that's what you're getting at, isn't it? Quantum entanglement? In simple terms, it's possible for a pair of particles, separated by hundreds of miles, to be connected, or *entangled*, so that an action performed on one prompts a change in the other. I'm guessing the swarm is like this, in that the spheres aren't independent of the system. They're entangled with each other. And with the mothership."

"This isn't quantum entanglement," Perez said. "But the comparison *is* appropriate. They may be separated by distance, but as far as we can tell, the drones form a single entity."

"An entity?" Owen queried. "You mean something *intelligent*?"

"An artificial superorganism, if you will," Mbye said. "Think of the mothership as the nerve centre, so to speak, and the drones as nerve endings, receptors that gather and send information back to the brain. It's simplistic, yes, and we know the spheres are far more than just sensory devices. But it's a theory; one of several we're working through."

Again, this was new and unexpected. Struggling to tie the various threads together, Owen kneaded his temples, hoping to ease the heightened throb that had caused a headache to bloom there. "So… going back to what we know about the crash… when the swarm fell to Earth, the impact created a gateway here in the Amazon, the Vent—a valve through which the megs and a host of plant life emerged. Later, we find this strange, 2,000-year-old organic material surrounding the sphere in Nevada—clearly, this is a related emergence, yeah? If, as you say, the swarm is entangled, then logically, the crash not only opened a vent here, but it opened one in Nevada, too, and all the other places that might be hiding spheres; like Jessy said, an action performed on one affects the other. But again, the question is *how*? How were the gateways opened to begin with?"

"It's a single anomaly, with several gates," Perez said. "As to how it opened, we suspect it was a glitch, an unintended consequence of the swarm's unique system of propulsion."

"You mean how it travels through space," Owen said.

"Space, dimensions… even time."

"Wormholes," Jessy reasoned. "That's what you're getting at, right? This isn't new. You're going to give us the wormhole theory."

"That, or something similar," Mbye replied. "A form of gravity warping, perhaps. You saw for yourselves the magnetic and electrical irregularities at play down here—"

"The moai," Owen murmured to Jessy. When Ed had placed his grandfather's disc in one of the statues, it set off an antigravity force. A *repulsive* force. According to legend, the T'aevans, the builders of Intihuasi, were able to harness the 'power of the sun'. Ed had since discovered this to be true, that they had not only accessed this energy, but had likely settled in the crater because this was where the power was most active. Owen looked at Mbye. "Ed thought the crater was a vortex, a convergence, a place where the energy was concentrated."

"And he was right," Jessy said, jumping in. "It's all of that, isn't it? And it's because of the mothership. The mothership is the source, and it's leaking something. It's leaking that energy."

She didn't reject the idea, but Mbye's expression implied there was more to it than that. "We suspect the mothership generates these space-time distortions to enable long-range travel, but in this case the system was damaged and malfunctioning, perhaps even before the crash. Either way, when it came down, one of these distortions stayed open for a period before seemingly collapsing. We believe that with this failure, most of the outlying spheres—N-439478 included—fell into hibernation. Others, like the two you found, stayed awake, trying to maintain a connection. Trying to boot up, as it were."

"The strange pulsing," Jessy reasoned. "The spheres were trying to start up, to turn over, like a car with a dead battery."

"More likely a broken starter, or an alternator, to borrow the analogy," Perez said. "The battery, for want of a better term, still has some juice."

Which would explain the energy leakage, Owen thought. "So, when Oliveira placed the rod into the statue, it caused a reaction, kind of kickstarted something, but the sphere couldn't engage, not fully. Oliveira had the keys, but the engine wouldn't start."

Biting her lip, Jessy spent several seconds mulling this over. "This is beginning to make sense… sort of." She swiveled in her seat to face Owen. "When Oliveira inserted the rod—the key, if you will—the smaller sphere, the temple sphere, started to suck everything towards it… that's the reaction you mentioned. The kickstart."

"A gravity field," Owen said, agreeing. "Generated and controlled by the sphere, as though it were a miniature black hole."

"Similar to a black hole, yes, but in effect, something else," Jessy said. She turned back to Mbye. "The aura, the gravitational pull swirling around it… that was something trying to open. That was the mouth of a wormhole."

Mbye gave a wry, knowing smile, tapping a finger against her nose as she did. "Perhaps they're one and the same. Some believe that black holes are openings to gravitational tunnels, that they *are*, in fact, the mouths of wormholes. It's been proposed these tunnels might even connect black holes to each other."

Sensing where this was heading, Owen leaned forward. "What we're really talking about is a network of black hole generators, tethered to each other by wormholes."

"The spreading tentacles of an artificial superorganism," Mbye said.

Jessy tilted her head. "You talk as though it's *alive*."

Mbye snuffed a laugh but didn't deny it. "There's a lot we still don't know. For instance, what's the swarm's purpose? Is it benign or hostile? Can it do more than what we've seen? Are the individual spheres, like the temple sphere, *meant* to generate their own gravitational fields, or is this usually the sole preserve of the mothership? These are mysteries. All we can say with confidence is that the swarm is connected across space, and likely time."

Jessy blew air through her teeth. "This is wild."

"That's the understatement of the century," Owen replied, leaning back. He spent a few moments collecting his thoughts. Where to begin? Conventional wisdom, no doubt, would argue the very concept espoused by Mbye and Perez was impossible, that the notion of artificially generated wormholes or black holes or gravitational tunnels that somehow remained tethered and stable and controlled was not only nonsense, but a violation of countless scientific laws. And he tended to agree. Hell, he wasn't a physicist and even to *him* it seemed farfetched. But something was going on, wasn't it? Something incredible—they'd seen it for themselves. And no matter how unlikely, Mbye and Perez were offering an explanation, something that seemed to fit. He wondered what would have unfolded that afternoon up in the temple if the system hadn't been damaged and the sphere had been able to operate as intended. What if the space-time distortion had kicked in at full strength and the wormhole had opened completely? Would it have stabilised? Or would it have continued to suck everything in, spaghettifying everything in the process? Maybe it wouldn't have destroyed anything at all and instead, even more bizarrely, spat it all out, fully intact, at some other location. He shuddered. Man, the T'aevans may have been able to harness the energy of the spheres, but they could never have known the true extent of that power.

Or the danger.

Belding deadpanned, "Which brings us, finally, to why you're here." He nodded at Mbye, who, accessing the laptop, opened a network directory on screen and started searching through various files.

As she did, Belding leaned over the table and continued. "I've read your reports and your resumes." Turning to Owen, he said, "Aside from your discovery of this very cave system, Dr Faulkner, you've spent several years as a field anthropologist for Brazil's National Indian Foundation, FUNAI. Most significantly, you recorded *verifiable* contact with the Yuguruppu tribe, whose existence had been rumoured but not previously been confirmed." To Jessy, he said, "And Ms. Baxter, I note your specialty is ancient Meso-American cultures, specifically the rise of towns and urbanism. You were instrumental in the discovery, and subsequent documentation, of several moai and the lost city of Intihuasi."

"We had help," Jessy said.

Ignoring this, addressing them both now, Belding said, "Make no mistake, these are significant findings, at the forefront of a substantial operation. The government, as you can see, is highly invested." With that, he straightened. "Already, we have good people on the ground, but given your expertise and first-hand experience with the phenomena, I'd argue the two of you are *uniquely* qualified to help."

Trading a subtle, knowing glance with Jessy, Owen said, "Admittedly, we were determined to stay involved."

"So, *how* can we help, Colonel?" Jessy asked.

Belding nodded at Mbye. "Major?"

Mbye located the video file she'd been searching for and clicked on it. To Owen and Jessy, she said, "You may find this of interest."

The monitor went black. In the screen's top left corner, a timecode rolled, and around the edges other graphics—mainly graphs and meaningless numbers—moved and shifted. Then the image distorted, flickering with interference before resolving. Close to the camera lens, shapes formed in shades of green, and Owen realised the jolting, unsteady vision was of dense vegetation—jungle—captured from a vehicle moving low to the ground, maybe a wheeled rover.

"This is pre-recorded drone footage from inside the crater," Jessy concluded.

"Drone footage, yes," Mbye replied, "but not from the crater. Like I mentioned before, everything goes both ways. Things emerge. And things can enter."

"*Enter?*"

"No way," Owen said slowly, incredulously. He looked at Mbye, then stared back up at the screen, this time with a vastly different perspective. "You opened the Vent. *This is vision from the other side.*"

31
α

Mbye nodded. "Thrilling, isn't it?"

Owen baulked. Thrilling, yes—infinitely so—but also perplexing, too. Before, Mbye had said the gateway had collapsed, that the Vent was closed…

Apparently sensing his confusion, Mbye explained, "We've engaged the anomaly several times. Six, to be exact."

"That can't be right," Jessy said with breathless wonder. "That's impossible."

Overwhelmed, his emotions swirling, Owen watched as the rover ploughed ahead, bumping over uneven ground, the vision on screen lurching fuzzily from rotting leaf litter to feathery underbrush and back again. Jessy was right. How the hell had they pulled this off? That they'd opened the Vent six times clearly suggested they were closing it, too, likely as a risk mitigation. But still…

On screen, the image distorted again.

"It gets clearer," Mbye assured them. "Of course, a UAV would be preferable, but the drones need to be tethered and grounded. Unfortunately, this also limits their range. Okay, here, it is."

The rover entered a clearing and halted. The image stabilised, and rotors whirred as the camera focused and then panned slowly from left to right. Low-lying ferns and broad-leafed shrubs dominated, but there were blade-like buttress roots, too, snaking from the shadows in all directions. Here, the forest floor was dark, almost swampy, and out of this murk rose gnarled, twisted trees draped in vine-like lianas and woody, parasitic growths. The jungle was gloomy and oppressive. Claustrophobic.

Watching that vision, Owen felt a stab of unease.

"So, this place… what we're seeing… this is where the megs came from," Jessy clarified. "And the spheres, too."

"The megs, yes, but not necessarily the spheres," Perez said. "The system was damaged, remember? The gateway could have opened to a random place, totally unrelated to the spheres. Either way, it's locked onto this location."

Owen's skin rippled in gooseflesh. Unrelated, random, it didn't matter. Whatever—*wherever*—the hell this was, be it another planet or dimension or something else altogether, it was nothing short of mind-blowing. *Next level* mind-blowing. "Goddamn," he said. "The megarachnid *homeworld…*"

Jessy squeezed his knee, a non-verbal confirmation that she, too, was equally stunned and inspired. "It's just like here, isn't it? The vegetation… it's the same. Just like Earth. I'm guessing the stratosphere must be similar as well… and the temperature, maybe a little warmer, but most likely steady."

Perez nodded. "Data confirms the surface temperature is conducive to liquid water. Rivers, at least, but likely oceans and lakes. If it's a planet, logic suggests it's positioned such that its sun doesn't evaporate the oceans or bombard it with too much radiation."

"The famous Goldilocks zone," Jessy said. "Not too hot, not too cold."

"We can go a step further," Mbye said. "Preliminary analysis suggests the chemical composition of the atmosphere is similar, but oxygen levels are higher. This is supported by the kinds of invertebrates we've seen."

"*Kinds* of invertebrates?"

Owen caught it, too, and shot a glance at Mbye. "You mean the megs, of course."

Mbye jutted her chin at the monitor. "Keep watching."

On screen, the image shifted as the rover started forward again, repositioning itself at the clearing's far edge. Here, the foliage was thinner, and the muddy ground fell away, affording the vehicle a wide-angled view across a shallow, jungle-covered valley. In the distance, beneath a sky blackened by lightning-wracked clouds, a shape rose above the canopy, straight edged and cube-like. The camera reframed, zooming in.

"What the hell is that?" Owen asked, removing his glasses and wiping them on his suit before thrusting them back into position. Despite his efforts, the strange shape remained sufficiently blurred and unclear. "It's a rock formation, yeah? A mountain?" It had to be. Some sort of natural landmark—

"No," Jessy said evenly. "That's not what it is."

"Sorry?"

Turning to Mbye, Jessy said, "That object… it's a structure, isn't it? Man-made. We're looking at a pyramid."

Hitting the pause button, freezing the ambiguously pixelated image on screen, Mbye said, "A temple, I'd suggest. And yes, it's sitting atop the truncated peak of a stair-stepped pyramid."

Holy shit, Owen thought, leaning forward and squinting. Now that he had context, a reference, he could infer more detail, maybe a series of columns and several dark, empty doorways. Below that, sitting just above the line of the canopy, an angular, tan-coloured wedge implied a long, sloping side, and perhaps even a set of regular-sized stairs. Incredible.

A temple-topped pyramid, just like the one in the crater above them…

"It's Mayan," Jessy stated, trying her best to contain her excitement. "At least, that's what it looks like."

"The similarities are apparent," Mbye agreed.

"But that means—"

"We don't know what it means," Mbye said.

Owen frowned. "You don't know?" Wasn't it obvious? According to legend, when the T'aevans lost their home—the mythical, lost Pacific continent of T'aeva—to cataclysmic floods, they fled to the jungles of South America, and there built the city of Intihuasi. The stories, at least in part, were true—the city was real, so too the distinctly Mayan-like pyramid at its heart. Looking again at the frozen image on the monitor before him, Owen tilted his head, the explanation all too apparent. "The T'aevans opened the Vent, and they crossed through."

Mbye shrugged. "I think it's *very* likely they crossed through, but the question is—"

"—from which *side*?" Jessy finished.

Surprised, Owen looked from Mbye to Jessy and stuttered, "Wait… you think they came here… from *there*?"

Although Jessy started to speak—Mbye, too—Owen heard nothing. Suddenly, his mind was spinning rapidly. If this was true—if humans had crossed through—then the implications were ground-shaking, not just for the origins of Intihuasi, but for all of humankind. Was it possible? Could it have happened? Had another race of humans migrated here from across worlds?

He realised he was rambling out loud. "But it can't be true, can it? I mean, before, you said of all the biota to emerge, of all the plant and animal life, the megarachnids were the dominant species, the alpha species—"

"Of all the *known* species to have emerged," Mbye said. She pointed at the image on screen. "Like I said, we don't know what *this* means, not ex-actly. But today—"

"—we find out," Belding interjected.

Tearing his gaze from Mbye to Belding, still scrambling to catch-up, Owen blinked rapidly. Today? He glanced at the countdown clock and its rolling red digits, which had now ticked beneath two hours. Refocusing, he said to Belding, "Colonel, what happens when that clock hits zero?"

Clenching his hands behind his back, Belding offered them a thin smile. "We go green for launch."

"You're reopening the Vent," Jessy reasoned. "Another drone mission."

"We're finished with drones," Belding replied. "As we speak, an advance team is prepping to go. They'll secure the area, set up base camp, then we'll send in the Mayflower."

Jessy's eyes widened. "Hang on… what?"

"You're sending *people* inside?" Owen asked.

Belding swiveled, jutting his chin at the monitor. "If there are humans in there, we need experts on the ground. People with knowledge of ancient cultures, people with experience in first-contact." Twisting back, he eyed each of them in turn. "People like you."

"*What?*"

"You're on team two," Belding confirmed. "You've scored a ticket inside."

Though he'd seen it coming, Owen felt the blindside's full force, a loop-ing sucker-punch that knocked the wind from his body. A ticket inside? That made no sense; he wasn't a soldier, wasn't trained for such a mission, and neither was Jessy. He turned to her, and although she, too, seemed un-able to speak—her eyes glistening with emotion—he realised this wasn't driven by fear but instead, something else: curiosity, intrigue, maybe even excitement.

She wanted this. She was ready.

This is crazy…

Glancing at the monitor, Owen wondered if the image on screen was accurate, if this was indeed proof of a lost human culture, maybe a lost tribe. Could there be humans living beyond the Vent right now? Were they even human at *all*?

As the questions ran through his mind, there was a rush of movement at the door. A soldier burst into the room, straightening and saluting. "Sir, we have a problem, a big one," he panted. "Nevada is offline."

Rebecca…

Before anyone could react, Owen heard commotion outside, followed, in the distance, by faint popping sounds.

The sounds of gunfire.

32
α

Rebecca poked her head from the underbrush, intent on avoiding the open road and in turn, the strange millipede-like creature. The opposing treeline seemed an obvious source of refuge, but a quick scan of the path forced a change of mind. The creature was nowhere to be seen, and with the coast clear, the faster, more direct route held greater appeal. With the brothers in tow she broke into a run, beelining for the shed. The roller-shutter was down, but to the right of it was a regular door which Carlisle held ajar with one hand. With her other, she motioned frantically. "Passcode worked! Hurry!"

At the fence, Rebecca paused, turning and holding the gate wide for the brothers before running for the door, which Carlisle slammed behind the group with a resounding clang.

"Man, we thought we'd lost you," Carlisle said, turning. "What the hell *happened*?"

Safely inside, gasping for breath, Spencer quipped, "We nearly bugged out."

Greeting the joke with an eye-roll, Wyatt, also panting, said, "So, I'm guessing you forgot to tell us something."

Carlisle's brow creased. "Forgot to tell you *what*?"

"Gee, let me see," Spencer blurted, "maybe something about the *giant frickin' bugs*?"

At this, both Naziem and Fitzgerald burst into the room from an adjoining space out back. The shed, Rebecca noted, was surprisingly spacious and well-maintained—hardly a shed at all, really. Shelves and lockers occupied the far wall, and along the ceiling, fluorescent lights and conduit dominated. A computer terminal sat flush against the right-hand wall. On the left, server racks and junction boxes.

Constructed almost entirely of concrete, it looked like an emergency bunker.

"Slow down a minute," Carlisle implored, palms up. "Giant *bugs*?"

Chewing faster than ever, Spencer scowled. "Yeah, a foot-long cockroach for one… oh, and a giant goddamned centipede!"

"Technically, it was a millipede," Rebecca corrected.

"Outside?" Fitzgerald asked. He, too, seemed short of breath, but in this new environment, perhaps away from potential triggers, his asthma appeared under control. "There were *bugs*? Are you sure?"

Perplexed by their reactions, Rebecca frowned.

"You're surprised by this?" Wyatt asked, equally confused.

Carlisle and Fitzgerald traded a hurried look—quizzical, and yet underpinned by something else, as though they'd just been presented with a long-lost puzzle piece.

Rebecca narrowed her eyes. "There are Carboniferous-sized arthropods out there, and I get the feeling you know why."

As she said this, Naziem scampered for the computer terminal, plunging into one of two swivel-chairs. He started typing furiously at the keyboard.

Carlisle addressed Rebecca. "There's nothing like that in here; at least, before *now* there wasn't. But there have been rumours."

"Idle talk," Fitzgerald added. "About the new habitats, H-7 and H-8. We thought the stories were a bit of fun, nothing verifiable—not by us, anyway, because we don't have project clearance beyond RC-1. Like I said, RC-2 is restricted, and RC-3 isn't even online yet."

"Or so we were told," Carlisle said.

"Yes," Fitzgerald agreed. "Or so we were told. But if something *was* going on in there, we weren't privy to it."

"Compartmentalisation of information," Wyatt mused.

Carlisle shrugged. "I guess. But H-7 and H-8 were always shuttered, which is probably why the rumours started. Some people swore there were assets in there under a classified program."

"Yeah, well they were right," Spencer said.

Wyatt pursed his lips. "It fits, but it doesn't explain how the creatures got from there to *here*, though, does it? And anyway, didn't Li say the new habitats were still under construction?"

"That was our understanding, and maybe hers, too, I guess," Fitzgerald said. "As you probably noticed, the domes are structurally complete, they just needed an internal fit-out." He glanced at Carlisle. "Or so we were told."

Suddenly, Naziem pushed back from the keyboard, spinning in his chair to face them. "I can tell you *exactly* how those creatures got here. Check this out." He urged them in, adjusting the angle of the monitor as they crowded behind him. "I had a thought, so I checked the system access for the last hour."

"You can do that?" Spencer asked.

"Naziem's good with computers," Fitzgerald explained.

Naziem waved his hand. "I learnt a trick or two at university. I can peek through the backdoor. Read-only. Admin access? Not a chance." He pointed at the screen. "This is a login usage report, time-stamped with today's date. You'll note the first login is 44 minutes ago."

Wyatt looked at his watch. "Just before we were thrown inside the habitat."

Rebecca studied the screen.

```
Systems Security Access Log, (RA)-71, 49/12T-F93203
```

Time	Operator	Action and Response
13:22:03	L2/C11/AS-09	Security camera disable command// SL1-6783 system shutdown
13:49:36	L45/C536/SR-02	Release command entered/Gate D opened
13:49:47	L45/C536/SR-02	Release command entered/Gate E opened
13:49:55	L45/C536/SR-02	Release command entered/Gate F opened
13:50:04	L45/C536/SR-02	Release command entered/Gate G opened
13:53:12	L45/C536/SR-02	Life support system access command entered
13:53:39	L45/C536/SR-02	Artificial atmosphere start-up command entered
13:54:17	L45/C536/SR-02	Constituent mixing ratio enacted

Naziem talked them through it. "The numbers in the middle there, they show the location and console that was used. Then we have the operator ID. The first one is AS-09, which must be someone in security. Looks like they shut down the cameras on Sublevel 1."

"Just prior to the attack," Wyatt reiterated, nodding. "What about SR-02?"

"That's a different operator," Naziem said. "Senior Researcher, Level 2."

"Li," Rebecca guessed. "Looks like she opened four gates in quick succession."

"Gates D through G," Carlisle clarified.

"Like I said, this report only goes back an hour," Naziem reiterated. "It doesn't show when the gates to the first four habitats—Gates A, B and C—were opened. That happened earlier this morning, prior to your arrival."

"Li wanted the megs to roam freely," Rebecca said, recalling Carlisle's previous comments.

"Right," Spencer said, chewing loudly, "so twenty minutes or so after Holtorf's attack on Beckett, and after we were already inside H-1, Li opened these other gates."

"Not Li," Fitzgerald argued. "She's a hostage, remember? Most likely it was Holtorf, using Li's login."

"Or Li at gunpoint," Wyatt said. He squinted at the screen. "These extra gates—D through G—I'm guessing they lead into H-5 and H-6?"

"The first two gates, yes," Carlisle said. "But the last two service H-7 and H-8. Li opened *everything*."

Spencer clicked his fingers. "Which explains the bugs. If those two habitats were secretly in use, if the bugs were in there, then obviously they escaped when the gates were opened. Some of them must have beelined down here."

Naziem nodded eagerly. "My thoughts exactly."

"It makes sense," Wyatt said. "What doesn't, is why Li—or Holtorf—opened *all* the gates? Why open *any*?"

Rebecca thought about that, but only briefly. To be honest, right now, she was less concerned with gates and systems and Holtorf's plans than she was with the bugs themselves. On that subject, she'd barely had a moment to reflect on what, exactly, these creatures were, or where they'd originally come from. Logically, they must have been roaming the jungle back in Intihuasi, hiding in or around the nest somewhere, having come from the same place as the megs. And when the military had later scoured the area, wrangling the scattering arachnids—Egbert amongst them—they must have stumbled on these other creatures, too.

A lost world of giant arthropods that she and the others had somehow missed...

Realising she'd dropped out of the conversation, Rebecca snapped back, turning to Carlisle. "The alphas. Where are they now?"

The consequences of multiple open gates had apparently dawned on Fitzgerald, too. Anxiously, he tapped Naziem on the shoulder. "Hurry. Check the pens."

Navigating to another menu, Naziem brought up a site plan, showing the habitats from above. He zoomed in on a cluster of red dots.

"Tracking signatures," Rebecca said.

Naziem nodded. "You're looking at H-5, which is the primary alpha pen. As you can see—" he zoomed in even closer, "the assets haven't moved." Leaning back, he released an audible sigh of relief. "They're all accounted for."

Carlisle, however, leaned closer. She jabbed a finger at the screen. "The alphas and the betas may not have moved, but see that? The *weavers* have. And the hunters, too."

"They've left their pens," Fitzgerald said, scratching his head. "And they've gone down to H-5."

This piqued Rebecca's interest. Immediately, she was reminded of her encounter beneath the pyramid, inside the nest, when the alpha female had called to her subordinates, summoning them to her side. Had that happened here, too?

"It explains why we haven't crossed paths, I guess," Spencer said. "The megs have skipped town for a family reunion."

"And we'll leave them to it," Wyatt said. "We only need to get to H-4. This is good news!"

"It is," Naziem said, typing again, "but I hate to rain on your parade." He brought the access log back on screen. "The last three lines. Look."

Rebecca narrowed her eyes. "Minutes after opening the gates, Li accessed the life support system."

"That got my attention, too," Naziem said, nodding. "We're talking about the habitats, of course—Li wouldn't have access to the overall system. But what concerned me was the last two entries."

"Shit," Carlisle said.

"What's wrong?" Wyatt asked.

Naziem swivelled to face them. "The habitats have an artificial atmosphere, right? Almost identical to ours. The breakdown of gases is like the troposphere, the lowest layer of the Earth's atmosphere."

"*Okay*," Wyatt said, shrugging. "So, what? Is there a problem with the atmosphere in here?"

Naziem held up a hand. "Let me show you." Turning back to the keyboard, he started typing again, speaking as he did so. "Filtered air has both permanent and variable components, just like the air outside. This includes trace amounts of various chemical compounds, as well as organic substances such as pollen and spores. That's normal, and not a problem. There's also water vapour, which is variable; the percent by volume in this hot, humid environment is high. But what I want to show you relates to the permanent components, so I'm going to remove the variables—water vapour and methane and carbon dioxide and a host of others—" he tapped the keyboard, "to give us the major constituents of dry air by volume, sorted by parts per million by volume."

"Um, Naziem, seriously… you've lost me," Wyatt said.

Chewing furiously, Spencer frowned. "Me, too."

In the zone, seemingly not hearing any of this, Naziem continued, typing faster than ever. "But concentration in PPM doesn't really illustrate my point, so now, let me sort that into a percentage." With a flourish, he hit enter, and adjusted the monitor. "Right. Here's the breakdown of principal gases inside the habitats, as of one hour ago."

Constituent	Percent by Volume
Nitrogen (N_2)	78.08
Oxygen (O_2)	20.95
Argon (Ar)	0.93
Neon (Ne)	0.0018
Helium (He)	0.0005

Wyatt frowned. "There's only five."

"It's the top five permanent components, yes. To be honest, I could have filtered it further, down to the top three, because beyond them, the trace gases hardly rate a mention. But look at the two major gases, nitrogen and oxygen. Both are stable—and at the same, natural levels you'd find out in the real world."

Spencer stifled a laugh. "So, you've gone to all this trouble just to tell us that everything is peachy?"

"One hour ago, everything *was* peachy," Naziem said. "But if I extrapolate the information using *current* data, we get a different result." He typed again. "This is the same breakdown, as of right now."

One specific line stood out:

```
Constituent                    Percent by Volume

Oxygen (O₂)                    23.36
```

"Oxygen levels have increased," Rebecca said.

"Exactly," Naziem said. "It's not pushing anything else down, just making the atmosphere denser and thicker. But the level is climbing."

"Is that dangerous?" Spencer asked. "Breathing that in?"

"Not in the short term," Naziem said. "We can breathe high levels of oxygen, even up to 100 percent, for hours."

"But long term, yes, it's a problem," Carlisle said. "Oversupply causes hyperoxia; it'll start with a dull headache, maybe some brain-fog. After that kicks in, you'll get some lung irritation, maybe a cough and some breathing difficulties and it'll continue until your body's so overwhelmed it can't deal with the toxicity. That's when you'll die."

"Well, that's grim," Spencer deadpanned.

"And Li did this," Wyatt said. "Or Holtorf, or whoever—but you can see it there on the log. They accessed the life support system, then the constituent mixing ratio, meaning the principal gases, and then they sent the oxygen levels soaring, which, come to think of it, probably triggered Fitzgerald's attack. You see what they're doing? It's an insurance policy. They're raising the levels in case the spiders don't get to us—they're *gassing* us to death."

"Also, grim," Spencer said.

Rebecca, biting her lip, thought about this. Li had said the habitats were essentially inhalation chambers; that in the event of an emergency, they could flood the domes with carbon dioxide. If Wyatt was right, then why not poison the air with excessive CO_2? Not only more efficient, but faster, too—hell, Holtorf could have had everyone comatose in minutes, and dead soon after. It didn't make sense.

Clearly, he had something else in mind.

"Rebecca?" Wyatt asked, trying to get her attention. "What are you thinking?"

She didn't reply, not at first, because when the penny suddenly dropped, she needed a moment.

Gases. Carbon dioxide. Oxygen.

"Rebecca?"

Still pondering, still biting her lip, Rebecca cleared her throat. "The bugs outside, they're oversized. The last time we saw arthropods that big was during the Carboniferous period, which is the comparison I drew a moment ago. Coincidentally, the Carboniferous is *also* when oxygen levels peaked."

"What? You think there's a connection?" Wyatt asked.

"Maybe," Rebecca said. "Think about it: the Carboniferous saw the emergence of immense forests, which removed huge amounts of carbon dioxide from the air—"

"Which in turn, pushed up oxygen levels to as high as 35 percent," Fitzgerald said, jumping in. "That's why the bugs grew so big—they could more easily oxygenate their blood."

Spencer clicked his fingers. "And with more oxygenated blood, activity levels increase. You think that's it? Holtorf's agitating them? Making them more active?"

"It's possible," Rebecca said. "But there's another thing peculiar to the Carboniferous period… a by-product of higher oxygen levels."

"*Flammability*," Naziem said.

Rebecca nodded. "Back then, everything was more susceptible to fire, everything burned easily, even wet vegetation. There were fires everywhere, all the time."

"Christ," Fitzgerald said slowly, an expression of realisation spreading across his face. "That's why he's here, that's why Holtorf opened the gates and is flooding the habitats with oxygen."

"He's sabotaging the project," Rebecca said, nodding. "I think Holtorf's mission is to destroy the research, the assets, the whole lot. He's going to burn it all to the ground."

33
α

Shadows crossed the threshold, one after another. Crouched, guns up, the men moved beyond the airlock and across the platform, fanning left and right.

The maintenance entry was designed for vehicular access, wide enough to accommodate a truck. No doubt when they were building this place, the construction crews had squeezed heavy equipment through here.

Davies only cared that the gate provided a suitable back door.

Thirty feet in, staring along the barrel of his suppressed MP5, he paused. It was dark inside the dome, but ultraviolet light bathed the surrounding foliage in waves of psychedelic colour. Apparently, the bugs fluoresced under UV, making them easy to locate, but he couldn't trust in that. Touching a hand to his earpiece, he spoke into his throat mic. "Hopkins, you're my eyes in here."

A voice crackled back. *"Scanner's clear. They're still in H-5."*

"And we're gonna keep it that way, yeah?" Davies replied. "Stay frosty and watch your six."

He issued further instructions and the bulk of the team slipped soundlessly deeper, forming a perimeter at the treeline. As the green beams of their laser sights bounced over the looming vegetation, seeking targets, he checked his watch. Thirty seconds. Using hand signals, he indicated this, and nodded at Reyes.

Slipping from his shoulder the canvas case containing the M112 demolition charges, Reyes dropped to his knees at the base of a huge tree. Amongst the roots, he placed several blocks of foil-wrapped C-4 and inserted a detonator.

One down, two to go…

Waving his hand—line formation, double-time—Davies urged them on.

Of course, they could have set the charges outside, could have blown the structures from out there, but the domes were like goddamned tanks; no guarantee they'd nail everything. If they'd wanted to bring them down, he reckoned they had enough composition to do it, but this was about cooking the insides. That shit had to burn hot and long, and if the domes maintained their integrity, all the better. Keep it contained.

So that meant heading inside. It also meant adding canisters of incendiary gel along the way, to ensure the spread. Holtorf dealt in absolutes—for that matter, so did he—and sure as hell they wouldn't get another crack at this before everything went south.

One hundred feet along, Reyes knelt at a similar tree, set the next assembly, and gave the thumbs up.

Ninety seconds.

"Hopkins. Sitrep."

Having inserted via a separate maintenance entry, Bravo was down in H-6, setting more charges.

No reply from Hopkins.

"Bravo. Sitrep," Davies repeated.

A voice rasped in his ear, but it wasn't Hopkins. *"You hear that?"*

Another voice. *"Hear what?"*

"Something… I don't know," Blake said. *"I swear… in the trees, on our six."*

Davies swiveled. Blake was the rear scout for *his* team.

Laser sights vaulted from tree to tree. No threats were apparent, and Davies heard nothing, either. No rustling, no movement. "Hopkins!"

Finally, a reply. *"Sarge, you're clear. They're still in H-5."*

"That's bullshit," Blake said.

"Hopkins. Confirm."

"I got 'em all on screen. There's nothing in your dome."

"I'm telling you, I heard something!" Blake insisted.

"Then you heard wrong! Nothing's gotten past us—"

The remainder of Hopkins' sentence was lost, engulfed in a rushing quake of leaves, loud and close. Behind them.

Again, Davies spun, aware the rest of his team had too, and although nothing but ghostly foliage showed through his NVGs, he guessed that something large had just leapt from one tree to the next—something *very* large. Wondering how the hell it had outflanked them, he scanned for it desperately and spoke fast into his throat mic. "Hopkins! North-eastern quadrant!"

"There's nothing there!"

Except there *was* something there, something in here with them. Davies was now certain of that, because despite an absence of further rustling, further movement, he did hear *something*; a kind of clicking sound, low and abrasive, maybe from the canopy above—

The sound stopped.

Davies' breath caught in his throat, and he held it for several beats. The hairs on the back of his neck prickled.

From the trees ahead, something watched them.

Time sped up, and voices exploded in his ear, jumbled, on edge.

"—you're goddamned missing something!"

"I'm not! I'm telling you the scanner's clear!"

When the sound came again, loud, close, it had morphed into something different, not quite a growl or a hiss, but a raspy cross between the two. Almost like a dog's bark, low and menacing.

"Fall back!" Davies ordered. Although he struggled to isolate the source, he sensed the sound was emanating from a single point directly in front of them…

In that area, in the overstorey, leaves shivered, and branches cracked, and then something moved, something immense shifting forward, towards them—

"—nothing on the FLIR!"

It won't show on thermal, Davies thought, hustling backwards. These things don't generate body heat, and they're masters of camouflage, too, meaning infrared—and night-vision—was probably just as useless. That'd explain why he couldn't see the animal now. Absently, he wondered why the thing wasn't fluorescing, or why the hell it wasn't showing on the tracker—

Davies raised his MP5, about to light up the dark, when he sensed the sudden change in air pressure, as though something had swooped close to his ear. Although it happened fast, he caught a blur of movement—an object, long and black and segmented—and his first impression was that it was an appendage of some kind, like a whipping tail, and then as it swept by, the head of the man next to him cracked open without warning, just seemed to split apart, and a fountain of warm, sticky wetness erupted out of it and splattered across Davies' face and goggles.

Shouting. And gunfire, muted by suppressors.

Davies whipped off his NVGs, and the tail-thing swooped again. Another man toppled, awkwardly, unnaturally, seemingly cut in half, because one side of him appeared to slough from the other. Not far from him a third man was already on the ground, facedown, unmoving, and beyond that man, yet another, crawling on one hand and both knees, aimless and clearly confused as to why his entrails kept slipping between his gloved fingers.

Davies fired blindly into the trees, and then the tail-thing reappeared, sweeping through the air once more, and he tracked it with his unloading MP5 and thought he might even have hit it, because there was a sound like a shell cracking, but the thing was fast and as it recoiled, disappearing back up into the trees, he caught a glimpse of a huge dark body and multiple legs, and then the thing was gone and Davies realised his point of view had shifted and now all he could see was the underside of white-glowing ferns and all he could feel, pressing against his cheek, was a sudden damp coldness.

More gunfire, and someone screaming, but distantly now, moving away.

Davies drew a ragged breath and spluttered, coughing again when he sought a second intake. An earthy smell, thick and cloying, assailed his nostrils, but that wasn't the cause of his distress. While he felt no pain—only tingling—a hollow whistling sound accompanied each breath, suggesting both his chest and lungs had been punctured.

Lifting his head, Davies gazed across the forest floor. One of his teammates was missing. Of the other four, which were close, one in particular caught his attention; not the man with the cracked skull or the soldier with the severed torso, not even Blake—who'd gathered most of his spilled intestines and shoved them back into his abdomen before dragging himself between the flared roots of a huge kapok, where he now sat ashen-faced and lifeless. No; of most interest was the other man, the one lying on his stomach, facedown and unmoving. Reyes.

The man with the C-4 remote clutched in his outstretched hand.

As darkness came creeping, Davies rolled over and started to crawl…

34
α

It didn't matter if Rebecca was right about Holtorf or not. Either way, they couldn't hang around. The maintenance shed was, on the face of it, a good place to hunker down, but according to Naziem it wasn't fire-rated. Even if it somehow did resist the flames, the smoke—trapped inside an enclosed dome with nowhere to go—would soon render the air toxic and unbreathable. On the other hand, if Rebecca was mistaken and they were simply faced with rising oxygen levels, the threat of hyperoxia loomed. Even the most defiant of them—Naziem at first, but also Fitzgerald and Carlisle—agreed that the smartest option was to stick with the original plan and get out while the assets were gathered in H-5. As it was, they had a clear run to H-4, which was more than they'd initially hoped for.

Now was the time to move—and move fast.

The men scampered to gather equipment, mainly herders and trackers from the storage room out back, but also anything else they could get their hands on. As they did, Rebecca rushed for the computer terminal. Apparently, they couldn't close any gates or open any doors from here; none of them had the appropriate clearance for that. They couldn't access the life support system either, just reports and general data—effectively read-only, like Naziem had said. Spencer had found an emergency phone, but it was dead. Unsurprisingly, Holtorf had sabotaged communications, too.

Still standing, peering at the monitor, Rebecca magnified the cluster of dots down in H-5. All the megs were there.

What the hell are they up to?

Suddenly, Carlisle appeared beside her. "I need to tell you something. It's important." She spoke low and fast and didn't wait for a response. "I wasn't going to say anything at first, not until I had time to think, anyway. You need to understand, she's never been anything but good to us. But all this talk about gates and oxygen levels and Holtorf's agenda—"

"Wait. Who are you referring to? Li?"

"I think she's part of this," Carlisle said. "I think she's working with Holtorf. That's why she went with him."

"Hold up," Rebecca said, straightening. "Went? I thought Holtorf took her against her will?"

"I'm not so sure," Carlisle replied. "Holtorf and those other men, the soldiers dressed in tactical gear… I heard them talking… or I heard Holtorf, at least… and he was speaking *Mandarin.*"

Rebecca frowned. "You speak Mandarin?"

"I'm taking a few classes at night school, I thought it'd be fun. I'm not fluent, but I know what I heard."

"What did he say?"

"It happened quickly," Carlisle said. "It was when you were unconscious and they were tying us all up and moving us into the cleanroom, and one of the men passed Holtorf a phone, likely an encrypted duty cell unless they disengaged the jammers, and then Holtorf was on the phone and it sounded like he was reporting to someone, giving a sitrep… I got the feeling he was coordinating something, and he was speaking in Mandarin."

Rebecca baulked. For sure, that was strange, but she couldn't make the connection. "What does this have to do with Li?"

"Li is Chinese-American, she speaks Mandarin."

"*So?*" Rebecca shot back, appalled at the insinuation. But before she could call out the younger woman, Carlisle, seemingly anticipating her reaction, held up a hand.

"I know, I get it," Carlisle said. "I'm not comfortable with it, either. But hear me out. If Holtorf had done his research, he would have known this, right? That Li speaks Mandarin. The thing is, why talk in another language unless you're trying to hide your conversation? And if you're trying to be secretive, why speak freely in front of someone who can understand every word? Why speak freely in front of *Li*?"

"He spoke freely in front of you."

"I wasn't meant to be on this shift," Carlisle said. "I only took it at the last minute; I'm covering for a sick colleague—which is just my goddamned luck. Point is, Holtorf would have known Li speaks Mandarin, and would have known she'd be here today. But he probably wasn't expecting me or anyone else who might understand him. But I did understand him, sort of, and one of the words he said really jarred with me, because it *wasn't* in Mandarin."

"What word?"

"*Odysseus*," Carlisle said. "I'm certain the word was Odysseus."

Rebecca tilted her head. "As in the Greek hero?"

At that moment Spencer emerged from the other room with a hard-case of equipment which he promptly dumped on the desk. "Wait, what did you just say?" Without pausing for an answer, he clicked his fingers. "That's it! Homer's Odyssey. The Trojan Horse!"

Carlisle turned to him, clearly hopeful for an ally. "Yeah, that's what I thought. Odysseus was the guy inside that big wooden horse, right?"

"One of them," Spencer said, visibly energised by the revelation. "You remember the story, yeah? How the Greeks pretended to surrender after a failed siege of Troy, staging a retreat and leaving behind a huge wooden horse, a gift, for the victorious Trojans? Falling. for the ploy, the Trojans wheeled the horse inside the gates, unaware it was hiding a force of men who, with Odysseus, ultimately sacked the city." He shook his head. "This is a classic Trojan Horse scenario."

"Holtorf," Rebecca said, blowing air through her teeth. "I thought he'd simply used the situation to his advantage, got himself a ticket inside and tagged along with the rest of us—but you're thinking he was *behind* everything, right from the start?"

"That's how you sneak into a top-secret military installation," Spencer said, nodding. "Trick your opponent into rolling out the red carpet. Hell, I bet 'Odysseus' was Holtorf's goddamned codename or something. The fact he even *said* that word suggests the smug bastard was toying with us all along. I bet he's still laughing."

It seemed plausible enough, the theory gelling with many of the conclusions Rebecca had already drawn. But if it were true, if Egbert's transfer, the cover story, the whole thing was just a ruse created by Holtorf, then the implications were significant. She blinked, realising Spencer was now talking to Wyatt, who, like his brother, had entered the room cradling a case of his own.

"And once inside," Spencer explained, "Holtorf's team hacks into the system, gains control of the security cameras, alarms, communications—"

"And opens the gates to a larger force waiting outside, hiding in the desert beyond the fences. Just like Odysseus," Wyatt said, nodding. "It makes sense. But Holtorf must have had inside help—the asset transfer, the research team, the cover story; none of that would have worked without authorisation."

"*That's* what I'm talking about," Carlisle said. "Li."

Rebecca's gut squirmed uncomfortably. "No, not Li," she said in a low voice. "Frank was the project leader, he authorised everything."

"You think Hayward's a *traitor*?" Wyatt asked.

Rebecca shook her head. "No. Frank wouldn't have helped willingly. Holtorf's people must have had something over him, must have somehow forced his hand; I don't know… maybe they took his family hostage, then made him seize my research as a ploy to get me and Egbert and the rest of us in here—"

"Along with Holtorf, hidden in plain sight," Spencer said.

Succumbing finally to the case's heavy bulk, Wyatt eased past his brother to place it on the desk, stacking it on top of the first. "I still think it makes sense, but it's kind of elaborate. If they got to Hayward, why not simply take his prox-card and sneak in?"

"Too many guards and fences and cameras," Spencer said, "and just a single, secure entry above ground."

Rebecca agreed. "There's no way Holtorf could have gotten inside without a cover story—without Egbert." She turned to Carlisle. "Holtorf had inside help, yes, but from Frank. Li isn't involved."

Carlisle shook her head. "Then how do you explain this morning? She opened multiple gates, remember? That's not standard protocol. Why did she do that? And then she gives half the team an early mark, gets them out of here. Convenient, yeah? But hell, even if I'm wrong about her, there's a bigger question. Why was Holtorf speaking in *Mandarin*?"

Spencer shrugged. "Because the person on the other end of the phone couldn't speak English."

He was stating the obvious, but at the same time alluding to something else: that Holtorf wasn't trying to hide the conversation at all.

"What, you're suggesting Holtorf's working for the *Chinese*?" Naziem asked as he and Fitzgerald joined the group, drawing up behind Wyatt.

"I'm not suggesting anything," Spencer said. "But hell, why not? Maybe they have an interest in what's going on here; you know, industrial or economic espionage, or maybe they're angling for some strategic advantage. If so, maybe Holtorf is their man—if he's CIA, he'd have international connections. I mean, the whole thing's not as farfetched as it sounds; we live in an era of military ambiguity—you've probably heard all the buzzwords, right? Hybrid, non-linear warfare? The grey zone? These days it's all about irregular, unconventional, unattributed forces."

"You mean proxy forces," Fitzgerald said. "Private military contractors, military 'advisors.'"

"Exactly," Spencer said. "Irregular forces have been used increasingly in regional conflicts all around the world: Syria, Ukraine, the Baltics, Venezuela. Lots of places, all led by Russia, China, Iran—and hell, us, too. It's a thing."

Always eager to support his brother, Wyatt nodded. "The use of regular forces is risky; it's clear who's involved, who's behind the action. But unattributable forces, that's different, because you can seed enough doubt for plausible deniability—you can disconnect the state from the action."

"Precisely," Spencer said. He turned back to Naziem. "So, yeah, why not? Maybe Holtorf's a private military contractor—and maybe he's working for the Chinese."

Rebecca shook her head. "Or by that reasoning, working for someone who wants to *frame* the Chinese, make it look like them."

"Equally possible," Spencer conceded. "I'm not suggesting the Chinese are involved; I'm just throwing out scenarios. But you know, that said, I read a report suggesting there are tens of thousands of Chinese spies here, and they say most of them aren't even of Chinese descent, they're actually Westerners—"

"They? Who are *they*?"

"It was a report, I'm just saying—"

Rebecca shook her head. "This is fake news. Mass paranoia at its finest. Just another urban myth."

"Spencer is an urban myth afficionado," Wyatt said.

"Yeah, I am," Spencer agreed. "Myths, legends… let me tell you about Sasquatch sometime, it'll blow your mind."

"It's too unlikely," Rebecca said.

"Sasquatch? She's real!"

"No, that the Chinese are behind this. It's crazy; entirely improbable."

"*Implausible*, you mean?" Spencer said. "That's my point! You said yourself that Holtorf's here to sabotage the project, and obviously someone's behind that, someone with knowledge and resources and who clearly wants to remain anonymous. So, whoever that is, they engage an unattributable proxy force to destroy the research—or steal it, or both; you know, some sort of economic espionage—before covering their tracks and disappearing, and the whole scenario is so audacious, so improbable, that the state has maximum plausible deniability."

"It might not be a state," Naziem said. "It could be a private organisation, a terrorist cell… it could be anything."

"Which is why we shouldn't jump to conclusions about who's behind this," Rebecca said, readying to move. "Including Li."

Throwing her hands in the air, Carlisle rolled her eyes. "They were speaking Mandarin! And I'm telling you, Hayward's their patsy."

Rebecca was desperate to leave, but that last comment hit home. Right now, she didn't care who Holtorf was working for, but the suggestion that those responsible for the incursion had actively set up Frank to take the fall for this made her feel sick to her stomach.

"And with their patsy in place," Carlisle said, perhaps sensing a chink in Rebecca's armour and aiming for it, "they pretend to nab Hayward's second in charge—someone who just happens to be of Chinese descent, who just happens to speak Mandarin, and who just happened to open the habitats against protocol and send the bulk of her staff home early." She paused, giving her argument a moment to sink in. "It's a little coincidental, wouldn't you say?"

Rebecca's head swam, and she shook it until it had cleared, even if only partly. "I find it less coincidental than racist, and you should be ashamed of yourself for suggesting it. We need to move."

Carlisle looked surprised and more than a little wounded, and this was reflected in the aggrieved tone of her voice. "Holtorf's American. He's a bad guy. Li's American, and she's a bad guy, too. Race is irrelevant. I'm telling you… it *fits*."

"It fits because you want it to," Naziem said, joining Rebecca in rifling through the hardcases.

Fitzgerald nodded, and said quietly to Carlisle, "The whole Mandarin thing, it's a red herring, just another layer to Holtorf's plan. He's seeding doubt. I mean, think about it: Holtorf mightn't have known about you, but *Li* did. She knew you were taking night classes; hell, I've seen the two of you practice together over lunch. If Li's in on this, she would have warned Holtorf from the beginning." Gently, he placed a hand on Carlisle's shoulder. "She's innocent. She's one of us, she's a colleague."

"Colleague, yes. But I'm telling you, something isn't right."

"Give it a rest, Carlisle," Naziem said. "Please—"

As the words left his mouth, a deep, ground-shaking rumble rose in the distance, swelling before peeling away like rolling thunder.

"What the hell?" Wyatt said. He turned to Fitzgerald. "A storm? I thought you couldn't replicate storms?"

"We can't," Fitzgerald deadpanned.

Rebecca rushed to the door and flung it open. Underfoot, the ground shuddered as though gripped by a mild earthquake, an aftershock, but then the tremor dissipated, and the thunder waned, too, before a new sound arose, a dull roar more akin to distant, crashing surf. As she peered into the darkened jungle, off to the east where the sound seemed to be emanating, an orange glow appeared, bleeding through the canopy. At first, it was dull and faint, yet incrementally it grew, looking like a fast-moving sunrise.

Her heart skipped a beat.

Oh no...

Of course, in here, deep underground, there was no sun.

This was the glow of fire.

35
α

More popping sounds, like suppressed gunfire.

Owen's mind raced. *We're under attack…*

"Stay here," Belding barked, bolting urgently from the room with the young soldier in tow.

It wasn't clear to Owen if Belding had spoken to all of them or just him and Jessy, but either way, Mbye and Perez also took off, hot on Belding's heels.

Jumping to his feet, Owen turned to Jessy. "You're coming, right?" The last time he'd delayed an escape, back when he and Sanchez had been captured by the Yuguruppu, he'd very nearly paid with his life. He wasn't about to repeat the error.

"Hell yeah," Jessy said as more rounds of muted gunfire reverberated outside.

Grabbing their masks from the table, the two of them made for the exit, the one taken by the others.

Just shy of the door, Jessy stopped and reconsidered. "No… this way." She pulled him to a side exit.

"Good idea," Owen said. There was no way to be certain what was going on out there, other than some sort of gun battle. How many assailants there were or how close they might be was a mystery. At the main exit, a hail of bullets might be waiting.

Unzipping the side-door quickly but silently, he and Jessy slipped from the shelter and back into the cavern. They were now behind the structure, which was mostly dark and shadowy, but a system of lights, including those surrounding the Vent, threw random illumination overhead. To Owen's surprise, the cave wall he'd expected to find was missing. In its place was a narrow riverbank which ran the length of the shelter and beyond, disappearing into yawning gloom. Extending from the edge of the bank and deeper into the cave was a broad expanse of still, black water, fed by the waterfall over which he'd earlier assumed the Sombra had tumbled.

Less gunfire now, and more shouting.

Sticking to the shadows, Owen and Jessy crept down the side of the shelter, along the riverbank. Jessy hobbled on her moon-booted leg but kept up. Gravel crunched softly underfoot.

Ahead, a long gangway, more like a wooden jetty, extended across the water, culminating in a large square deck loaded with several shipping containers. The area was partially lit, but for the most part deep, coiling shadows had taken residence.

At the end of the shelter, Owen drew to a halt and stole a peek around the corner.

Mbye and Perez were nowhere to be seen. What he did see was a group of four men standing several yards away with their backs to him. The men were dressed not in hazmat suits, but in black wetsuits with scuba gear and masks and night-vision goggles. In their gloved hands were grasped modern-looking automatic weapons. Obviously, the men were part of an unfriendly military unit that had inserted via the river, quietly and undetected. Owen got the feeling they'd neutralized several soldiers and scientists in full stealth before launching a more direct assault. He couldn't be certain of the size of the force but sensed more of them at the Vent.

Not good.

They had Belding. He wasn't complying. He was standing defiantly, resisting them—

One of the frogmen pulled his sidearm and put a round into Belding's head. A red mist puffed outwards, and Belding crumpled to the ground.

Oh my God…

"We've gotta get out of here," Owen whispered to Jessy, ducking back as bile rose in his throat. "*Now.*"

Jessy mumbled something, but he missed it. She sounded afraid.

Owen frantically searched for options. They couldn't head back up to the cavern above because the path was too well lit, and they'd be in full view of the frogmen. And anyway, it was likely they'd already closed off that exit in anticipation of reinforcements from above. He looked to the dock. Several vessels were moored there, including rigid-hull inflatable Zodiacs, and what looked like a shallow-draft barge.

They must ferry supplies and equipment via the river, Owen thought. The Vent was deep underground, no doubt it was easier to transport everything by the Sombra, which could accommodate large machinery. It made sense—the rock tunnel was too narrow for large vehicles and drilling it wider would be expensive and time consuming. But if the river was being used as a highway, then clearly it led to the surface. Which meant it was their ticket out of here.

"This way," Owen whispered, heading for the dock.

"What about the others?" Jessy asked. "Mbye and Perez… and everyone else?"

They're already dead, Owen thought, but he kept his fears to himself. He stopped and turned. "There's no way we can fight these guys. What we *can* do is raise the alarm and send for help."

Jessy looked back. "Who the hell are these people, Owen? And why are they doing this?"

"I don't know. Come on."

Taking Jessy's hand, Owen kept to the shadows and crept along the curving beach, beelining not only for the dock, but the nearest and fastest boat tied up there—a Zodiac Hurricane with a centre console and twin outboard motors.

They made it to the jetty unseen. Stairs led up to the dock.

We might just get away with this, Owen thought, climbing them and moving swiftly for the Hurricane.

They were nearly there when a spray of high velocity rounds zipped their way, sparking off the shipping containers and splintering the timber at their feet.

36
α

A low groan rumbled overhead, sounding like the precursor to an earthquake. It was an apt comparison, because a moment later, the walls shook, and motes of dust dislodged and rained from the rock-hewn ceiling. Standing at the edge of the dark, underground cavern, Charles L. Holtorf glanced upwards and spoke into his throat mic. "Davies? Report."

Cold silence.

"That was an explosion," Boor said in a thick Dutch accent. Forsaking the hand-truck and its load of crates, Holtorf's white-haired second-in-command paused in the middle of the chamber to check his watch. "Something's wrong. They set it off early."

Before Holtorf could respond, a burst of static erupted in his ear, followed by a flood of words. Holtorf recognised the voice. "Hopkins… say again?"

A stuttered reply; fragmented, unclear. Down here, under layers of rock and close to the anomaly, communication was problematic. Regardless, Holtorf gleaned enough and issued instructions. Receiving an immediate response, he terminated the conversation, not caring to delve deeper into what had happened up there, or why, or even how. It didn't matter. His job, now, was to deal with the repercussions.

"Major?"

Holtorf turned to Boor, who stood awaiting orders. "Davies is dead. Bravo's on clean-up. Once they're finished, they'll meet us as at the rendezvous." He gestured deeper into the cavern, past the blood-spattered walls and bullet-ravaged bodies of the security team and the lab-coated scientists, to the object pulsing and shuddering in the darkness not thirty feet away. "We need that thing loaded, and *fast*. We're about to have company."

Boor nodded and dashed into the chamber, barking orders to the rest of the team.

As he went, Holtorf checked his G-Shock and set the timer. Boor was right. The detonation was ahead of time.

And now, the clock was ticking.

37
α

Rebecca turned from the jungle and its distant orange dawn, slamming shut the door and dashing across the room. "We're in trouble."

"Situation normal," Spencer said, hinting at the military acronym.

Naziem was already at the computer terminal and bashing at the keyboard. "SNAFU is understating it. We've got fires in H-3, two, by the looks. And spreading."

"You were right," Wyatt said to Rebecca. "Holtorf's plan is in motion."

"Gather the equipment," Rebecca said to him, then ducked behind Naziem to look over his shoulder. "What about the sprinkler system?"

"Fire sprinklers are disabled," Naziem said. He was sweating. "I'd turn on the irrigation system, make it rain, but—" He hesitated, typing furiously. "Nothing's responding. I can't get in. You ask me, the system's corrupted… like it's been hit with a virus or something."

"Another trojan," Spencer said, clicking his fingers. "I bet Holtorf's uploaded a virus… it's like that cyberattack years ago at the Iranian nuclear facility. He's throwing everything into chaos, maximising the damage."

"It looks that way," Naziem said, speaking fast as he continued to thrash at the keyboard. "But… check this out." He jabbed a finger at the screen. "ATC-B, same habitat. It's *open*."

Carlisle's face screwed up. "Open?"

"It wasn't before," Naziem said, still pointing. He spun to Rebecca. "Half the habitats—including H-3—have these entries which were used in the initial construction phase. Now they double for maintenance access, and Asset Transfer and Control." He looked back at the screen. "But surely there's not a control team in H-3…"

"You think they're looking for us?" Fitzgerald asked.

Rebecca shook her head. "No… that entry, that's how Holtorf got inside. Him, or his men, so they could start those fires."

"But why haven't they closed it?"

"Who cares?" Carlisle said, back to her usual, brusque manner. "It's open, so the plan's changed, right? That entry isn't far; maybe a few hundred feet at most. That's our exit."

"That's where the fire is," Fitzgerald said.

"And *here* is where it's headed," Carlisle said.

Naziem nodded and stood. "She's right. If that fire gets through the gate and into this habitat, we'll be cut off for g—"

A low rumble reverberated through the shed walls, causing them to shudder. It was the same sound as before but not quite as loud. Underfoot, the ground thrummed.

Still standing, but with a hand on the desk for balance, Naziem turned to the monitor. "No way… we've got another fire… this one's in H-6."

Fitzgerald blanched. "They're setting off *detonations*…"

"And there could be more to come," Rebecca said. "We've gotta hustle."

Urgently, the group dragged the last of the equipment from the hardcases the brothers had earlier placed on the desk.

Passing out flashlights and two-way radios, Rebecca bounded for the exit with Wyatt and Spencer in tow. Wyatt had armed himself with an ultrasonic prod—the device looked like a cross between a shotgun microphone and a cattle prod; effectively a two-foot-long wand with a trigger grip at one end and a unidirectional, grilled head at the other. No doubt it was designed to emit a high-intensity ultrasonic blast, inaudible to humans but distressing for arthropods. If it worked as well as the X40s they'd used down in Brazil, it could prove a handy acquisition. Still at the desk, Carlisle grabbed another of these, as well as a rectangular, metallic box with a curved handle on top. Clearly, the box was an ultrasonic repeller, too, likely one of the portable herders they'd talked about earlier. Looking more like a standard X40, the device probably emitted a sustained, omnidirectional soundwave, unlike the powerful, one-off burst no doubt delivered by the prods.

From a different crate, Naziem seized a tablet with which they could track the assets. He and Carlisle ran for the door.

Fitzgerald was the last to move. Looking confused, he spun about.

Spencer, who carried nothing but a flashlight and his sharp-edged stone, wrinkled his face into a frown. "What's the hold up?"

Apologising, Fitzgerald moved to join them, then paused as though struck by an idea. Turning back, he lifted a fire extinguisher from the wall near the desk.

"Seriously?" Carlisle whined, brandishing her prod impatiently.

Fitzgerald shrugged. "You never know."

Rebecca flung open the door and the group charged into the darkness.

38
α

Owen ducked, startled by a sharp zipping sound—and, even more concerning, a sudden change in air pressure—as a bullet sizzled past his ear.

That was close.

"Get in!" Jessy cried, releasing the Hurricane's dock line and leaping aboard the sleek, black vessel.

Hot on her heels, bullets chomping at the jetty behind him, Owen soared high and landed heavily, almost slipping over. As Jessy made for the stand-up console, the Zodiac rocking underfoot, he called out to her. "So… you know how to drive this thing?"

Wasting no time, Jessy engaged the ignition, gunning the twin motors and pulling from the dock in a fast, sweeping U-turn that kicked up a high wall of spray behind them.

"I guess that answers my question!" Owen said, nearly swept from his feet by the wild maneuver. As they sped into the darkness, he threw a hurried glance backwards. A succession of rounds ricocheted off the dock's metal railings in a shower of sparks.

Then he and Jessy were gone, zooming out of range.

Owen exhaled.

Way too close.

"No time to relax! They won't be far behind!" Jessy called back to him. As she spoke, she flicked a switch and the Hurricane's powerful spotlights sprang to life, searing across the Sombra's black, mirrorlike surface. "Owen… see if this thing is hiding any weapons!"

A brief search of the stern boxes revealed nothing of the sort, only flares and chemlights. Owen spun, glancing desperately about. Wind buffeted him. On both sides, the cavern walls sped by; hazy, indistinct. The ceiling, while shadowed and unseen, felt close and somehow too low; he sensed a mountain of rock up there, hanging over his head.

Almost immediately, as expected, the roar of multiple outboard motors rushed up at them from behind and at least three spotlights appeared, reflecting off the water and carving a path through the gloom.

"They're coming!" Owen said.

Jessy gunned it, and the Hurricane responded in kind. Although the rigid-hull inflatable had been the largest of the Zodiacs moored at the dock, it was packed with horsepower and undeniably fast. Owen hoped that if nothing else, it was faster than its pursuers.

Ahead, bathed in light, the cavern walls narrowed, then suddenly blended into a single, solid mass.

A dead end.

"There!" Owen called, pointing to the right, and a vertical, jagged shadow that suggested an opening in the rockface. He needn't have said anything; Jessy was already aiming for it.

The noise from behind swelled. The three boats looked to be gaining. Owen anxiously turned from them, back to the approaching crevice, hoping desperately that this was, in fact, the way out. If it wasn't and they hit a blockage at this speed…

The Hurricane hurtled into the cleft. The walls blurred, so close they seemed within touching distance. In the tight space, the motor-roar was deafening.

Thankfully, the tunnel was open-ended.

Riding high, the Zodiac shot through the opening and out the other side, bursting into another wide section of river.

Jessy didn't slow. She couldn't, because behind them, the noise of their pursuers intensified, sounding like thunder from an approaching storm. Owen looked back. For an instant, light bloomed inside the fissure, then blasted outwards as the smaller boats were disgorged. The sight caused his breath to catch sharply in his throat; suddenly, the distance between the two groups was alarmingly narrow. Feeling trapped, Owen baulked, wondering how he and Jessy had found themselves in such a predicament, and with that thought rode a hot flush of anger. Why were these people after them? The answer, of course, was irrelevant. These assholes had killed Belding, and probably others, too; clearly, they weren't taking prisoners. Right now, that's all he needed to know.

From behind, flashes of light erupted out of the dark, and sharp zipping sounds cut through the air like a swarm of angry insects. On both sides of the Hurricane, a thunderstorm of rounds sliced into the water.

He and Jessy were back in range.

Not good…

At the console, Jessy hunkered down, minimising her profile. Owen, looking back, did the same. As the smaller boats cut back and forth, changing formation, he saw detail in the diffused light, and swallowed hard. Having spent months traversing remote jungle rivers, and a lifetime surfing at home and abroad, he knew watercraft. The three boats on their tail were CRRCs, or Combat Rubber Raiding Craft. Military vessels. Much lighter and more agile than the craft they pursued.

"They're gaining!" he said.

"Tell me something I don't know!" Jessy called back.

More rounds zipped past them. Jessy zigzagged, trying to confuse their pursuers, throw them off their aim. It worked, but it was only a stopgap. The Hurricane was nimble, but it couldn't keep the smaller craft at bay forever. They needed a plan, and fast.

"We gotta lose them! Maybe—"

Jessy yanked down on the wheel, catching him by surprise and nearly costing him his footing.

Their pursuers, equally surprised, took a moment to react, and lost ground as the Hurricane spun in a tight arc—like before, almost a U-turn. Water sprayed high. Pulling sharply out of the turn, Jessy rocketed away on a new course. Owen saw what she was aiming for.

Ahead, the river split, forking around a rocky outcrop. On closer inspection, there appeared to be multiple exits out of here—not just in the direction they had previously been heading, but on all sides. As they zoomed closer to the outcrop, Owen saw more detail, and felt a stab of concern. A line of jagged rocks, like pointed fangs, hung from the ceiling. Below them, an inverted row jutted from the river. Together, the formation resembled a tooth-filled maw.

Jessy headed straight for it.

It looked to be a tight fit.

It *was* a tight fit.

"Jessy?" Owen yelled.

More rounds zipped by. A couple sparked off the Hurricane's overhead rail.

Jessy accelerated, still weaving. Clearly, she intended losing the CRRCs amongst the treacherous outcropping.

"Jess, not a good idea!"

Another storm of bullets. Some peppered the Hurricane, others zinged past, impacting with the jagged teeth and sending powdery shards flying in all directions.

"Jess!"

She wasn't listening. Owen threw himself onto the floor, almost flat on his belly, and covered his head with his arms. The outcrop was most likely a cave-in, maybe hundreds or thousands of years old, the stone having sheared from the ceiling to form the sharp peaks below.

As the Hurricane flew amongst them, those peaks whizzed by.

But not all of them.

With a metallic scream, the roof above the centre console abruptly vanished, ripped free by one of the overhead fangs and hurtling past Owen's head to crash into the water behind. At the same time, the Hurricane collided hard with one of the lower teeth, jolting heavily to the side, and with it came an instantaneous, deafening bang, a puncture sound, which may have been a hull breach—

Blackness. Sudden and total.

Jessy had killed the lights.

Oh my God...

Smaller and nimbler, the CRRCs could have sliced through the gap. But for whatever reason, be it the sight of the Hurricane impacting with the rocks and vanishing into blackness, or simply a deliberate flanking maneuver, they pulled out. One of them diverted left, around the outcropping, the other two went right. Perhaps realising the formation wasn't surrounded by water—that behind the toothy mouth was a long throat that extended deeper into the rock and that there was no other way in—they doubled back.

But they'd lost crucial time.

The CRRCs shot inside the formation, tracking the path already carved by the Hurricane. They caught up to the vessel at the far end of the dark passage, in the exact place it had slammed into the cavern wall at high speed.

The place where it now lay broken and sinking.

39

α

Already, the smell of smoke was distinct, but not overpowering. Not yet, anyway. The domes were at least 200 feet high, and whatever fumes had travelled this way from H-3 were for the most part drifting towards the ceiling. But the presence of haze, even unseen, suggested that H-3 might already be engulfed, the air already unbreathable. The thought of what lay ahead, of what they were now hastening towards, terrified Rebecca.

The jungle was strangely silent. To the east, where Gate B and the entrance to H-3 lay currently concealed, the orange bloom had intensified, hemorrhaging through the glowing foliage.

Immediately ahead, just a few yards away, lay another steel-mesh walkway. The path cut through the vegetation on a direct line to the gate.

Their route, at least, was clear.

"Come on!" Rebecca urged, hitting the path at a fast jog.

The others followed, and under the boots of six people, the grating clanged loudly. No time for stealth, not anymore. Rebecca thought about the megs and wondered if the noise of their passage would attract attention.

It will, but it doesn't matter. The flames are going to drive things this way, regardless.

Not good.

She turned to Naziem. The group was aligned single file, and he was in the middle, behind the brothers. "The scanner… is it working?"

"We're online," Naziem called up to her, holding the tablet in front of him as he ran. He reverse-pinched the screen. "Just so you know, it's proximity-based—the ping rate will increase the closer they are to us, like an electromagnetic parking sensor on your car. Right now, I can see the assets… they've scattered, but I can get a lock on most of them… looks like some are still in H-5."

Some?

"What about that centipede-thing?" Spencer asked.

Naziem shrugged and called up to him. "You tell me. As far as I know those bugs aren't tagged, or if they are, their signatures are restricted. We can't track them."

"Who cares?" Carlisle blurted from behind Naziem. "The herder is on. That should keep everything away."

Rebecca wasn't worried about insectivorous millipedes or giant cockroaches, but she did wonder if anything else had escaped.

Keep moving.

She quickened the pace, glad for the ultrasonic device and the minor comfort it afforded.

The gate was close. Rebecca could tell, because suddenly the smoke thickened, strangling the light ahead. Already stinging, her eyes started to water.

She heard a wheezing sound and turned.

Fitzgerald. He'd lagged several yards behind Carlisle and had now drawn to a halt. Coughing, struggling to draw breath, he thumped a fist against his chest, overwhelmed as much by the brisk tempo of their march as the poor quality of the air.

"You okay?" Rebecca called down the line, concerned she'd pushed him too far. She started back towards him, but Carlisle and Spencer beat her there.

"Here, let me take that for you," Spencer offered, relieving the larger man of the fire extinguisher.

Fitzgerald thanked him, hacked again, and waved the rest of them away. "We gotta move… I'm good."

He didn't sound good, but he was right—they had to go. As Fitzgerald stubbornly pushed forward, the group went with him. This was literally a race for their lives…

More smoke, darker and thicker now. Like a shadowy apparition, it slid through the trees, its creeping tendrils searching. Rebecca's eyes wept painfully, and her vision blurred. Now she, too, struggled to breathe. Coughing, she pulled her shirt up over her nose and mouth. She was at the front again, trying to force the pace.

Maybe forty feet ahead, obscured by foliage but still cutting through the haze, a bright light bloomed, the epicentre of the orange glow she'd seen from the maintenance shed. Rebecca felt a strange mix of hope and trepidation. This had to be the gate. Beyond that was H-3, and then a short dash to the exit. But as she burst from the underbrush and stole her first unobstructed view of the opening, her anxiety skyrocketed.

Oh my God…

It looked like the entrance to Hell.

The fire hadn't yet crossed into this habitat, but tongues of flame licked hungrily at the exit, shimmering in orange and yellow and white. Inside the adjoining habitat, the blaze was in full flight.

Forced to a halt, Rebecca glanced over her shoulder, her gaze met with ashen faces and fearful eyes. No words were said, but a conversation passed.

Turning forward again, Rebecca eyed the gate. The mouth of the dragon yawned back, wide and menacing, ready to unleash its deadly breath.

It took every ounce of her courage to face it down, but with the support of her companions, Rebecca steeled herself… and charged towards it.

40

α

There was a gap, just beyond the gate. Just enough to squeeze through. Rebecca aimed for it.

A wall of heat rushed at her, searing, like a furnace, singing the hairs on her arms and battering her face with real force. Light flared, blinding her.

Burying her eyes in the crook of her elbow, Rebecca plunged for the gap, hoping she'd lined it up right, that her aim was true.

It was. She was through, they all were—inside H-3…

She stole a glance. Ahead, a mountain of white-orange reared, looming several stories high. Within its belly, dark shapes shrivelled and died, silhouettes of trees and vines and broad-leafed shrubs.

Keep pushing.

Which way?

Rebecca hesitated, her eyes weeping and straining through the heat and smoke. Though they seemed to be surrounded, the more she looked, the more she realised there were in fact gaps, openings all around her, places where the flames hadn't quite reached because even in the face of higher oxygen levels, the vegetation was too green and moist.

There was still a chance…

"This way!" Carlisle yelled, coughing and spluttering. The younger woman ran for one of these openings, leading them north through raining embers, her eyes wide, her nose and mouth concealed in her tee-shirt.

Tightly bunched, the group swept forward. Fitzgerald tripped and fell. Rebecca helped him to his feet. On the way up, he said something to her, little more than a murmur, and as she turned her ear to catch it she thought she heard something else, an alarm, way off in the distance, but clearly it was her imagination because over the roar of the flames and the crackle and pop of vegetation she could barely hear anything—

To the left, another breach in the flames, narrow, but big enough. As the group approached, sparks billowed, hot and glowing, warning them to turn back. Taking no heed, the group rushed through.

Rebecca's heart thumped harder and faster, working overtime. It was almost impossible to draw a clean breath now, the air thick and poisonous and choking. She grew dizzy, and oddly detached, confused as to why her legs now seemed to be slowing, resisting her, but she bent them to her will and kept them pumping because her instinct for survival was strong. She sensed it was the same for her companions, too, and though it wasn't clear how long they ran like this, pushing themselves beyond their limits, they eventually caught a break. Shimmering through a haze of heat and light and beyond the questing tendrils of smoke and flame, the exit appeared.

Rebecca felt a surge of adrenalin. It raced through her veins, shocking her, jolting her back and clearing her mind.

Move!

She ran faster.

Like the previous two gates, the opening was wide, big enough for a truck, and this was certain because parked within it, facing into the habitat, was a large black vehicle, an armoured personnel carrier of some kind.

Absently, Rebecca thought that this was most likely an ATC vehicle—Asset Transfer and Control, like Naziem had said—and while at first it seemed out of place, she got the feeling it was always parked here, ready to go. Still, she couldn't dismiss the possibility that Holtorf or his men had driven it here, the soldiers who were now conspicuously absent, and she felt a spike of alarm, fearful of an impending ambush. Thankfully, this never eventuated, and before she knew it, she was alongside the vehicle, running the length of its solid steel flanks. The others came with her, pounding through behind, and then she was past it, bursting into a large, open space filled with air; fresh, glorious, clean air, and as it whooshed into her lungs, filling every part of her, Rebecca drew to a halt and realised she'd in fact exited the habitat and was now standing on the outside of the plexiglass dome, back in the huge subterranean cavern…

41
α

She was right, after all. There were alarms.

Alarms are good. Help is coming...

Rebecca collapsed.

Rolling onto her back, coughing and spluttering and straining for air, she tried to clear her lungs. She heard the others doing the same, although some of them made different sounds—retching, vomiting sounds.

You need to get up.

She did. Sitting, still purging, she wiped her eyes, firstly with the back of her hand, then her palms. It was dimly lit in here, but above the maintenance entry amber warning lights flashed and rotated and she could see well enough. Across the polished concrete floor, on all sides, multiple pallets were stacked high with polycarbonate crates. This was a storage area, a warehouse. Its extremities were cloaked in shadow.

An orange glow began to drift from the maintenance entry, and with it, wisps of smoke, seeping towards her from both sides of the personnel carrier. The doors—there were inner and outer vacuum-sealed roller-shutters, one in front of the vehicle and one behind in the manner of an airlock—were still open. She wondered why these hadn't slammed shut when the alarms had triggered. Same with the gates between each habitat. She guessed that multiple systems had been compromised, not just the fire sprinklers, but the entire fire alarm system, and probably more. If Holtorf had indeed uploaded a virus, then it was likely nothing would operate as intended or expected.

He's causing chaos and confusion. It's all part of the plan. That's how you mask your escape.

As she considered this, Rebecca saw the smoke start to darken and clot; before long, the warehouse would be overwhelmed.

No time to waste.

Still coughing, wishing she had water to soothe her stinging throat but now with more pressing matters to deal with, Rebecca dragged herself to her feet and spun about. The others, seemingly unaware of the encroaching smoke, were variously sitting or lying as they recovered. Collectively, they appeared okay; singed and sooty and generally banged up, but superficially. No doubt they needed medical attention, especially for smoke inhalation, but right now she couldn't help with that.

Scrambling towards the formidable black form of the ATC vehicle, Rebecca called back over her shoulder. "The smoke is getting thicker… you need to get out of here, all of you. Get somewhere safe and hunker down. Help is coming."

"Wait!" It was Wyatt, spluttering as he dragged himself to his feet. "Where are you going?"

At the vehicle's door, Rebecca paused. "Frank is in there." With that, she grasped the handrail and hauled herself into the driver's seat.

The personnel carrier was heavily armoured; it might be flame resistant, too.

As she moved to close the door, a hand caught her wrist.

"Bec… no. He's gone," Wyatt said. He'd leapt up behind her, onto the step board, his eyes moist and red-rimmed. "No-one can survive that. *You* can't survive that. Going back in… it's suicide."

"Just get somewhere safe," Rebecca said, easing from his grip and nodding towards the opening. "The roller-shutters are equipped with a manual crank handle. When I'm through, seal the exit."

Wyatt could have tried harder to stop her, to change her mind, but he didn't. Instead, he simply shook his head and ran his gaze over the vehicle's interior. "Can you even *drive* this thing?"

The carrier—somewhere between a ridiculously oversized, six-wheeled SUV and an armoured truck—was big and daunting, no doubt about it. Rebecca glanced at the dashboard and its myriad of gauges, unsure if she could drive it or not—to be honest, she hadn't thought that far ahead.

Blowing air through his teeth, Wyatt cleared his throat. "This is a BAE Caiman MRAP variant, repurposed and customised, by the looks. Ballistically tolerant medium tactical vehicle, nearly twenty tons. Run-flat tyres. Ten-crew capacity. I can drive it."

"You can?"

He shrugged. "Well… it's just a big truck, right? Fully automatic transmission… how hard can it be?" He looked at her sheepishly. "Point is, you can't go by yourself."

"No, she can't, and neither can you." It was Spencer. He stood below and behind his brother, on the ground in front of a row of open lockers lining the airlock's interior. From one of them, he'd retrieved a yellow polymer hazmat suit with a full-face mask and self-contained breathing apparatus, which he held aloft. In his other hand was a compressed air tank. He grinned up at them. "You always need a Plan B, right?"

Unable to refrain, Rebecca returned the grin with a smile of her own.

42

α

The other lockers held more suits. Rebecca and the brothers dressed fast, slipping the garments over their regular clothes.

The suits themselves were of limited value, but the masks would protect them from the heat and smoke. A continuous supply of compressed air would be useful, too.

Moving swiftly, Rebecca hoisted a cylinder for herself and procured several spares. Carlisle gave her a hand. Together, they loaded the extra tanks and suits in the rear crew compartment. A moment ago—while quickly rehydrating with bottled water, also from the lockers—the two women had agreed the lab-techs should remain here for when help arrived. In the meantime, Naziem could focus on the sprinklers, maybe get them back online.

With the equipment stowed, Rebecca headed up front. Carlisle had already briefed them. Apparently, the nest was small. If they stayed parallel to the path, they'd hit Gate C in short time. Straight again, and they'd hit the feeding grounds—which was where the megs nested, and where Rebecca believed Frank had been taken.

She could only hope he was still alive. The chances were slim, she knew that. But she had to try.

As Rebecca climbed onto the step board, Naziem passed her a pair of night-vision goggles; again, also salvaged from the lockers. "Here. These won't fit inside your mask, but they're Gen-3, which means they're equipped with thermal technology. If the fire hasn't spread into H-4, use them. They'll penetrate everything—smoke, trees, even silk." His eyes glistened sadly. "If the professor's there, if he's okay, there'll be a heat signature. You'll see him." Finally, he passed her the tablet. "Good luck."

Thanking him, Rebecca slid into the passenger seat. Wyatt, facemask on, was already at the wheel. Now that she had the goggles and the tablet, riding shotgun made even more sense.

As Spencer strapped himself into one of the rear jump seats, Wyatt gunned the engine and the Caiman growled throatily. The keys had been in the ignition, maybe where they were always kept, or maybe left there by Holtorf or his men—she was certain they'd been here.

Were they still inside the habitat?

"Ready?" Wyatt asked.

"Wait!" Carlisle leapt onto the step board. Through the window, she handed Rebecca the ultrasonic herder.

Rebecca placed it in her lap next to the tablet, then fitted her mask. "Remember, be careful with the radio. I get the feeling Holtorf is still out there. He might be listening."

"For now, we'll stay silent and monitor the emergency channel," Carlisle said. "No need to break cover over an open line." With that, she jumped clear, causing smoke to swirl about her. As she waved it away, Rebecca glanced at the inner door, where Naziem now stood with one hand on the crank, ready to seal the exit as she'd urged. Raising his other hand, he stuck up his thumb. Fitzgerald, at the outer door, did the same.

"We'll keep the doors closed until you're back," Carlisle said. "But you need to be quick."

"Don't worry, we will be," Wyatt said.

And with that, he planted his foot and the truck blasted into the habitat.

Crimson light bloomed, and embers swarmed like fireflies.

Accelerating, Wyatt ploughed headlong into the blood-red inferno. He swerved right—to the left, the flames formed an impenetrable wall, but on the western side the blaze had yet to assert itself. Here it was mainly spot fires, smaller and intermittent, which meant there was space to maneuver. Rebecca wondered about this. Had Holtorf erred? Clearly, the oxygen levels weren't high enough—the fire was spreading, yes, but perhaps not as quickly as Holtorf might have hoped.

Maybe he'd been interrupted.

"There! The path!" Spencer said, raising his voice over the combined roar of flames and engine, perhaps forgetting the masks were fitted with a mic and speakers. He pointed left.

Rebecca looked that way. Through the shimmering heat, she discerned a streaking blur, the black silhouette of the steel-mesh walkway leading to H-4. The flames had claimed it.

Wyatt gunned it. The Caiman bellowed, shooting forward, meeting little resistance as it rocketed into the trees. The vehicle had surprising speed and excellent ground clearance, which Wyatt used to fearless effect. Staying parallel to the path, he raced across the forest floor, over snaking flames and through fallen logs, not slowing for anything. Against the blast-proof windows, foliage slapped, not only leaves and hanging vines but thick branches, too, some of it ablaze, some of it still green, but all of it relenting, parting and snapping. He may well have been behind the wheel of a supercharged bulldozer, the Caiman making short work of all that stood before it.

Soon enough, through the trees, a clearing appeared. Wyatt eased onto the brakes. To their left, the wall of flame diminished, not quite disappearing but weakening, pulling back to the treeline. As it shrank, it sucked heat from the vehicle, and Rebecca realised just how hot it had been inside the cab.

In front of them, at the clearing's opposing edge, was the gate.

Like before, the blaze hadn't passed through the opening—again, it was just spot fires; low, irregular, skirting the entrance. Ash swirled about, and embers, too, riding the smoke-clogged air.

Crawling now but not stopping, Wyatt slipped beyond the gate and into the adjoining habitat.

H-4.

Rebecca gazed about. There was a clearing on this side, too, and several yards ahead, a line of tall trees: massive kapoks with thick boles and bladed roots that snaked like giant woody ribbons through the soil. Nestled amongst them, as though seeking the protection of their larger cousins, smaller vegetation reigned, featherlike ferns and shrubs with broad, waxy leaves. Notably, none of the foliage glowed—the jungle here was dark, the UV lamps either damaged or simply not operating. Even so, Rebecca realised the area was, in fact, illuminated, but this time with regular light; low-level, no more than soft starlight. She recalled Li's comment about retaining the visible spectrum for night simulation.

With no flames to light the way, Wyatt moved to activate the Caiman's LEDs, but at the last moment stayed his hand, perhaps worried about drawing attention. Consolidating his grip on the wheel, he urged the Caiman towards the dark treeline, carefully, slowly.

An eerie stillness descended.

Rebecca shivered. At this speed, the engine had quieted, and now that the roar of flames had also diminished the sudden change in sound was unnerving.

"Something isn't right," Spencer whispered.

Staring at the impenetrable wall of green, Rebecca agreed. While the fire had yet to cross the threshold, the smoke was already here, and within its searching black tentacles, every gnarled root, every branch and leaf and stem took on a sinister form.

"The scanner," Wyatt urged.

Cursing her oversight, Rebecca lifted the tablet. Onscreen was a bird's-eye view of the habitats, depicted as a modest graphic overlaid with gridlines. She reverse-pinched the display and the image zoomed out. Naziem had said the system was proximity-based—the range no doubt limited but for now encompassing all eight habitats. She saw no blips; the screen was clear.

The megs, as expected, weren't here, not in H-4.

Not anywhere else, either.

That concerned her. Was the scanner working? Was she reading it right?

She was certain the answer to both was yes. Maybe the megs had perished trying to escape H-5 where they'd previously amassed, unable to get beyond the flames in H-6. Or perhaps they'd fled somewhere else entirely and were now simply out of range.

Both were possible.

Or maybe the heat is masking the signal, or the smoke is, or both, and they're still around.

"Bec?"

Rebecca jolted back, unsure if the scanner could be trusted but committing to it anyway. "Sorry… it's clear. We're good. Keep going, straight ahead, just like Carlisle said."

From the rear compartment, Spencer pointed a gloved finger at the treeline. "There's a gap, see it? It's narrow, but I think we'll scrape through."

Rebecca searched it cautiously. Without light, the slender opening would be near impossible to negotiate, and the last thing they wanted was to get hung up on a root or stuck between two thick boles and unable to pull free. Wyatt, clearly of the same opinion, turned to her and shrugged. When Rebecca shrugged back, Wyatt leaned forward and flicked on the LEDs.

Powerful beams blazed outwards, searing the trees. Spencer was right; fully illuminated, the gap looked passable. Accordingly, Wyatt squeezed inside, slowly, carefully, branches clawing and scraping at the Caiman.

Rebecca's heartrate spiked. The nest can't be far, she thought.

Frank can't be far.

The ground—muddy, uneven—shifted beneath them. Despite its massive weight, the Caiman jolted and slid, fighting for purchase. The rough ride was short-lived; almost immediately, just beyond the first line of trees, the ground levelled out and the vegetation thinned again, giving way to another clearing. Wyatt jammed on the brakes.

"Oh, *shit…*" Spencer murmured.

43
α

Ringed by large kapoks, the flat, circular space was at least eighty feet in diameter, entirely devoid of vegetation, and wholly engulfed in silk. Sheets of it swept in from the surrounding trees, converging in the middle where it formed a twisting, vertical cylinder more than a dozen feet wide. Rooted to the ground, the silken tube, dark grey in colour, towered into the canopy and disappeared into darkness.

"What the hell is *that*?" Wyatt asked breathlessly, his voice preceded by an amplified click. "It looks like a funnel cloud."

"More like a tornado," Spencer said. "Just sitting there, in stasis…"

Rebecca hesitated. Clearly, this was the nest, but unlike any she was familiar with. Had there been something like this down in Brazil, something they'd missed?

Surrounding the funnel was a huge mat of silk. It looked like a large, flat plate. The floor of the clearing was covered in it.

What is that?

"Bec… are they here?" Wyatt asked nervously.

Rebecca checked the scanner. Again, nothing. She indicated this with a shake of her head, slipping her mask free at the same time. The air was smoky but breathable, at least in the short term—certainly long enough for a quick scan with the NVGs. Flicking them to thermal, she slipped them over her eyes.

Heart thrumming, Rebecca scanned the funnel, sweeping her gaze about.

At first, nothing, just shades of blue and purple, indicative of cooler temperatures… background readings, no more. She was looking for orange or red or—

There! Low to the ground, suspended within the silk, an elongated, faint yellow blob; indistinct, unmoving, but undoubtedly a source of heat. Rebecca's breath caught in her throat. "I think I've got something."

"The professor?" Wyatt asked. "Or one of *them*?"

Struggling to keep her emotions in check, Rebecca didn't answer. Whatever it was, it wasn't an invertebrate. Arthropods don't generate heat—they simply retain the temperature of their surroundings. Inside the funnel was something warm. "I'm heading in."

Whipping the goggles free, she reached for her mask.

From the rear compartment, a flurry of movement; Spencer, unclipping his harness. "I'm coming with you."

She didn't try to dissuade him. She was prepared to go alone, but Spencer had insisted on accompanying her, declaring his intent back when Carlisle had briefed them about the road ahead. Now, he seemed determined to keep his word.

Refitting her mask, Rebecca adjusted the valve on her tank, fine-tuning the flow of air. Satisfied, she jumped from the Caiman, Spencer in tow. As planned, Wyatt remained at the wheel with the engine running.

Outside, it was warm; Rebecca could feel the heat against her suit. She turned. The Caiman's lights washed across the clearing, blasting towards the funnel and throwing harsh shadows to the rear. In some ways the interplay of light and shadow was confusing, but it was better than full darkness. Hesitating a moment, she ran her gaze up the huge vertical tube, perplexed once more by its shape and stunned by its height. Out here, it looked inherently foreign, like something from another world; weird, alien.

It's exactly that.

She turned to Spencer, who gave her the thumbs up.

"Wyatt… you copy?" Rebecca asked over the two-way.

"Loud and clear. There's nothing on the scanner. You're all good."

"Let's do this," Spencer said with mock confidence. Clutching his prized stone in his right hand, he made a tentative, sweeping gesture with his left. "After you, of course."

Lifting the portable ultrasonic device, which she could feel vibrating softly through her gloves, Rebecca threw him a faint grin… then stepped cautiously onto the mat.

She half-expected a trap to trigger. Back in Brazil, the megs had employed silken trip-lines to alert them to intruders, and for a moment she feared the mat was an alarm system, maybe even a giant trapdoor. Thankfully, the ground didn't open beneath her, but she paused in any case, waiting, watching for something to scurry out and investigate.

Nothing did, and she took another step. Then more.

Underfoot, the ground was soft, spongy. Fortunately, the silk wasn't the kind used for catching prey; this was more akin to swathing silk, a non-sticky variety designed for wrapping or immobilising victims. Still, as she moved across it, aiming for the vertical tube, her footfalls were careful.

Perhaps too careful.

You need to pick up the pace.

She did so, and said back to Spencer, "You still with me?"

"God knows why, but yeah… still here." He sounded short of breath. She could hear him chewing madly.

That must be driving Wyatt wild.

Rebecca pressed forward. All suited up, breathing courtesy of the tank on her back and listening to the click of the regulator, she felt like an interstellar explorer on some strange, far-flung planet. As well as the repeller, she carried a flashlight, which she now swept to the places not covered by the Caiman's headlights. Through the beam, wisps of smoke drifted lazily, looking like thick fog. Beyond the haze, it was oppressively dark and quiet, and though Rebecca heard nothing of concern and saw nothing other than the trees, for an instant, her imagination got the better of her, convincing her that unspeakable horrors crouched in the shadows, behind the darkened fronds—

Her hands shook.

Get a grip.

Spencer's voice floated over the speaker. "Everything okay?"

"All good," Rebecca said, frustrated by her moment of weakness. Lifting the ultrasonic device, she flexed her fingers on the handle. Now that she was away from the Caiman, she could hear the repeller's gentle hum; it was comforting. "Come on. We're almost there."

She took another step, and something crunched underfoot.

Rebecca froze. At first, she feared she'd finally triggered something—they were only a few feet from the funnel, right where you'd expect a trap to be.

"Bec?" Spencer asked. He'd stopped, too, and was looking down at his feet.

Rebecca knelt. The sound had come from beneath the silk. Placing the repeller on the ground, she reached out a gloved hand and pressed her palm onto the mat, applying gentle force. There was resistance, but inconsistent.

"*Bec*?" Spencer repeated anxiously.

Focusing the beam of her flashlight, Rebecca speared her fingers into the mat, tearing a hole and reaching underneath. Probing, she pulled her hand free.

Grasped between her fingers was an object, long and thin and covered in mud.

"Oh man," Spencer said. "Is that what I think it is?"

Twig-like, the item was smooth and discoloured. Rebecca plunged her hand back to the hole, ripping it wider.

Beneath the silk lay a carpet of bones.

"Holy shit," Spencer said, swallowing. "The goats, right?"

Rebecca nodded. "Carlisle said the megs nested at the feeding grounds… that's what she called this place."

"She also called it the goddamned chow hall," Spencer said, his voice trembling.

Wiping her hand on her suit and retrieving the repeller, Rebecca stood.

"*Guys, what's the holdup?*" Wyatt asked.

"Nothing—we're good," Rebecca replied before turning to Spencer and whispering, "You okay?"

Spencer nodded, juggling his stone and chewing rapidly, nervously.

Together, they turned to the funnel.

Long lines of thick silk, like scaffolding, held the structure in place. These threads splayed out from the nest, interlacing with the surrounding trees.

The funnel itself was comprised of coarse silk which, like the mat, was no doubt a non-sticky variety. It was opaque, too dense to see through, but Rebecca assumed that on the other side was a hollow core—Carlisle had said the weavers roosted here, so logically, there had to be space to move about.

She and Spencer stood less than six feet away.

Rebecca couldn't see an entry. Maybe there wasn't one. Not at ground level, anyway. Maybe it was somewhere higher up, towards the canopy.

It doesn't matter. You don't need one.

"Here, do you mind?" She passed Spencer both the repeller and her flashlight. "Wyatt, we're still clear?"

"Confirmed. There's nothing there. But can you hurry it up?"

Rebecca reached for the funnel. There was no trick to this, no method beyond brute force, and that's what she used. Desperately, she ripped at the silk. It was tough and fibrous—vaguely reminiscent of coconut husk, or even hair—but no tougher than the silk she'd shredded moments ago. Tearing a fist-sized hole, she grasped its edge, pulling with both hands and peeling back a large flap. Devoid of the glue-like proteins of viscid silk, it didn't stick to her gloves.

Once the hole was big enough, she retrieved her flashlight and drew a sharp breath. "Here goes."

Ducking, Rebecca squeezed inside the nest.

44

α

Darkness.

As suspected, the tube was hollow, but there were thin strands through-out, or at least in the space immediately beyond the hole. While not large enough to entangle her, they did fall across her mask, obscuring her vision and clinging to her face-shield like jellyfish tentacles. Flailing at them, the beam of her flashlight jolting madly, Rebecca dragged her trailing leg inside, only for the tank on her back to snag on the hole and force her even lower. Heaving that through, too, she drew herself upright.

Beckett stared back at her, only inches from her face.

Shit…

Rebecca stumbled backwards, her heart leaping into her mouth, and when she heard Spencer call out, asking if she was okay, she realised she may have yelped in fright.

She answered him, and Wyatt, too, whose voice had also crackled through the speaker, and once she'd convinced them she was fine, she stead-ied herself and returned her light to the pallid visage before her.

"Oh my God."

Beckett's eyes were open and staring, but lifeless. Suspended inches above the ground, his body floating within the sea of silk, he hung with his head angled towards her. They'd strung him up there, swaddled him, so it looked like he was in a cocoon, but only partially, as though he was in the middle of breaking free from his silken prison.

The threads around his torso had been clawed away.

Underneath, his fatigues had been slashed and stripped, only fragments remaining, and his chest was a sorry mess of torn skin and gristle. Notably, there was little blood; he wasn't quite desiccated, but most of the fluid had been drained from his body.

Rebecca swallowed, barely able to suppress the bile rising in her throat.

Oh man…

There was no way of knowing if Beckett had been alive when the feeding had commenced, no way of knowing if he'd suffered. She hoped not, choosing to believe the stab wound Holtorf had delivered to his neck had proven fatal and he'd expired long before any of this had occurred.

Reaching gently for his face, she passed her fingers over Beckett's eyes, closing them. "You may have been an asshole, but you didn't deserve this."

"Bec!"

Rebecca jumped, and although Spencer's voice had barked sharply through her speaker, she sensed he was close. He must have followed her inside.

"Quickly! Over here!"

She directed her flashlight. Spencer stood on the other side of the nest, through a floating sea of gossamer. Beside him was another cocoonlike mass, human-shaped, wrapped like a mummy…

Frank…

She scampered over, pushing through the silk, which spun around her in wisps. Her heart thumped in her ears. "Frank!"

Like Beckett's, Frank's face was bloodless, his torso partially exposed. His eyes, however, were closed—

Spencer thrust a hand up to Frank's neck, searching for his carotid, and as Rebecca drew beside him, he turned and nodded excitedly. "He's alive…"

Rebecca let out a relieved whimper, her voice cracking involuntarily, her vision already blurring with tears. "Frank, it's Bec… I'm here! You're going to be okay! You hear me?"

Desperate to release him, she instinctively reached for the cocoon, about to tear at it, but was reminded of when Ed had been captured by the megs, when she'd found him in similar fashion, all bundled up, stored for later. Back then the swathing-silk had acted like a bandage, keeping Ed's wounds clean and protected. The megs liked to keep their victims alive for as long as possible.

Reconsidering, she shifted her hand higher, reaching instead for the support threads. "Please… help me get him down."

Together, they set to work. As she pulled at the strands, her heart thudding in her chest, her pulse beating so fast and hard it caused discomfort, Rebecca felt a growing sense of detachment, as though she wasn't really in this space anymore, not really in control of her actions. Fueled by adrenalin, barely cognisant of her surroundings, she spent the next few minutes in a dreamlike blur. She remembered extracting Frank, and with Spencer's help carrying him back to the Caiman, remembered easing him into the rear compartment and taking a seat in that same area with him cradled in her arms while Spencer dashed back to search for Beckett's cohort, the missing soldier, the fingernail-clipper. She remembered Spencer returning sometime later, not with the soldier, but with Wyatt, who must have gone out to help, and between them they had Beckett's body which they carried gently, with respect, placing it in the Caiman beside her. Then Wyatt was behind the wheel again, spinning the huge vehicle around, heading back the way they had come, back through the heat and smoke and flames.

Soon after, Frank finally responded to their desperate attempts to rouse him, finally responded to the compressed air, finally opened his eyes. When he realised she had come for him and he was no longer alone, the look on his face made her heart soar. When she told him he was safe, that they were getting out of here together, he found comfort, but in truth he'd been more pleased to learn that *she* was safe. That's all he wanted, and he told her that.

Her memory of that moment was the strongest. But she remembered, too, how quickly her soaring heart had crashed when she realised that something was amiss, that this time was different to before, that it wasn't the same as when she'd rescued Ed all those weeks ago and everything had turned out okay.

This wasn't going to end like that.

It only took minutes for the Caiman to roar back through the flames, back to the maintenance entry, but halfway there, somewhere between the two gates, Frank took his final breath.

Rebecca remembered sinking to the floor of the Caiman, dropping to her knees next to Frank's prone form, along with Spencer, the two of them trying desperately to revive him, but these memories were scant.

Later, she'd recall some of their race against the flames, of Wyatt's heroic effort in getting them out of there and back to safety, of Spencer's continued attempts to rouse Frank back to life even when he knew he was gone.

But again, these were just moments in time. She wouldn't remember everything.

What she did remember, slumped on the floor of the Caiman with Frank's head cradled in her hands, were other moments in time, memories of her mentor. Fond memories. Good memories. And as these came to her, she cried for her friend.

Then her new friends were helping her out of the Caiman, drawing her close, and someone covered Frank, and Beckett, too, with a foil emergency blanket, a mark of respect, while another closed the rear door to the vehicle because for now, that was the best place for them, at least until help arrived. And while the others talked softly about this, standing there in a group, heads bowed, Rebecca started walking. She walked until she couldn't anymore, which, in the end, wasn't far at all.

In the darkness behind one of the pallets, she slumped to the ground. There, on her back, she cried, allowing herself that moment, allowing herself to release it. As she lay, she thought absently that she could hear drumming rain somewhere in the distance but somehow close, too.

It was a comforting sound, and as she listened to it, she cried some more.

45
α

The truck rumbled into position, backing up to the substation below.

As it entered the cavern, Major Charles L. Holtorf hurried across the metal observation deck, heading for the stairs. Again, he checked his watch.

Time to move…

"Security team inbound, north-eastern quadrant," Boor confirmed, hustling beside him and thumbing the screen of the mini tablet at the same time. "Delta's on intercept; two minutes."

Light towers loomed over the partially excavated space, bathing the area in a harsh white glow. Buried deep within the complex, the cavern was surprisingly large, housing an array of buildings and metal pylons connected by high-tensile power lines. From up here, it looked like a switchyard.

Hitting the stairs, descending two at a time, Holtorf said back to Boor, "There's an art to drawing attention to your left hand, so that the right goes unnoticed." He wasn't referring to their own use of misdirection, but to that of their opponent.

Boor understood. "It's the team you can't see…"

Holtorf said nothing more, and as they hit the cavern floor, boots echoing on the galvanised steel path underfoot, Boor issued instructions to one of the other men. As that man moved out, taking two more with him, Boor turned back to Holtorf. "You know… what Davies said… and Hopkins, too… there's something out there, something we weren't expecting. And now Bravo's gone dark—"

"As planned," Holtorf reminded him. Without stopping, he glanced at his second-in-command. "Whatever's out there, they'll deal with it."

The truck ground to a halt. Men darted towards it. Holtorf headed for it, too. Of course, Boor's concerns weren't without foundation; Davies' loss was a setback, no doubt, and Hopkins' radio silence was ahead of schedule. The latter wasn't necessarily a problem, but the comms window had now closed, as ordered. Of greater concern was the unfolding counteroffensive; already, some of the systems were back online, and multiple strike teams were converging. Naturally, they'd planned for that, but the noose was tightening.

Holtorf reached the truck and leapt onto the step board, reminding himself that they were on track. In fact, if anything, the response time of the enemy had been slower than expected. The plan was working.

Stick to it.

As he opened the door, the driver gave him the thumbs up, confirming the cargo was secure and they were good to go. Holtorf turned to Boor. "Finish the job, and I'll see you at the rally point. Don't be long."

From the ground, Boor looked up at him. "What about the hostages?"

Absently, Holtorf's hand went to the object in his pocket, his fingers tracing the spiraling grooves of the palm-sized stone disc, flat on one side and slightly curved on the other. It was warm to the touch. "We have what we came for. We don't need them anymore."

With that, the driver revved the engine and took off. As the truck rumbled away, Boor reached for his sidearm and grinned.

THE
HUNT

46
α

At first, the hole had seemed like a good place to hide. It was away from the heat, which was dangerous and had to be avoided. The hole was cool and dark and quiet. It liked this. This was what it had always known.

But now it liked new things, too. Things it hadn't known before. There were many of these, and they were arousing; smells and sounds and even tastes, and as it was reminded of these new things the deadly heat was forgotten.

There was more, too. Something that stirred it beyond a simple and yet deep hunger, beyond a basic desire to eat. This was what it knew now.

The warm things were getting closer. It could hear them. It had seen these creatures before, but always from afar and never within reach. Until recently, it had never hunted them. Now, as they approached, it grew wary, but it wasn't afraid. The warm things were dangerous—it had learned they could spit and sting—but they were also slow and easy to catch. The reward outweighed the risk.

One after another, its senses fired, overloading. Almost unbearable. Still, it was patient, and it waited, because this was what it knew. The things were noisy—they were always noisy, even when they were trying to hide—and as easy to track as they were to catch. It wouldn't lose them, even though they were deep beneath the ground.

It knew how to get down there, through the tunnels.

For the moment, however, it could wait.

Still, as the vibrations intensified, swarming around its body, it wasn't long before it reached the limit of its patience. It could no longer deny its most basic instincts, nor its newest—the one that liked to *kill*.

It wanted more of what it had not known before.

As it moved from its place of darkness, drawn from its hole, it scurried after the warm things, and suddenly, it knew the meaning of excitement.

47
α

"Bec… wake up."

Wake up?

A hand gently shook her. Rebecca opened her eyes. Kneeling over her, a concerned look on his face and a forefinger pressed to his lips, was Wyatt. Sitting up, she looked around. She was still in the dimly lit nook behind the pallets—the private place she'd retreated to earlier—and although she couldn't remember closing her eyes, it appeared she *had* fallen asleep back here. Either that, or she'd passed out. She opened her mouth but before she could say anything, Wyatt stopped her, shook his head.

Something was wrong.

"You need to come see this," he whispered. Standing, he helped her to her feet before leading her back to the maintenance entry, the beam of his flashlight jolting side to side, scattering the shadows. The place was deserted.

Where are the others?

"This way," Wyatt said.

The inner roller-shutter was down. Warning lights still flashed and rotated, but the alarms had stopped, the silence broken only by a muted pattering from somewhere beyond the gate, inside the habitat. This was what she'd heard earlier. "The sprinkler-system," she said. "It's on."

Wyatt nodded, but once more thrust a finger to his lips. As he did, he glanced at her hazmat suit, which made swishing noises as she walked. He'd ditched his own suit for his regular clothes, and sensing his unease, Rebecca slipped from hers, too. As she hurried after him, deeper into the warehouse, she threw a glance at the Caiman. A lump rose in her throat and she swallowed hard, but there were no more tears—she'd already purged herself, and her despair, it seemed, had morphed into something else: anger, and a desire for justice.

She hustled to catch up.

Together, they continued around a corner and into an area Rebecca hadn't earlier ventured. Here, weakly lit by overhead fluorescents, was a yawning concrete floorspace. Rows of tall pallet racking stood at the edge of the light, with more extending into the shadows behind.

"Wyatt," she whispered, clasping his arm. "What's going on? And where is everybody?"

Drawing to a halt, sheltering behind a dormant forklift, Wyatt murmured, "We searched the area… turning on the lights, but it seems we're on emergency power only, which is why it's still so dark, and…" He hesitated, then gently pulled her forward, around the side of the vehicle. "And, well… we found this."

Running the beam of his flashlight across the floor, he highlighted a series of glossy red splotches, like spilled paint, except it was clearly blood, lots of it, and not just drops but arterial spray and elongated smears, too, like drag marks. He ran his beam higher, along the storage racks. More blood was there as well, glazing the surrounding crates and pallets, some of it still wet, still dripping.

"Wyatt, whose blood is this? Is everyone okay?"

He didn't answer, and simply took her hand in his. His fingers shook. With the beam of his flashlight leading the way, he hurried forward, following the trail around the corner.

"*Wyatt?*"

The others were here—they were standing in a group with their backs to her, in what looked to be a caged elevator hall. Rebecca shuddered with relief. Everyone was present—and as far as she could tell, physically unharmed—but fear hung in the air, thick and heavy. She could feel it.

"Bec, look at this," Spencer said, his voice trembling as he turned to her. He swung back to the service elevator in front of him, his flashlight pointing the way. The trail of blood that she and Wyatt had tracked went right up to the elevator door, where it abruptly ended. The door was closed, but unstained.

"What happened here?" Rebecca asked. Above her, one of the emergency fluorescents buzzed and flickered.

"Something escaped," Carlisle said, her gravelly voice, like Spencer's, barely holding under the pressure.

"I told you already, we don't know that," Fitzgerald said sharply.

"The hell we don't!" Carlisle shot back. "Look at all that blood! I'm telling you, it's the only explanation! Something got out… used the same exit as us… and not just one. Maybe *all* of them got out. That's why they didn't show on the scanner."

"Naziem," Rebecca said urgently, turning. "The tablet… where are the megs now?"

Looking as though he might be sick, Naziem shook his head. "I don't know where they are… the scanner… it won't help, not here."

"What do you mean?"

"I mean it won't work!" Naziem snapped. "It's useless… there are no sensors out here, the sensors are *inside* the habitats. The system wasn't designed to track the assets out here because they shouldn't *be* out here. This is unprecedented."

"Not good," Spencer murmured.

Yeah, not good, Rebecca agreed. She noticed that Spencer had her flashlight in addition to his own. Easing it from his grip, she turned and stepped from the hall, scrubbing the gloom as she went.

"Bec, we broke radio silence," Spencer whispered after her. "We didn't want to, but we did… we didn't have a choice. Emergency frequencies… security channels… but we heard nothing back, there's no-one out there—"

Just beyond the range of the faulty fluorescent, Rebecca halted. Quietly, she spoke over her shoulder. "Wyatt… hit the call button."

"What?" Carlisle said. "The elevator? I'm not going in there. Let's go back to the Caiman and lock ourselves inside, wait for help. Someone will come eventually… a security team, a fire response team… someone. And anyway, you can't use elevators during a fire."

"Technically, that isn't true," Fitzgerald said, speaking fast. "You can use them, it's just that the stairs are generally safer—if a lot of people are trying to evacuate, the elevators might overload, or take a long time to arrive, or even divert altogether—"

He was rambling. Rebecca hardly heard him. "Wyatt," she repeated, again without turning, "*hit the call button.*"

Murmurs of unease, and nervous shuffling. "Are you sure?" Wyatt asked. "I mean, the blood… we don't know what might be in there…"

"Maybe we should do as Carlisle suggested," Spencer said.

Ignoring them, still with her back to the group, Rebecca lifted the beam of her flashlight from the floor—where the small, metallic shell casings had glinted like a scattering of diamonds—and slowly followed a dripping trail of blood up the pallet racking and to the ceiling. There, she paused.

"Oh my god…" Carlisle breathed.

48

α

The bodies hung above them, several stories up, at least four of them suspended by the feet on individual strands of silk. Despite a cocoonlike casing, it was clear they were dressed in tactical gear. These were soldiers. Holtorf's men.

"The elevator," Rebecca whispered, backing away slowly but still craning upwards. "*Now.*"

She couldn't see beyond the bodies because shadows clung to the ceiling, dark and impenetrable and out of range, but within that inky realm something shifted. Something large. She heard it. Everyone must have.

"Oh, no," Fitzgerald whimpered. "Please no."

The Caiman was too far away. They wouldn't make it…

The group contracted, everyone—except for Rebecca, who remained a few paces out—pressing flat against the elevator door. Wyatt punched the call button, not just once, but multiple times. The others did, too.

Ahead, a dull thud broke the hush, something landing on the ground, followed by a loud crash; things toppling, maybe crates or pallets tumbling from the shelves somewhere in the darkness. As the objects settled, a scurrying sound echoed faintly, something large and heavy brushing against the floor. Then silence.

"*What was that?*" Spencer blurted, as flashlight beams crisscrossed the murk. "I can't see anything!"

Behind them, in the elevator shaft, the sound of movement. The cab, heading slowly towards them.

"*Come on!*" Naziem cried.

Dead ahead, more skittering. Closing in.

Panic rippled through the group. Rebecca retreated another step, still facing out from the cage in the direction of the pallet racks. She sensed that whatever crept amongst the shadows was sizing them up, maneuvering into position; she could feel its predatory gaze, could feel its multiple eyes staring back at her from the gloom.

She wasn't going to turn from it. If she did, she was certain the shadows themselves would come alive—

Behind her, a ping sounded, and the elevator door slid open. Someone gasped.

"Oh, *shit*," Fitzgerald said.

Rebecca didn't mean to turn, but compelled by the reactions of her companions, she did.

The cab was bathed in blood, splattered from top to bottom. On the floor, amidst a sea of spent shell casings like those on the ground out here, lay a human torso; again, a soldier, dressed in the same tactical gear worn by Holtorf's men. He must have run in here, trying to escape…

He didn't run far.

Where the hell are his legs?

Rebecca realised her error. When she spun back to the warehouse, it was already too late.

She didn't see it, but she sensed something pounce from the blackness, something large soaring towards her. At the same time, a hand fell on her, grasping her and hauling her backwards into the elevator. On the way through, her left shoulder collided hard with the door, sending a sharp bolt of pain lancing through her body, the impact spinning her around, towards the back of the cab, and as she went, she heard voices.

"Close the door!" Fitzgerald screamed.

"Shit! This thing only goes *down!*"

"*Just punch it!*"

Someone did. The door started to close, but not fast enough.

A spray of silken spittle zigzagged through the opening. Some of it caught the door on the way through, spattering across it in a viscid glob and sticking there, but the majority made it inside, and although she was sure it had been aimed at her, Rebecca's collision had spun her off course and out of the way. The phlegm-like substance struck Naziem square in the chest, the force of the impact hurling him against the rear of the cab with a bone-shattering crack. He slumped to the floor, pinned there by the sticky mess.

Rebecca had barely registered this before the terrifying, frenzied face of the huge meg appeared at the door, pressing against the half-foot gap that remained there. Hissing, the creature loomed large in the flickering light, its eight mirrorlike eyes as smooth as black glass, its jaws spread wide to reveal rows of toothlike serrations and a set of curved, four-inch fangs swinging with threads of venom.

The door started to open again.

Reflexively, Rebecca scrambled backwards. Behind her, someone fell, and someone else screamed—the sound long and thin, and Rebecca couldn't tell if the source was male or female—and as she recoiled, she turned and saw Wyatt mashing his fist against the control panel. Once more, the door started to close. Backpedaling, the creature disappeared… only to suddenly return, this time leaping flat against the opening and forcing four of its legs inside. Two went left, two right, the long spindly appendages thrashing about, scraping against the floor, the ceiling, ripping at the walls—which were padded, because this was a freight elevator. As the creature tried to squeeze its body through the gap, a female voice came over the speaker, politely asking the passengers to *please stand clear of the closing door*, and with that the door started to reopen. Rebecca ducked as a flailing limb came for her, whipping over her head, only for another to slam against her thigh and knock her off balance. Slipping in the pool of slick blood, she crashed to the floor… and came face to face with the dead soldier.

Clutched in the man's bloody, outstretched hand was his weapon, a suppressed MP5. Rebecca tore it free and spun onto her back, intent on sending a hailstorm of bullets pointblank into—

Click.

No ammo…

Oh no…

Unhindered, the creature burst fully inside the elevator. It came straight for her, leaping onto her legs and pinning her with its thick abdomen, and she tried to hit it but it was too heavy and then it raised its head and body and forelegs high, fangs glistening and poised to strike—

—just as Carlisle leapt forward and hit it in the sternum with a blast from the ultrasonic prod.

Stunned, the meg recoiled, flying backwards out of the cab.

Not dead, but gone…

As it went, the door closed—finally—and wails of relief erupted as the elevator jolted downwards, descending at last.

"*Okayyyyy…*" Spencer said over the noise, hands on knees, panting heavily. "That's enough for me. Seriously, I'm ready to go home. Like, right now."

"*You're* ready?" Rebecca blurted, swallowing hard.

Spencer moved to help her up, but before he could get to her the cab stopped abruptly and the lights died, plunging them into complete darkness.

49

α

"Like I said, I'm ready to go *now*," Spencer murmured.

Flashlight beams jumped about.

Repulsed, Rebecca pushed back from the torso, standing with Spencer's assistance and shouldering the MP5. Blood from the floor had smeared her all over; it felt tacky on her skin, and its coppery reek caused her to gag.

Elevators, she thought absently, trying not to breathe too deeply. *What is it with me and goddamned elevators?*

Thanking Carlisle for her quick thinking, she hurried to Naziem, for the moment ignoring the sudden loss of power.

"I told you the crawlers had escaped," Carlisle said, going with her. "Didn't I tell you?"

Rebecca said nothing in reply. Together, by torchlight, she and Carlisle cleared Naziem of the rubbery spittle and helped him to his feet. He was dazed, maybe concussed, but otherwise unhurt. Cradled protectively in his hands was the ultrasonic herder, the device Rebecca had left in the Caiman. He must have retrieved it when she'd wandered away. It wasn't on. She moved to ease it from his grasp, but he hugged it closer, wide-eyed and confused.

"I need to get out of here," Fitzgerald said, dry retching, and verging on panic. "I mean… there's half a freaking man on the floor…"

Wyatt, his flashlight trained on the control panel, was already punching buttons. "Nothing. The power's out. You think it was *cut*?"

Spencer joined him at the panel. "Holtorf… maybe he wasn't up there with those men, or this one here. Maybe he's still alive, and *he* cut it."

"Him, or the crawlers," Carlisle suggested.

As she said this a low, dull boom reverberated through the elevator walls, causing them to shudder.

"What was *that*?" Spencer asked.

Another boom, this time vibrating up through the floor.

"Could be the filtration system," Fitzgerald said, distracted by this new development. With his thumb and forefinger, he pinched his nose against the smell, giving his voice a nasal tone. "Subterranean fans—part of the ventilation system."

"Or maybe it's the emergency power trying to boot up," Wyatt said. "Backup generators or something."

"I thought we were *already* on emergency power," Spencer said.

Naziem reached gingerly for his head. "There are multiple backup systems. They could all be struggling… chances are, Holtorf's cyber bomb is still wreaking havoc, causing compounding disasters." With the help of both girls, he got to his feet. He seemed lucid enough, perhaps fueled by adrenalin. "I think that's what's happening here… a compromised system can trigger a disruptive chain of events. Once one system crashes, it puts pressure on the next, and then that system fails, and so on."

"The Cascade Effect," Fitzgerald said.

Wyatt shrugged as another boom shook the walls. "That, or Holtorf's attack was designed *specifically* to cause chaos, maybe circumvent the backup systems and make everything go haywire."

Rebecca had reached this conclusion already. Earlier, the fire alarm system hadn't behaved as expected; the gates hadn't shut to isolate the habitat fires, and the sprinkler system, which had initially failed, had later activated.

"Everything's compromised," Naziem said. "And chances are it'll get worse."

"Great," Carlisle said. Thumping a fist against the wall, she let out an angry groan. "And so here we are. Trapped. I told you we shouldn't use the elevator."

"You're kidding, right?" Spencer blurted. "You'd prefer to be topside with that thing? You know it's not dead, yeah?"

"Don't start on me! I just saved your ass!" Carlisle fired back. "But yeah, we should still be up there—we should have run for the Caiman when we had a chance."

"Well, we're here now," Wyatt interjected, aiming for calm. "There's no going back. That thing is up there, and its friends are probably up there, too, hiding in the shadows. Gives me chills just thinking about it."

Absently, Rebecca wiped her hand on her clothes, her fingers still sticky from the congealed silk that had netted Naziem. Wyatt was right; there were more up there. The individual that had attacked them through the door was a jumper, a hunter—it couldn't have spat at them; only the egg-layers possessed the specialised glands and mouthparts for spitting liquid silk. Which meant that, as previously suspected, the assets were no longer segregated, that the alphas had indeed summoned the other group. Most likely they were *all* up there now, just as Wyatt had suggested, roosting together in the shadowed warehouse, having evaded the flames by crawling across the domed ceilings and then exiting—most likely minutes earlier—through the same opening she and her companions had used.

"You've gotta wonder what Holtorf's up to," Spencer murmured. "Surely he didn't mean to release the megs… what they did to his men… I mean, this couldn't have been part of his plan."

"Something went wrong," Wyatt reasoned.

Rebecca agreed. Obviously, the megs had crossed paths with Holtorf's crew—probably the same team responsible for setting off the charges—and there was a fight. She hadn't heard gunfire, none of them had, but that wasn't surprising; the encounter would have been quick, probably over in seconds, and the MP5 in her hand was fitted with a suppressor, no louder when fired than a human voice at normal speaking level. After the fight, the victorious megs had likely retreated, perhaps to recover. She shivered.

They were up there the whole time, clustered on the ceiling, just like they had been back in Intihuasi, back in the pyramid—

Suddenly, a great bulk pushed past her—Fitzgerald, heading for the door. "Hell, enough with the talk already… who really gives a toss about what happened? If the fuzzies are up *there*, they can't be down below, right? What are we waiting for?"

"Good point," Naziem said as he, too, pushed to the front of the cab. In his haste, he nearly lost his footing in the slick blood. "The smell is making me sick."

"Me too," Spencer said, joining them at the door. "Let's see if we can't pry this open."

As they set to work, Wyatt caught Rebecca's gaze in the dim light. "In other news, I found this." He lifted his hand. In it, attached to a retractable lanyard, was a blood-smeared prox-card. "It was lying here on the floor. Half-man must have dropped it." He passed it to her.

Rebecca took it, and her eyes welled unexpectedly with tears. There was a good chance this was Frank's card; Holtorf's men would have needed one of these to move about. Obviously, the guy on the floor had tried to use it but hadn't gotten far; maybe he'd dragged himself in here after losing his legs, or maybe one of the megs had followed him in.

"Okay, on three," Spencer said, oblivious to this exchange.

"Just a crack," Carlisle cautioned. "Enough to see through, but no more. We don't know what's out there."

Slipping the lanyard over her head, Rebecca wiped her eyes while Spencer counted the men in. Together, they heaved. Without power, the door opened with minimal resistance.

"Yes!" Fitzgerald said. "This is promising… the door restrictor hasn't engaged, which means we must be all the way down, or close to it."

At a cursory glance, it was too dark to know for sure; shadows pressed at the narrow opening, even blacker than those inside the cab.

"Only one way to be certain," Spencer said. Tentatively, he stuck his flashlight—and then his head—through the gap.

"Careful," Wyatt said.

Almost immediately, Spencer's voice floated back to them, echoing faintly. "Good news… we're in the landing zone." He popped his head back inside the cab. "Just a small jump down."

Relieved, Wyatt shone his flashlight at the control panel, then glanced at Carlisle. "Sublevel 2. What's down here?"

Carlisle shrugged.

"We've never been here," Naziem explained.

"Great," Wyatt said, looking at Rebecca. "Deeper into the rabbit hole."

Again, Spencer stuck his head outside, flashlight probing the gloom. "The coast is clear… for now, anyway. I suggest we move."

They pulled the door wider. The floor was only a couple of feet below.

"Watch your step," Spencer cautioned as Carlisle exited, leaping down. Fitzgerald went next, then Naziem.

As they disappeared through the opening, Rebecca dropped to her knees beside the dead man and started rifling through his vest.

Wyatt knelt beside her. "You think Holtorf's down here somewhere? Him, or the rest of his men, waiting for us?"

At last, Rebecca seized upon what she was looking for and stood, helping Wyatt to his feet as she did so. She then checked the object in her hand. During her time at Camp Delta, she'd learnt a thing or two about self-defence. Lifting the magazine, she punched it into the MP5 with a swift, sharp-sounding smack. "It doesn't matter. *Whatever's* down here, we'll be ready for it."

50

α

Rebecca was the last to exit. Her search of the torso was grim work, but worthwhile. In addition to the last-remaining mag, she'd found a radio and earpiece. She considered sending Holtorf a message.

I'm still here, asshole. And I'm coming for you.

She didn't do that, and simply pocketed the radio. If Holtorf wasn't up with current events—if he hadn't caught them over the airwaves before—then she still had the element of surprise. Better to keep it.

And anyway, this isn't about him. This is about getting everyone out of here safely. Remember that.

Joining the others, Rebecca looked about. Multiple flashlights swept the murk, the lurching beams bounding over concrete walls lined with crisscrossing steel struts. Underfoot, steel-mesh grating extended into the distance. They were in a narrow passage; functional, like the warehouse above.

"Even the emergency lighting is out," Wyatt murmured. "Looks like this place has suffered catastrophic power failure."

Rebecca wondered if this was a random effect of Holtorf's cyber bomb as proposed by Naziem, or something more deliberate.

"There must be some stairs around here," Fitzgerald said, directing his flashlight. "An exit up to the ground floor. I'm guessing we can bypass Sublevel 1 altogether, get past the fuzzies that way."

Stepping forward, Rebecca added her light to the others, thrusting the powerful beam through swirling motes of dust as she probed deeper into the shadows. There were no stairs in the immediate vicinity, but halfway along the passageway were two doors, one on each side. At the end of the corridor was a T-junction, at the head of which was another door, this one comprised of semitransparent plexiglass. Rebecca's ray of light bounced from the reflective surface and into her eyes, making it impossible to see into the space beyond.

Spencer threw her a glance, and then a shrug. "I guess we gotta check that out."

Conjuring a half-smile, Rebecca swept out her hand. "After you."

"Touché." Returning the grin, his stone in one hand and his flashlight in the other, Spencer led the group forward. Boots clanged softly on the steel mesh, disrupting an otherwise deathly silence. As they passed, Rebecca tested the two doors. Service doors, apparently. Both padlocked.

They reached the end of the corridor. On the translucent door, in large white letters, were the words, 'Restricted Area'. Directly beneath them, 'LAB 14'.

Rebecca turned to Carlisle. "What's this lab used for?"

"I don't even know what this *level* is used for," Carlisle replied.

Acknowledging this, leaning closer, Rebecca squinted through the frosted glass. There appeared to be a workspace beyond, but it was blurred and shrouded in shadow.

"Seems like a strange place for a secret lab," Wyatt murmured. "Directly beneath a dusty old warehouse and all."

"Seems like the *perfect* place to me," Spencer said.

Rebecca glanced left and right; there looked to be more doors in both directions, maybe more labs. Again, she wondered if Holtorf was down here somewhere. Him, or more of his men. She sensed a gaze upon her.

You're imagining it.

"Hey, turn it on," Carlisle whispered, nodding at the herder in Naziem's hands. "Just in case."

Naziem did so. "Sorry… I forgot I even had this." Emboldened—or maybe regretting he hadn't used the device earlier and was now seeking to avoid the judgement of his companions—he split from the group, the herder humming gently as he moved tentatively down the left corridor.

Wyatt went right. Both men returned in short time.

"No stairs that way," Naziem whispered.

"More doors to the right," Wyatt said. "Padlocked, as well."

"So, what's the plan?" Spencer asked.

Realising she was tightly gripping the MP5, her knuckles white with the strain, Rebecca eased off a little. Even so, she couldn't shake the feeling they were being watched. "We need to get out of sight, for starters. Maybe the lab has a phone."

"Or somewhere to hunker down a while," Wyatt said. "Catch our breath, regroup."

To the left of the door was a reader. Rebecca pressed the prox-card against it but got no response.

"There's no power, remember?" Carlisle said.

"We mightn't need it," Fitzgerald said. He grabbed the edge of the door and pulled. It opened a crack, and he looked back at them. "I figured it might release in the event of an emergency, like a fire exit." Wrapping his fingers around the edge, and with the assistance of both brothers, he forced it wider.

The group entered, flashlights darting.

51

α

Spotlights scoured the water as the three boats combed the river, zigzagging through the subterranean cavern. The rocky throat was long, but it was narrow, too, and the drone of motors reflected off the walls, angrily buzzing its length as the assault teams searched for bodies.

They wouldn't find any.

Unseen, Owen returned to his hiding place, ducking beneath the overhang and pressing against the rock wall behind him. The submerged space was tight and claustrophobic, but above the waterline there was enough clearance for his nose and mouth. He moved by feel; it was pitch black in here, and though he couldn't see Jessy, he found her hand and clasped it in his own. Her teeth chattered, and she trembled violently, maybe due to a surge of adrenalin, but more likely the cold. The water was freezing. Owen shivered, too. He worried about hypothermia, but for the moment, pulling Jessy closer, he held his nerve.

They're looking in the wrong place…

He and Jessy were dozens of feet from their stricken vessel. Moments before the Hurricane had crashed into the cavern wall, Jessy had eased back on the throttle and they'd leapt free. Although they'd hit the water hard, losing each other in process, Owen was quick to crack one of the chemlights he'd earlier absconded from the stern box. The slender crevice had presented itself, and together they'd swum for it, squeezing inside and diving beneath the rocky overhang that lay on the other side. The Zodiac had stayed its course and there was a loud bang just before the CRRCs had thundered past.

Now, perhaps concluding the bodies they sought were trapped beneath the sinking Hurricane, the assault teams terminated their search. Owen guessed this to be the case because the motor-noise swelled a final time and then rapidly diminished, fading into the distance.

"They've gone," Jessy whispered, water bubbling around her mouth. "We've lost them."

Owen hesitated a moment, listening. On the other side of the crevice, back in the main cavern where the Hurricane was slowly sinking, water dripped from the ceiling, making an eerie pinging sound. Other than that, silence. "Come on," he said, removing the chemlight from the folds of his suit, where he'd stashed it to hide its glow. Still holding Jessy's hand, he ducked beneath the surface, leading her beneath the overhang and out the other side. Turning, he climbed on top of the jutting rock and helped Jessy out of the water.

They stood on a narrow shelf in a small chamber.

Owen passed Jessy the chemlight, then cracked another for himself. He'd stuffed half a dozen of the glowsticks into his suit.

"Who the hell were those people?" Jessy asked as she pressed against the wall.

"Saboteurs," Owen said. "This has something to do with the Vent, I'm sure of it."

"Earlier, that soldier… he told Belding that Nevada was offline. You think this is connected? You think Bec's in danger?"

"I'm certain it's connected," Owen said. "Just as certain as I am that Bec can handle it."

Shivering, hugging herself, Jessy inched towards the slender crevice through which they'd squeezed—it rose from the waterline like a jagged bolt of lightning, continuing up the rock face for several feet above their heads—and peered through the narrow opening, chemlight held high. "We've lost our ride."

"And it's an awful long swim home," Owen murmured. He rubbed his arms to encourage the blood flow, then raised his own chemlight, panning it about. "Speaking of our ride… where'd you learn to drive like that?"

Jessy turned back to him. "What? You forgot? I used to ski, remember?"

He had forgotten. Waterskiing, of course. Not snow.

As though reminded of this herself, Jessy glanced down at her leg, and the moonboot encased by the clinging material of her dripping suit. Perhaps wondering if she'd ever get the chance to pursue the sport again, her eyes glazed over, but then she snapped out of it and cast her gaze beyond him, to the opposing end of the rocky shelf. "Hey, what's that?"

Owen turned. At the edge of the light, maybe twenty feet along the shelf, a tall shadow blotted the wall like a black stain. Raising his chemlight, he moved towards it. It looked like a cave mouth; maybe an exit…

When he heard a soft clicking sound emerge from the narrow opening, he paused.

Click-click…

What the hell?

Abruptly, the sound paused, too, and Owen felt compelled to glance from the opening to the ground beneath his feet. All around his boots, crisscrossing the rocky shelf and looking like a maze of cracks, was a series of serpentine threads. He lowered his chemlight. The threads— sprouting from the cave mouth like dozens of strands of crimson spaghetti—stretched in all directions.

Step on a crack, break your mother's back.

He used to recite the rhyme as a kid. Back then, he'd avoided cracks in the pavement because he'd been told it was bad luck to step on them. The branching capillaries, some of them as thick as his little finger, resembled blood-red fissures.

"Is that mold?" Jessy asked.

Owen wasn't sure. Some weird, cave-dwelling fungus, maybe. Either way, he got the feeling it was something to be avoided, just like cracks in the pavement.

Careful not to tread on the spidery strands, he retreated.

From a safe distance, he glanced back at the mysterious cave. The strange clicking sound hadn't restarted, as though whatever had made it had been spooked into silence by the light. He considered a second approach, but at the mere thought of this his skin tingled. "We don't know where that cave leads, if anywhere at all. I suggest we find a different exit."

"My thoughts exactly," Jessy said, already on the move. "Let's head back to the rocky outcrop; that formation that looked like a set of teeth. We can watch from there for passing traffic."

"You think there'll be any?"

Jessy nodded. "Those frogmen caught most of us by surprise, but not everyone. There was a gun battle, remember? I'm guessing there's a good chance that someone got a message out, maybe called for reinforcements. There'll be a response soon enough. And we have flares, right?"

Owen patted his breast, nodding. "We'll have to swim back there, and we have no way of getting warm."

"We can't stay here."

That was true. If they had their facemasks, they could hunker down and attempt to raise the surface via the in-suit comms, but they'd lost those when they'd leapt from the Hurricane. It wasn't a big deal; the system probably wasn't designed for long-range communication anyway. Accepting that Jessy's plan was the only viable option, Owen retook her hand. "Come on, then. If someone comes by, we don't want to miss them."

They both had watersport backgrounds and were strong swimmers, which was fortunate because they needed to be quick. At the crevice, Owen slid from the jutting overhang, gasping as the frigid water stole his breath. He couldn't recall the water being as cold as this the last time he was submerged in the dark dozens of feet below the surface, back when he and Sanchez had traversed a subterranean lake to escape the megarachnid nest. He suspected the Sombra lay deeper underground, even farther from the warm jungle above. Wondering how he'd landed in an almost identical dilemma—but glad, in any case, that he didn't have to deal with any angry arachnids—he helped Jessy into the water. She, too, gasped involuntarily.

"We don't have much time," Owen said, guessing their adrenal glands were already releasing cortisol into their bloodstreams. "At this temperature, I figure we've got twenty minutes before we lose control of our limbs. Hopefully, that's enough to get us back." Even now, he sensed the surging stress hormone was causing his heartrate to accelerate. He hoped he wasn't slipping into shock.

Jessy led them through the opening. As they emerged into the larger cavern, the Hurricane's nose slid beneath the waterline in a mushroom of bubbles.

Shame we couldn't have salvaged something…

Quickly, the two of them headed for the toothy maw, swimming back the way they had come with strong, smooth strokes. A dozen yards in, Owen drew to a halt, treading water and cocking his head. A moment later, he got moving again.

Clearly, his imagination had gotten the better of him, but he could have sworn he'd heard a faint clicking sound bidding them good riddance.

Shivering, he swam for the exit as fast as he was able.

52
α

As stated by the sign on the door, this was indeed a laboratory. Upon entry, Rebecca realised it was also an office space.

Lab 14 was cloaked in deep shadow, and accordingly, flashlight beams jumped and flitted. Rebecca stood at the front of the group, in a small foyer with workstations to the left and a viewing gallery to the right. There, a large glass window overlooked the adjoining science lab, where several white laminate benches topped with electron microscopes, robotic arms, and other equipment in molded white plastic were drawn from the gloom by the probing lights. The space appeared modern and new; in fact, the contrast to the utilitarian, concrete walls outside was stark: Lab 14 was a showcase of glass and steel.

It was also a vacuum, devoid of life and sound.

"It's warm in here," Wyatt said.

"No air-conditioning," Fitzgerald whispered.

Indeed, the background hum of extractors, now absent, only deepened the unnerving quiet.

"It looks clear, but we need to be sure," Carlisle said. "Spread out."

Rebecca nodded, and moved left. "Keep your eyes peeled for exits, phones… anything."

"I'll look for the electrical panel," Naziem said, heading back to the entry. "I'm sure I saw a maintenance closet outside—if the circuit breakers were tripped, I might be able to get the lights back on. There are some other doors I want to check out, too."

"You want company?" Spencer asked.

Naziem hoisted the herder and shook his head.

As the group dispersed, combing the shadows, Rebecca realised the MP5 was again firm in her grasp. Bringing it to bear, she pressed her flashlight against its muzzle, then looked back over her shoulder. As her companions searched, multiple darting beams threw a dizzying combination of abstract shadows and reflected light; all at once, bright shards sprang from mirrored surfaces, and dark shapes seemed to duck and weave.

Tightening her grip on the MP5, Rebecca glanced forward again, moving deeper into the room.

"Where are the workers?" Spencer asked, his voice now emanating from somewhere near the large glass wall of the viewing gallery.

"Skeleton staff, remember?" Wyatt said, his own voice echoing through the empty space.

"Yeah, but there's no-one here at all. Where's the night crew?"

"Maybe there isn't one," Wyatt mused. "I get the feeling this isn't a key operational area."

Rebecca listened to this exchange as she methodically probed her surroundings. For the most part, the area was open, with individual workstations defined by frosted, polycarbonate dividers. Oddly, she found no phones on any of the desks—not only were the surfaces uncluttered, but they were curiously devoid of personal effects. *Sterile*, in fact. This was apt, because a sharp, antiseptic smell hung in the air and underfoot, the floor was coated in a non-slip resin like that favoured by hospitals. A similar material, maybe polyurethane, paneled the few walls not made of glass. To these were affixed long banks of dead-faced monitors.

"Clear," Carlisle called from across the room.

From elsewhere, Spencer's voice: "Clear."

Confirmation came from all quarters. Lab 14, at least on this side of the glass divider, was empty.

"We should check the science lab next door," Fitzgerald said. "Just to be certain."

"There's an entry over here," Wyatt called from the far end of the workspace. He stood to the left of the observation window. "Looks like there's a hatch in there, too, maybe a cleanroom entry. There must be another—"

A metallic clang echoed loudly. Rebecca jumped.

What the…?

The sound had come from inside the science lab, from the maze of ventilation ductwork affixed to the ceiling: a single quick thump, followed by silence.

"Air pump?" Spencer whispered.

"Maybe a fan rebooting," Fitzgerald offered.

Rebecca feared it was neither of those things. The rectangular, galvanised-steel shafts, hidden in shadow but now glinting in the lunging beams of multiple flashlights, were large and numerous, which wasn't surprising; this deep underground, air filtration—and a substantial exhaust system capable of limiting airflow contaminants—was a necessity. When the sound came again, her fears were realised.

Oh no…

On the other side of the glass, the metal conduit pushed in and out of shape. Not once, but several times.

Something was moving through the ductwork. Sliding. Skittering. Something large.

Rebecca ran for the lab entry, pulling Wyatt into a crouch and dropping beneath the observation window. Pressing her back against the wall, she mouthed to the others, "Get down!"

Desperately, Fitzgerald followed her lead, diving beneath the window with Spencer and Carlisle in tow. As they killed their flashlights, the skittering stopped, and Rebecca's breath caught in her throat. She got the distinct impression that whatever was up there had heard them and had paused to listen. There was a crashing sound—a metallic object falling to the ground, maybe a vent cover—on the other side of the glass, followed by a heavier, padded thud as something dropped through the opening and into the lab.

"Where's Naziem?" Carlisle whispered.

With a violent shake of her head, Rebecca thrust a finger to her lips. Inside the lab, movement; unhurried, methodical. The thing was searching, skulking through the shadows.

It knows we're here.

Rebecca tensed. Whatever it was, the animal was big. Bigger than the dog-sized weavers or jumpers. She could tell because its movement was heavy.

An alpha?

Maybe. She doubted it was one of the large females, like the pseudo-Queen that had attacked them back in Intihuasi, atop the temple. That individual, with her obscenely bloated abdomen, had squeezed through a narrow vertical shaft not unlike the ductwork above, but she'd been accompanied by a host of egg-layers. The thing in the lab was alone. Logic suggested it was a large male, then, like the alpha that had tracked them to the river and attacked the *Tempestade*. That specimen had been built differently to the egg-layers; more streamlined than the females, designed for speed and agility. A hunter. But he'd had a reason for tracking down Rebecca and her team—he'd been searching for his mate. And anyway, he'd come with subordinates, too.

If this isn't an alpha, then what the hell is it?

There was a sudden, hefty scurrying, and something thundered to the floor, equipment of some description, shattering on impact, and then on the other side of the observation window, directly above them, a face pushed hard against the glass and froze there.

Rebecca froze, too.

Oh God…

She couldn't see the creature, but above the thump of her own heart, she heard it. Its breaths—although they weren't quite breaths, not in the traditional sense—were loud, which was surprising, because the air flowed through gill-like openings in the creature's abdomen, where its book lungs were located. To hear it like this, from another room and through the pane of glass, suggested the thing was even bigger than she'd imagined.

Keep still…

Another intake of air, long and deep, followed by a snorting exhalation. Long legs crept up the glass—again, she couldn't see them, not from down here—but as they searched, they made padded, scratching sounds. Testing. Tapping. Then they fell silent.

Rebecca sensed a roving gaze above her as the creature, stock-still, scanned the gloomy office space.

Don't panic, it can't see us…

Beside her, someone whimpered.

Rebecca glanced left. It was Fitzgerald. He wasn't alone in his distress; barely concealed terror rippled through the group—even in the darkness, Rebecca could see the whites of her companions' eyes, moist and glistening. Again, Fitzgerald moaned, almost a sob, and she grasped his trembling hand and squeezed.

Don't move. That's what it wants. It wants us to move because it can't see us.

In the absence of visual stimuli, the thing would feel for vibrations with which it could form a sonic image of its surroundings. An image of them.

And in the absence of movement, it had a final option to fall back on.

As the familiar, tingling intrusion washed over her, Rebecca's eyes fell shut in resignation.

No…

Releasing Fitzgerald's hand, opening her eyes, Rebecca lifted the MP5, wondering how strong the glass was and if the thing on the other side of it would break through before she had a chance to open fire, but before she could turn and get above the line of the window there was a shuddering sound in the walls, and a thrum of machinery and extractors kicking into gear, and then across the room, the wall-mounted monitors softly beeped, rousing as one from their slumber.

Rebecca baulked—

—Naziem—

—and then reached for the lanyard around her neck. Unseen, she slid her arm up the wall, towards the faintly glowing touchscreen panel to the left of the window and to the right of the door.

She pressed the prox-card—gripped between two fingers and un-spooling on its reel—against the reader. A series of ascending beeps rose agreeably.

Inside the lab, long banks of suspended fluorescents buzzed and flick-ered and then came alive, flooding the room in a burst of cold white light.

On the other side of the glass, a rush of movement. With a shriek, the thing fled the window, and there was a succession of crashing sounds—more equipment falling—and Rebecca suddenly realised she had turned on her haunches and had poked her head over the sill, and so had Wyatt. Inside the lab, a darting, dark blur—a black shadow—retreated deeper, leaping for the ceiling and the ductwork above, aiming for the place through which it had entered: the vent. It was gone in two or three seconds, maybe even less than that, so Rebecca failed to capture any true detail, anything other than con-firmation of multiple jointed legs and a dark carapace. But what did catch her attention—much to her puzzlement—was the presence of a long limb, maybe a tail. The trailing appendage was the last thing she saw before it, too, was gone, whipping up through the vent, and then the ductwork trembled a final time and there was silence.

"Holy shit," Wyatt said, turning to her. He grabbed her by the arm, his fingers digging deep. "What in God's name was *that*?"

An eruption of panicked voices followed, including Spencer's, rising above them all. "You scared it away by turning on the freaking lights? I mean… goddamned *lights*?"

As if to punctuate his point, the lights in the office space came on as well, so that now, the entire floor was bathed in a stark, white brightness.

"Naziem," Carlisle said. "He did it—he found the circuit breakers."

"Where is he?" Wyatt asked, gazing about. His grip on Rebecca's arm loosened and fell away.

Rebecca barely noticed. Blinking, her attention still focused on the other side of the observation window, she drew upright on unsteady legs. The creature had left a mess in its wake: a mobile cart lay on its side, its contents—computer hardware, mainly, but also other odds and ends, maybe an imaging camera—lay strewn across the floor amidst a sea of twinkling, broken glass. Several feet beyond this lay an upturned chair, and farther down, yet another. A bank of suspended fluorescents, still swinging gently, strobed on and off. Another bank had been ripped from the ceiling altogether and lay dark and broken across one of the white laminate benches.

Significantly, there were doors in this room, a couple at least. The steel hatch was at the room's far end.

"That thing… it's gone, yeah?" Fitzgerald asked, panting heavily and thumping a fist against his chest. "I mean… it moved deeper… deeper into the ventilation system. That's what happened, right?"

"It's gone," Wyatt confirmed. "I saw it go."

"What if it comes back?"

"It won't," Spencer said, wheeling on Rebecca. "It won't come back, because it doesn't like the light, does it? It's scared of the light."

Rebecca said nothing, still blinking, still trying to gather her thoughts when Naziem casually entered the room from the corridor outside. He looked pleased with himself. In one hand was a Dr Pepper, and in the other, a Snickers.

Through a mouthful of both, he bowed and said, "I know, I'm good, right? The power. I got it back on." Oblivious to the sea of blank faces staring back at him, he took another swig, and another bite. "So… did I miss anything?"

53
α

When the lights had gone out, catching him by surprise, Boor had moved fast. Guided by his NVGs and with his Glock out and leading the way, he'd swiftly but silently climbed the stairs to the control room overlooking the cavern where Pank was guarding the advisors. At first, he'd figured the blackout was an unintended consequence of the payload but concluded it could just as likely be part of the counteroffensive; one of the inbound security teams cutting the power before a breach and clear. Either way, the outage wasn't part of the plan, and when he hit the control room his fears were confirmed. Pank wasn't in position. He wasn't anywhere, for that matter, and neither were the two government employees.

Spinning about, Boor cursed.

The hostages had escaped.

54
α

"Naziem, I need you to find a computer terminal," Rebecca said urgently. "We need to access the CCTV."

Blinking myopically, still reeling from the news that another of the assets was on the loose, Naziem stammered, "I thought we were safe down here…"

Rebecca took him gently by the shoulders. "We are, okay?" The assurance sounded hollow, even to her. She couldn't promise they were safe, couldn't be sure of anything right now other than the need to stay calm and act fast. "Please, you need to do as I ask."

"What do you want with the CCTV?" Fitzgerald asked, frowning. "We have to get out of here!"

"I agree," Carlisle said. "Why are we wasting time?"

Releasing Naziem, Rebecca turned. "That animal was different. I'm guessing it was another of those secret projects, like the millipede. But I need a closer look."

"*Why*?"

"Because we should know what we're dealing with," Rebecca said. "Just in case."

"Just in case it comes back, you mean?"

"Didn't we agree it *wasn't* coming back?" Fitzgerald asked, his voice tightening. "If that's your thinking, all the more reason to get out of here *now*!"

"Let's stay calm, okay?" Wyatt implored.

Rebecca turned back to Naziem. With any luck, the shutdown had reset the camera system, got it online again. Hopefully Holtorf wasn't monitoring it. "The lab will be equipped with motion-activated cameras, so there'll be a recording—it should be saved to the DVR," she said, speaking quickly. "But I also want to know where that thing is *now*, so see if you can access the live feed, maybe get us a layout of this place."

"I've got a better idea," Fitzgerald said. "Let's stop wasting time and *blow* this joint!"

Scowling, Spencer wheeled on him. "And go *where*?"

"In there," Carlisle said, nodding through the observation window. "We've searched everywhere else, and there are doors in there, not to mention that hatch."

"No," Fitzgerald said. "No way I'm going inside that room. And I'm not going through it, either. That thing… maybe it didn't go as far as we thought. Maybe it's waiting for us… or something else is. We should double-back, that's what I meant. We don't know what's behind *those* doors."

"And we don't know what else might be out *here*," Wyatt said. "We can't double-back, and Bec's right. We gotta check the entire floor, check the CCTV. Do it right. Secure the area."

"And specifically, that vent," Rebecca said. As far as she was concerned, the plan hadn't changed; no doubt they'd missed vital features along the way—stairs, elevators, exit signage—and until they found those things, or somehow got a message topside, they were stuck here. Most likely the way out *was* through the science lab, but she was no longer content to stumble about blindly. The visit just now, and those bodies upstairs—and in the elevator—had brought everything into sharp focus.

As though arriving at the same conclusion, Naziem snapped from his stupor. "Outside, I found a maintenance closet. The electrical panel was in there… like I thought, the breakers had been tripped, and that's how I got everything back online. Next to the closet was a data center, a server room; I bet the DVR's in there."

"Where's the herder?" Rebecca asked.

Naziem's hands were still full of sugary plunder. "There's a staff room… I must have put it down…"

"I need it."

Nodding, looking more focused now, Naziem said, "And the server room? When the power returned, it probably locked us out."

Moving to the science lab entry, Rebecca thrust the prox-card against the reader—much to Fitzgerald's horror—and pushed open the door. Sticking her foot in the jamb, holding the door ajar, she slipped the lanyard free and threw it to Naziem. "Let's hope Frank had access to everything down here."

Naziem caught the card in the same hand that held the Snickers. Like Fitzgerald, he wavered, his eyes dimming with uncertainty. "And to be sure… the asset… it's gone, right? I mean… the light chased it away?"

"Like I told Fitzgerald, it's gone," Wyatt said. "For now, anyway." Urgently, he turned to Rebecca, and then glanced at the vent. "I think I know what your plan is. I'll get you the herder."

Looking increasingly anxious but resigned to the fact he wasn't going to sway any of them, Fitzgerald scanned the ductwork. "If the creature used the ventilation system to get down here, then the others can do the same."

"Which is why we need to do this," Rebecca said, hefting the MP5. "And fast."

Conceding this, offering to accompany Naziem but perhaps simply wanting to escape the room and the open door, Fitzgerald suggested they look for schematics as well, something that showed the entries and exits, maybe even a layout of the ventilation system. With a sense of urgency and purpose, the men, minus Spencer, scampered through the foyer, their voices trailing as they departed.

"And so, you found a vending machine?" Wyatt asked Naziem, the two of them almost at a jog.

"In the staff room."

"They have Mountain Dew?" Fitzgerald asked, panting to keep up.

"That, and Fanta Grape."

The three of them disappeared. Spencer, chewing rapidly, looked torn.

"I'm sensing you need a sugar hit," Carlisle said to him.

"No. I'll stay until Wyatt's back with the herder."

Rebecca opened her mouth, but Carlisle, brandishing the ultrasonic prod, interjected. "We've got it covered. Go get your fix."

Spencer hesitated. "You want anything?"

Both women asked for water. Nodding, promising a speedy return, Spencer dashed after the others.

As soon as he was gone, Carlisle wheeled about. "The CCTV—it's a good plan, but I know what you're thinking."

"Sorry?"

The younger woman's features, normally hard, grew even more severe. "You're not just looking for that asset. You're looking for *him*."

"Holtorf, you mean."

"I get it," Carlisle said. "I really do. After what he did to the Professor… to your friend… it's understandable. But I won't let you do this."

"Do what?"

"Put a personal vendetta ahead of the group."

Still standing in the doorway, Rebecca broke eye contact to scan the science lab. "Holtorf and his men are as much a threat as any of those assets. We're not safe until we're certain this place is clear, and that nothing is coming for us. Human, or otherwise."

"And that's all? Nothing more?"

"I'm not putting anyone at risk, if that's your concern." Once more locking gazes with the younger woman, Rebecca lowered her voice. "Now, are you gonna help me or what?"

For several beats, Carlisle held the look, perhaps searching for the truth, or simply a modicum of reassurance. "So… what do you need me to do?"

55
α

"We've got power," Naziem said. "That's promising."

The server room was small, dark and cold. Data cabinets and racks laden with the usual hardware lined the walls. Some of the equipment whirred, and a sea of lights flashed sequentially from red to amber to green.

"System's rebooting," Fitzgerald said. "The UPS must have failed, probably before it could switch power sources—I'm guessing a voltage surge stressed the power supply."

"Or the cyber bomb nailed the capacitors," Naziem said. "Okay, here it is." The DVR was a small black box with a dedicated monitor, located at a standing workstation towards the room's rear. He pulled out the keyboard and mouse. "Cross your fingers."

They sourced the interface easily enough. The lab's recordings, however, couldn't be accessed with Naziem's login, and they had no luck with Fitzgerald's, either. Figuring they could spare a few seconds and maybe jolt it with a reboot, they shut it down.

As the system restarted, Fitzgerald unhooked the radio from his belt. "We should give this another go."

"Radio silence, remember? Unless it's an emergency."

Fitzgerald snuffed a laugh, but the sound was choked and uneasy and anything but mirthful. "We're trapped underground with a bunch of fuzzies on the loose. Trust me, it's an emergency."

"You heard Wyatt just now," Naziem said. "Let's stick to the plan."

"The plan," Fitzgerald replied, hefting his trousers. "You think it'll work?"

"Using the herder to create an ultrasonic barrier… it's a smart idea," Naziem said. "But right now, I'm just as worried about Holtorf. If he finds us…"

"Half-man's radio hasn't chirped since Bec found it," Fitzgerald said. "Maybe the fuzzies got Holtorf, too. He could be dead… or gone."

"Or maybe he wants us to believe that."

"You think?" Fitzgerald said, and shrugged. "If you ask me, it's too quiet out there. Fuzzies aside, I get the feeling we're alone down here."

"Then there's no point using the radio, is there?"

"By that rationale, there's no harm, either."

Naziem leaned forward, squinting. "Okay, system's back up." He took hold of the keyboard and typed, but unsurprisingly, the result was the same. At least they had access to the live feed, which went straight to the monitor in full-colour high definition. So long as they could locate the creature in real time, he figured it didn't matter that the recordings were unavailable. Accordingly, he clicked the mouse and the screen split into a large grid, each section devoted to an individual camera. Even though these were labelled, Naziem struggled to get his bearings—to him, the various rooms and corridors of Sublevel 2 looked identical. Shadowed and empty. Quiet.

Probably a good thing.

"Wait!" Fitzgerald said, pointing. "Go back. That camera there."

Naziem clicked again, bringing the relevant feed to full screen.

Adjusting his glasses, Fitzgerald leaned closer to the monitor. "Um, Naziem… what the hell is *that*?"

56
α

"It's a cleanroom," Spencer called from the far end of the science lab. Pressing closer to the hatch, he peered through its acrylic porthole. "There's an air shower in there. I can't see anything else."

Standing below the vent, Carlisle appealed to Rebecca. "A cleanroom. It's gotta be safe, right? Whatever's on the other side will be sealed tight."

"Whatever's on the other side will have ductwork," Rebecca replied, nearly at the top of the stepladder they'd procured from the maintenance room. "This deep underground, you can bet on it."

Carlisle frowned. She seemed impatient, wanting to get going. Maybe nervous. "You know, I didn't see the creature, but if it's using the ductwork to move around, it can't be as big as you say."

"Trust me, it's big," Rebecca replied. At the top of the ladder, she drew a steadying breath and fixed her gaze on the vent above. The opening couldn't be sealed; already, the creature had slammed the rectangular cover free and even refitted, could do so again. Her best bet was to discourage further visits. "Okay, I'm ready."

Ascending the lower rungs, Carlisle raised the herder. Rebecca clasped the device and hesitated.

The vent was a black hole almost four feet wide.

What if the creature's still in there? Hiding? Waiting?

Before she could talk herself out of it, Rebecca stuck her head inside. Her heart thrummed. With her flashlight, she scoured the gloom; left, then right. A draught of cool air struck her face. Nothing else came for her.

"All good?"

"Clear."

Placing the herder into the empty duct, Rebecca hit the on switch. The device hummed to life.

Carlisle was talking. "You say it's big, but those ducts aren't wide enough."

"I saw it, too, remember?" Wyatt said, passing Rebecca the damaged vent cover.

With a grunt, Rebecca maneuvered the lightweight metal grille above her head. Just moments ago, a closer inspection of the ventilation system had confirmed her fears; the ductwork ranged across the ceiling in all directions, disappearing into the walls on all sides. The creature could have fled through any number of outlets, or even quietly returned. As she slid the misshapen grate into position—some of the spring-clips were damaged, and it fit loosely at best—she heard a low, metallic buzz. The ultrasonic herder was causing the conduit to vibrate.

Good. Just as she had hoped. With any luck, the ductwork would carry the pulse throughout the entire system, deterring not only the strange creature, but the remaining assets from Sublevel 1. She felt herself relax a little.

This might just work.

"Are we good?" Carlisle asked.

Rebecca nodded. "That should buy us some time. And some breathing space."

This seemed to put Carlisle at ease, too, but she wasn't finished with Wyatt. "So, what did you see?"

"I don't know," Wyatt replied. "But it was bigger than that hole. Much bigger."

"That's impossible."

"Don't be fooled," Rebecca said, descending quickly and grabbing the MP5 from the laminate bench. "Ever wondered how spiders get into rooms with closed windows and doors? They find alternatives: cracks, plumbing lines, air vents… anything. And they can flatten themselves, often dramatically, to squeeze through the smallest of gaps. In fact, there's a genus of Australian spider, *Dolophones*, otherwise known as the wrap-around spider, that squashes itself so flat it can fold around tree branches like a strip of ribbon." Checking the MP5 but keeping it safetied, she slung the weapon. "Point is, I've seen these animals contort themselves into all manner of shapes, and into exceedingly small spaces."

"I can vouch for its size," Wyatt said as the three of them hurried for the hatch, "but I'm not convinced it was a spider. I mean, it had eight legs, or at least I think it did. But I also saw a tail. Spiders don't have tails."

"A tail? Like a scorpion, you mean?" Carlisle said. "You think that's what it was? There were giant scorpions back in the Carboniferous, right?"

Transferring his flat stone from hand to hand, Spencer turned at their approach. "Scorpions aren't afraid of the light." Chewing fast, he looked at Rebecca. "So, what happened before? Did the light really spook that thing?"

Hurriedly, Rebecca peeked through the now-vacant porthole. The chamber beyond was dimly lit, but like Spencer had said, there was an air shower in there—she could see multiple jets housed within a stainless-steel cubicle. Beyond that, in the opposite wall, was another hatch. Ignoring the question, she asked, "And for certain, you checked the other doors?"

"Like I told you already, storerooms and lavatories," Spencer said.

The hatch was all that remained. In anticipation, Rebecca moved a hand to the prox-card Wyatt had reclaimed from the boys when he'd gone to collect the herder. Just as quickly, she moved it away.

"Bec?" Spencer urged. "The light?"

Rebecca hesitated. Clearing the area was vital—and that included the area beyond the hatch—but until she got the go-ahead, she could do no more than clear her throat.

You owe them an explanation.

"The megs are light-sensitive," she said, turning. "Particularly the egg-layers, which spend their lives inside the nest. That thing wasn't an egg-layer—and at the time, I had no reason to think it was anything other than a meg—but I figured it wasn't comfortable with artificial light, either; at least not a sudden burst of it." She glanced at Spencer. "So, the light might have confused it, or even hurt it, but that's not the reason it fled."

"So, what *is* the reason?" Carlisle asked.

Rebecca lowered her voice. "Egbert," she said.

"What?" Wyatt asked.

"I don't understand," Spencer said. "You mean your *pet*?"

"I consider him a research companion," Rebecca said, moving around, triple-checking the room. "My work—the work I was conducting back at Camp Delta and was brought here to continue—was spawned by an early encounter with the megs. Egbert's central to that work, and my theory."

"By encounter, you mean when you were attacked down in Brazil," Wyatt clarified. "Inside the pyramid."

"We were briefed," Spencer explained. "Sort of."

Rebecca nodded. "I had a couple of close calls down there."

Only a couple?

"And your theory?"

Cognisant of the time, Rebecca wondered if she should radio Naziem for a sitrep but decided against it. She spoke quickly. "Inside the pyramid, there was a huge central chamber at the top of which was a ball of spiders. I suspect that we encountered something similar up in the warehouse just now. Point is, when we entered that chamber back in Intihuasi, I felt a kind of vague, mental intrusion."

"I don't follow," Carlisle said.

"There was another man with me," Rebecca explained. "Oliveira. He felt it, too. Soon after, when the megs woke, I sensed it again. And when the alpha male had me underwater—"

"Hang on, back up," Spencer interjected. "A mental intrusion? You're suggesting they were inside your head? Reading your mind?"

Rebecca squirmed. "At first, that's what I suspected—that they were poking around in there. But it didn't sit right. Afterwards, I wondered if what I'd felt was a simple chemical reaction, the effects of a pheromone used to attract prey, for instance. That could still be true, but I no longer believe the animals are sentient. I'm certain they're electrosensory."

"Like sharks!" Spencer said.

"Great," Wyatt said, facepalming. "Not them again. Always with the sharks."

"Sharks, and other fish," Rebecca said to Spencer, nodding. "No doubt you've heard of the ampullae of Lorenzini?"

Spencer could barely contain his excitement. "The ampullae are sensing organs—they help sharks detect the electrical impulses of their prey. You're saying the megs have a lateral line?"

"Of sorts," Rebecca said. "There's evidence of sensory organs—electroreceptors—behind the eyes, protected by the carapace. I believe they use these to detect electrical and magnetic impulses."

This seemed to pique Wyatt's interest. He clicked his fingers. "All living things create an electric field, and our brains produce electricity. The megs weren't reading your mind, in the sense that they could understand your thoughts, but they were reading the electrical activity of your brain."

"It's less passive than that," Rebecca said. "I suspect they send out a pulse, like echolocation, actively seeking disruptions in the electric field. And I think our bodies react to that."

"Like the feeling you get when you're being watched," Spencer said. "Puts a new spin on *spidey-sense*, yeah?"

Carlisle shook her head. "I've been around the crawlers. If any of this is real, then why haven't *I* felt it? Or Fitzgerald or Naziem?"

"Maybe you have, but failed to recognise it," Rebecca said. "I've become more attuned to it myself. But chances are you haven't been close enough."

"Close?"

"Air is a poor conductor of electricity," Rebecca explained, "and environmental conditions play a part. Then there's the plexiglass. So, proximity is important—you have to be close."

"Or underwater," Spencer said. "Water is a more efficient conductor. That's why electrosensory abilities are more common among marine animals."

Rebecca nodded. "When the Male had me underwater, the effect was heightened. But some terrestrial animals use these abilities to observe their environment, including insects like bees and cockroaches. It's rare, but it isn't unknown. This is what I'm researching. And Egbert is helping me."

Carlisle screwed up her face, apparently far from convinced. "Okay… but *why*? The crawlers have exceptional vision, acute vibration sensitivity… why do they need this?"

Pacing, rubbing his chin, Spencer turned on his heel. "Maybe it's something else entirely; I mean, some fish communicate by generating an electric field, they vary the wavelength, the frequency and delay… and this, in turn, is interpreted by the receiver. Maybe this is how the megs talk to each other."

"It crossed my mind," Rebecca said. "No pun intended." She shrugged. "My work is still in its infancy. Everything is on the table."

Wyatt nodded thoughtfully. "So, going back to what happened here… I think I know what drove that thing away. Fluorescent tubes glow when an electric field excites mercury gas. When you turned on the lights, the sudden appearance of a large, electric field overwhelmed the creature's senses. That's it, right?"

"Seemingly," Rebecca said. "I had hoped the field generated by those fluorescents might camouflage us, maybe mask *our* electrical fields. But we got lucky: the sudden burst of energy seemed to spook it."

Carlisle smirked sarcastically. "Well, that solves everything. We just keep the lights on."

Rebecca didn't bite, and instead, simply nodded her agreement. "I think the field will continue to mask us."

For a while.

It wasn't a long-term solution, that much was certain. Once the creature was attuned to its environment and had learned to filter the various sounds and vibrations, they'd lose their stopgap.

But for now, the others didn't need to know that.

Just then, Fitzgerald's voice came over the radio, speaking fast. "*Good news—we've got ourselves an exit. Trouble is, we might have company.*"

57
α

Beyond the hatch and adjoining cleanroom was a dark passageway. With Carlisle and the brothers trailing closely behind, Rebecca crept its length, MP5 at the ready. "Talk to me," she whispered over the hand-held.

"*Go left,*" Naziem directed. "*There, at the junction.*"

She wasn't thrilled about breaking radio silence; as stated earlier, her preference was to avoid the airwaves altogether. But Fitzgerald had warned them it was a maze out here, impossible to navigate unaided, and he was on the money. Long concrete corridors—most of them braced with criss-crossing steel struts—intersected each other at intervals of roughly a dozen yards, forming an endless grid. Each new passage extended into darkness. In the spaces between were rooms, locked and windowless. Rebecca was surprised at the scale; she'd thought there'd be a simple lab beyond the hatch, maybe another research centre. She hadn't expected this.

"Some kind of storage facility," Spencer said in a low voice.

It felt like that. Rebecca was reminded of the basement archives back at the museum in New York, whole floors filled with artefacts hidden from the public eye. This place was equally vast and just as quiet.

What are they hiding in here?

Preceded by a burst of static, Naziem's voice crackled over the radio. "*Okay, you're clear. At the next junction, go right.*"

"And the creature?"

"Like I said, you're clear."

To discourage eavesdroppers, they'd chosen one of the lesser-used frequencies. That had been Naziem's idea. Now, he and Fitzgerald were the group's eyes and ears, tracking them via the network of cameras from the relative safety of the server room. The two men had pieced together a rudimentary floorplan; turns out the elevator down from the warehouse was more of a backdoor, likely a service entry for maintenance staff. Presumably, the scientists and lab staff would enter from the front—being the other side of the vast chamber to the one in which Rebecca and her companions now found themselves—so the boys had concentrated their search there. They'd promptly located stairs and an elevator hall. Certain this was their ticket topside, Rebecca had opened the hatch, the group entering via the air shower. The presence of a cleanroom suggested this was a controlled environment, but the air filtration was minor, maybe ISO Class 7 at best. Most likely, the workers wouldn't be required to wear protective bunny suits in here, perhaps getting away with just their regular gear and lab-coats. Not that she cared right now about dust or microbes or cross-contamination.

She continued forward. Once she and the others were safely topside, they'd send the cavalry back for the boys. That was the plan, anyway. Currently, they were on a slight detour. Earlier, Fitzgerald had caught something on one of the cameras, something that needed immediate investigation.

He thought he'd seen people in here.

"You're almost there," Naziem said. *"Straight on."*

At the junction, Rebecca maintained her course. The others followed, boots quietly scuffing the epoxy flooring. Overhead, stirred by the group's approach, a bank of motion-activated fluorescents awoke, only to time off seconds after the four of them had passed. The lights clicked with the change of status.

"Okay, at the next intersection, turn left. Then take another right, and you're there," Naziem said. *"That's where they are."*

Rounding both corners, Rebecca entered an open area dominated by a standalone structure of shuttered plexiglass. There, she drew to a halt. Behind her, the others did, too.

"Christ…" Spencer said.

Fitzgerald was right. There *were* people here. Four of them, face-down on the ground in a pool of dark crimson.

"I think I'm going to be sick," Carlisle said.

Long sprays of red patterned once-white lab-coats. These weren't Holtorf's people. These were researchers. Civilians.

"*It wasn't the creature, right?*" Naziem asked. "*This is something else? Like we thought?*"

Her stomach squirming, Rebecca forced herself to look closer. The lab-techs, three men and a woman, lay side by side, as though before death they'd been lined up shoulder to shoulder. Open wounds gaped at the back of their heads. Empty shell casings littered the floor.

"These people were executed," Wyatt said.

"Holtorf," Spencer said, turning away. "Goddamned murdering bastard."

"*Bec?*" Naziem pressed.

"Confirmed," Rebecca said into the hand-held, trying hard not to gag at the sharp, coppery reek coursing thickly through the air. "No survivors. This is Holtorf's handiwork." Shaking, she lowered the radio and cursed under her breath. When Fitzgerald had stumbled upon the horrifying image, he and Naziem had realised they were looking at corpses but had questioned if there were more people in here, survivors hiding in a blind spot or beyond the range of the cameras. If there were, they probably needed help, maybe urgent medical attention.

But there was no-one else. Holtorf had made certain of that.

A few feet away, Carlisle—still doubled over at the waist and with her hands on her knees—swallowed hard. She seemed rattled, perhaps all too aware of how close she and the rest of them had come to a similar fate. She gave no indication that these people were known to her. Running a hand over her mouth, she straightened. "We should go."

"Agreed," Wyatt said.

Rebecca lifted the radio. "Naziem, we're gonna make for the exit."

"Wait," Spencer said. He'd moved several yards along the adjoining corridor, towards a long window fixed into the wall of the plexiglass building. He jutted his chin. "Before we go, you might want to check this out."

Hurrying over, Rebecca followed his gaze through the glass, and then once more lifted the radio. "Naziem, strike that last comment. We're gonna need you to stand by."

58
α

So, this is what they're hiding…

As she stared through the glass, it dawned on Rebecca that the large, shuttered structure, positioned in the centre of the maze, was likely the focus of operations down here. Beyond the wide observation window, bathed in muted red light, was a large room—more a cross between a hangar and a greenhouse—extending lengthways into the distance. Its low ceiling, curved and domelike, was braced with a series of steel ribs that ran to the floor on both sides. Several feet below the ceiling's arch, running horizontally, was a hanging scaffold, effectively a long, mesh grid, and dangling from this, attached by vertical threads of silk, were dozens—maybe *hundreds*—of white spheres. Each of these was the size of a small soccer ball.

Eggs sacs.

"This is a hatchery," Rebecca whispered, awestruck.

"The megs… they're breeding them down here," Wyatt said.

Rebecca thought back to Intihuasi, and the nuptial chamber inside the pyramid. That room, too, had been filled with egg sacs, but it had also been home to a host of protective mothers, including an alpha.

Were there egg-layers inside this room? Was there an alpha in here?

Spencer turned to Carlisle. "You knew about this?"

"The breeding program?" Carlisle clarified, shrugging. "I knew of its existence. But the details? No. It wasn't my job."

Glancing at the bodies, Wyatt said, "It was *their* job. Compartmentalisation of information."

Rebecca, too, shot her gaze that way, perplexed as to why Holtorf had murdered the techs but hadn't sabotaged the hatchery.

Returning to the window, she stared through the light sheen of condensation hugging the pane. Inside the room, connected to an array of pipes running the length of the metal scaffold, were tall aluminum tanks, one per row. They looked like carbon dioxide cylinders. Each was marked ARP-44.

"Alpha Retinue Pheromone," Carlisle explained.

"The Queen Substance," Rebecca said. "This is the synthetic version that Fitzgerald told us about, the chemical infused into the habitats upstairs. They're infusing it in here as well."

"Tricks the weavers into thinking the alpha is present," Carlisle said. "I guess it keeps the eggs viable, too."

Chewing loudly, Spencer moved to the right of the window, where a card-reader sat inches beneath an eye-level touchscreen interface. With his index finger, he swiped the screen and frowned. "Bec, the card. Do you mind?"

"I don't think you should be playing with that," Wyatt said, seemingly less bothered by his brother's noisy chewing than the dangers his brashness might unleash.

Ignoring him, catching the card as Rebecca tossed it his way, Spencer touched it to the reader, then swiped the screen once more. "Just as I thought," he said, shifting his gum from one side of his mouth to the other. "All the relevant data: temperature and humidity control, biometric information, egg viability. Lots of different menus. Hey, this is interesting."

"What's that?" Wyatt asked, suddenly curious.

Spencer drilled deeper, reading aloud as he went. "Duration of embryonic development: eight days at 77 degrees. Post-embryo, still cocooned, three days. Emergence from the cocoon and first instar: three days. Post-cocoon: two more molting instars, defined by morphological changes, seven days each. Full maturation in 28 days." He looked up. "This is the megs' life-cycle, from embryo to adulthood."

Wyatt peered over his brother's shoulder. "Go back," he said. "There… that's the current crop… still in the first eight days." He jabbed a finger at the screen. "Bec, what's this?"

Both men moved aside, allowing Rebecca an unobstructed view of the screen. The full-colour monitor was filled with random graphs, numbers and letters. It took her a moment to get her bearings.

"There," Wyatt said, pointing. "The embryos are numbered by column and row. But what are all those letters next to them? DH, EH, PBAN… and here, AKH? They're all different. What are they? Chemicals? And what about these? Prothoracicotropic? Sesquiterpene? Again, more letters… JH?"

Rebecca leaned closer to the screen.

"Bec?"

"Um, JH… juvenile hormone," Rebecca said, only half-listening as she worked her way through the data. "Inhibits adult growth. Belongs to sesquiterpenes."

"What about this one? 20E?"

"20-Hydroxyecdysone. Another hormone. Controls the molting process in arthropods." Her interest climbed as other ecdysteroids caught her attention. Struck by an idea, she swiped the screen and delved deeper, scanning days and dates. Navigating back to the current cycle, the megs' embryonic stage, she spent a few seconds skimming various enclosed file notes. She then stepped back and blinked. "Those letters, they're acronyms for hormones. The figures beside them are dosages." She looked at the brothers in turn. "The researchers are introducing—and in some cases, denying—hormones to the embryos."

"Hormones," Spencer said slowly. "So, what… the spiders are getting acne and growing hair in extra places?"

Wyatt rolled his eyes.

"They're conducting experiments down here," Rebecca said.

"On the embryos?" Wyatt clarified.

Rebecca nodded, and started to talk her way through it, as much for her own clarification as for her companions. "So, the megs… they're eusocial, right? There's a division of labour. This is unique; no other known species of spider has a defined caste system. So, in that sense, they're more like ants."

"We already know this," Carlisle said.

"I know, but hear me out," Rebecca said. "Ant larvae develop into specific castes as determined by hormones. The introduction of a specific hormone—essentially, a certain chemical—at a particular point in time determines whether a larva will become a worker, a soldier, or even a queen."

Wyatt pursed his lips. "So, you think the researchers were trying to manufacture more weavers? I mean, this is one big biofabrication lab, basically a silk farm—that's what Li told us. By playing with hormones—flicking the chemical switches, so to speak—they could ensure a greater yield of workers, and in turn optimise silk production. It makes sense."

"It does," Rebecca said, "but by flicking those chemical switches, they can also create jumpers, trapdoors, egg-layers… or *soldiers*."

"Soldiers," Spencer said slowly. "That's it, isn't it?"

"That's *what*?" Wyatt asked.

"They're not producing weavers down here," Spencer said. "They're producing bioweapons. They're producing an army."

Carlisle scoffed at him, her eyes widening in open ridicule. "Bioweapons? Trained *spiders*? I know you like your conspiracies, but that takes the cake."

"What? You're *surprised* by this?" Spencer countered.

Rebecca interjected. "I wasn't suggesting bioweapons, but there's a reason I mentioned soldiers. Some ants have a size-variable worker caste—basically, there are minor workers and major workers. The majors are often referred to as soldiers. But there are a few species that have a third caste: the supermajor caste."

Carlisle laughed. "This is too much. You're kidding me, right? That's a real name? They call them *supermajors*?"

"The supermajors are essentially large soldiers," Rebecca said. "Technically, they're a distinct caste in themselves, and morphologically different. But for all intents and purposes, they're an extra-large version of the majors. Fearsome looking: giant heads, huge mandibles."

"Supersoldiers," Spencer said, turning to Carlisle. "See! I told you! They mucked around with the embryos and created a supersoldier caste. Bioweapons!"

Carlisle shook her head. "No. Weaver production I can understand, maybe even silk enhancement, like those guys who edited spidersilk proteins into the silkworm genome to produce genetically modified silkworms—you know, to create strains of stronger, lighter, more flexible silk fibres."

Now it was Spencer's turn to scoff, and he embraced his opportunity with gusto. "Pfft. Seriously? We're not talking about transgenic silkworms. It's bioweapons for sure. All this stuff about silk production, farming… it's a smokescreen. This is a military facility, for Christ's sake."

"Guys," Rebecca interrupted. "I'm not talking about bioweapons *or* weaver production. All this mucking around with chemical switches… it tells us something else. It tells us about that creature with the tail."

59

α

The radio hissed as Naziem interrupted them. *"Hey, what's the holdup? You've been there a while."* Neither he nor Fitzgerald could hear what was going on.

Rebecca checked her watch. "We should go."

"No, this is important," Spencer said. "You've worked out what that thing is? The creature?"

"We can talk on the way," Rebecca said.

"No, wait," Wyatt said. "Naziem and Fitzgerald have us covered; we have a minute."

Hesitating a moment, Rebecca lifted the hand-held and issued instructions before elaborating on her theory. She spoke fast. "When I saw that creature back in the lab, when I saw the tail, I wasn't sure what to make of it, not at first. A few things sprang to mind, but I can tell you, there was nothing like that in Brazil. Of course, there were no giant millipedes or cockroaches down there, either."

"So, you thought this was like them, something new and undiscovered," Spencer said. "A giant scorpion."

"I still thought it was a spider," Rebecca said. "Tailed spiders exist—there's an Australian species, for instance, aptly named the Scorpion-tailed spider. The females have a tail and when disturbed or threatened they curl it over their body—just like a scorpion. I thought it might be something similar.

But I couldn't discount the fact that it *mightn't* be a spider—there's an early arachnid, *Uraraneida*, for example, that lived nearly 400 million years ago; not a spider, but it looks like one, with eight legs and spigots that may have excreted silk. And it has a tail. And then there's *Chimerarachne*, which may be a relative of *Uraraneida*, or may be something else entirely—the jury's still out—but again, it's spiderlike, and it has a tail."

Carlisle's face creased into a frown. "I can't say I'm any clearer on this," she said. "You're hedging your bets. Sounds like you're saying it *could* be a spider… or it might not be."

"It's a meg," Rebecca said, removing any shred of ambiguity. Turning to the screen, she tapped it. "Now that I know they've been experimenting down here, flicking switches, I'm certain of that. In fact, I'm guessing they've unlocked an evolutionary throwback."

"What?" Carlisle asked. "An ancestor?"

"You've heard of atavism?"

Spencer inclined his head. "The reappearance of ancestral traits that have been lost over time."

"Effectively, yes," Rebecca said. "I think that by flicking all those hormonal switches, by playing around with embryo development, they've reawakened a previously dormant state."

"They flicked the wrong switch," Wyatt deduced.

"More likely, the wrong combination of switches," Rebecca said. "There's a lot of information here, too much to go through now. Maybe they introduced an artificial hormone into the mix. I don't know. I need to study their notes. I need more time."

"We don't have it," Carlisle said.

Rebecca nodded, agreeing. "Either way, the reason I never saw that creature in Brazil, is because it wasn't there. This is new. This has been engineered."

Wyatt shook his head, looked through the window at the hanging egg sacs, and then turned back. "They woke something. Question is: *what*?"

"I can't answer that," Rebecca said. "But with atavism, when something lost comes back, it often comes back… differently."

"Sounds ominous," Spencer said.

"It can return in unexpected, potentially dangerous ways," Rebecca explained. "Take the supermajors, for instance. A few years ago, there were some scientists—they were studying a class of ants, the Pheidole genus—and they were doing the same thing as the researchers here; you know, flicking switches to create throwbacks in the lab. And they were successful. But for some reason, the supersoldiers weren't tolerated by the colony. The other ants *killed* them."

"They knew they were different," Wyatt reasoned. "They sensed the supermajors were throwbacks, that they weren't natural."

Rebecca nodded. "So, like I said, this thing's a meg, but it's not part of the group. Like those Pheidole supermajors, it's different, it's unnatural, and the other megs know it. I think the alphas sensed an intruder and rallied the others, called them down to H-5."

"The family gathering," Spencer said. "The megs were distracted, focused on the imposter instead of us."

As though the subject was a large jigsaw puzzle in need of a collective solution, Wyatt added another piece. "And so, you've got this aberration that's been brought back from the past, suddenly released into a world that's entirely different to everything it knows—or is conditioned by instinct to know—and it's surrounded by enemies; the other megs, *and* us. It's a loner, it's confused, and so it does what it must to defend itself. It resorts to violence. Kill or be killed."

"Sounds a little unhinged," Carlisle said.

"Maybe it is," Spencer mused. "That's why the researchers kept it isolated in H-7 or H-8 under a restricted program. That's why no-one knew about it."

"Well, we know about it now," Wyatt said. "And the secret is out of isolation."

Glancing fitfully about, Carlisle swallowed hard. "Question is, where is it *now*?"

Spencer threw his gaze about, too. "If you're alone, confused, and surrounded by enemies, where would you go?"

"You'd retreat," Carlisle answered. "Maybe find a place to hide."

"No," Rebecca said, shaking her head. She thought back to the incident in the lab and couldn't help but feel there was more to this thing's actions than a simple desire to survive. "This thing isn't going to ground—that's not how it's programmed. Something tells me it's a killer. A predator." On that subject, she was suitably qualified; predator-prey dynamics was her specialty.

Wyatt seemed to understand. "A predator doesn't hide."

"No, it doesn't," Rebecca said. "A predator hunts."

60

α

Groaning, Owen dragged himself from the water. For the most part, the rocks forming the toothy maw were jagged and angular, too slippery to find purchase, but hidden amongst the peaks was a flat shelf of granite. Shivering with cold, his arms numb and weakened by the exhausting swim, he clawed fully onto the ledge and then turned for Jessy. Out of the river, she sank onto her back, equally drained, her chest heaving.

Owen craved rest, too, but he didn't pause. "You're freezing," he said, helping her up and throwing his arms around her. Beneath his hazmat suit, his soaked clothes squelched, the garments chilled and heavy and clinging. Earlier, he'd considered ditching the suit—not only was it unwieldy, but without the mask it couldn't be sealed. Despite this, it was made of polymer, which had given him an idea. "We need to get out of our clothes."

Her teeth chattering, Jessy raised her eyebrows, perhaps tempted for a joke but too cold and fatigued to bother. "What are you proposing?"

"Our clothes… they're sapping the warmth from our skin," Owen explained, trembling. "We need to take them off… put our suits back on. You go first, I'll turn away."

Already, the resistant suits were sloughing the last of the water; they were nearly dry.

Understanding, shivering hard, Jessy nodded and moved behind him. "No peeking."

A series of swishing, shuffling sounds followed, as Jessy slipped firstly from her suit, then her clothes, the latter landing in a growing wet pile to Owen's left. Feeling his face flush warm, he fixed his gaze on the black mirror of the Sombra as it snaked through the supercavern. This was a perfect vantage point: it was dark in here, but the rocky outcrop—the result of an ancient cave-in—sat in the middle of the river, at the head of the long, water-filled throat through which they'd just swum. Any responders to the incursion would have to pass this way, and when they did, racing to the aid of those back at the Vent, he and Jessy would flag them down with flares and glowsticks.

That was the plan, anyway.

He heard Jessy slipping back into her suit, probably not the easiest of tasks with her calf encased in a moonboot. "You okay back there?"

She sat down beside him. "All done."

Once Owen had added his own clothes to the wet pile and had climbed back into his suit, he huddled next to Jessy, enfolding her in his arms.

She hugged him back. "That was a good idea. I'm feeling better already."

"Me too," Owen said. Though he could feel the heat returning to his limbs, he continued to tremble, and suspected the cold and lingering adrenalin was only partly to blame. "Still, a fire would be nice."

"Shame we can't burn our clothes."

"No, I'm glad they're wet. That Hawaiian shirt is one of my favourites."

A moment passed in silence before Jessy broke it. "Hey… up there. Look."

By now, Owen's eyes had adjusted. Realising the cavern wasn't as dark as he'd first thought, he followed her gaze to the ceiling, which was awash with pinpricks of white-blue light.

"Glowworms," Jessy said breathlessly. "They're beautiful."

The ceiling was covered in them, both here inside the rocky outcrop and throughout the supercavern at large, like a sprinkling of stars in a night sky. Awestruck, Owen glanced about. He'd seen glowworms before and wondered if these were the bioluminescent beetles common to cave systems around the world. Keen to fully appreciate the sight, he stuffed their glowsticks under the wet clothes and waited for his eyes to adjust further.

Almost immediately, the shimmering lights intensified. *That's weird,* Owen thought, unconvinced that his vision could have improved so quickly or markedly. It was as though his and Jessy's presence—or perhaps even their undivided attention—had excited the creatures, causing them to glow more brightly. The bioluminescence was so brilliant, in fact, that Owen could now clearly see his surroundings. This shocked him, and squinting, he questioned if these were glowworms at all. On closer inspection, the lights were in fact white-blue strings; they hung from the ceiling in long threads, like chandeliers of twinkling ice crystals.

Or—even more weirdly—the trailing blue tentacles of a swarm of gleaming jellyfish.

Owen blinked. As though adrift in an ocean current, those tentacles gently waved.

You're imagining it.

No, he wasn't. They were moving. Was there a current of air blowing softly through the cavern?

Maybe. Or they could be waving of their own accord.

Don't be ridiculous.

He tensed, suddenly fearful that one or more of those glowing appendages might reach down from the ceiling to grasp him.

Get a grip, Owen.

That's exactly what I *don't* want.

"Some subterranean glowworms trail glowing, sticky threads to attract prey," Jessy said, apparently sensing his unease.

Owen wondered how she knew that, but then started to relax. Jessy was right. They're just bugs. Entirely normal. *Natural.* He shook his head, and for some reason, an image of the strange, capillary-like fungus from the other cave sprang into his mind's eye.

Was that organism normal and natural, too?

He shifted closer to Jessy, and she leaned into him, burrowing her head against his neck. Her trembling subsided. So did his.

"You know," Jessy said, still nestled in place, "when I was a kid, maybe ten or eleven, we took a family vacation to Maui, a whole week of surf, sun and sand."

"My idea of heaven."

"Mine too," Jessy replied. "Every day, Dad and I would go out snorkelling, in the harbor just out from the resort, and I'd practice my breathing techniques, you know, so I could hold my breath longer and dive deeper. I got really good at it and one day, I'd swum a little farther out, beyond the shore reef, and below the surface there was this wall of rock, almost like a bommie, but it was deep, deeper than I'd ever gone."

"Let me guess… you went for it."

"I was certain there was adventure to be had, and I was right," Jessy said, nodding. "On the way down, I remember seeing this crevice in the wall, like a tall vertical crack, and I was convinced there was something exciting in there, like long-lost pirate treasure or some secret underwater kingdom, and my heart was thumping, my lungs burning, but I didn't care, I was bursting with excitement. Then I finally reached the wall and peeked through the crack, inside the crevice, and at first, I didn't see it, which was probably why it startled me so much, but there was this tentacle poking out, and in fright I nearly sucked in a lungful of water right then and there. I never did see the creature itself—its body was inside the fissure—but the tentacle seemed huge, and then it moved, lunged for me, and I was sure it was trying to grab me and maybe pull me through the crack, even though I was too big to fit in there. Obviously, I got out of there fast, before this massive sea monster that was most likely just a small octopus could drag me to my death, and as I hit the surface, swimming like crazy back to the shore reef and certain the creature was hot on my tail, I remember having this flashing thought… a kind of panicked realisation that I'd intruded on this thing's domain and if something bad happened, it was all my fault. I was an imposter… I had no right to be there in the first place. It sounds dramatic, I know, but I felt lucky to have escaped."

Owen realised Jessy's grip on him had tightened, her body tensing at the memory, and gently, he stroked her hair. The point of her story wasn't lost on him, and he thought about the Vent before glancing nervously at the blue tentacles above.

When Jessy spoke again, her voice was low. "The Sombra extends from the Vent," she said slowly. "Perez claimed it was part of a huge underground river system, along with the Hamza. That's what he said, right?"

Owen nodded. "That's what he said."

"But he hinted at something else, too," Jessy said. "Another river, the Amazon's secret twin; a huge waterway running beneath the Amazon and out to the Atlantic, just like its famous sibling."

"Two mouths, one above ground, another below," Owen said, guessing where she was heading. "The Amazon disgorges more at its mouth than the next eight biggest rivers in the world combined. If there's a secret river beneath it, the volume of fresh water exploding into the ocean would be off the charts."

"And its true source untraceable," Jessy said. "I mean, you'd assume all that water was coming from the one outlet, from the Amazon itself, but that's only half the story…"

Owen hesitated. He hadn't previously considered the deeper implications. "If Perez is right, if the Amazon does have an underground twin fed by a vast system of tributaries, including the Sombra, then anything that might have escaped the Vent—"

"Would have direct and undetectable access to the ocean," Jessy said. "Free passage on a huge, subterranean highway."

Christ.

This was big. Fresh water spewed so powerfully from the Amazon's mouth that it could be found more than 160 kilometres out to sea; such unbridled force could flush all sorts of things far and wide. Again, he thought of the capillary-like fungus at the opposing end of the rocky throat, that strange organism that had initially struck him as unusual but now seemed inherently foreign. A sliver of ice coursed down his spine.

What else had escaped to the outside world? And what had stayed close, making its home in these very caves, or in the Sombra itself?

Reflexively, he drew his legs from the water's edge.

Jessy did, too, and with that action, she started to shiver again. "Owen, what if no-one comes for us? What if those men at the Vent were part of a larger force that's also taken control of the pyramid? What if everyone up there is *dead*?"

It began as a wrinkle of unease, a small ripple of dread, but soon it was growing, swelling into a wave of despair that may well have been spawned by the Sombra itself, driven from below by some unspeakable horror. As it hit Owen, he didn't react, managing to mask his concerns before the wave could drag him down, but Jessy's words had highlighted the stark reality of their predicament. Suddenly, he couldn't help but feel they were as far from home as they could ever be, stranded and alone in the cold and dark and with no hope of return. Determinedly, he resisted those thoughts and clutched Jessy tighter. "We can't think that way. Someone will come for us, I know it."

Even to him, those words sounded hollow, but they proved oddly prophetic. Almost immediately, a low drone buzzed from afar, the sound of a motorboat heading their way, and promisingly, from the right direction.

Owen stood. Someone from the surface was approaching.

Trouble was, there was no telling who.

61
α

"We gotta go," Wyatt said. "Now."

He got no argument. With a final, troubled glance at the murdered scientists, the group departed the plexiglass hatchery and hurried for the exit. Guided by Naziem, Rebecca led Carlisle and the brothers through the grid-like corridors with speed, but also stealth. She sensed in her companions an ever-growing edginess, something for which she herself had no immunity. The notion that a large predator might be down here somewhere, not only skulking in the shadows but actively on the hunt, was at best unnerving.

Let's hope the ultrasonic herder is still doing its job.

Moving level with her, Spencer made small talk, perhaps as a distraction. "You know, you keep mentioning all these unusual, Australian spiders; wrap-arounds, spiders with tails. You guys seem to have a lot of them."

"Spiders? About 2,000 different species," Rebecca said without stopping.

"Australia is scary."

"Wait till I tell you about the snakes."

Spencer seemed to shiver. "*Snakes…* Wyatt won't be vacationing there anytime soon." Subtly, he shifted topic. "There was something else you mentioned. Just before. Something about the alphas, and how they summoned the subordinates."

Rebecca nodded. "They did the same down in Brazil."

Spencer acknowledged this with a nod of his own. "All this talk about alphas and betas… it got me thinking. The tailed creature… I think it's an omega."

"Sorry?"

"Wolves," Spencer explained. "Like the megs, a wolf pack has alphas and betas, but it also has an omega. The omega is solitary, the lowest-ranking member—it's usually pushed to the periphery and bullied by the others. This new creature is an outsider, but it's still a meg; it might be an omega."

Rebecca bit her lip, turning to him. "I guess you could think of it that way. Maybe—"

She jumped as the radio in her hand hissed loudly, Naziem's voice yelling, *"Guys! Stop!"*

Rebecca halted. Ducking, she waved the others into a crouch, right at the intersection of two corridors. "Naziem, what's wrong?"

Before he could answer, a bank of lights—one corridor over, and several cross-corridors down—flickered… and then burst to life.

"Oh no," Wyatt whispered.

The lights are motion-activated…

"Naziem?"

"We're working on it… we thought we saw movement at the entry, but we were watching you—"

She cut him off, promptly muting the radio as Wyatt, peeking ahead, motioned desperately for quiet. As he did, the first bank of lights died, and the next activated—same corridor, but this time closer to their current position.

Something was heading towards them, from the exit at the end of the room.

"Bec," Spencer mouthed, pointing upwards.

Rebecca lifted her gaze to the bank of fluorescents blazing overhead.

Nowhere to hide.

Raising the MP5, flicking off the safety, Rebecca caught Carlisle's attention, jutting her chin at the junction and hooking a thumb to the right. Hefting the ultrasonic prod, Carlisle nodded, understanding.

"Wait here," Rebecca whispered to the brothers. Her mouth was dry, and her heart thudded loudly in her ears as she rose and scampered forward with the younger woman in tow, resigned to the fact they had no choice but to meet their adversary front on, and then they were around the corner and in the next corridor, the same corridor as the approaching enemy.

There, Rebecca stopped dead in her tracks, which was precisely the response of the person at the passageway's opposing end; the woman with jet-black hair tied in a no-nonsense bun and a white lab-coat draped over a dark pantsuit.

"Li?" Carlisle whispered.

62

α

For a moment, all three women stood rooted in shock. Then Li's eyes widened, and she stumbled forward, limping. "You made it out!"

"Sandy?" Carlisle asked, her voice laced with both surprise and suspicion. "How'd you get down here?"

Li didn't answer. She was a dozen yards or more away and intent on closing the gap, but slowly, because her left ankle seemed to be injured. As she hobbled forward, she latched a watery gaze on Rebecca and started to ramble. "This is incredible… he told me this would happen, that you'd escape… he said that if anyone could get out of there alive, it was you. And he was right."

What?

"And the others?' Li asked. "They're okay?"

"Sandy," Carlisle said. "How about you hold up a moment… *what's that in your hand*?"

Rebecca dropped her gaze. Grasped within Li's right hand was a gun, possibly a Glock semi-automatic, and as she wondered how the hell Li could be in possession of such a thing, she realised there was blood on that hand, too, and even more on Li's lab coat. "Sandy, are you hurt?"

"He hoped you'd understand," Li said, still hobbling. "But he had to take the chance. Holtorf was going to kill you… his men were going to execute you, shoot you, and there was no way out of that, but he said he'd only cooperate with Holtorf if they threw you in the habitat instead, like they did with Frank and the others…"

"Sandy, wait!" Carlisle said. "You're not making any sense…"

But Li didn't wait. "He took a real beating for it, but he didn't care, he said that otherwise, he wouldn't give them what they wanted, and I guess he had them over a barrel because they needed his help… he must have known this, and Holtorf must have known it, too, because of what happened next."

"Next?" Rebecca asked.

"He gave you a fighting chance," Li explained, "and later, he told me that's all he wanted, to give you that chance… and he said he didn't care if Holtorf had beaten him to death right then and there, so long as he'd done everything in his power to give you that chance. He'd have given his life for you, that's what he told me. And I believed him."

"Sandy, please… I don't understand," Rebecca said, her mind spinning, trying to fill the gaps. "What are you talking about? *Who* are you talking about?"

Finally, Li drew to a halt. "He said you'd find a way, that you'd get out of there, and he was right. *He was right!*" Her eyes flickered, the pupils narrowing suddenly, snapping into focus. "I'm sorry, Bec. I couldn't stop him."

"Stop *who*?" Rebecca asked.

"Ed," Li said flatly. "He's gone after Holtorf."

Rebecca rocked back on her heels. She felt faint.

Ed?

"Sandy… the gun," Carlisle said. "Where'd you get the gun?"

Li glanced down at her hand just as Wyatt and Spencer hurried into the corridor, having obviously overheard the exchange. Li didn't seem to notice their arrival, and slowly lifted the pistol. As she did, her expression soured, dimming with distaste. "I don't like guns," she murmured. "I didn't want this thing to begin with. When the lights went out, we jumped our guard, that's when I rolled my ankle, and maybe got cut, it was all a blur, and then we made our escape, and Ed told me to take the gun for protection. I don't want it anymore." She offered the Glock to Carlisle, who took it with evident relief.

Rebecca barely perceived this. "Ed," she whispered to herself, her thoughts racing. *He's here… I did see him earlier.* She looked at Li. "You said he… *Ed…* is working for Holtorf?"

"Not *for* him," Li said, shaking her head. "Holtorf had him hostage, those other soldiers brought him down from the surface when they brought down Frank. I'd never met him before that moment, but it was clear that Holtorf needed him, just like they needed Frank, and then they threw Frank inside, and then…" She lowered her gaze, fighting tears. "Well, like I said, Ed and I escaped. He told me to get help, to raise the alarm, to find you guys and open the hatch… and I came here looking for a phone while he went after Holtorf." Her face creased with concern. "Holtorf got his hands on the research."

"We know about Holtorf's plan," Rebecca said. "We know he came for the research, to steal what he could and to sabotage what was left. What I don't understand is Ed's role in this, or why Holtorf needed him. What's Ed got to do with the Farm?"

Li tilted her head, her expression shifting from concern to confusion. "The Farm? Holtorf isn't here for that. He came for the sphere."

"*Sphere*?" Spencer blurted. "What sphere?"

Li answered, but Rebecca didn't actively listen—she didn't need to. With that single word, the pieces fell swiftly into place. In hindsight, it all seemed rather obvious, and she guessed she should have tied the threads together earlier; hell, subconsciously perhaps, she *had*. Either way, Li's revelation was confirmation of another project, another black budget operation running parallel to the meg research. It made sense; realistically, it could never have been just about the spiders, could never have been just about the habitats or silk harvesting or biofabrication. Those things were relevant, no doubt, but from the get-go there'd been even bigger fish to fry. Obviously, the military had extracted the Intihuasi sphere—the one buried beneath the pyramid, because the smaller sphere had been destroyed—and flown it out on one of the dozens of choppers that had for weeks buzzed over Camp Delta. Ultimately, they'd brought it here. At the same time, they must have brought Ed on board, too, just as they'd brought her on board to continue her research with the megs. Again, it made sense. It would also explain why Ed had recently fallen off the radar. Everything was connected, right? She'd suspected as much from the start, or at least from the moment she'd figured out that Beckett was moving her and Owen and Jessy into place like pawns on a chess board. There was a bigger picture, and there always had been.

Now, as the pieces coalesced, she heard Li tell the others that she hadn't been privy to this other project, that she hadn't known of its existence or what, exactly, it was about, and again, Wyatt mentioned compartmentalisation of information, and then Li told them that despite this, she *had* seen the sphere—only moments before her escape—and that Ed had access to it and had in turn unwillingly given *Holtorf* access to it, and then Holtorf had loaded it onto a truck and fled. And now, perhaps to make amends, Ed had gone after him.

Rebecca listened to this quietly, glancing at the MP5 in her hands before lifting her gaze to Carlisle and the brothers. "You need to go with Sandy."

"What?" Wyatt asked, frowning.

"The exit's just over there," Rebecca said. "Get Dave and Naziem, and then the six of you get out of here."

"You're going after him," Carlisle said. "Why am I not surprised?"

"No time to argue," Rebecca said bluntly. She turned to Li. "Ed and Holtorf… where will I find them?"

Li must have sensed the depth of Rebecca's resolve, because she didn't attempt to talk her out of her plan. "Holtorf's got a head-start; I don't know if you can catch him. But if you're quick, you might catch Ed." Gesturing over her shoulder, back the way she'd come, she explained that there were fire stairs just off the elevator hall; she'd used them to get here. Directly below, on Sublevel 3, was a maintenance facility, as well as a parking garage. With any luck, Rebecca might be able to commandeer a vehicle. There were tunnels down there, too, and apparently an exit to the surface, a service tunnel that Ed believed Holtorf was aiming for.

As Li finished, Spencer placed a hand on Rebecca's forearm. "Just to be clear, we're coming with you."

"And don't try to stop us," Wyatt blurted. "If there's a garage down there, and vehicles…"

"No, not again," Rebecca said, shaking her head. "I can't ask you to do that."

"You're *not* asking," Spencer said. "We're telling. And anyway, Wyatt loves to drive."

"I do," Wyatt said.

"Go," Li urged. "Daisy and I can handle it from this end."

Rebecca turned to Carlisle. "Daisy?"

"Surprise," Carlisle moaned, her eyes rolling apathetically. "Bec… can I have a word?" Without waiting for a reply, she pulled Rebecca out of earshot, her voice low. "I'm not comfortable with this. Remember what I told you earlier?"

"You mean Li," Rebecca murmured. She was more conscious of the time now than ever before and didn't mince her words. "Listen, you need to deal with it, okay? You're wrong about her, trust me. She gave up the gun, right?" As Rebecca glanced at the Glock in Carlisle's left hand, she couldn't help but wonder if the younger woman was the right person to be in control of it. "You're all good? With *that*?"

Carlisle lifted the pistol. "If you're asking if I can be trusted with this thing, or with *her*, let me allay those fears. I'm good. I won't do anything stupid." Reciprocating, she glanced at Rebecca's MP5. "And what about *your* intentions? I mean, are you going after your friend… or *Holtorf*?"

Faced with the irony, Rebecca half-smiled, but the expression held no mirth. "I guess we have to trust each other."

At that, Carlisle's gruff demeanour softened, her features lightening. "That won't be an issue," she croaked. "Thanks, Bec. Thanks for getting us out alive."

We're not out of this yet, Rebecca thought, but the sentiment humbled her. "I had help… I should be thanking *you*." With that, she turned and unmuted the radio, relaying the plan to Naziem and Fitzgerald. Now that the exit was clear and in sight, the boys were free to come through. Li was alarmed to hear that the megs had escaped, but she wasn't surprised.

Turning back to Carlisle, Rebecca placed a hand gently on the younger woman's shoulder. "Stay safe, and good luck. I'll see you topside."

They moved out.

63

α

Fortunately, Li had biometric access to this level. She and Carlisle would meet the boys at the hatch, then escape together. As the women headed back through the maze of corridors, Rebecca and the brothers hustled for the elevator hall and the adjoining fire exit. Beyond the door lay a set of stairs; these spiralled upwards into semi-gloom—only dimly lit by emergency lighting—and downwards into a similar, amber-tinted veil. Several levels were evident beneath them, and Rebecca wondered how deep the base ran. She didn't ponder this for long. One floor down, they exited.

The door to Sublevel 3 opened into an empty service area, maybe a maintenance facility as Li had surmised. Directly across the concrete floor was a small, windowed building like those found on a construction site. To the left was a concrete wall braced with strutted steel and lined with thick pipes and conduit, partly cordoned by a wire-mesh fence. The place was uncomfortably hot and smelled damp, almost earthy, and Rebecca found it difficult to breathe. Beelining for the small building, which, on reflection, was more like a shipping container, she peeked beyond it. Cutting perpendicularly across the space ahead was a large, road-like tunnel at least two lanes wide and maybe thirty feet high. Both ends of the tunnel extended into the distance. On the other side of the road was another windowed building, this one more like a toll booth, complete with a boom gate and a sign bearing the words 'Waste Management'. Here, Rebecca saw other signs, too. One of these, labelled 'Loading Dock', had an arrow pointing right.

She peered through the window of the building beside her. A security office. Unmanned.

The place was deserted.

The deep, guttural roar of an engine startled her. Rebecca turned as the lights of a large vehicle sprang to life across the road, temporarily blinding her. With a lurch, the vehicle sprang forward, accelerating through the boom gate towards her. It pulled up with a hiss of airbrakes.

She hadn't realised Wyatt had snuck off, but it was him behind the wheel. She shook her head. "Are you kidding me? We're in a top-secret military installation, and *this* is your vehicle of choice?"

Wyatt leaned out of the driver's-side window and shrugged, slapping a loving hand on the door of the side-loader garbage truck. "What were you hoping for? A tank? Get in!"

Rebecca climbed inside, closely followed by Spencer. As soon as his brother had closed the door, Wyatt hit the gas, speeding down the concrete tunnel in the direction of the exit signs.

It might not have been a tank, but the truck handled like one. It took a while for Wyatt to get it up to speed. Once he had, it ran okay.

The tunnel was well maintained and looked newly constructed—the asphalt was a deep black colour and mostly unworn. Overhead, the ceiling was a hive of interlocked girders, marked by a central line of lights and an array of air filters—giant fans housed in engine-like cylinders—spaced every hundred feet or so. Despite appearances, Rebecca doubted the tunnel could have been built in the two months since the incident in Intihuasi. It must have been constructed years ago.

Wyatt kept his foot to the floor, trying to make up for lost time. According to Li, Holtorf was aiming for an exit off this tunnel. Along the way, other tunnels appeared, branching in different directions and clearly offering access to various parts of the base, but they ignored these. The exit signs pointed straight ahead.

Before long, Spencer leaned forward, squinting. "Hey… slow down. What's that?"

In the distance, a long, dark shape materialized; an obstacle blocking the path ahead. Wyatt slowed as it grew larger.

Jackknifed across the tunnel, running lengthways wall to wall, was a large semitrailer; an eighteen-wheeler, like a Mack or something similar.

"Goddamnit," Wyatt said.

"You're kidding me," Spencer moaned, punching a fist against his seat. "It's a roadblock. Holtorf got through and blocked the exit behind him. We can't get past."

The semitrailer wasn't the only obstruction. Parked in front of it, haphazardly abandoned, were two vehicles—a black Hummer, and an MRAP, just like the ATC Caiman they'd procured earlier. The driver's-side door to the Caiman was ajar.

The trailer door to the larger rig was open, too, and beside it stood a figure. A man. He stepped towards them, out of the shadows of the truck and into the light.

He was dressed in jeans and a polo shirt, his clothes disheveled and bloody. His thick brown hair was messed, as was his beard.

"Ed," Rebecca whispered, leaping from the truck.

64
α

Their gazes met, and for a single breath locked… and then Rebecca was running. Ed, too. They flew into a tight embrace.

"*You made it*," Ed said, pulling her close, his voice soft in her ear. "I knew you would… I knew you'd escape. I'm so sorry, Bec. For everything."

"You're here… you're *okay*," Rebecca said, scarcely able to believe it. She held him tightly, her head against his chest, his heartbeat racing in her ear. "We found Li, she told us what happened." She lingered a moment before easing from his arms and stepping back, and as she did, a stinging mist clouded her vision. She wasn't sure if her tears were borne more of relief or shock; a great weight had lifted at the mere sight of him, but Ed's cruel and obvious mistreatment was also deeply distressing. Just like Li had said, they'd beaten him badly; his face was cut and bruised, and his left eye was swollen shut. Distraught, she reached up to caress his cheek.

Ed flinched, and lowered his one good eye. He wasn't embarrassed at his condition, but he was clearly anguished and ashamed.

Again, Rebecca drew him close. "Ed, it's okay… you did the right thing."

"I'm sorry I put you in that position. And I'm sorry I couldn't save Frank. I tried. I really did."

Once more, she lifted her gaze, and when she spoke, her voice was low and even. "Don't apologise. This is all Holtorf's doing."

"And the others?"

"They made it out. They're okay. I'm okay. You believed in me."

"You've always believed in me. I missed you so much."

"I missed you, too," Rebecca said, and as she again drew him close, a calmness soothed her, a momentary sense of peace edging through the swirling emotions; it was as though order had been restored, or something missing had been returned, and in a sense, it had, and she could have stayed like this forever but for a final time she eased away, wiping her eyes with the back of her hand. "We should go. There's nothing more to do here. Holtorf's gone. It's not up to us to fix this mess." Clasping Ed's hand, she moved to lead him away, but he held firm.

"Holtorf's gone, yes," Ed said, "but still… something's not right."

"What do you mean?"

"When I pulled up in the MRAP, the Hummer was already here, but there was no-one in sight. And the truck… I mean, the trailer door was open, so I came round and saw this. Look."

He led her to the back of the truck and the open door. The trailer was empty, except for several long, aluminum tanks. The cylinders—lying loosely on their sides, their nozzles open—were each stenciled with letters and numbers.

ARP-44…

Rebecca's breath caught sharply in her throat. "Ed… run! It's a trap…"

65

α

Naziem pressed his ear to the server room door and listened.

"Open it!" Fitzgerald said. "Let's go! They should be at the hatch by now."

"No! Wait!" Naziem replied. "Did you hear that?"

"Hear what?"

"I don't know," Naziem said. "Something. Maybe nothing. Let me check the cameras." Rushing back to the CCTV monitor, he fumbled with the keyboard and mouse.

"Oh, *shit*," Fitzgerald said.

Naziem turned. Eager to get moving, Fitzgerald had already opened the door and now stood unmoving at the threshold, looking out.

"What is it?" Naziem asked, his view of the adjoining corridor blocked by Fitzgerald's large frame. Before Fitzgerald could reply, Naziem was already dashing back, dreading what he might find and suddenly wondering about the clicking sound he could now hear, and then he was at the door, peering over his companion's shoulder.

Outside, the corridor was alive with movement. A carpet of bugs, *huge* bugs, rippled and heaved. Naziem was stunned; some of the creatures were up to a foot in length. Most of them ran low to the ground, but many had taken to the walls, and a few even buzzed through the air, looping erratically on wide, veined wings. Naziem's initial thought was that they were cockroaches—they had flattened bodies and skittering legs, and he was reminded of the insect carcass Spencer had told them about earlier—but even so, they were unlike any roach he'd ever known, size notwithstanding. At a minimum, roaches were brown, but these were strangely colourful, with alternating black and yellow bands on their hard, shell-like bodies—

With a shriek, Fitzgerald stumbled backwards into the room, arms flailing. Unable to get out of the way, Naziem tripped and crashed to the floor.

Fitzgerald screamed again. "Get off me!" he cried, looking down at his left leg, his eyes wide and crazy. Somehow, he was still standing, but he was hopping about, furiously trying to dislodge the roach that had latched onto his trousers. Soon enough, he lost his balance and toppled—nearly crushing Naziem, who was still on the ground—as more bugs swarmed for the open doorway, the antennae atop their domed heads waving excitedly. Several of the creatures skittered into the room before Naziem could get back to his feet, and a few more flew through the opening, right past his face. He recoiled as their wingbeats thrummed against his ears, causing him to flap wildly himself, and then he was standing again and at the door, looking out.

More of the creatures had swarmed into the corridor; the surging mass growing in waves. Naziem had a flashing thought about the ultrasonic herder inside the vent; clearly, it was doing its job, but it was doing it *too* well. These things must have been inside the ventilation system. In the walls. Everywhere.

The herder is flushing them out.

The spider must have been perched on the corridor's ceiling, just above the door; he hadn't seen it there earlier, and only guessed this to be the case when the juvenile—and yet dog-sized—arachnid leapt from its place of ambush onto the heaving mass below. As the smaller creatures scattered, the spider snatched one at random and sank its fangs into the helpless animal.

Naziem recognised the body type. A hunter.

How did it get down here?

In terror, he slammed the door shut, which wasn't easy given the tide of roaches pressing against it, and he could only hope the distracted and inexperienced subadult hadn't sensed him. He wasn't sure. It dawned on him that the megs usually hunted in packs, so there may have been others out there, including adults, but he tried not to think about that, mildly comforted by the solidness of the door behind him as he thrust his back against it. Trembling, his heart thumping a million miles an hour, he thrust a finger to his lips.

Panting heavily, Fitzgerald nodded, so hard and vigorously that his head looked in danger of flying off. His shoes and trousers were splattered in a gooey, dark ichor and the shell-like remains of multiple smashed insects.

The odor of those crushed bugs was pungent, like ammonia. Choking, Naziem whispered into the radio. "Sandy, Daisy. There's been a breach, and we're pinned down. Turn back. You need to send help."

As he said this, something banged hard against the door outside, making it shudder.

Still struggling for breath, Fitzgerald's eyes flew wide, and he thrust a hand to his chest, wheezing now, just like he had earlier when his asthma had flared. "Naziem, tell them to hurry, *please*. We mightn't have much time."

66
α

Rebecca ran. Behind her, something struck the side of the semitrailer hard and loud. She flinched, but she didn't look back. Reaching the Caiman—she'd been aiming for the garbage truck, but the MRAP was closer—she dived inside with Ed hot on her heels. Frantically waving to Wyatt and Spencer, urging them to get down, she turned back to the truck.

At first, she saw just a single leg rising from the rig's far side. In slow motion, the segmented limb lifted high into the air, straight up, then down, caressing the trailer's roof. It was joined by a second limb, and after that, still more. Under the creature's weight, the truck rocked gently.

"Christ," Ed whispered. "The megs… they escaped?"

Effortlessly, the omega drew itself fully onto the roof of the trailer, where it paused, testing its environment. Its long tail swished lazily behind it, slicing through the air, catlike. Though terrified, Rebecca was transfixed; this was her first unhindered look at the creature. Similar in size and shape to the alpha male she'd encountered in Brazil, the animal had a long, segmented body and cigar-shaped abdomen. Its exoskeleton was heavily armoured, and it had an enlarged head, which was common to supermajors. Its downward-striking, paraxial fangs were currently unsheathed, looking like curved swords and extending from immense, jaw-like chelicerae. Atop its head sat three rows of huge, obsidian-like eyes. Again, just like the alpha, the thing was sleek and aggressive looking. Unlike the alpha, however, this creature was dark in colour, almost black.

And then, of course, there was the tail.

"This is new," Ed said breathlessly, and as the words exited his mouth, the omega dragged something up from below with its back legs, something long and dark that it proceeded to shuffle and roll forward. "Is that…?"

Rebecca swallowed hard. "I think so."

Clutched now in the omega's pedipalps—the hand-like appendages on either side of its mouth—was a person. A man.

The omega dropped the body onto the roof of the trailer, where it landed with a sickening wet slap.

Bile rose in Rebecca's throat, and she bit it back. Her stomach rolled.

"That man," Ed whispered, "He's base security, judging by the way he's dressed. That explains the Hummer. He would have come here with a team; they must have been chasing Holtorf. Looks like they got hunted down themselves."

It sounded plausible. Clearly, this was part of Holtorf's escape plan; he must have known that something had gone wrong, that the megs had escaped, and so he'd turned it to his advantage, setting up an ambush for anyone daring to come after him. The aluminum cylinders in the back of the truck were filled with Alpha Retinue Pheromone, which was the chemical infused into the habitats, as well as the hatchery upstairs. Holtorf must have acquired the canisters from there—which would explain why he'd murdered the scientists but hadn't hung around to sabotage the hatchery itself—and then opened the valves to let the substance permeate freely. Most likely, he'd been trying to attract one of the alphas. It was a clever tactic. Back in Brazil, an alpha had tracked Rebecca and her companions by virtue of powerful chemoreceptors in its legs, which had locked onto the signature scent of the creature's mate, the alpha female. This time, however, the pheromone had drawn in something else.

Without warning, the omega lowered itself, spreading its legs wide and flattening its body onto the roof of the trailer.

Hunting behaviour.

"Ed," Rebecca said, buckling up, "we've gotta go."

Slowly, the omega rotated, turning to face them with its cluster of shiny black eyes. Its gaze didn't shift as it again lifted its catch, its rear legs now moving gently back and forth, like spindles. As the omega calmly wrapped its prey in swathing silk, saving it for later, it continued to look in their direction, and Rebecca couldn't help but feel the animal was staring straight at her…

"Ed… go *now.*"

The omega discarded the body and leapt from the trailer, soaring through the air towards them. It landed only a few feet away, right on the roof of the Hummer, just as Ed turned the key in the ignition and gunned the engine.

"Shit! Go!" Rebecca screamed.

The omega swiveled and leapt again, but Ed was already swinging the Caiman about, and the creature struck the side of the armoured vehicle with a loud thud. Wyatt—who had clearly watched the scene unfold—had already started up the garbage truck, but that vehicle wasn't nearly as maneuverable, and by the time Ed had brought the Caiman a full 180 degrees, Wyatt had only just started to reverse.

"Where is it?" Rebecca cried, spinning about.

In the ensuing commotion, Ed inadvertently rammed the garbage truck, the two vehicles connecting nose to nose. Perhaps panicking, Wyatt accelerated backwards, and Ed continued forwards, as though pushing the garbage truck along. In this manner, the two vehicles hurtled down the tunnel, the throaty growls of both machines reverberating loudly off the walls. Neither attempted to disentangle, because already the omega had scrambled back to its feet. Rebecca could see it now. Behind them.

It came for them.

Skittering with blinding speed, it leapt again. This time it soared high and landed on the hood of the Caiman, and Rebecca let out an involuntary cry as the creature's fangs came for her, scraping the bulletproof windshield not once but repeatedly. It was crazed, rabid, and then its face was there, looming large, its black eyes like pools of ink fixing upon her with cold, hard intent. Those eyes startled her; they were glossy and reflective, and so deep they seemed to be pulling her in, holding her transfixed, and as she and the creature stared at one another through the glass, Rebecca wondered what the animal was thinking, if it could think at all, and then the moment passed and the omega's legs were suddenly scrabbling again, scratching furiously at the windshield, the claws at their tips giving rise to a high-pitched squeal like fingernails down a blackboard. The creature's jaws widened, its obscene mouthparts not only squealing along the glass like its claws, but also spreading venom and digestive juices in long sticky smears. Then its tail started to whip furiously, slamming hard upon the roof and against the window next to Rebecca's head. Like the windshield, the impact-resistant glass held, but Rebecca recoiled as the window shuddered under the blow.

Without warning, Ed jammed his foot on the brake. Wyatt kept reversing.

The omega flew clear of the Caiman, soaring through the air. It dropped well short of the garbage truck, crashing heavily onto the asphalt between the two vehicles, and then continued to tumble end over end. As it struggled back to its feet, stranded in the middle of the road, Ed planted his foot. But the omega was too fast. It skittered sideways as the Caiman thundered by.

You've got to be kidding…

Still, the move had bought Wyatt some time, enough to spin the truck in a wild arc, but the vehicle was heavy and slow to accelerate. Ed had to swerve hard to miss it, the Caiman's tyres squealing in protest, and Rebecca wondered if Ed could see properly with only one good eye and through a badly smeared windshield.

The Caiman shot into the outside lane, past the truck, blasting ahead.

Rebecca twisted to look back over her shoulder. Already, the omega was on the move, scurrying up the tunnel towards them, starkly bathed in light and growing larger through the rear window. "It's catching us!"

The animal pounced sideways. It landed heavily on the back of the nearest, slowest target. The truck.

Shit!

As the truck thundered forward, the omega pulled itself onto the top of the box—the container used for storing and compressing trash—and scuttled ahead, towards the cab. Rebecca's heart skipped a beat. Unlike the Caiman, the truck wasn't ballistically tolerant, its windows weren't bulletproof.

No match for the creature.

"Slow down! Get me alongside!" Rebecca yelled desperately, turning forward to push open the side-window.

Ed did as asked, pumping the brakes hard, abruptly slowing to match the truck's speed. But just as he started accelerating again, he was forced to take evasive action when the garbage truck veered perilously towards them. Wyatt had either panicked, or he was trying to shake the omega free. In keeping with both scenarios, the truck swerved back the other way, towards the wall, but Wyatt must have misjudged the maneuver. With a scream of metal, the truck grazed the tunnel wall, causing orange sparks to billow and fly. Having already skittered safely away, the omega scurried to the truck's opposing side just as the vehicle rebounded off the wall—as though Wyatt was compensating for hitting it. Rubber wailed, and the truck swerved back towards the Caiman, fishtailing, threatening to roll. Again, Ed had to act, this time jamming both feet on the brakes to avoid being sideswiped and crushed.

The truck shot ahead.

Ed planted his foot, catching quickly.

Astride the cab, the omega held firm, moving forward, the impact of its multiple legs causing huge divots in the roof of the cab as though the animal was walking in sand. As it went, its tail whipped about, looping from side to side, but then the appendage momentarily stilled, lifting vertically before striking over the omega's head, hooklike. In that moment, the resemblance to a scorpion was indisputable. The blow connected with its target and the windshield shivered into a maze of squarish cracks. Brake lights flared, and the truck again veered dangerously.

Rebecca let loose with the MP5.

She'd shoved the weapon through the open side-window. As the burst flew wide, pinging off the side of the truck in a shower of sparks, she cringed, fearing that one or more of those stray rounds had penetrated the cab. *"Ed, keep her steady!"*

Ed raced forward. Undeterred by her previous failure, Rebecca held her nerve, loosing another burst. This one hit home, spraying the omega in the carapace and opening a crack near to its lateral line. Maybe stung, but most likely confused, the creature backpedaled, stumbling onto the box body.

Wyatt's reaction was swift. The hydraulic arm used for clamping onto trash bins was already on the move.

The omega rotated, dodging it easily and striking out with its tail, hitting the arm with multiple blows like a rearing, fevered snake. The clamp at the end of the device opened and closed, snapping at the omega, but the arm wasn't fast enough to bother it. Still, the animal was forced to dodge it, and had to scramble down the side of the box, the side nearest the Caiman. Ed didn't hesitate. Swiftly, he yanked down on the steering wheel.

The Caiman lurched savagely sideways, crunching into the truck with an ear-splitting screech of metal. Rebecca was thrown hard in her seat, her harness digging into her flesh. Ed kept his foot planted, and Wyatt did, too, the two vehicles scraping forward together.

Like a drumbeat, footsteps stuttered over the roof.

The omega had escaped. Damn it!

Realising this, Ed steered away, pulling clear of the truck, and the Caiman juddered and whined as it pried itself loose.

Overhead, more trampling. Unlike the unprotected truck-cab, the Caiman's armoured exterior held firm, withstanding the assault. Rebecca wondered where the tail was, just as a dark blur appeared in her peripheral vision. Too late, she realised she'd forgotten to pull the window shut. She was lucky. The tail had been aimed at the gap, but instead struck the doorwell, bouncing harmlessly away. But the strike had been close, and loud, and Ed had reflexively ducked, again pulling hard on the steering wheel, this time in the opposite direction and with less control. The Caiman swerved, tilted alarmingly, and grazed the opposing wall, causing sparks to shower the hood, and then it was bouncing back the other way. Oversteering, Ed struggled for control.

Holding on, her knuckles white, Rebecca dared to hope that the last hit may have brushed the omega free, because suddenly, she could no longer hear it on the roof. "Where is it?"

As if in answer, the creature's horrifying face appeared right beside Ed, at his window, mouthparts gnashing, spraying slobber.

Rebecca screamed, and Ed swerved, this time deliberately. Again, the Caiman slammed into the tunnel wall. It was quick, and it appeared the omega's luck had finally run out. The creature hit the wall, pinned there momentarily as the MRAP scraped along. Then it sagged below the line of the window and disappeared.

Rebecca glanced back over her shoulder. A dark shape lay sprawled in the middle of the road. The omega, unmoving.

The two vehicles sped down the tunnel. This time there was no catching them.

67

α

"It wasn't just bugs," Carlisle mused as they hustled into the elevator hall. "Naziem said there were crawlers, too, which means they're already down here. They could be anywhere."

Li said nothing in reply. Carlisle knew that like her, Li had heard the rumours of bugs and other organisms being housed in the shuttered habitats, but Naziem's terrified report had come as a shock. Anxiously, Li hit the elevator call button; not once, but several times.

"You think that's a good idea?" Carlisle asked. "It's only two levels up. Let's take the stairs."

Hesitating, Li glanced at her ankle.

"Your injury," Carlisle said, slapping a palm to her forehead. "I forgot."

Stoically, Li shrugged. "I guess we're better safe than sorry. Come on." She hit the fire-door's crash bar and pushed through.

Carlisle felt a twinge of guilt, but it was fleeting. No doubt the stairs would be tough on Li, but the alternative—an enclosed metal box with an unreliable power supply—wasn't an option. Once already, she'd been forced into an elevator against her better judgement and nearly paid the price; she wasn't about to repeat the mistake. Li could manage.

The stairs were the same set that Rebecca and the brothers had taken. While that group had gone down, she and Li would head up, with the intention of bypassing Sublevel 1 altogether and exiting straight onto the ground floor. It was a simple plan, and this pleased Carlisle; she was so close to freedom she could taste it. A moment ago, when the boys had called through with the bad news, that freedom had been challenged and she'd had to refrain from going ballistic. She was done with this place, period. In fact, as soon as they were out of here, she was resigning, effective immediately. They could take their job and shove it.

She and Li ascended.

As they climbed, Carlisle looked up. *Okay, stay cool. Only two levels.* On the face of it, that sounded good. Unfortunately, the distance between those levels was vast.

For now, Li seemed to be managing okay. She was strong.

Low-level emergency lighting bathed the stairwell in a faint amber glow. Their shoes scuffed the concrete stairs with soft swishing sounds.

They'd been going for several minutes when Carlisle's fingers brushed something sticky on the metal handrail. She halted and jerked her hand away. "Hey, wait up," she called to Li, who despite her injured ankle was several steps above her and still climbing. Raising her hand to her eyes, Carlisle wiggled her fingers. They were coated in a dripping, viscous goo. She put them to her nose and smelled. Acrid. Vinegary.

"What the hell is *this*?"

68
α

A safe distance along the tunnel, Ed slowed the Caiman and pulled over to the side. Looking traumatised by their ordeal, Wyatt eased alongside them.

Spencer leaned out the window, also shaken, but as irreverent as ever. "You've got a flat. Right rear."

Rebecca couldn't resist a half-smile. "And you don't have any windows."

Both statements were true. The tyre wasn't an issue; the MRAP was fitted with run-flats. The garbage truck, on the other hand, was a broken mess. The windshield was gone, and the passenger windows were also missing, blasted out when the roof had collapsed. Both wing mirrors had been ripped free, and the driver's-side door was hanging by a thread. Casting his gaze over the wreck, chewing fast, Spencer glanced back at Rebecca and shrugged. "I guess this is why we can't have nice things."

After a quick introduction and an even quicker discussion, they decided to make for a different exit. There were plenty of tunnels down here, and there had to be another way out. It was agreed they were better off in a single vehicle. The Caiman was the only option.

As Wyatt and Spencer slipped from the broken rig, Rebecca reached for Ed's hand. "If nothing else, we have a knack for attracting trouble." She was expecting a light-hearted reaction, something to calm the nerves. She didn't get it.

"I'm sorry I went after Holtorf," Ed said, "instead of coming for you."

"Ed…"

He squeezed her hand. "I'm not proud of that decision, but something told me you were okay, that you'd escaped. Call it intuition, a gut instinct, whatever. Somehow, I knew. And there was a part of me… well, in the heat of the moment, I just couldn't let Holtorf get away with it. I'm sorry, but I didn't think ahead. Just as dumb and reckless as always."

Rebecca hesitated. She had wanted to go after Holtorf herself, and figured she was in no position to criticise. There'd be time for talk later, and she told him that. "I do have one question, though. Why are you here? What's your involvement in this mess?"

"That's two questions."

Rebecca rolled her eyes but was cheered by his smile.

"Have we got time?"

"A little," she said. "But hurry."

"They call it Project Cold Sun," Ed began. "All very cloak and dagger. Top-secret operation. Pentagon-approved black budget funding. Super mysterious and all."

"Cold Sun," Rebecca said. "The sphere."

Ed nodded. "The spheres are the key to everything. At a minimum, we're talking antigravity research, propellantless propulsion, mass reduction technologies. They're reverse engineering everything."

"You said *spheres*," Rebecca said. "Plural."

The Caiman's rear door flew open. The brothers hopped inside.

"Ready?" Spencer asked, his sharp-edged stone, as always, cradled in his hands.

Ed nodded, then turned back to Rebecca. "There's more than one sphere, Bec."

"*What*?"

"And there's more to the project," Ed continued. "I'm not privy to the bigger picture, I only came on board at the tail end, and in a limited capacity. You've heard of compartmentalisation of information?"

"Have we ever!" Spencer blurted, leaning forward excitedly and popping another stick of gum in his mouth. "What are we talking about? You said project… top-secret, yeah? Classified research. That's it, for sure. Is that your job?"

Rebecca threw Ed a knowing smile. "Spencer loves this stuff."

Turning to Spencer, Ed said, "I have a feeling we're going to get along nicely."

For the next few moments, he brought them up to speed, giving them an abridged version of events beginning with his recovery in hospital two months ago. Back then, he'd had a visit from a pair of government-types who'd advised him they were heading up a brand-new project, something hush-hush but involving a clean energy source that would address climate change and save the planet and grand stuff like that, and they'd spouted all the buzzwords and told him it was right up his alley. Of course, he'd known it was bullshit, that they were simply feeding him what he wanted to hear, but in the same breath they'd offered him a job, a consultancy position, and he was smart enough to realise this was the only way he could stay involved, the only chance he had of keeping tabs on the Intihuasi sphere.

And that, Rebecca knew, was the crux of it. They'd had Ed over a barrel, just like they'd had her; he was never going to let go of the sphere, not then, not after spending so long searching for it, not after coming within a whisker of having it firmly in his grasp. And they would have known this; they would have made him an offer he couldn't refuse, because that's what they always did.

"And ultimately, they wanted the disc," Ed said. "I got the sense they were going to take the disc no matter what I said."

"The disc," Rebecca said. "Your grandfather's. Where is it?"

"Holtorf's got it."

"Oh, Ed."

"That's not why I went after him," Ed said. "Not solely, anyway. Whoever Holtorf works for, they're well-funded, that much is certain. Which means they have the resources to do real damage with the tech they're developing here. I couldn't let that happen."

"Tech?" Wyatt asked. "What kind of tech?"

"I can't say for sure," Ed said. "Rumours, mainly. But it's got nothing to do with saving the planet. They're building a weapon."

Of course.

That Rebecca wasn't surprised by this saddened her immensely. Intihuasi's power—the power of the sun, as the legends had referred to it—was a gift. The world was going to shit, and fast, and here was an answer to some of those woes: a naturally occurring, free, clean, and renewable source of energy that could end humankind's dependency on fossil fuels, could put the brakes on global warming and climate change and save the planet like Ed had always hoped and dreamed. But with any great power came the potential for abuse, and the fact they were going down *this* path instead of trying to make a difference for good was as predictable as it was disheartening. "Holtorf came here with a plan," she said. "Right from the start, he knew what he wanted. He wanted that weapon."

"He doesn't just want it," Ed said. "He has it."

Rebecca nodded. "It makes sense."

There was a moment of silence. "Does it?" Spencer asked, biting his lip.

"What?"

"*Does* it make sense?" Spencer challenged. "I don't think it does."

"Which part?" Ed asked.

"The part about the weapon," Spencer said. "You said you'd heard rumours, which means you haven't *seen* this weapon."

"No."

"So, how do you know Holtorf's got it?"

"Because Holtorf's got the sphere, and—" Abruptly, Ed cut himself off. "Son of a *bitch*."

"Ed?" Rebecca asked. "What's wrong?"

"I can't believe I fell for it," Ed said, shaking his head.

"Fell for *what*?"

"Holtorf's smokescreen," Ed said. Gunning the engine, he slipped the Caiman into drive. "Holtorf wants us to believe he's gone, that he escaped and blocked the tunnel behind him. But he's still here, and I know exactly where to find him."

69
α

Hesitating in the stairwell, Carlisle wiped her hand on her shirt, repulsed and worried by the strange, foul-smelling slime.

"We need to keep moving," Li said.

Carlisle knew this, but cocked her head, waiting for the faint echo of Li's voice to die in the empty space. Hearing nothing else, and with no clear indication of what the substance was or where it came from, she nodded, and reluctantly pressed on. Reaching Sublevel 1, the women pushed higher still, and were nearly topside when the sound first came to Carlisle's ears. The buzz was low and thin, almost a hum. "You hear that?"

Li nodded. "I can, but… I can't tell if it's above us, or below."

It's above, Carlisle thought, but she didn't say this to Li. Above is where they had to go. She thought she sensed a faint tremor in the handrail, and again jerked her hand away.

Another flight up, they encountered more of the sticky goo, this time underfoot and pulling away in strands as they crossed the landing. They found the source of the humming, and the sludge, soon after.

The amorphous glob was attached to the sloping underside of the stairs and wedged tight against the wall, looming ominously above their heads. More than ten feet wide and maybe five feet deep, the strange blob was dark grey in colour, almost black, and slightly mottled. It looked like a lump of semi-hardened clay. Its extremities, however, were still in a partly liquified state, and like a weave of searching tentacles, some of these extended further afield. It was from these that the globules dripped, some falling onto the floor, others down the void of the stairwell.

"Dear God…" Li whispered, drawing to a halt and pressing the back of her hand against the strong, vinegary stench. "What the hell *is* that?"

Carlisle guessed it was a nest. It had to be, because squirming across its surface, held secure by strands of mucus, were several maggots. The white larvae were about six inches long and as thick as a man's thumb; smooth and faintly segmented. Beneath their writhing forms, the shapeless sludge heaved, expanding and contracting like a slowly beating heart, but this wasn't because it was alive. Clearly, the nest was swollen with young.

Nauseated and yet awestruck, Carlisle gagged, wanting to run but unable, and she sensed that Li was grappling with the improbable sight for a similar reason.

What else had escaped? What else had used the vents to get in here and—

Movement, overhead. Upside down on the railing above their heads, a large, winged insect scurried into view. At first, Carlisle thought the two-foot-long creature, with its jointed antennae and narrow waist, was a huge wasp, but its bulbous, multifaceted eyes and elongated abdomen hinted at something else, maybe a dragonfly. In an instant, more of these creatures appeared, and absently, she realised they were the source of the humming sound. Most of them were already airborne, and suddenly they were coming for her and Li, and instinctively she turned to run back down the stairs, but a hand latched hard onto her shoulder, pulling her back.

"No! *Up!*" Li shouted, and then the creatures were upon them, buzzing around their faces like a cauldron of bats, and Carlisle felt herself being dragged through the swarm, upwards by the arm, past the nest and higher into the complex, and there were deafening cracks of thunder, much louder than the angry buzzing, and she realised she was firing back down the stairwell, firing blindly, in a panic, and bullets zinged and ricocheted and sparked and she didn't think she'd hit anything at all, anything other than the stairs and the metal handrail. Then there was a door, and as they burst through it, Carlisle realised that even on a busted ankle, Li had hauled her the entire way.

With an echoing thud, the door slammed shut behind them.

This is the ground floor…

They were topside! Relief shuddered through Carlisle's body, almost painfully, and she slumped to the floor, panting hard.

Li had saved her…

Wanting to thank her, wanting to rejoice, Carlisle looked up at her colleague, who remained on her feet, breathless, with her back pressed against the door. When Carlisle noticed an angry red puncture on Li's forearm, her heart sank. "One of them got you."

"Yeah… tell me about it," Li said, grimacing and wiping at the blood weeping freely from the hole. "Man, they pack a wallop."

Carlisle noticed another opening on Li's neck, and her heart dropped even further. "Shit… you think they're… poisonous?"

"*Venomous*, not poisonous," Li corrected, wincing as she lifted a hand to the second wound. "I hope not."

Surreptitiously, Carlisle checked herself. She was uninjured. Again, a wave of relief shook through her, but this time it was marred by guilt. "Thanks for getting me out of there, Sandy. I lost it… panicked. I'm sorry they got you, but you really stepped up. I never should have doubted you."

"You doubted me?" Li said, the comment appearing to pack more of a sting than the insects.

"Yes… no… I mean… forget it," Carlisle said, feeling her face flush hot with shame. She felt like a fool, and realised this was a lesson, something to take forward. *It's okay to be wrong sometimes.* "Just know that I'm grateful for what you did. Thank you. I mean it. I really do."

Still looking perplexed, Li smiled faintly. "You're welcome." Wincing, but bravely pushing her personal woes aside, she helped Carlisle to her feet. "Come on. We're not done yet. The boys are still down there. We gotta find help, and fast."

70
α

Untroubled by the flat tyre, the Caiman hurtled down the tunnel, deeper into the complex. Along the way, Ed explained his theory to the others.

"Right," Rebecca said, stunned by this new information. "So, where are we *now*, then?"

"We're still in A-71. We don't need to leave this area but if we were to keep going this way—" he pointed at an upcoming sign, "we'd emerge into A-70."

"What's the 'A' stand for?" Spencer asked.

"Area," Ed said. "The numbers are a grid reference."

More cross-tunnels. The deeper they went, the older the tunnels became. Many of these were just a single lane, with a mix of old and new lighting. Ed told them that some of the tunnels were 1940s era.

Another sign, this one with an arrow pointing left. A-51 to A-60.

"You're kidding me," Wyatt said.

"A-51," Rebecca said. "Are you thinking what I'm thinking?"

"It can't be," Spencer said, shaking his head. "I mean, the distance is too great, there'd have to be a massive network of underground tunnels connecting everything. Is that even possible?"

Without warning, Ed slowed the Caiman. Drawing to a halt, he killed the lights and the engine. "This is the place I was telling you about, the place where they keep it."

"The object," Wyatt said.

Ed nodded. "Object N-439478. The Nevada Sphere."

71
α

Ahead, the decades-old, brick-walled tunnel ended abruptly. Beyond it, a large, natural cavern opened wide.

"So, again, to be clear… what is this place?" Wyatt asked.

"Like I said, it's part of Area 71," Ed answered. "I understand that N-439478 has been rehoused once or twice, but this here is the original site, the cave where it was found back in the 40s."

Rebecca was still trying to wrap her head around the idea of multiple spheres, all originating from a single, catastrophic event in which they'd crashed to Earth in scattered locations. Ed had only just explained this, and she'd barely had enough time to consider the ramifications.

"We go on foot from here," Ed said, easing open his door.

Still gathering her thoughts, Rebecca followed suit and hurried to the back of the Caiman. Amongst the jump seats, Wyatt and Spencer had found an equipment locker. "Anything useful?"

"This is an ATC vehicle," Spencer answered. "Asset Transfer and Control." He removed a rifle case and opened it. "A tranquiliser gun, maybe?"

Rebecca opened a separate hardcase, this one filled with silver cylinders. "Transponders, by the looks."

"Maybe they shoot them into the assets to help with tracking," Spencer mused. "In case there's a microchip failure."

"Who cares?" Wyatt said, lifting out a couple of ultrasonic prods. "You can have those. I'm taking these."

"Well, I'm taking *these*," Spencer said, lifting pieces of body armour, including a tactical vest. "Cool as. Hey, what's *this*?" He passed the garment to Rebecca.

Built into the vest, up near the neck, was what looked like a radio, or at least the face of a speaker. It was no bigger than a smartphone. Rebecca bit her lip. "Looks like a personal ultrasonic repeller. How many have we got?"

"Just the one."

"Guys, we gotta go," Ed said.

They took what they needed and followed Ed to the end of the tunnel and into the cave. Its fringes were mostly dark, but in the centre of the cavern was a lighted space, and in the middle of that, a single huge dome; another habitat, just like those on Sublevel 1. This was just as big as those structures, more than 200 feet high and longer than a football field. Galvanised steel walkways were affixed to its exterior. In front of it, on stilts dozens of feet above the ground, was a large circular platform. Flanking the platform towered racks of powerful LEDs, all facing the dome. There were other buildings, too, placed around the outskirts, as well as metal towers latticed in steel and connected by a complex web of overhead cabling; high-tensile powerlines, perhaps. Interspersed amongst the buildings and tower bases were dozens of grey metal boxes. They could have been generators or transformers, or circuit breakers of some kind.

"What the hell is this place?" Wyatt asked. "A power plant?"

"It looks like a switchyard," Spencer said. He pointed at a building. "*That* looks like an electrical distribution centre."

"I'd say it's a transmission substation," Wyatt said. "I think those grey structures are power transformers, used to increase or decrease voltage. Electrical power comes in here from a generating facility, probably somewhere above ground, and when it gets here, the voltage is either stepped up or down, and then distributed elsewhere."

Rebecca frowned. She didn't know about power stations or switchyards but didn't think either of those ideas was on the money. She had her own theory as to the purpose of this place. "They're experimenting with the sphere," she said, turning to Ed. "That's it, right? They're learning how to harness the sphere's power."

"Not learning," Ed corrected, urging them forward. "Like I said, they've already done it."

Creeping ahead, Ed drew to a halt in the shadows of the nearest building. It was surprisingly cool in here, almost frigid. He gestured towards the dome. Unlike the habitats above, there were no shutters on this structure, and Rebecca could see movement through the transparent acrylic. Men, and vehicles.

"Just as I thought," Ed whispered. "Holtorf's in there. He's after the prototype."

Just moments ago, in the Caiman, Ed had brought them up to speed. The prototype, as he called it, was a generator, a device reverse-engineered from materials recovered from the crash site in Brazil. The scientists had found a way to replicate Intihuasi's mysterious power, the repulsive force that, at the very least, could levitate large objects and push them about. Ed had said there was more to it than that, of course, and proceeded to tell them crazy stuff about wormholes and something the scientists referred to as the Tether, which apparently tied the spheres across space and time. He wasn't privy to most of it, but even the basics of his story perplexed Rebecca; the whole thing was outlandish. But she believed him, and she trusted him. More than that, she could see that he was worried. That concerned her. He'd said that possession of a single sphere was one thing, but control of the Tether was another. *That* was how you weaponised the power. And that's what Holtorf wanted.

"You do realise," Spencer began, "that we don't have a plan, right? Holtorf's men are armed. We can't stop them."

"No, you can't," came a voice.

Rebecca turned… to find a gun pointed directly at her face.

The man holding the Glock smiled and shook his head, which was topped with a shock of pure white hair. "Now this just takes the cake, don't it?" he said in a thick Dutch accent. "You came back, and without a plan, no less." Still shaking his head, he chuckled, and even though the sound was unpleasantly rough and discordant, it was tinged with genuine amusement. "I gotta say, if there's a history of dumb mistakes, then hands down, this one tops the list."

·   ·   ·

The man was Boor; Ed acknowledged him by name. Accompanying the mercenary were two other men, both dressed in tactical gear and armed with submachine guns.

"Where's your friend?" Boor asked.

"Li?" Ed replied. "She's gone."

"You should have gone with her," Boor said. As he did, he relieved Rebecca of her MP5, slinging it over his shoulder before collecting Wyatt's twin ultrasonic prods. With his pistol, he waved them ahead. "Get moving."

Rebecca fell into line and glanced about. One of the soldiers led from the front. The other man trailed Boor, who was second from the rear. Boor was speaking into his throat mic, ordering a sweep of the area. No doubt he was concerned that Li and the others were out there somewhere, lurking in the shadows.

Single file, they walked to the dome and through a large open gate. There were trees in here, a jungle ecosystem like that inside the habitats. This struck Rebecca as odd. The habitats upstairs she could understand, but why replicate everything down here? Was this a backup facility? An off-site storage area? Looking about, she noted the trees weren't as dense as those on Sublevel 1, nor bathed in ultraviolet. But it was just as hot and humid, the air thick and syrupy.

It could be a greenhouse. A terrarium for plants.

From nowhere, a thought flashed into her mind, an image of the strange, algae-like plants she'd encountered beyond the alcove in H-1. She could see none of those in here, but she was curious as to why her subconscious had dredged it up. Was there a connection?

It doesn't matter. Either way, we're in trouble. Again.

In the centre of the dome, the vegetation had been cleared. Here, several men stood beside a parked truck that may once have served as a troop carrier. If Ed was right, inside that truck was the sphere from Intihuasi. Prior to coming into Holtorf's hands, the sphere had been stored in a lab beneath the habitats.

Of greater interest was what lay *beyond* the truck. On the inside of the clearing, aligned in the shape of an octagon, were several huge, shadowy forms. The statues, eight in total, had large bodies and oversized, tapering heads. From beneath brooding browlines, narrowed eyes peered, as though intently watching the humans gathered nearby. Several weeks ago, down in the Brazilian Amazon, Rebecca had encountered these very carvings. They were similar, if not identical, to the famous moai of Easter Island.

She turned to Ed and whispered, "They stole them? Brought them back from Intihuasi?"

"You're surprised by that?"

With his Glock, Boor clipped Ed behind the ear. "Shut up and keep moving."

On either side of each of the stone carvings, staked to the ground, was a cylindrical metal rod at least ten feet high and more than a foot across. Each moai was connected to its pair of rods—and in turn, to the other statues—by taut, thick wires that loosely resembled the ropes of a boxing ring. These wires, however, were more like strong powerlines. Together, the rods, wires and moai formed an enclosure with the bulk of the clearing at its centre. In the centre of the clearing was a sphere.

The Nevada sphere, as Ed had called it.

N-439478.

The object was similar in size to the orb Rebecca had discovered beneath the pyramid of Intihuasi, the very sphere now stored within the truck. N-439478, however, was dormant; it didn't pulse or flare with energy, and its crystal protuberances were dark and lifeless. It was supported several feet above the ground by a smooth, metallic pillar that seemed to eddy with movement, as though phantom drifts of smoke were floating across it.

Ed had said that the two spheres, N-439478 and the Intihuasi sphere, had intentionally been kept apart; something to do with the Cold Sun experiments, apparently. Most likely, this was the closest the two spheres had been to each other since their recovery.

Outside the ring of statues surrounding N-439478 was a larger octagon, a steel-mesh walkway marked with yellow and black warning stripes. Within this area was a tall object, an obelisk maybe eight feet high. Not only did it look like a giant version of the crystal rods protruding from the latent sphere, but it seemed to be comprised of the same obsidian-black alloy. Rebecca had a flashing thought of the temple atop the pyramid in Intihuasi, the interior of which had also been lined with the mysterious material.

The obelisk, no doubt, was the prototype device Ed had spoken of.

As they drew to a halt at the edge of the clearing, a voice rose from behind them.

"Rebecca, so nice to see you again." The voice was Holtorf's.

Rebecca wheeled towards him. "Fuck you."

Boor raised his Glock, about to strike, but Holtorf stayed his comrade's hand with a wave of his own, crossing the ground to stand before the group.

He was dressed as he had been when Rebecca had first met him on the Hercules: cargo trousers, polo shirt, glasses and a baseball cap. That first meeting had seemed like weeks ago. It had only been several hours.

"Impressive escape, I'll give you that," Holtorf said. "Can't say I was planning on those assets joining you on the outside, but hey, here we are." He shrugged, stroking his goatee and throwing Wyatt and Spencer a nod and a wink. "Gentlemen."

"Chuckles," Spencer replied, returning the greeting. He then tilted his head, as though recalling a message he'd been tasked with passing on. "Oh, yeah, I almost forgot. Chuckles, you're a prick."

This earned Spencer a stinging rebuke from Boor, who moved too quickly to be stayed a second time. Not that Holtorf had any intention of stopping him, it seemed. Boor's blow was vicious, the Glock whipping so hard across Spencer's face that the blow busted his lip and sent his chewing gum flying in a looping stream of blood and spittle. Spencer collapsed to the ground.

Bristling, Wyatt moved towards Boor, but Holtorf lifted a hand in warning. "I let the first one go, but I suggest that from now on, you keep that shit to yourselves. This can get bad fast. Don't make it worse than it needs to be."

Rebecca didn't react to Holtorf, but broke ranks to help Spencer to his feet. "Are you okay?"

Spencer nodded, but said nothing as he massaged his jaw, clearly rattled by the brutish blow.

"What do you want?" Ed asked Holtorf.

"To be honest, nothing," Holtorf replied. "I already got what I needed from all of you. This isn't your fight, and never was. The tragedy for you is that you escaped and came back. Trust me, you should have stayed away."

"Who are you working for?" Rebecca demanded.

"That's none of your concern," Holtorf said. "*I*, however, *do* have a concern. Like I said, you shouldn't have come back." He tapped the face of his watch and nodded at Boor.

"On your knees," Boor spat, kicking Spencer from behind and causing him to buckle and fall.

"No!" Rebecca cried.

To Ed, Boor said, "You can stay on your feet." He then waved his Glock at Rebecca and Wyatt. "But not you two. Get down."

Rebecca felt a boot strike the depression at the back of her knee, one of the other men forcing her to kneel. "You don't have to do this," she pleaded as she hit the ground.

Raising his pistol, Boor aimed it between her eyes. She flinched. Tormenting her, he then moved the weapon towards Spencer, and finally Wyatt, who was also on his knees. Boor grinned. "Eeny, meeny, miny—"

Swiveling, Ed said to Holtorf, "Please, don't."

Holtorf ignored his plea but addressed him, nonetheless. "Your intrusion is a pain in the butt, I won't lie. But it does afford me an opportunity… a chance to try before I buy, you might say. And there's a bonus: it also saves my employer from having to source their own test pilots. Volunteers, no doubt, will be hard to come by."

With that, he nodded to one of his men, who promptly hurried to the obelisk. Rebecca hadn't taken much notice of the workstation connected to the device but looked closely at it now. The trolley was laden with unrecognisable hardware, save for a ruggedized laptop. Accessing this, the man typed a series of commands—Rebecca guessed those commands were stolen, no doubt during the incursion—before inserting a short crystal rod into the obelisk's base.

The taut wires ringing the sphere started to hum; a low, droning sound over which a series of muffled booms rose, seemingly emanating from the metal poles flanking the statues. With each boom, the ground beneath Rebecca's feet shook, and she wondered if the poles were in fact giant electromagnets. Soon enough, the humming wires began to quiver, and a sound like crackling electricity filled the air, causing the hairs on Rebecca's arms to rise and stand on end.

The moai started to shimmer. The sphere, too, had woken, pulsing now. Blinding lights—like solar flares leaping from the sun, but at the same time looking like flaming electricity—arced out of it, and as they intensified, a golden aura formed around the sphere.

"It's a wormhole," Holtorf explained. "Or it soon will be." He glanced at Ed, then at the truck. "Don't worry, the other one's in its box, it won't wake up. I hear you've gotta be careful with these things."

He got no reaction from Ed but smiled anyway, apparently enjoying himself. Gone was the awkward persona from the Hercules; here was the true Holtorf, the unmasked version Rebecca had sensed lurking beneath the surface back when the two of them had first met. She could never have guessed what was truly hiding in there, could never have known how cold and dangerous he was, not then. But now, it was all too apparent.

As though aware he'd been exposed, maybe even playing up to it, Holtorf grinned once more, his eyes flickering, his façade morphing yet again. Looking back to the pulsing sphere, his tone was suddenly helpful. "I'm yet to see one of these in action, of course, and I must say, I'm looking forward to it. Oh, and in case you're wondering, we're quite safe out here. The wires are a barrier. Electromagnetics, or something like that. I'm not good with that physics stuff. But it's an ingenious contraption, I hear, and like I said, we're safe. Except for you, of course." Again, his eyes flashed, and he shoved Ed hard in the back, pushing him towards the sphere. "In you go. Let's see what this thing can do."

No!

Desperately, Rebecca threw her gaze about, looking for options as Ed, herded by Holtorf, stepped unwillingly towards the ring of statues. The golden halo around N-439478 continued to grow stronger, solidifying. Inside the octagon, on the ground, dirt and debris started to rise, swirling and coalescing, moving towards the sphere.

Just like in Intihuasi when Oliveira activated the smaller sphere in the temple atop the pyramid.

Ed drew to a halt just shy of the yellow-and-black safety zone. He knew what was coming. He'd been down in Brazil; he'd seen what had happened when the temple sphere had activated, when it had started sucking everything in. He'd perhaps seen *this* sphere in action, too.

What happens when a human enters a wormhole?

Behind Ed, one of Holtorf's men had begun filming the proceedings on a smartphone.

This is a demonstration for Holtorf's employers, Rebecca thought. *Proof of the sphere's power, something to tide them over until they had the goods.*

Maybe.

Perhaps it wasn't that simple. It dawned on her that her group's sudden appearance may have caused Holtorf to stray from his plan. Delaying his exit was risky; he had the spheres and the obelisk—his best bet was to get out of here fast. And yet here he was, tempting fate. Why? Had he gotten greedy? Did he think a demonstration of the sphere's power would allow him to squeeze more out of the deal? Or had he reneged on that entirely, figuring he could now offload the tech to the highest bidder? A working demonstration would make for a stellar sales pitch—

Forcefully, Holtorf shoved Ed in the back. Ed bristled, and turned to look over his shoulder. He caught Rebecca's gaze, anxious now, but trying to stay strong. *It's okay*, he mouthed silently.

Still on her knees, Rebecca closed her eyes. An instant later, she opened them and mouthed back, *I know*. Ed frowned at her response, perhaps surprised by her demeanour.

Rebecca tore her gaze from him and looked up at Boor. "You know, you were wrong about us."

"Oh?" Boor asked, raising an eyebrow. "Wrong? In what way?"

"You said we came here without a plan."

Boor laughed, just as unpleasantly as before. "A plan? If you had one, I guess it went to shit, eh?"

"Plan A went to shit," Rebecca replied, and as she did, she tossed Spencer a discreet wink. "But you always need a Plan B, right?"

And with those words, all hell broke loose.

Boor's chest burst open with a horrific rending sound, a fountain of blood splattering far and wide. Almost immediately, the long, segmented tail that had ripped through the newly created cavity reversed, and as it did, Boor's lifeless form crumpled to the ground, eyes frozen wide in horror.

Gunfire erupted, upwards into the trees. The omega fled into the cover of the canopy from which it had attacked, leaves shaking violently in its wake.

Rebecca and the brothers were already on their feet, running for the truck and diving beneath it as a fresh volley of rounds zipped their way, causing clumps of dirt to erupt on all sides.

The hailstorm was short-lived. Holtorf's men were exposed. The omega returned… and came for them.

Rebecca's plan, if she could call it that, had worked. She'd planted the active transponder—the one she'd found in the Caiman's locker—into the empty mag of her MP5, the submachine gun Boor had taken from her and slung over his shoulder. *That* had been a bonus; she'd initially intended on stashing the weapon elsewhere, at whatever time and place proved the most appropriate. Her plan—her *hope*—was that the signal emitted by the transponder would be strong enough to draw the omega's attention and stoke its curiosity. She'd known the creature wasn't dead when they'd left it sprawled on the road, back in the tunnel, and she'd known it'd come for them again, just like the alpha had come for them down in Brazil. She'd been close to the open canisters of ARP-44 in the truck trailer, and in that moment the powerful scent had attached itself to her and Ed. There was no avoiding that; the pheromone was *designed* to bind itself to things, that was how it spread. In Brazil, the alpha male had tracked them for miles through dense, rain-soaked jungle; here, the omega—unable to fight its attraction or simply seeking a showdown with the female—had an even more concentrated scent to follow, and a much shorter distance over which to do it. The transponder, then, was an insurance policy, something Rebecca had hoped would divert the omega's attention when it *did* come for them. She hadn't told the others about this; they would have resisted, and with good reason. The plan was risky, most probably stupid—she was essentially using herself as bait, drawing the omega in, and then hoping to confuse it at the crucial moment—but it was all they had. The game-changer, in her mind, was the ATC vest Spencer had given her. The compact ultrasonic repeller had been running the entire time beneath her shirt, tucked into her bra. In tandem, the two items—the transponder, and the repeller—had been enough to deflect the omega's attention from her and push it onto Boor's standing and more prominent form. To the omega, in full hunting mode, Boor would have been a beacon....

When she'd heard the shiver of leaves in the canopy above—the omega's approach masked by the sound of the opening wormhole but not going unnoticed by her, because she'd been actively waiting for it—she'd closed her eyes, overcome by a fierce stab of doubt and an almost paralysing fear. But she'd held her nerve. Only barely.

Now, she stuck her head out from under the truck.

The sphere's golden halo, the wormhole, was almost fully open. The sphere itself, in the centre of that radiance, had started to shimmer and glitch, as though losing its grip on time and space.

Detaching and reattaching, Rebecca thought. *That's what it's doing, right?*

The rising debris—leaves and dirt, mainly—started to fly into the anomaly, but only from the sphere's immediate surroundings. The wormhole was trapped, confined within its electromagnetic prison, and nothing outside the octagon seemed to be affected by its gravitational pull, as though an invisible wall occupied the space between the wires. On the outside of these wires, beyond the walkway with the yellow and black stripes, Ed and Holtorf were fighting, fists flying. Holtorf was supremely fit; Rebecca recalled the immense strength that had radiated through his bone-crushing handshake. For now, Ed was holding his own, but ultimately, he was no match for Holtorf and judging by the way his shoulders drooped, he was already tiring. As both men circled each other, Rebecca figured it was only a matter of seconds before Holtorf finished Ed and threw his unconscious form beyond the barrier and into the sphere's gaping mouth.

The omega leapt from the ground, where it had just torn one of Holtorf's men viciously apart, and landed on one of the moai, perhaps attracted by the two moving targets, or even intrigued and aroused by the strange electrical activity within the octagon. Either way, it seemed to stumble, perhaps misjudging the leap, or maybe going too close and catching the edge of the sphere's growing gravitational pull.

The sphere's confusing it… it attracted the omega, and now its warping its surroundings, setting the omega's electroreceptors on fire.

She didn't realise it at first, but Rebecca was running. Already, she'd scooped up the ultrasonic prods dropped by Boor. Now, she was aiming for Ed and Holtorf.

The omega, having ventured too close to the anomaly, was now almost certainly caught in the sphere's pull, its tail already drawn tightly towards the centre of the octagon, and its rear legs, too, and she had a flashing thought at the irony of a spider being drawn into a trap, being ambushed, and then she was nearing Holtorf, and he hadn't seen her coming, because he'd overcome Ed, who was on the ground, dazed and confused, and Holtorf was about to deliver the final, crushing blow, fist raised, ready to crash down, and then she hit him hard around the waist, knocking him a step or two forward, closer to the octagon. There was no future in that move, other than offering Ed a momentary stay, because like Ed, she wasn't a match for Holtorf, either. She and the brothers combined, however, *were*.

Together, all three of them overwhelmed Holtorf, and the impact sent them careening as a group to the edge of the anomaly, beyond the yellow and black safety zone, tumbling into one of the moai, and she felt something tug at her, a strong pulling sensation, like being caught in a rip in the surf, and she also saw that her foot had passed through the wires, through the invisible field. At first, it had felt like plunging into a pool, like breaking the surface tension of water, although now she felt nothing other than the tugging sensation, and then the omega was there, coming for her, coming for them, because that's what it did, it kept coming, it would always keep coming, and she hit it with a blast from the ultrasonic prod, right in the leg where it had grabbed her, because that's where its ears were, in its legs, and at the same time she rammed the other prod into its lateral line, right where she'd hit it earlier with the burst from the MP5. Its other legs had already clasped around Holtorf, and it could have been trying to ensnare him, or it could have been simply grabbing at anything, trying to save itself, trying to pull itself away from the sphere. Either way, she didn't use the prods to save Holtorf. Later, this played on her mind, caused her doubt and division, but in that moment, in that single snapshot of time, she dealt with it, dealt with *him*, the only way her emotions would allow.

"This is for Frank," she said. And with that, she kicked Holtorf through the wires, through the powerlines, and he disappeared.

72
α

The omega went with him. Perhaps it had chased him, blindly following its predatory instincts to the very end, to its ultimate demise. Or perhaps it had simply lost its battle with gravity. Either way, when Holtorf flew towards the swirling vortex, the omega went, too.

Rebecca remembered little of what had happened next, immediately after Holtorf and the omega flew into the anomaly in a flash of blinding light. She had broken memories of running for Ed, of embracing him and the brothers, and a sense of relief and elation and sadness and exhaustion so overwhelming, so consuming, that she could no longer think straight. There was an inevitability about this; she'd always strived to control her emotions, to keep them contained, but no-one could do so forever. This was a time for release.

She remembered almost nothing of Ed and the brothers powering down the sphere, or of their escape to the Caiman, or of their rise back to the surface. Not at first, anyway. Later, bits and pieces returned.

Later.

For now, she needed to think of nothing.

Nothing at all.

73

α

Rebecca hung up the phone just as there was a knock at the door.

She answered it. It was Ed.

With an excited squeak, Priscilla leapt from Rebecca's shoulder, bounding into Ed's arms and nearly bowling him over.

"*Another* hug?" Ed asked as the tiny monkey nuzzled closer. "I just saw you yesterday!"

Rebecca invited him in and closed the CHU's door. "Good news. I just got off the phone to Owen. Looks like they'll be discharged tomorrow." As she said this, Priscilla launched from Ed's arms, soaring towards her, and Rebecca caught her and shifted the monkey onto her hip like a mother juggling a small child.

"I was about to tell you the same thing," Ed said. "I just got off the phone to Jess."

"I spoke to her yesterday," Rebecca said, nodding. "I'll phone her again tomorrow, once they're out of the infirmary. All things going well, they'll be back in the States in a couple of weeks." She looked at Ed. "Jess is in a good place. She's happy."

Ed nodded.

Again, Rebecca shifted Priscilla, this time up to her shoulder. Yesterday, she'd spent an hour or two on the phone, chasing as much information as she could lay her hands on. Up here, the recovery effort was still in its early stages, which meant that facts were difficult to gather, and it was the same down in Intihuasi. There'd been an incident there, too, some sort of incursion, which by all reports was related to Holtorf's assault on Area 71. Owen and Jessy had escaped the attack and had been rescued on the banks of an underground river. They'd suffered mild exposure, nothing serious, but they'd be in hospital for a night or two. Apparently, the incursion had resulted in several civilian and military casualties, but exactly how many people had lost their lives, Jess didn't know; for now, at least, there were no official figures. She *could* confirm that a pair of colleagues, a man and a woman she'd had dealings with, had both survived. She'd been comforted by that. Otherwise, details were sketchy. Rumour had it the assault had been met with extreme prejudice, and control of the site had been regained. That was the official line, anyway.

It was unlikely that the true story would ever find the light of day.

Jessy had promised Rebecca other news, too. Big news, something mind-blowing, something about the origin of the megs. But she couldn't tell her yet, not over the phone.

Rebecca couldn't wait to see them again.

"Once they're out, they'll be stuck in isolation for a while," Ed reminded her. "Just like us."

Rebecca nodded. She'd been able to tell Jessy some of the news from this end, but OPSEC was listening. Most of it, she'd had to keep under wraps.

The habitats had been severely damaged, but the destruction had been contained to less than half the domes. This would set the project on its heels for an indeterminate period. Rebecca was opposed to the project continuing at *all*; as far as she was concerned, it was simply too dangerous, and too many lives had been lost already. Her assertions, however, had fallen on deaf ears; ultimately, she had no say in what happened moving forward. If they kept her on board—and if she decided to stay—she might be able to exert some influence, maybe get them to see reason. She doubted she could get them to shut down the project, but maybe she could convince them to scale it back. Still, for now, all that was moot; she had no idea if there remained a role for her here or not. On that front, no-one would tell her anything.

Like before, the interviews had started. One-way traffic, for the most part. What she did learn was that the assets had been *contained*. She guessed that meant they'd been rounded up. She'd asked about Egbert. He was apparently fine; the transfer pens hadn't been breached. He'd since been rehoused, or so she'd been told. She'd also been told that soon, when she got out of here, she could see him. She'd taken that to mean that maybe there *was* a role for her if she wanted it. Part of her *did* want that; she still had questions, loads of them, not only about the arthropods from H-7 and H-8, but about the strange plants in H-1, and the habitat on Sublevel 3. And on top of that, there was Li's cryptic comment about the megs' silk having *unexpected* properties. She hadn't seen or spoken to Li since their escape.

So, there were plenty of good reasons to stay, even if a large part of her wanted out.

Her immediate outlook, on the other hand, was much clearer. More isolation, for a start. Ed had his own housing unit, but it was right next door, and they were permitted to move freely, which meant she could visit him whenever she wanted. And the brothers, too, for that matter. She was pleased about that; she felt a deepening connection to them and enjoyed their company immensely. In fact, tonight, Spencer was hosting a game of Texas Hold'em. Everyone was invited; Carlisle and Naziem and Fitzgerald, who were in the same complex, and Li, too, who by all reports was getting out of the infirmary tonight. One big happy family, really.

Rebecca offered Ed a coffee and a seat at her small kitchenette table. He took the chair but declined the former. Sitting across from him, she fell into a moment of silence before reaching over to clasp his hand. "You know, when I think back to that day on the river, when you were suffering from the envenomation… you know, the fever, the abdominal cramps—"

"Don't remind me," Ed said. "I thought the spiders had laid eggs inside me."

Rebecca grinned. "I'm glad *that's* not part of their lifecycle."

"Not as glad as me."

"Anyway… when you were in the Zodiac, when you'd lost consciousness and they took you away, I came to a realisation."

"Yeah?"

"I didn't want to lose you. I *couldn't* lose you."

Ed squeezed her hand. "You haven't."

Rebecca smiled faintly. After a time, she eased her hand away and leant back. Perhaps subconsciously, she glanced across to the bathroom and the amber pill bottle on top of the basin.

Maybe I can finally do away with those, she thought. *Maybe everything is good now.*

Maybe.

Deep down, she knew she wasn't there yet. Not quite. These things take time. All things take time. She was okay with that. They were going to be here a while. Time was something she had plenty of.

Priscilla seemed bored and started chittering restlessly. In a flash, she hopped from Rebecca's shoulder and disappeared beneath the bed. She returned clasping not only a bag of pistachios, but a bag of choc-chip cookies, too.

"Are you kidding me?" Rebecca blurted as the monkey leapt high onto the table. "Should I even bother asking how you got these?"

Priscilla lifted her shoulders, mimicking a shrug.

Frowning, Rebecca turned to Ed. "You know anything about this?"

Ed shrugged, too, a perfect imitation of Priscilla. "I had nothing to do with it. I guess she found a way into the chow hall."

"There's no doubt about you," Rebecca said to him, rolling her eyes. "Or *you*." She tickled Priscilla under the chin and busted open the bag of cookies.

As they eagerly dipped in, munching away, Rebecca grew serious. "I keep thinking about Holtorf."

"Me, too."

"I know we've already talked about this, but what happened to him? I mean… *there was no trace*."

Again, Ed shrugged. "Like I said, I doubt we'll ever know for sure."

Rebecca nodded and thought about the Tether, the strange connection shared by the spheres. The research into this phenomenon remained in its infancy. Ed had told her what he knew about it, but that hadn't equated to much, and she'd sensed an underlying reservation.

Sometimes, she wondered about the group Holtorf had worked for, and if they would return.

Of course, none of it mattered right now. She hated that her thoughts kept circling back to Holtorf. He wasn't worthy of her time, wasn't someone she *wanted* to think about, mainly because whenever she *did* think of him, she was reminded of Frank's last moments. That wasn't how she wanted to remember her friend. That painful wound, like everything, needed time to heal. It was difficult to allow that process to begin because she was still full of anger. But she had to let it go, she knew that. She owed that to Frank.

And if nothing else, Frank would want her to be happy. She wanted that, too.

Leaning forward, Rebecca gave Ed a peck on the cheek. His whiskers bristled against her lips.

An expression of pleasant surprise passed over Ed's bruised but healing face. "What was that for?"

"No reason," Rebecca said, but that wasn't true. She'd lost one friend, but at the same time another had returned. Reaching across the table once more, she studied Ed. "You know, bruises aside, with that beard and longer hair, you look a little like you did when we first met."

"Is that a good thing?"

Rebecca didn't answer. Not with words, anyway. She just clasped his hand and smiled.

EPILOGUE
α

FIELD CAMP 2, JUST OUTSIDE KUNLUN STATION
EAST ANTARCTIC ICE SHEET, ANTARCTICA
AUSTRALIAN ANTARCTIC TERRITORY
SIX WEEKS LATER…

Ray Drexler paused.

"This is the place," Nico said from behind him, hurrying forward as the chopper powered down. "The body bags are a dead giveaway."

Ahead, across the ice, a couple of RDS inflatables fluttered in the howling wind, barely retaining their hold on terra firma. Beside them, a yellow track vehicle with an integrated drilling rig sat abandoned and encrusted in ice. Beside that, at least half a dozen body bags lay side by side, covered in a layer of loose, windswept snow.

"You know, it's been nearly two months," a voice said.

Drexler turned as a figure hastened from a recently erected field tent; Langdon, who he'd already spoken to over the phone.

Introducing himself to the rest of the team, Langdon gestured to the body bags. "Like I said, nearly two months, and they're still perfectly preserved. Professional hit. Heart and head. We brought them up from below." Despite layers of cold-weather gear, Langdon hopped around as though trying to get warm. The man was OGA, a field agent, but his fidgeting suggested he'd prefer to be back in D.C. pushing pencils.

Turning again to the neat row of corpses, Drexler said, "Surveyors, right? Chinese? This is Australian territory."

"They had clearance."

"Clearance, maybe. Question is, what was a survey team doing down here, and with a drilling rig, no less?"

Langdon smirked. "Does it matter? The bigger question is: who killed them?"

It mattered. And this was a pointless game of cat and mouse. Drexler was aware of what had happened down here. Langdon, too.

The OGA man seemed to agree with the sentiment. "Anyway, the real interesting thing is down below. This way."

Drexler sensed that as much as anything, Langdon wanted a reprieve from the biting wind.

Calling back over his shoulder, Langdon said, "When we found it, your name came up. The brass thought it was right up your alley, given your specialist expertise with... *unusual* phenomena." He stopped and turned to Drexler. "And especially in light of your recent work."

He turned forward again and led them beneath a freshly erected tarpaulin, to an array of ice-encrusted halogen lights surrounding a large round hole about six feet in diameter. A ladder descended into the hole. There was another shelf in the ice below, and another ladder, and beneath that, a deep void.

Drexler and his team followed Langdon into the angular-walled cavern. It was empty. Over to the side was a large opening to the sky.

"The sphere was in here," Langdon said. "They cut it out and hauled it through that opening. Must have taken a while, and a lot of effort."

Drexler was less interested in that, and more intrigued by a series of strange ripples in the surrounding ice. Much of it had been destroyed when the sphere had been extricated, but some remained intact. Clearly, the ice had melted and refrozen.

How could something melt down here?

Crusting the ripples, and running beneath them, was a green-black stain. Again, much of it destroyed.

"This will interest you," Langdon said.

Deeper into the cavity, in an adjoining void filled with more rippling ice, more recent excavations had occurred. The ice here had been dug to a lower depth, then meticulously chipped away in the delicate manner of an ancient archaeological dig. It was perfectly clear.

From behind Drexler, Nico's stunned voice rose. "What the hell?"

In the ice below their feet was an ominous dark shadow. A huge animal, by the looks, with multiple, wide-spread legs.

"It's a bug," Box said, shaking his head and blowing air through his teeth. "I told you, didn't I goddamned tell you? Another bug hunt. It's *always* another goddamned bug hunt."

"It's not a bug," Quinn said, pointing. "That there, behind it. That looks like a tail. Bugs don't have tails."

"It's an arachnid," Langdon said. "A spider, to be precise."

"You're shitting me," Wolfe said.

"A goddamned spider," Box said. "Of *course* it's a goddamned spider."

Quinn shook his head. "Well, here's a fun fact for you, Box. Did you know that spiders can be found on every continent *except* for Antarctica?" He looked down at his feet and chuckled. "I guess that little nugget's been blown out of the water."

Drexler ignored them and knelt, leaning closer. The specimen was interesting, sure. But there was something else of even greater interest. "What about *him*?"

The figure wasn't immediately apparent, because it was entwined with the larger form, but frozen in the ice, looking up at Drexler with wide, lifeless eyes, was a man. Drexler thought he could make out the man's goateed face, perhaps even a baseball cap on his head.

"Now *that* is freaky," Nico said.

"Look at how he's dressed," Merc added. "No layers, no cold-weather gear. Looks like he's just stepped off the golf course."

Drexler looked up at Langdon. "How old is this ice?"

"Two thousand years, give or take."

Not only had Drexler heard about the spheres and the related black budget project involving time and space experiments, but he'd been explicitly briefed. Despite appearances, the lifeforms beneath his feet had only been here for six weeks. Just prior to the sphere's removal.

The drill team hadn't gone this deep.

"We performed a deep scan," Langdon said. From inside his thick jacket, he pulled out a tablet, danced his gloved fingers across the screen, and passed it down to Drexler. "The man's carrying an object. It might be known to you."

The palm-sized disc with spiraling grooves was indeed known to Drexler. He'd been briefed about it. He also knew the name of its rightful owner. "You can extract this? You can get it back to him?"

Langdon nodded, then cleared his throat. "Major, let's not beat around the bush. We know what Cash has done. What we don't know is where he is now. He's vanished, along with the sphere. We can't locate its signature, but we're working on it. I understand you've been briefed about Outpost 43."

Drexler stood. Cash was well known to him. The mercenary was a crafty bastard, and a cunning adversary. He wouldn't stay hidden forever, but obviously, he had an agenda. Drexler wondered if that agenda highlighted a connection between the sphere's disappearance and the strange events reported at the nearby Chinese outpost. He didn't ponder this for long.

Everything is connected.

Glancing a final time at the twisted mess of arachnid and man beneath his feet, Drexler jutted his chin. They headed topside, where he spoke privately with Langdon before rejoining his men. Across the ice, the chopper had started to power up, its rotors whining above the howling wind.

"So, this research station," Merc said to Drexler, raising his voice. "I guess we're heading there?"

The Antarctic Treaty prohibited military activity down here. Drexler knew that.

This should be interesting.

Merc seemed to take Drexler's silence as confirmation. "Glad I packed my winter woolies."

Drexler clapped his friend on the back, and with haste, the team hustled across the ice, heading for the chopper.

THE
FACILITY
A.
H-1
H-4
H-5
I-B
CROSS-SECTION OF SUBLEVEL-1
EXACT LOCATION, PURPOSE, AND DIMENSIONS OF FACILITY >> CLASSIFIED <<
SUBLEVEL-1 >> EXISTENCE CONFIRMED << | FURTHER SUBLEVELS >> UNKNOWN <<
A. CONTROL ROOM AND OBSERVATION DECK | H = HABITAT. H-1 = HABITAT-1.
THE ABOVE IS AN ARTIST IMPRESSION ONLY, BASED ON EYEWITNESS ACCOUNTS.

ACKNOWLEDGEMENTS

For obvious reasons, there are two people I couldn't thank in the opening Acknowledgements.

First, a big thanks to Charles Holtorf for the generous use of his name. Charles, I did warn you in advance…

Thanks also to Robert Thienes for the use of his comic book character, Egbert.

ABOUT THE AUTHOR

WW Mortensen is the international #1 bestselling author of EIGHT and SLITHERS.

He lives in Brisbane, Australia. He has a passion for writing, and devotes his spare time to honing his skills, being with family, and indulging a love of horror movies, adventure stories and action-thrillers.

For more information about the writer and
his books visit wwmortensen.com